JOHNNY COLE

Maskwa

◄DIVERGENCIES►

First published by Divergencies 2025

Copyright © 2025 by Johnny Cole

Divergencies.Com

Venice Ca

90029

Copyright © 2025 by John P. Cole

Library of Congress TXu- 2-523 -729

Print ISBN 979-8-218-86710-2

First edition

ISBN: 979-8-218-86710-2

This book was professionally typeset on Reedsy.
Find out more at reedsy.com

There are no words to express my heartfelt love and appreciation for all my teachers, especially Mother Earth, our ancestors, allies, and all children. Maskwa is dedicated to all of this beauty.

My skin is kind of sort of brownish
pinkish yellowish white. My eyes are
grayish bluish green, but I'm told
they look orange at night. My hair
is reddish blondish brown, but it's
silver when it's wet, and all the colors
I am inside have not been invented
yet – Shel Silverstein

Contents

Music

Author's Note on Music: Music serves as both an atmospheric soundtrack and a tool for character development throughout this novel. Each song reference is carefully chosen to reflect the emotional landscape of scenes and the inner worlds of characters. Like a film score, these musical cues are meant to enhance the reading experience and provide deeper insight into how characters process their experiences through sound, rhythm, and lyrics. While not essential to following the story, readers may find that listening to these songs during or after reading enriches their connection to the characters and settings. A complete playlist and QR codes for the songs are available at the end of the book in the Music playlist section. Streamers are also linked below for those who wish to experience the novel's whole sonic landscape.

Qobuz Playlist

Maskwa Novel

Spotify Playlist

Qobuz Playlist https://tinyurl.com/maskwaQobuz
Maskwa Novel https://divergencies.com
Spotify Playlist https://tinyurl.com/MaskwaSpotify

1

The Rebels

Nestled between an electronics repair kiosk specializing in phones, computers, and robots, and a bio-hacking health salon offering the latest health and longevity techniques, the Creatrix Gallery's exterior was decked out with cracked neon signage and an eclectic charm. Behind its unassuming steel door, the gallery smelled of spray paint, sass, and rebellion. The shelves were filled with banned manga, forbidden books on surveillance hacks, radical climate activist zines, Eco-science studies, anti-fascist manifestos, and handmade jewelry made from crystals and recycled metal. Inside, erotic sculptures, exotic plants, a dolphin-shaped fountain, and art-covered walls celebrating nature set the stage for three rebels as they prepared a different kind of artwork.

In the art studio tucked away in the back, which served as both altar and battle bunker, *Disco Inferno by the Trammps*, one of their warm-up songs from fifty years ago, slapped through the air. Gemini Moon grooved to the beat and leaned over a protest sign. The sharp swish of aerosol filled the room as she sprayed in violent pink across the warped canvas:

RISE UP! PERIOD!

Gemini, their natural and unelected leader, always felt as if she came from everywhere on Earth and from ten thousand light-years beyond language. Her appearance only reinforced this otherworldly quality. From afar, Gemini looked mid, but up close, her skin was light blue and softly glowing under the gallery's UV track lighting, shining like the inside of a conch shell. Gemini covered her face with streaks of purple and yellow protest paint, and her long orange seaweed-like dreadlocks stuck out like wildfire from beneath her signature white top hat. Imprinted on the chest of her hoodie were the colorful characters from the children's TV show *Sesame Street*, standing together under a banner that read:

THE RESISTANCE

Lastly, but not least, Gemini's mismatched eyes sparkled like David Bowie's long-lost star cousin or a cross-bred, bluish-green sea creature. That was legit, her overall aura. Gemini held the protest sign aloft, made some odd clicking sounds between her teeth and her cheek, and sang out, "You like?" She tossed the line away with the confidence and childlike innocence of someone who had created these on the reg.

Lucia Sky, deeply immersed in her dance moves, beamed at the sign, her lips wrapped around a blunt she wasn't supposed to smoke indoors. But what was rebellion, after all, if not ignoring or breaking the rules? That was her motto. Lucia looked like a riot wrapped in glam-punk and a schoolgirl fantasy-nightmare. Short tartan kilt, mesh sleeves, scratched combat boots that screamed "try me." She was radical and had the sharp bullshit detector of a street-smart alley cat. If she had a strain of Northern California coastal weed named after her, it would be called 'Truth Serum,' because that's what it would bring out in those who got too close to her innate Puerto Rican smoke.

Lucia dance-stepped over and handed the joint to Rachel Lamont, who took a long, practiced inhale, shook her booty, and raised her middle finger in appreciation of Gemini's sign. Her deep red beret angled over her forehead, daring gravity to defy it, and she pulled out her phone, setting her location and the anti-AI surveillance app to 'Fuck off!' Barely concealing her nerves, the joint flickered between her fingers, as she raised and adjusted her phone's focus, then snapped a group selfie. She grinned, her eyes sparkling, and shouted over the music, "You know I have to say this," her voice lilting nonchalantly with her thick French-American accent.

Lucia groaned, "Uh oh, gurl. Here we go again."

"Like clockwork," Gemini mouthed.

Rachel inhaled, posed proudly, shimmying her shoulders, turning down the music slightly on her cell, and exhaled her lines like a manifesto. "More than I love the planet. More than *j'adore la vie*. Even more than I like red wine on Wednesdays, there are no two people I'd rather storm the Bastille with than the two of you, *chéries*."

She passed the blunt back to Lucia, who took it and inhaled, belly deep. Out of plain curiosity, Lucia exhaled, rolled her eyes, and asked, "You never did say exactly what happened at that Bastille thing, anyway? Spill."

Rachel's riff turned righteous. "Well," she declared, "my French ancestors stormed the fortress, which was a symbol of the bloated power of the king, and sold the rubble in the markets. And with that, *La Révolution commença.*"

Gemini raised her sign and called out, "*La Révolution* works for me. Ready?"

Lucia nodded, stubbing the last of the weed into a ceramic ashtray shaped like a swirling mermaid. Rachel was already slipping gas masks into her tote bag, along with a camcorder, a bundle of compact protest signs and stickers, and illegal drone disruptors. The trio rolled out of the gallery, mounted their scooters like brujas on silver brooms, and started their engines, which purred with purpose. They synced their rear-mounted speakers and cranked up the volume on *Can't Hold Us by Macklemore & Ryan Lewis (Feat. Ray Dalton)* and lip-synced the words they knew off by heart, because what was a revolution if it didn't have beats to remix? That was their motto. This was their 20s, and this was their moment.

They tore through the city as if they were flying on the wings of an omen: past LED-lit Korean noodle bars and shuttered AI confession booths, past blinking surveillance drones spiraling through the sky, past hunchbacked pedestrians with faces buried in their screens and carrying ineffective, dusty umbrellas, past a roaming gang of coyotes, and past rolling delivery robots wearing Santa hats strung with festive icicle lights — the bots didn't ask for or particularly need.

Ahead of them, a wind rose from nowhere, carrying a burgeoning dust storm that spiraled between the mirrored buildings like a spirit conjured by the protest itself. The three amigas didn't slow their roll and rode straight into the storm. Like everyone else, they were used to the dust. Its bland taste and acrid smell had become a near-daily vibe kill, coating their mouths, eyes, and hair like a second skin. The dust rose slowly at first from the earth's increasingly parched and poached landscapes, but now it could, on a whim, sprinkle, shower, blanket, twirl, cut, or clear the atmosphere – all as if it had a mind and meaning of its own.

2

The Bounty Hunter

The lone desert highway simmered under the blazing eye of the midday sun, and a mirage of heat peeled off the asphalt in slow, hungry swirls. In the distance, the sound of a slow grind began to rise, mechanical and predatory. A coyote paused at the edge of the highway, ears perked and nostrils flaring, sensing that an infrequent, loud intruder was approaching.

A black motorcycle with a sidecar punched through the haze, its torque trailing heat and attitude, and its fairing-mounted speakers blared *Gone Surfing by Sixteen Wheelers* at full volume. On the bike, a lone figure rode, wrapped in dust-proof armor, a face masked tightly under a scratched retro helmet. An unmistakable tribal bear claw insignia stretched across the back of the rider's cracked leather jacket. On the sidecar platform, a man crouched, shirt torn, eyes hidden behind antique motorcycle goggles, wrists lashed and bound with heat-cured rope. He shifted uncomfortably, sunburned and restless, but he didn't dare complain. The rider didn't seem the type to tolerate chit-chat or chatter.

The motorcycle sped past the spot where the coyote had

already vanished and headed toward a concrete outpost that loomed on the horizon. The structure stood alone and partially concealed in the desert, surrounded by razor wire and sagging military tents — serving as both a temporary prison and a checkpoint. On its rooftop, a security turret spun. Its camera lens zoomed, locked on, and tracked the rider who slowed down, turned off the engine, as dust curled around its wheels like smoke rings.

They dismounted, quickly removing their helmet and face wrap, revealing a Skrillex side-cut and the sharp, weathered features of a Métis biker baddie. Those eyes — they hunted prey that didn't necessarily bend, bleed, or break easily. A single feather earring gently swayed from her left ear, hinting at her Cree roots and her femininity — both kept close to her chest but not entirely hidden. She looked up at the scanner device on the roof turret, which scanned not just her face but her ID chip — mandatory for movement through sectors of the American Landscape since the regime enacted the Emergency Powers Act. It beeped, and her profile appeared on its screen.

ALASKA RAINMAKER — Bounty Hunter #11.16.85

The door swung open, and Alaska yanked the man from the sidecar as if he were a bundle of butcher's meat, dragging him toward the entrance. Before stepping inside, she pointed her key over her shoulder and pressed a button. The bike rattled, and the sidecar folded like an accordion, snapping flat against the chassis and locking into place with a metallic clack.

Alaska entered to meet a wall of stale air, trapped by its artificial coolness seeping from a squeaky AC hanging from the room's only window. Bounty hunters of various shady backgrounds loitered like sun-lizards at a wooden table cluttered with greasy playing cards, half-empty ashtrays, and day-old sandwiches. She knew and nodded to all the bounty hunters passing through the outpost, not by name but by their distinctive features: the old cowboy hat guy with the face scar, the rookie with a permanent plastered-on smile, the one-eyed discharged army vet who hunted with his trained doberman which slept loyally at his feet, the guy who couldn't stop coughing up his frequent dust-storm runs, the cocky kid with the missing earlobe she tore off for crudely propositioning her, and the new bounty bots who always seemed predictable and inadequate, though they were becoming increasingly deft at the gig. To enhance the surreal vibe, *Rudolph the Red-Nosed Reindeer* elevator music played instrumentally from a lonely speaker that had seen better decades.

Alaska led her catch toward a dark-tinted wall that had all the warmth of a steel shark trap. Her fingers hit a button, and a robotic arm unfolded with goggles attached to the spot where its hand would be, if it had one. "Eyes open," the robot commanded, its voice emotionless and cold.

The prisoner ducked, then instantly lunged, headbutting the goggles and bumping Alaska off balance.

Bad move.

Alaska spun him like a drunken doll and slammed him against the side wall. Her fist cocked back, but it shook and activated a subtle tremor that betrayed a deeper wound. She clenched her hand, rubbing her thumb against her forefinger, trying to control the shaking which, if left unchecked, could rumble into a full-blown seizure and leave her helpless. He noticed, and his eyes darted to the door, but she clocked it, grabbed him by the hair, forcing his face toward the goggles.

Still, he resisted, and he squeezed his eyes shut like a child afraid of ghosts, or playing the game of *'I can't see you, so therefore you can't see me.'*

Alaska's tremor had now lowered, threatening her hips and legs. She desperately steadied her arm, reached down behind the prisoner with her free hand, and without ceremony or concern grabbed his balls in a punishing grip, squeezed, and demanded, "Open sez me."

He grunted, and his eyes flew open.

The robot voice barked, "Bill Perkins – Domestic Violence and Rape."

A green light beeped and flashed above a side door, which slid open. Without untying the rope, Alaska shoved her prisoner, and the door slammed shut, taking the man and his restrained future with it. Above the door, a digital bounty display scrolled out:

$2,192.58.

Alaska looked up and scoffed, "Cheapskate," then quickly waved her wrist device over the display. It zeroed out, and the robot arm retracted through its slot like a bored bank teller.

Alaska stepped back, her body now trembling fully, leaned against a cool pillar, pulled a well-worn pill bottle from her belt pouch, and dry-swallowed one. Her breathing slowed, and limb by limb, her body calmed, but her teeth remained clenched as she steadied herself. Her eyes drifted to the 'Most Wanted' bulletin board, cluttered with faces: some monstrous, some normal, hung alongside posters of rogue and untethered robots.

Alaska generally only hunted the AWOL humans, as they

were easier to catch and paid more than their mechanical look-alikes. The world, her world, didn't give her much time to linger. It only presented targets, then new ones, then the next. So she pushed off the pillar, quickly peeled a few of the fresh bounties from the board, tucked them under her arm, and headed for the exit, nodding to the bounty hunters and bounty bots as she passed. As she neared the door, she glanced up at the blinking television in the corner. The volume was low, but the face of a news anchor filled the screen – smooth, polished, and utterly detached.

"In national news, with the melting of the A-78 iceberg, evacuations continue throughout the Florida Keys and Dade County as rising sea levels worsen, and Hurricane Harry sweeps through the Carolinas. Meanwhile, the drought and heat wave persist across the Midwest. Seniors are advised to stay indoors. In other news, border crossings through Tijuana and Buffalo have reopened momentarily – permitted goods and vehicles only."

3

The Protest

The news anchor image pulled back, widening to reveal a wall of televisions in a city's storefront window – all of them showing the duplicate headlines, the same anchor with the same soulless smile. On the sidewalk outside, a single protester, his face covered with a bandana, reached into his knapsack, pulled out a Molotov cocktail, lit the cloth fuse, and threw it. And then, a crash. The cocktail blasted through the window like dragon's breath, and every screen exploded in sync, until they all shattered, silent. The protester quickly turned and ran away – an image of an animal-filled Noah's Ark was printed on the back of his jacket, with a caption that read:

OLIGARCH – FREE ZONE

Deeper into the city's core and surrounding streets, crowds erupted in chaos as thousands of protesters clashed in a furious mosh pit – fierce as ancient, disgruntled, and pissy gods. The planet's rising heat showed in their eyes, burning

with rage. Bodies crowded the side streets – some marching,
others lying flat with orange slogans painted across their
chests:

OIL IS CRUDE
LOVE IS LOVE
STOP THE MASS EXTINCTION
JUSTICE IS PEACE

A giant inflatable whale floated overhead, tethered to a dozen
defiant fists. Across its belly, the words blazed like prophecy:

SAVE THE OCEANS – SAVE OUR HOME

Through the smoke and bodies, a blur of green and silver
cut between the barricades on a monowheel like a mercurial
pixie – blue cape, glitter boots, 'Captain Climate Change'
logo shimmering on her chest – and was gone before anyone
could catch her attention. Distant sirens screamed like hungry
jackals over the skyline, while nearby police helicopters
circled low and security drones zipped between buildings
like mechanical hornets. City Hall loomed, surrounded by
police barricades like a medieval fortress. Its steps were
buried under a flood of protesters spilling from alleys – one
group pulling a flat trailer loaded with refrigerator-sized
speakers blasting out *Riot by Three Day.* Some protesters wove
through the middle of the crowd, costumed in full frivolity
and mockery: clowns, cartoon characters, inflatable frogs and
birds, realistic-shaped hot dogs and hamburgers, fairies and
gnomes, anime, manga, and comic book hero-ines.

At the fringe, Gemini Moon stood beneath a rust-stained

awning, its metal frame providing momentary cover. She handed makeshift gas masks to Lucia and Rachel – one by one. Rachel adjusted her retro-camcorder, clipped to her chest rig, and powered it on. The red light blinked, ready. "We're at the 'Water is a Human Right' protest," Rachel announced, pointing the lens toward the others. "Whatcha got, Gem?"

The camera found Gemini's protest-painted face, and her eyes burned through the lens. "It's all connected," she insisted. "Fuck with the Earth and the Earth will fuck with you – no caps."

Lucia jumped into frame like the camera diva she was, another blunt flexing between her lips, and a laser jammer already in hand. "It's all one rise," she announced. "Climate justice, gender-queer rights, and Indigenous people's rights. Human rights, civil rights, workers' rights, immigrant rights, your rights, my rights, and our rights to fly our own personal Philadelphia Freedom flag."

Gemini raised her voice in solidarity with her practiced growl, emerging, "Heal ourselves. Heal the Earth. Heal the future."

Lucia aimed her laser jammer at the dark, dusty sky above. "So we target the underbelly, jam the sonar, and earn fifty bucks for every drone we drop, right?"

"Plus a shot of tequila," Gemini added.

Lucia and Rachel laughed and echoed each other. "We're about to be totally unhinged tonight."

They slipped on their masks, made of plastic visors, cloth, and duct tape. They grabbed their courage and protest signs, spray-painted with hope-fueled rage, and stepped into the chaos – joining a small, pre-arranged protest group designed to prevent kettling by riot cops. Each moved with the tide of bodies, pushing against the barricades, swallowed by the surge, their voices rising with the collective chant.

"WATER IS LIFE! WATER IS LIFE! WATER IS LIFE!"

From the mouth of a nearby alley, an older woman in a baseball cap, clutching a walking cane, watched the crowd. She was silent, still, and mostly unnoticed, yet she was keenly observing Gemini's movements. She glanced at her watch, then looked up as the sirens grew louder, surround-sound encircling the protesters.

Then the vans arrived: black, unmarked, and efficient. Riot cops poured out in layers of armor, eyes hidden behind mirrored visors. Behind them, machines advanced in unison. Eight-foot-tall riot bots, cube-headed and rolling on tank-like wheels, pressed forward with mechanical indifference, shoving and tossing bodies like trash cans to the curb.

"Disperse and clear the streets!" a voice barked through a bullhorn.

No one moved.

Lucia's eyes narrowed. "Holy cop-crap!" she yelled, "HERE THEY COME!"

Gemini raised a fist and whistled loudly, "RISE AND RE-SIST!"

Rachel shouted, her voice wild with defiance, "VIVE LA RÉSISTANCE!"

The protesters erupted. Rocks flew first from the left flank, then smoke bombs and makeshift firecrackers popped in the air like snare drums. From rooftops, squads launched rubber balloons filled with gooey glitter, which hit and blinded more than a few cop visors. Ground crews pulled steel cables up from the pavement, jamming a half-dozen riot bots and rendering them useless. Rachel slapped a bright red sticker on a nearby cop bot's leg as it rolled past. The sticker read:

FASCISM – NOT EVEN ONCE

The riot cops responded with tear gas, rubber bullets, and water cannons. From above, drones buzzed down like locusts over a cornered wheat field. These particular Valkyrie drones had changed markings three times in two years: from police to homeland, then to something without insignia at all. Lucia spotted one, aimed her laser, and zeroed in on a scout drone – zap. The drone sparked, glitched, and spiraled in a dizzy tailspin as Lucia let out a triumphant whoop, pumping her fist for the win. Gemini smiled at her and nodded her hand repeatedly, as if tossing back shot after shot of tequila.

The trio surged forward just as a riot battalion barreled into them. A metal arm swung out like a renegade piston, narrowly missing Rachel but hitting Gemini across the shoulder, sending pain screaming down her side. Her top hat flew away as she hit the pavement, her gas mask cracking and ripping halfway off. She rolled to her side, dazed, blinking through the smoke, and surveyed her injuries – dislocated shoulder, bruised shin, and swollen eye. In rough shape, she searched for her friends, calling out, "Rachel?! Lucia?!"

Crickets.

Only the rush of panicked boots passing by, ear close. Gemini staggered to her feet and pushed through the screaming, coughing crowd, which spun around her, squeezing her into a side street and a momentary safety, where she peeled off her mask, winced, and cradled her shoulder.

Captain Climate Change cut back through the smoke on her monowheel, her shoulder-harnessed speaker rig rolling out *We've Got The Power by Sunny Luwe*. Like an eagle, she spotted and scooped up a wallet from the curb, flipping it open to reveal Rachel's ID. Eris scanned the crowd, eyes squinting, but couldn't see anything. She climbed onto a mailbox and pulled a brass telescope from her belt. She panned left, right, and frowned. No luck. With a curse and a kick, she sprang off the mailbox onto her monowheel and sped down the block.

Gemini caught sight of the familiar 'Captain' and limped after, trailing around the corner where the air felt lighter but still warped by heat, dust, and protest smoke. She stumbled past an older woman who stood at the edge of the alley — the same one from earlier, wearing a baseball cap and holding a cane. The woman carried a box of oranges and opened the side door of a white van that was idling. As she stepped forward, she tripped, spilling the oranges on the ground and into the gutter. Gemini's breathless voice called out from behind her, "Let me help you with those." The woman nodded, and Gemini knelt to gather the fallen fruit. The woman gestured toward an orange that had rolled into the back of the van, and Gemini waved her off. "I got it."

As Gemini reached past the threshold to grab the orange, a cloth-covered hand suddenly clamped over her mouth. Her eyes widened; she thrashed and elbowed, but her injured arm gave out. She kicked in the direction of the woman as the smell of chemicals flooded her senses — sweet, synthetic, and wrong. The sound of bells rang in her ears, her vision narrowed, and the last thing she saw was the woman's blurry face, while the last sound she heard was the jarring slam of a door, locking her inside.

Unaware of the van pulling away or the muffled thud coming from inside, a solitary Salvation Army Santa rang his bell on the corner. His red hat sagged, along with his sweat-soaked T-shirt, and his bell's determined clang echoed through the street and faded from Gemini's eardrums. Torn paper swirled through the air: missing person notices, most-wanted posters, climate action bills, and garage sale flyers floated upward. On a lamppost, a sticker flapped loose:

FIGHT FOR WHAT YOU LOVE

At the dawn of a rising revolution, and amid the illusion of pixel-thin progress and 'tis the season bustle, the van and Gemini Moon disappeared like the dust that once upon a time would have been falling snowflakes.

4

The Missing

The two-story apartment complex sat quietly in the late-afternoon haze, its stucco walls cracked from years of heat, with paint flaking and wrinkling like dried Florida skin. A wilted aspen leaned over the roof as if it, too, had given up, and a lone crow hopped along the roof line, observing.

Inside 2B, dim light leaked through closed blinds, highlighting a ceiling fan that ticked like a metronome. Scattered across the floor were half-read books, piles of clothes, and a city map with places circled in purple felt pen. The more routine decor was modest: a threadbare couch, old movie posters on the wall, a shelf half-filled with zines, mostly unread self-help books, a framed picture of a cat, a yoga mat, and camera gear. One corner, hidden behind a curtain, was reserved for an elaborate livestream-podcast setup, designed to produce and spit out content. Throughout the apartment, the smell of Nag Champa incense clung to the air, masked by something sharper – nerves, maybe.

Rachel paced around her living room, clutching her phone during a video call with Nick Durell, her on-again, off-again, and now-off-again live-in boyfriend. Nick, his boyish charm tarnished by one too many dreams that got away, clutched a skateboard like a security blanket and tried to soothe her. "We put out flyers all around the neighborhood, blasted their face across our social media platforms. I mean, Gem's skin is blue – they won't be hard to miss." He pulled his hoodie off over his twenty-something, thin frame, battered by repeated run-ins with cracked sidewalks and late-night escapades, and propped up Rachel with a few more niceties. "Don't stress, Moon knows their way around." and "Everything's going to be alright."

Rachel offered a soft, "Thanks," then hung up and walked toward the kitchen. She stopped and stood in the doorway, tense, fingers tapping against the door frame. She stared at Lucia, who leaned against the kitchen cupboard with her arms crossed. Rachel's anger flared as she mirrored Lucia's stance and said, "Where the hell is Gemini? What about filing a missing person report?"

Lucia stepped closer, sunglasses pushed up into her hair, the edges of last night's eyeliner still clinging to the corners of her eyes, and she sighed. "Cops? I don't think we should invite them into Gemini's life," Lucia insisted.

Rachel stepped into the kitchen and resumed pacing, heat rising under her skin. Her voice cracked, not from anger, but from the sharp edge of fear she hadn't named yet. "Lucia... Gemini's always looked out for us. Remember that time you literally ghosted us after your operation, and we all thought you croaked?" She stopped and faced her. "Gemini tracked you down. It turned out you were just on a bender in the Bronx with your new friend, Pablo."

Lucia grimaced, but a hint of guilt hid behind her facade.

"Alright, alright. But I'll do it anonymously." She raised her arm in the air like a surrendered white flag. "I don't want to hear about it from Gem when they come storming through the window all big mad."

Rachel softened. "Call me if you hear anything?"

Lucia nodded. "Same," she said as she walked to the front door.

They hugged briefly, their arms entwined as they clung to each other, sharing a mixed cocktail of hope and despair. Then Lucia opened the door, stepped into the hall, and went down the stairs – carrying the weight of her worry on her hunched-over shoulders.

Rachel double-locked the door behind her, peeked through the peephole, and waited until the footsteps faded. She pushed back against the heavy silence and looked around the room for something to ease the dread. She pulled up Gemini's last social media post, saved before the platform purged 'unauthorized political content.' This latest form of censorship had been creeping, then sudden, then absolute. She shook her head, crossed the room, and turned on the TV. A grainy, subtitled horror movie flickered to life – a Japanese Christmas-themed slasher where a green-faced Grinch with a kabuki grin hunted carolers through a frozen forest. Rachel watched it briefly to catch a few breaths and distract herself, then lowered the volume and looked around for her next fix. Her gaze landed on the ceiling, where a heavy punching bag swung slightly in the draft.

She took off her rings and cracked her knuckles. Then she slammed her fist into the bag.

Once.

Twice.

Her nerves settled, and her heartbeat slowed; the only sound remaining in the apartment was the thud-thud of pain with nowhere else to go. She punched again, and the bag swung back as if purposefully dodging her. Sweat beaded and gathered on her temple as she kept punching out of frustration and rage: for her missing friend, for the collapsing climate, and her own crumbling personal life. She punched toward the elusive place called mind-numbing nowhere.

* * *

Lucia didn't take her direct route home; she instead chose to pass by some of the familiar haunts where she thought Gemini might be: places where she might bump into Gemini's friends or lovers, most of whom she knew, and some she didn't. As she rode her scooter through the backstreets and alleys, the heat smelled like Washington Heights in the Bronx – pernil and exhaust, cumbia from a third-floor window – the block alive even at midnight because the block was always alive. *Cáncer by Bad Bunny* drifted from someone's speaker two floors up and followed her down the street like a memory she hadn't finished and refused to relinquish.

Riding deeper into the dusty city, Lucia obsessed on how desperately she wanted to find Gemini and how she also desperately wanted to delay calling the cops for help. She recalled that long ago, they had made a blood-sister pact that no matter how dire their circumstances became, they would never 911. They vowed never to cooperate or collaborate with their opps in advance – Immigration, cops, FBI, DHS, ICE, or any agents of the regime. Their mistrust of these authorities was well earned: jail time, broken bones, and bruises that they had both endured at the regime's hands only reinforced their views. She remembered all the rubber bullets, batons, tear gas canisters, and water cannons they had faced together as she navigated through the city's edges, wrapped in a holiday veneer: neon ads of gleeful-looking children looping silently, billboards of used electric car salesclerks hawking their wares, AI-generated holiday vacations promising happiness, and 50% off sales of robotic maids with the caption:

NEVER CLEAN AGAIN

Christmas lights blinked above shuttered storefronts, and the dust caught a hologram snowman dancing in endless laughter – a laughter as far removed from her mind as Christmas, or the feeling of Christmas itself. Somewhere out there, behind the tinsel of the gift-wrapped city, Gemini Moon remained lost in a city that kept moving, the way cities do – indifferent, luminous, and utterly unbothered by all the seasons and tidings it swallowed whole.

5

The Cabin

Miles and eons away from the city's fast, relentless chaos, Alaska zigzagged her way down winding country roads to avoid the closed official crossings between Canada and the United States. She knew and took the back roads into and through one of the few Indian Nations that straddled the border, and one of the few remaining ways to enter and exit America, from Canada or anywhere. The reservation was small, but still sovereign land that the regime couldn't quite breach – not yet. Alaska paid her passage in tobacco and cash to the crossing guides who remembered her mother, and sped on through dirt roads that she knew by heart and by the light of stars when necessary.

Alaska guided her motorcycle along the 'homestretch' coun-try road, bordered by hills covered in pine trees and lush, green grass. Wildflowers nodded in the breeze, and birds scattered as she rode by, slicing through the peace in a streak of leather, metal, and speakers playing *Aguila y Condor by Arthur Mena* – an ode to a Q'ero prophecy from the Peruvian Andes she'd heard about. It was a vision of the Indigenous peoples of the Americas uniting under the wings of the condor and the eagle, ushering in an era of peace and prosperity. Although that vibe was currently beyond her personal reach, she reflected on that possibility as she turned onto a familiar dirt road. At the end of the trail, she entered a vast meadow filled with memories: hers, her ancestors', their ancestors', and the ancestors of Mother Earth.

The meadow opened onto a small lake that mirrored the sky so perfectly that it felt like she was riding into an in-between world. It was a blend of spirit, earth, and imagination that let her escape or dream whatever she wanted. At the water's edge, a cabin stood like an old friend: rustic, weathered, and cozy. She pulled in close and parked, kicked the stand, unstrapped her helmet, and took a long, deep breath – the kind that comes from deep within her heart and the earth itself. She looked around, feeling and knowing she was home.

Alaska entered the cabin and pressed a small button near the door. With a click, the shuttered windows opened together, flooding the cabin with natural light. The cozy space was simple and felt like a warm bath. The living room featured a fireplace, a couch, a coffee table, a flat-screen TV, speakers, and shelves cluttered with gear and keepsakes. The familiar air carried the faint scent of cedar and sage, and the lingering smell of burnt firewood bled from the walls.

She dropped her saddlebag and hung her lasso on a wall rack filled with other ropes, each intricately knotted and worn from use. Her jacket came off next, revealing a faded Buffalo Calf Road Woman T-shirt. The image shone from her chest in printed defiance in honor of the Northern Cheyenne warrior woman, who, as legend has it, was the one who downed General Custer at his last stand during the Battle of the Little Bighorn. Alaska could relate to buffaloes, calves, roads, women, and being someone else's last stand.

Alaska looked around, then instructed, "Abacus, light the tree." A beep responded. Abacus, her cabin's computer system, powered up and lit the Christmas tree in the corner; ornaments reflecting the light like trapped stars. Alaska then crossed the room with a stack of 'Most Wanted' posters she had taken from her bag and pinned them on the wall, arranging them beside older bounty posters – her gaze already calculating the odds. Next to the posters were pinned crime-scene photos and clipped, yellowed newspaper headlines about a crime she generally preferred to ignore, but kept up anyway.

She stepped back, lit a bundle of sage, and the flame crackled softly. The smoke curled through the air as she swept it over a small altar of family photographs. The picture at the center depicted her mother, Taino Rainmaker, in her mid-thirties, with old-soul eyes and three tattooed lines extending from each corner – Cree markings of her lineage and story.

The sage smoke drifted across the room and out the open window, where a child's laughter, faint and distant, danced through the meadow. Alaska walked over to the window and squinted through the curtain at a dreamy flashback:

A little girl running barefoot through the tall grass, her yellow summer dress fluttering behind her. A long feather dangling from her left ear, the seven-year-old Alaska laughed and spun in circles, fingers trailing over wildflowers. Her joy flickered like an old reel from a home movie.

Then the flashback faded and dissolved.

Alaska's hand trembled, and her attention was immediately drawn back inside the cabin. She reached into her jacket, pulled out the pill bottle, and shook it. It was empty, and a spike of panic pierced her chest. She ran to the bathroom and flung open the medicine cabinet.

Nothing.

Then to the kitchen, rifling through drawers, pushing aside jars and boxes.

Nothing.

Her vision blurred as her legs wobbled out. She grabbed a wooden spoon from the counter, dropped hard to the floor, and her body twisted as she shoved the spoon between her teeth and bit down.

The seizure hit violently, her body arching as foamed saliva spilled from the corner of her mouth. Her eyes rolled back into darkness as her inner awareness floated outside to observe the meadow buzzing with cricket songs in the tall grass, soft as feathers. She could perceive the bees dipping between the sweet nectar of wildflowers and the distant, dreamy blessing of the crystal-clear creek beyond the trees. From above, she watched:

Her seven-year-old self was hidden behind a low berry bush, bare feet stained red with fresh juice and fertile dirt. Her cheeks were smeared with the same deep crimson, like finger paint applied spontaneously or by accident. She licked her fingers slowly, savoring the last succulent burst of sweet-tart flavor on her tongue. For a moment, there was only sun, sugar, and bliss.

Then a shadow blocked the sunlight, and young Alaska's eyes blinked upward. Her mother, Taino, stood over her, still and quiet like a dawn about to break. She wore her hair in braids, and a hand-beaded pendant swung close to her heart. "Oh, there you are, Alaska," she whispered in Cree, with amusement.

Alaska jolted upright, her sticky fingers clutching the empty berry basket as she slid it behind her back. Her mouth twisted with guilt, opposing her eyes, which feigned innocence. She quickly wiped her face with the hem of her dress, but the red only smeared wider and clown-like.

Taino crouched down, eyeing her closely. "I see you've been collecting berries for us again."

Alaska shook her head too quickly. "No, mama. I didn't find any."

Taino raised an eyebrow. "I can see that. They must be all gone." Her voice dipped, gentle but heavy with knowing. "I wonder what'll happen when there's no more berries?"

Alaska squinted up at her. "Will the bears go hungry?"

"Yes. Our Maskwa Ancestors." Taino tilted her head. "And?"

Alaska fidgeted. "And the foxes will have empty tummies. And the birds'll stop singing, mama."

As if summoned, a pair of foxes stepped out from the grass. Cartoonish yet alive, with sleek fur and amber eyes. A bluebird swooped down and landed on a stalk nearby, and the meadow opened up like an animated storybook, colored in rich acrylic.

Taino nodded. "What'll happen to us if we just take, take, take and give nothing back?"

Alaska bit her lip. "Will the Wetiko come?"

The foxes nodded, and the bluebird tilted its head and blinked at her.

"And what about Mother Earth?" asked Taino.

Alaska solemnly said, "She'll get sick and sad."

Taino smiled, something older behind it. "That's right. That's why we take care of each other and all our relations."

Taino reached out, lifting Alaska and her empty basket, and they walked hand in hand through the waist-high grass. On Taino's back, embroidered into her shirt, a bear danced among constellations. When Alaska glanced over, the bear winked at her. "Mama," she asked nervously, "have you ever seen a real live Wetiko?"

The sun dimmed, and clouds rolled in like wolves as Taino leaned in close, her voice low and mischievous. "Oh yes," she said. "It has dead black eyes and pale, sickly skin, with claws sharp enough to skin and possess the spirit from your bones. It can barely breathe and continually gasps for air. Its chest is a hollow cage, because no matter how much it eats, it's always hungry. So hungry it will even chew on its lip and eat itself, even after it eats you." She twisted her face, bared her teeth, and playfully lunged. "Rawrr!" Taino growled gleefully. Alaska squealed with delight, then bolted toward the cabin. Taino chased after her, growling like a cartoonish, possessed beast.

Taino and the young Alaska suddenly stopped and stood still in the meadow, observing the forest. Its trees, once serene, now twisted into silhouettes, clawing at the sky. The forest floor seemed to vibrate with something dark and ancient. Above, a coven of crows exploded from the trees, cawing as a warning. Near the edge of a forest, at the far end of the meadow, a real bear appeared – massive and silent. Its ears twitched as it turned to face the woods, then it rose on its hind legs. It let out a deep growl followed by a vicious snarl, then bolted, crashing through the tree line. The forest gave way to the loud sounds of a territorial battle: flesh hitting flesh, claws against hide, and branches cracking and thundering to the ground.

Taino and Alaska leaned in to listen to the whimpering and snarling roar of the bear. "Mama," Alaska gasped, staring at the tree line, "Bear is in trouble."

She hesitated before taking a step toward the forest, her small hand reaching out, but Taino grabbed her arm. "Get inside," she ordered, cold and fierce. "Quickly."

Then it was gone.

Still on the cabin floor, Alaska jolted alert as her spirit slammed back into her adult body. Her hands trembled as if the electricity hadn't entirely left, and her chest rose sharply beneath her sweat-soaked shirt, as her breath tore back into her lungs like a whip crack. Her eyes snapped open: wild, disoriented, and re-awakened. Her tongue felt like steel wool, and her brain became a storm of scrambled signals. The wooden spoon clattered from her mouth as she ripped it free and dropped it on the floor. Strings of saliva trailed from her cheek, which she wiped away with the back of her trembling hand. She looked around, and the cabin felt distant, as though it had pulled back to give her space to return from wherever she had gone.

Still breathing hard, she staggered over to the open cabin door, looked out, and surveyed the meandering meadow to see if she could remember anything. Pulling off her boots and socks to reveal her blistered, bare feet, she instructed Abacus to play *Save It For Later by Eddie Vedder* through the cabin's outdoor speakers and stepped outside. Her toes felt refreshed as she walked across the music–filled meadow, which she had done countless times since the day she went out to collect the berries.

Her memory was sparse, coming in inconsistent flashes of what had happened that day: the berries, her dress, her basket, the birds, her mother, fragments of the Wetiko story, a bear in the meadow, and monstrous sounds, all foggy and vague at best. Memories, especially excruciatingly painful ones, require both reliance and mental fortitude from those who venture into their unpacked depths. Alaska sometimes had that strength, but she mostly directed her available resources toward her own present-day survival. She mainly chose to keep her mind 'focused' on the twin flames of dissociation and distraction, whether she realized it or not.

Alaska continued wandering through the meadow, found the berry patch, offered a small amount of tobacco from her pouch, picked a handful, and ate them – still tart and sweet. She licked her fingers and rubbed her thumb over her forefinger, picked a few more berries, then gazed out over the deep forest longer than usual. It was a place she hadn't entered since childhood, and only then, guided by the gentle hand of her mother.

She turned and walked back into the cabin, stepping toward an old cedar trunk tucked in the corner by the window. Her fingers brushed over the carved lid before lifting it, releasing a scent of earth and animal. Wrapped in a faded wool blanket was a bearskin. She touched its snout, traced the fur between its glass eyes, and ran her palm down the spine of the pelt with reverence. Her family had told her long ago that the bearskin came from an ancestor's hunt – a bear taken in ceremony, not in conquest. As Alaska slowly closed the lid, she couldn't quite remember if what her family told her was true or if anything was true anymore.

Her gaze moved around the walls, cluttered with more memories and questions. To reorient herself, she examined the bounty posters and the crime scene photographs curled at the edges – her makeshift display of yellowed newspaper clippings with headlines underlined in Sharpie:

Cop's Wife Missing
Indigenous Woman Found Dead

The Roach Walks Free

A painting hung on another wall of her grandmother, Halona 'Kokum' Rainmaker, with eighty-one years of stories and storms behind her. Her gray braids draped over her shoulders like river lines, and five bold, vertical tattoos ran from her bottom lip to her chin — Cree markings of her initiations, medicine, and ancestors. Next to the painting was an old black-and-white photo of her grandfather, enlarged to match her grandmother's size and stature. Achahkos, or Archie 'Moshom' Rainmaker, appeared young, maybe 25, crisp and sharp in his military cap and pressed shirt. She couldn't remember if it was WWII, Korea, or the Vietnam War he fought in and never returned from. Those war names all seemed the same to her, but as she thought more about it, maybe it was her great-grandfather who fought in WWII, or was it WWI? Either way, she could never fully grasp that her grandfather looked younger than her in the photo — sometimes she thought of him as her younger brother. And as such, she often imagined going into battle with Archie to protect him, riding shotgun and fighting alongside him — lasso in one hand and a *rat-tat-tat-tat* machine gun in the other. She looked deeply into her grandfather's eyes and quietly asked Abacus to play *Who Says That's Not American by Raye Zaragoza.*

Alaska then moved closer to her grandmother's portrait and made a mental note to visit her the next time she felt strong enough for another trip to the city and across the border into America. She lit some sage, smudged it over her grandparents, and her elbow nudged a leather-bound book tucked underneath them in the overflowing bookcase. It wobbled and fell to the floor, and she bent down to pick up the well-thumbed book:

EARTH TRADITIONS

Alaska never had a particular reason to look at it before, but this time, she opened it up. On the inside cover was a simple handwritten note that read, "For Taino." She scanned the table of contents, which led her to a single word etched in bold script: The Wetiko – pp. 41-50. She quickly flipped through the pages until she found it, but it was missing; someone had ripped out the chapter. Only one page remained – an old charcoal drawing of the Wetiko: all shadow and bone, a pale face with a rib cage gaping open, black eyes – empty and endless.

She paused, then flipped back through the pages, thinking she might find some insight there in place of the missing Wetiko chapter. She turned over more chapters in the book, which covered various Earth-based traditions, including some from her own Cree heritage.

Alaska didn't wholly understand or embrace her heritage, and all that it entailed. She knew bits and pieces, and mostly cherry-picked what made sense to her. From what she could remember, her mother loved using plants, herbs, and remedies, and often shared stories about their Cree culture. When her grandmother visited, she taught Alaska how to connect with plant spirits and about some of their medicinal uses. Her grandmother also showed her how to use sage for clearing and how to offer tobacco or tobacco prayer ties before receiving anything, including the teachings she herself received from her grandmother. Alaska enjoyed doing these things, although she still had much to learn – like the night stars, the teachings never end.

Although Alaska continued to make progress in practicing her ancestral Cree language through an audio app, online classes, and conversations with her grandmother, it remained a challenge. It's not that she lacked opportunities to speak Cree face-to-face with others or to attend numerous gatherings, ceremonies, and Manitoba powwows; it's just that she preferred to spend time alone – not lonely, like most of the people she met, but simply alone. She sometimes went to the powwows intending to dance, but her anxiety about her mother would flare up when she saw all the women and children celebrating. As a result, she would usually step aside or leave altogether. It's not that Alaska didn't like the people she encountered out there in the big smoke; she just preferred to study and observe humans, any human, from an arm's length – unless that is, she was lassoing them and collecting their bounty-bling, in which case she entertained them.

Alaska primarily resonated with being Cree because that is who her mother and grandfather were, who her grandmother is, and what the land beneath her feet was and is. Her father was American, Welsh by ancestry – which made her part of that too." If anyone got too close, invaded her personal space, or probed too deeply into her background or the origins of her skin color, she would often say, "I'm an ocean whale." That usually made any stranger or opp look at her as if she were loco and back off immediately, which made her think her family from Wales couldn't be all that bad. She would keep them, and maybe even would like to meet them someday – from a distance.

As for the Earth Traditions book, Alaska wasn't sure what all these chapters and words referred to. To her, they mainly

seemed part of a different, much larger world than hers −
or maybe even from the distant past. When she needed to
research, it was usually about criminal psychology, bounty
hunting strategies, motorcycle mechanics, gaming techniques, or computer hacking − words that actually paid for
her own world to exist.

When Alaska did read, she had to really concentrate on
the words, as reading was not one of her superpowers, even
though it was one of her passions. Maybe it was because she
had **this neurodivergent** trait she was told she had, or maybe
it was just because they were written words. They didn't align
well with her bloodline's oral tradition on her mother's side
and perhaps even on her 'whale people' side − who knows.
Either way, Alaska was generally more of a physical, tactile,
experiential, visual, intuitive, and dreaming type. She usually
relied on written words afterwards, mainly as reference points
and frameworks for her direct experiences. Alaska was an
after-the-fact arrow. 'Shoot first, ask questions, and figure
it out later, maybe,' was her motto.

Alaska was ready to put the book back when she flipped
through and saw a charcoal drawing of a bear with a caption
underneath that said:

BEAR MEDICINE

Alaska had always liked bears. As a child, her teddy bear was
her favorite. Although initially inspired by a 'female' black
bear at the London Zoo, she found the adventures of *Winnie the
Pooh* and 'his' band mates: Christopher Robin, Piglet, Eeyore,
Kanga, Roo, Rabbit, Owl, and Tigger, incredibly amusing.
She enjoyed touching the bear skin in the trunk. She wore

her mother's leather bear claw motorcycle jacket and often watched the bears cross the meadow in the spring with awe. So, she took a closer look at the words on the page, tracing them with her finger and reading aloud – both effective hacks for her to understand any material she read patiently.

Here are some words she read about Bear Medicine:

The bear (maskwa) holds deep significance in Cree spirituality as a powerful healing spirit, a master teacher of plant medicines, and a guide for those who work with herbal healing. Bear medicine people are often specialists in root medicines and healing practices, and believe bears teach humans through dreams and visions.

Exhausted from the road and still foggy from her seizure, Alaska stopped reading, her finger and her mind growing tired from processing too much strange, yet somehow familiar data. Her hand trembled as she closed the book, made a mental note to return to it later, and set it down on the coffee table. She turned back toward the center of the room, to what she knew best and for sure. "Abacus," she directed her voice now steady. "Review the recent chase." The wall projector screen lit up, displaying footage from her bike camera of the recent bounty hunt in sharp detail: her motorcycle weaving through traffic and the distant figure of the fugitive riding ahead. The recording paused on a truck, caught just as she passed it.

Abacus pointed out, "Had you veered left instead of right, you would have gained three seconds."

Alaska clenched her fists and turned her attention to what she knew second best. "Play *Hellblade*." The walls responded and shifted around her. Her cozy wooden cabin dissolved into a holographic hellscape of twisted trees, foggy moors, and stone altars. Alaska slipped on her headset and gripped her sword-console, its cool plastic feeling familiar against her palms. On-screen, she became Senua, a Pict warrior woman burdened by voices and mental illness. Alaska had always felt a special connection with Senua, as she, too, had experienced more than a few of these diagnoses, having been told by professionals trained to deliver them. Before slamming the door and leaving the words and whatever the latest professional said in the dust. But not before raising her palm and saying "whatev." She only remembered their words: Epilepsy. Dyslexia. Complex dissociative disorder. Nervous dysregulation. And her personal favourite, delivered with the gravity of a sentencing: Oppositional Defiant Disorder. She had framed that one internally and hung it above her bed. Her grandmother told her that another diagnosis explaining her fire, seizures, and spontaneous storms is that when she was born, lightning struck the cabin – she carried that lightning spirit with her, and maybe sometimes too much of it, but lightning nonetheless.

Like Senua, Alaska fought and kept fighting her way out of any boxes or anyone who tried to box her in. If she had been an actual boxer, she would have most likely been the kind that *'Floats like a butterfly and stings like a bee.'*

For Alaska, *Hellblade* wasn't just a game; it was her therapy – a visceral, brutal way to confront her shadow, reflected on the pixelated landscape. She swung *Senua's* blade mercilessly at the approaching demons. She lunged, a silent scream ripping through her virtual throat, meeting the first creature head-on. Their eyes resembled the Wetiko her mother had warned her about: hollow, greedy, and starving. They collapsed beneath her blade, one after another. The clash of steel rang in her ears, a phantom pain in her phantom limbs. She fought, grunting with effort, twisting, parrying, and striking. The kill-tracker, a subtle digital overlay, counted upward: 1... 2... 3... in her peripheral visicn. Each kill carried something deeper than pixels – like a promise of justice, an elixir for healing, or at least a few moments of relief.

6

The Cellar

Somewhere in an American city, the air in a cellar was musty and putrid. The only light came from a single bare bulb hanging crooked from a rusted chain, swaying like a noose from the ceiling. Gemini Moon lay strapped to an old wooden table, wrists and ankles bound in cracked leather restraints. Bruises darkened her ribs and cheeks, and a strip of duct tape covered her mouth, pulled tight over split lips. Her eyes darted around the cellar, searching for a way out, for hope, for a weapon, or anything.

In the corner of the room, she could see a workbench lined with knives – some old, others surgical, with blades dulled and nicked from use, not time. Beyond the workbench was a scatter of stolen identities: dozens of IDs from lives long gone, with names scratched out and faces faded. Above the bench, the brick wall had shelves built into its mortar. On them stood rows of mason jars, the glass clouded and yellowed with age. Inside the jars, things floated: a squirrel, a human foot swollen and pale. One jar held something unmistakably male and mutilated – severed and curled genitals floating in yellowed formaldehyde. Gemini's breath hitched, and her limbs pulled against the straps in vain.

Then came the creak of stairs. The figure from the van stepped onto the concrete floor and peeled off their latex mask with a wet, stretching sound, though the angle of the light made their face hard to see. All Gemini could see was hair: thin, dark, and lifeless. The figure moved to a wall lined with mannequin heads, each wearing a different, unrecognizable rubber or molded-leather face. They carefully placed their mask among them, like adding another delicate doll face to their collection. The killer pressed play on an iPod, and *Bandit by Juice WRLD (Feat. YoungBoy Never Broke Again)* filled the dank air. They danced back and forth, tracing their fingers over the knives one by one, whispering to each of them in a whiny, child-like voice. "Eenie... meenie... miney..." The killer stopped on a single blade, their fingers curling around its hilt, "Mo."

Gemini's mind jackhammered... *who is this... is it even human... how do I... the children, the animals... get out... the water... how do I... Mother Earth...* her thoughts spiraling outward even as her body pulled inward against the straps.

The killer raised a knife. Gemini's mind blanked, and her muffled, sonar-like screams filled the cellar. But the walls were thick, and neither the killer nor the world outside cared. The killer worked quietly, then placed the bloody knife back on the bench. They walked out and up the way they came in, closing the door to the cellar and Gemini's life behind them.

7

The Cop and The Robot

In the mostly uninhibited part of the city, a repurposed gas station stood as a relic from another time. Its once-bright red-and-white paint was now faded and peeling, and the iconic Phillips 66 sign above the door flickered unpredictably. The space, which its occupants called Phillip or The 66, had been transformed from a garage into a living space, a lab, and a detective's office. Its gravel yard, serving as an outdoor laboratory, was a chaotic collage shaped by utility: concrete bones, forgotten machine parts, and rusted robot prototypes. Makeshift crime-scene setups were scattered randomly: mock-ups, ghost stories retold in plastic blood and mannequin limbs, and training areas including a weapons range in the far corner with paper targets riddled with bullet holes. A row of old cars, some marked with stray bullet holes, each in various stages of disrepair, sat behind the brick wall that guarded the premises like a junkyard dog. A wall built for privacy and to keep its contents safe from looky-loos and the city's growing legion of recycling scavengers and metal thieves.

40

The inside bays, once bustling with mechanics, were now filled with clutter: machine parts, an old couch, a vintage fridge, metal desks, and overflowing filing cabinets. Ama, a robot, rolled through the front bay on pink roller skates, her wheels clicking rhythmically across the dirty concrete floor as she navigated around broken tiles and oil stains. Ama was a patchwork robot – homemade and incomplete. Her skin looked synthetic, with a brown tone and uneven texture in some spots. Her bald head reflected the fluorescent lights, seamless except for faint lines of panel seams, weld scars, and a tuft of shocking pink hair. Her body was incomplete, like a portrait left half-done by someone who ran out of money or parts before finishing. One arm swung freely, while wires dangled from the other socket like loose nerve endings. She looked about thirty years old, maybe – if she had been human.

Young Americans by David Bowie blared from a circular speaker embedded in the place where Ama's heart would be – if she had one. She moved to the music, spinning, gliding, and doing slow figure eights past a rusted engine hoist and a pile of stripped-down motorcycles. She danced as if American dreams or a dream for America were coming alive in scrap metal. Her single good arm made exaggerated pop-star gestures, her eyes sparkling with digital joy. She twirled, her laughter slipping into a pre-coded trill. But then, just as the chorus hit, a red light pulsed in her iris like a faint heartbeat, and the music dropped into a drone note, replacing Bowie's voice.

She pivoted and rolled toward a rusted steel door marked OFFICE, in faded black stencil. On the other side, Detective Sam Morse sat behind a metal desk propped up by engine parts and old military crates. He was in his mid-fifties, thickening around the middle, and he looked grizzled and road-worn like he'd seen too many ghosts – or was haunted by the ones that got away, or both.

His office smelled like stale coffee, gun oil, and the intangible residue of those he couldn't or didn't protect: his daughter, his late wife, himself from himself, the crimes he couldn't solve, and the killers he failed to catch. These residues mingled with his series of contradictory personal choices, which he couldn't or wouldn't understand, etching lines on his forehead.

Sam kept the office lights as low as night, as if the sun were his mortal enemy, and he covered the concrete walls with grainy crime scene stills of murders, victims, and killers. Some images were new, some old, and some still there because he had simply forgotten to take them down, but each one was frozen or warped in time and horror. Strings connected the tracks of the Copycat Killer, one of his many assigned cases, linking photos to clues like a cracked spiderweb. One wall was nothing but a list of missing persons. Another held maps with multi-colored thumbtacks hammered in like wounds, over the last decade or so. A faded 'Defend Democracy' protest sign hung behind stacks of mandatory bureaucratic assessment forms he'd been ignoring for weeks. A Green Bay Packers flag drooped across another wall like a totem for victories and losses that also wouldn't leave him alone – in both good and not-so-good ways.

Sam was old school. He preferred to see everything laid out in front of him with tangible objects he could touch or move, but he grudgingly embraced new tech when necessary. Although he relied on Ama for her precise data recall, he reconciled his dependence on her because she sort of resembled a human being. He never quite asked himself what that said about him. However, modernizing his operation by purchasing a few second-hand computers still felt like cheating. He kept them out of the way. One of these monitors bled footage from a sterile morgue. Another displayed the inside of a strip mall in thermal imaging.

To balance things out, a vintage record player spun vinyl slowly behind him, *Robert Johnson*, the bluesman, preaching *Hellhound on My Trail* through speakers connected to a turntable with a used needle older than half the compound's inventory. Sam clicked his Zippo lighter open and shut to the music. It was the last remnant of his smoking days, the tiny flame sparking to the beat – a habit, too comfortable to quit cold turkey.

Ama opened the door and rolled in, sound vibrating softly from a valve in her throat. She offered him a cup of coffee in a cracked mug that read, "WORLD'S OKAYEST COP," a cherished gift that still tethered him to a life raft floating across his memories. "We got a report of a body," she announced in a clear, cadenced voice.

Sam took the coffee cup without looking up. "Location?"

"At the shoreline..." Ama's head rattled and paused, her body freezing. The red light in her eye twinkled, then stopped, and her voice cut out, leaving silence behind.

Sam looked up. "Ama?"

She rebooted mid-sentence. "... of Lake Walton."

He raised his coffee cup and nodded his thanks.

Ama spun on her skates, pirouetted once, and slid out the door without another word, as if it was just another Thursday. Sam took a long sip of his coffee. It was cold. Ama had never quite figured out the coffeemaker's temperature settings, and if he was being honest with himself, neither had he. He didn't care, and he winced at the bitter taste from the grounds as he drained his cup. He grabbed his old, worn-out bulletproof vest − the one he refused to replace because it had the three bullet holes that kept him on the right side of the grass. When asked about it, he'd end the conversation with, "Why mess with a good thing?" He holstered his battered sidearm, took a deep breath, and clicked his Zippo on and off, signaling − *'here we go again.'* He left the vinyl playing as he walked out, believing that the more the needle carved the grooves, the richer the sound, and the better the quality. Maybe he thought that about himself, but he never really explored that idea.

He stepped outside where the sun hit like a gut punch. His eyes squinted like Clint Eastwood in a showdown, and if he could have kept them closed, he would have. He scanned the yard − no dust today. He acknowledged to himself that none of this climate, both the weather and the political, had a discernible pattern or motive, two things that he banked his existence on − but here, it was beyond his pay grade to solve. He then climbed into his ride − a black, heavily modified, reclaimed 1973 Plymouth Satellite. He turned the engine. It coughed awake, loud and stubborn.

The compound's metal gate slid open with a rattle and slammed shut behind him as he pulled out onto the road to where Lake Walton was waiting, along with its problem.

8

The Livestream

Sun flares sliced across Sam's cracked windshield as dust clouds that had just formed rolled on the distant horizon. Right ahead, a line of people stood quietly for their water rationings that had been temporary, then permanent, then the new normal. Now even that was slipping. They sweat under the sun, each holding jugs, buckets, and canisters, waiting behind a battered water tanker with peeling paint and a dripping hose. The side of the tanker read:

WILLIAM'S WATER DELIVERY – 1-888-WET-GULP

Sam slowed, his eyes scanning over the faces with their parched lips and hollow cheeks. The world had changed. The air was hotter, water was scarcer, red tape was redder, and his job of hunting killers was more complex than he remembered. He had a few spare gallons of water in the trunk, but no time to hand them out, so he drove past without stopping. Whatever awaited at Lake Walton, it wasn't going to solve itself.

He drove ahead, checked his travel authorization on the

dashboard display – still valid for another week. Detectives got thirty-day rolling permits; civilians got seven. Cross-county required approval, cross-state required sponsorship. If the price was right and you knew who to bribe or hook up with a quality forger, then that was usually enough to get anyone through these hoops. He generally ignored and lost track of the shifting regulations, and followed them only after his boss nagged him when signing his renewals. He had one hand on the wheel while pressing a button with the other on a touchscreen monitor he had awkwardly anchored to the faded dashboard with screws and Gorilla Glue. The monitor and a familiar theme song came to life – *A Good Day to Fight the System by Shungudzo.*

Sam turned up the volume with his thumb as he drove through the city's outskirts, passing rusted factories, stacked shipping containers, and graffiti-tagged walls. He only slowed down to stop at a variety of familiar checkpoints to show his credentials. Even though most of the human guards knew him and waved him through without question or concern, the guard bots, or 'time wasters' as he called them, always, always checked.

The theme song faded, and Rachel sat upright in her makeshift livestream studio tucked behind a curtain in the corner of her apartment. The space was a tech shrine: communication books were piled high, along with old radios, computers, and monitors tracking God knows what. Rachel toggled through three proxy servers before going live; a standard practice she learned by rote since the crackdown on 'misinformation' and unsanctioned media platforms. A large screen behind her displayed the MISCHIEF logo – a stylized fist gripping a microphone. She sat before a halo of light, her face carefully made up, looking as if she hadn't just cried herself sick. Her voice cut in, crisp and cucumber cool, betraying none of the inner turmoil she felt, "I'm Rachel Lamont, and you're listening to Mischief." She leaned closer, her lips brushing a silver mic as if revealing a secret manuscript. "Today we're launching a new mini-series on violence in America," she announced. "Our first guest is Dustin Guidry, the curator of the Museum of Modern Murder. Welcome to Mischief, Dustin."

The livestream split screen revealed a man sitting comfortably in his macabre room, cluttered to the brim with killing collectibles: movie posters, books, photographs, old weapons, and serial killer memorabilia filling his windowless office. Fifty, going on forever, he exuded the languid confidence of a New Orleans ghost tour guide – which is where he landed his first job in the dark, underbelly business. His voice was smooth as bourbon and twice as buttery. "Thanks for having me on," came the drawl.

"Your museum is very unique," Rachel prompted, forcing a smile. "You collect artifacts from serial killers, murderers, acts of terror, and historical atrocities. Why don't you tell our Mischief audience a little bit about your gig?"

Dustin leaned back in his chair. "As you mentioned, I buy, sell, and collect items and artwork related to the history of violence and murder, not just in America, but worldwide. I buy and sell in person and online, and I also run a fairly active online community where we discuss all things brutal. The museum also has an online fan club called M & M's, where we sell fan club 'merch' including T-shirts, hoodies, coffee cups, postcards, and fridge magnets. Oh, and a shameless plug here – we're running a Christmas special right now. Enjoy 25% off select items in our online catalog."

Rachel leaned back, finishing a sip of her coffee. "You can make money with all that, and support yourself in *this* economy? Sounds sus."

Dustin barely held back his laughter. "You're kidding, right? I just heard that OJ's black glove sold for two million to a private collector. Anything related to victims, murders, or crime, especially involving any kind of celebrity, never goes out of style, especially the big-ticket items. As we like to say at the fan club, "Murder may bury ya, but it never dies.""

Rachel nodded her head, convinced. "Alright, we'll put your website info in the show notes. How did you get into all this anyway?"

Dustin looked at the ceiling, activating his recall. "Long story short, it started when I was a kid, during a time when there was a surge of serial killings across the country, often called the 'golden age of serial murder.' If you grew up in the seventies through the nineties, you'll know what I mean. I became terrified and wanted to understand what made these monsters tick. My parents sure as hell couldn't explain it."

Rachel raised her eyebrows, incredulously. "The golden age of serial murder?"

Dustin responded, "Yeah, there were reports that showed up on all the news cycles, seemingly 24-7, and that's when we just had nine channels. Not much different, really, than the golden age of cinema, the golden age of the internet, the golden age of mass shooters, or even the golden age of mass species extinction. The last two are the ages we are in now."

"I've never thought of it that way, as micro patterns within larger cycles," Rachel interjected.

Dustin thought it over, recalled a memory he preferred to

keep buried, then replied, "I mean, I was terrified as a kid, but at least we didn't have to endure active school shooter drills. Didn't have to practice hiding under desks, or be a parent sending your kids to school with the fear that they might never come back. What a nightmare that must be.

Rachel brought it back home and asked, with a mix of skepticism and fascination in her voice, "Alright, let's unpack this. How'd you go from a terrified kid to opening a murder museum? That seems like quite the leap."

Dustin adjusted his glasses. "I saved up my allowance, and the first thing I bought was Jeffrey Dahmer's high school yearbook. It kinda snowballed from there, and I started collecting and trading all kinds of serial killer memorabilia. I bought and sold online, and went to Crime-Con to collect what I could. Eventually, as I got older, I was doing so much volume that I could barely move around my apartment."

"So you started with Dahmer? Sounds like a next-level obsession," Rachel probed.

Dustin replied, "I suppose. To understand it. To catalog the human capacity for cruelty. To learn from it, perhaps. And, let's be honest, for the morbid fascination. When Marie Antoinette's guillotine came up at an auction, I realized I'd outgrown my apartment. Time to get a bigger boat."

Rachel smiled. "You have the actual guillotine. I might want to come down and see that."

Dustin mimicked the guillotine coming down with his hand. "Chop chop! We're open to the public seven days a week, except on Halloween. I mean, a guy's gotta go out and have some fun now and then."

Sam veered past a collapsed warehouse. On the screen, Rachel kept the momentum going and jumped in. "Let's cut to the quick. Why do you think America has so many serial killers and mass shooters? Do we need stricter gun laws? What's the deal?"

Dustin shrugged his shoulders and replied, "Giving citizens easy and unlimited access to bazookas, low-key, never ends well for anyone."

"Yeah, the bazooka bag is pretty big business for the owners, shareholders, and the political class. But why is this? What makes 'We The People' so violent?" Rachel sighed.

"I'm no historian or psychologist," Dustin directed into his mic, "but violence is in our blood. It's forged in the very fiber and fabric of our DNA. It's in the dirt under our personal and cultural fingernails. Ya know, the last time I checked what time it is, we didn't settle the American Revolution and the fight for independence over tea and biscuits; we settled it at the end of the barrel of a gun. Sometimes, the use of force or the threat of it to gain your freedom is the only option available, and when it is, make it count."

"That sounds Shakespearean," Rachel said as she refilled her coffee cup from the pot and took another sip.

Dustin mused, "Yeah, we can't ever seem to exit the stage. And now America's got more bullets than brains, along with a mountain of half a billion guns to fire them. If we're not the ones pulling the triggers, we're sitting back nursing watered-down beer and munching popcorn, watching the rockets and fireworks go off in real time. That, and we seem to love our Bibles even more than our booze or our bombs."

"Religion?" Rachel interjected.

"In spades," Dustin continued, calm and distant. "We just don't practice the preach. Working for the man and shopping till we're dropping are really the only true religions and rituals we have left around here. All that can lead to some gnarly behaviors. Combine that with the extreme summers, dust storms, and Florida-like winters," he added, "I'm surprised we all haven't sliced and diced each other by now."

"Yeah... I miss winter," she said, half-joking, half-not. "What do you think the roots of all this are?" asked Rachel.

Dustin leaned closer to his mic. "I'm no anthropologist either, but I had a great uncle Charlie who claimed some Cherokee heritage – just like half the folks seem to do in this country. Maybe legit, maybe not. He said that America was like a psych ward where everyone's competing to be the craziest and loneliest patient with the tightest straitjacket. His view was that America isn't a land of immigrants, but a land *with* immigrants – big difference."

"A land with immigrants? I've never heard it put quite like that," said Rachel.

Dustin waved his arm across his body and opened his palm upwards. "The Cherokee and the Indigenous peoples of the Americas have been here since time immemorial. The immigrants, including mine who arrived here, whether by force, freewill, or around a fence, didn't just bring our luggage, we also brought baggage: trauma from famine, war, poverty, persecution, indentured servitude, chattel slavery, along with greed for land, gold, and silver, and some sort of M.O. about converting or controlling souls. Instead of healing our baggage, we just spread it around and passed it down – sometimes at the end of a barrel of a gun. That was his take on it, anyway."

Rachel leaned in, "Your uncle sounds like a wise man. He reminds me of the philosopher, Jiddu Krishnamurti, who said, 'It's no measure of health to be well adjusted to a profoundly sick society.'"

Dustin chuckled and mused, "Your philosopher sounds like a wise man."

Rachel smiled, "On that note, we'll be right back after a word from our sponsor. This is Mischief."

The theme song kicked in again, and Sam lowered the volume just enough to let the music fade out. In the silence, he briefly thought about this younger generation with their music, their hopes and dreams, and their precarious futures, then turned his attention back to something he could manage – following the coordinates to the crime scene as they rolled down the monitor's screen.

9

The Crime Scene

Sam drove past an old, burnt-out shell of a church that loomed by the roadside. With boards nailed over the windows, a half-collapsed steeple, and the grounds overgrown, it looked like it had absorbed too many prayers or confessions and caught fire trying to release them. He looked at it, nothing more — just long enough for a few memories to pass by him like a backdraft. Then he slowed down into a lakeside parking lot, stopping beneath a row of blinking yellow caution lights. Flashing beacons lit up the marshy shoreline, where what was left of the once-deep, majestic, and drinkable Lake Walton merged into the dark, damp mud. Strips of warning tape fluttered in the gentle breeze like police-issue prayer flags. EMTs and hazmat technicians in full-body suits moved slowly and carefully, their faces hidden behind shields. Above, a helicopter circled lazily in the sky, its thermal radar pulsing through the lake's shallow, muddy water.

Sam stepped out of his car and took off his sunglasses. He inhaled deeply, the air heavy with the smell of diesel and lake rot. At the edge of the perimeter, a humanoid security bot with a police badge scanned him from head to toe. "Detective Morse. Confirmed." The machine's voice buzzed like a dental drill. Sam passed through the checkpoint, pulled on black nitrile gloves, and cracked open an ammonia inhalant beneath his nose with the ease of ritual. It hit sharply, clearing his sinuses and banishing sleep, almost as effective as caffeine, but not quite. He ducked under the plastic sheeting and crime tape, eyes already scanning ahead, spotting the crime scene marker fluttering beside a half-submerged log. And there, splayed like a broken mannequin, was the mangled body.

Carlos 'Carly' Hernandez, sixty-four and hardened in a wrinkled shirt, knelt near the body with a clipboard in one hand and a camera in the other – captain, on paper, seasoned workhorse in practice. Although half the forensics team had quit when the administration demanded pre-approved conclusions, Carly was one of the few who stayed, documenting everything twice – once for the official record, once for history.

"Whatcha got, Carly?" Sam's voice was flat as a forgotten soda, hung out to dry in an August sun.

"More shit show, Sam," Carly announced without looking up. "Floated in sometime last night. Deceased less than a week, give or take. Water pushed her to shore, stiff as driftwood."

Sam crouched beside the corpse. It looked like a woman, naked except for the lakeweed clinging to her shoulders. Her skin was a patchwork of light and dark shades of cobalt blue, although it did not appear to be from drowning or decay. Sam leaned in. "Lividity?"

Carly responded, "Nope. The skin's just blue. Like, blue." With gloved fingers, Carly peeled back part of the lakeweed covering the chest. "Also, with teeth marks. Something gnawed at her post-mortem." Carly pointed to the forehead, then rose to his feet. "There's your cross," he said. "Carved clean, just like the others."

Sam stood up, his joints cracking as he rose, clicked his tongue against his upper front teeth – false, but passable. "Copycat."

"Matches the pattern. Almost too clean," the Captain offered, then pulled Sam aside. "Look, the department's saying we need to close this fast. Some federal liaison called the chief, saying too much attention on serial killings undermines public confidence in safety and homeland security. They want us to blame it on immigration, or drugs, or domestic terrorism, or weather, or whatever." He waved his hand. "Anything but what it is."

Sam nodded, ignored him, and looked out over the eerily silent, slow-motion crime scene. "Sweep the area like your mama's kitchen," he barked, loud enough for the techs and uniforms to hear him. "Seal off a full mile radius. I want everything: blades, rope fibers, footprints, blood smears, fingernail shavings, DNA flakes, haystack needles, mystery turds. Don't miss a goddamn freckle." He pointed at a pair of sluggish-looking cadets loitering near the second perimeter. "And stay hydrated!"

One of the idealistic cadets raised a water bottle and waved at the renowned, seasoned detective, calling out, "Hey, General," which was Sam's nickname given to him by his colleagues in the field. Sam smiled, mirrored the gesture, and took a pull from his hip flask, which maybe contained whiskey and maybe didn't. What mattered to him most was that it was wet.

A sleek drone whirred to life from the back of a nearby cruiser, lifting off like a metal hawk. It hovered briefly, then shot upward and outward, its wide lens scanning the shoreline, the church ruins, and the distant tree line. Watching it go, Sam felt the knot tighten in his gut, recognizing the familiar pattern of the crime scene — and snarled to himself, "Who and where the fuck is this son of a bitch."

10

The Hellblade

Alaska was deep inside the *Hellblade* simulation, locked in a pixelated nightmare that mirrored much of her real life, yet one she felt she had more control over. Senua, or rather Alaska, gripped her sword-console, and streaks of digital ash and blood painted her face. Her sword, heavy and elegant, sliced through the horde of demons pouring out from cave mouths. Alaska moved as if she had been born for medieval times, ducking, parrying, spinning the blade through necks and spines with a precision that felt disturbingly real and natural to her, while the kill tracker tapped out the rising body count.

As she stood barefoot on cracked digital earth, a hologram flickered into view in the upper right corner of her HUD. Sam's face appeared rough and tired, with a hint of stubble across his chin that emphasized his infrequent shaves. "Hey, kiddo. What's going on?"

Alaska didn't look up, her focus locked into the dance of slaying and slaughter. "Annihilating some mutants. What's up, Dad?"

Sam scratched his chin and squinted as if he was trying to see through her ambivalence. "Ah, you know, I thought maybe you could spend some time with the old man. Come down for Christmas?"

"I can't do the city or America again right now. I just got back from driving through the desert dust." She decapitated another demon and sidestepped the spray, then kicked a flaming imp off the edge of a cliff. She mused, "Why don't you come up to the cabin?"

A pause hung in the air, and Sam sighed, "You know I can't."

Alaska gutted another demon and flung its body into the abyss.

"Also," Sam added, "I'm knee-deep in a case."

Alaska finally stopped moving, her sword dripping virtual gore. "I thought you were done chasing after Looney Tunes."

Sam insisted, "I am. I mean, I was. This is the last one."

"You said that about the last one," she reminded him.

Sam raised a hand like a man swearing on a bad Bible, knowing he broke his oath before he could make it. "It's the last, last one."

Alaska looked up and peered behind him. The background wasn't a department office or a dusty garage; it was scorched wood and blackened beams that hadn't held a roof in years. "Is that St. Mary's?"

Sam gave a slow nod. "Yeah. Come to think of it, I could use your help on this one."

"Yeah, but no." Her voice cooled quickly, returning her attention to the demons at hand.

He shrugged as if he already knew her answer. "Alaska, you were first in your class at the academy; you know how to do this work blindfolded."

"Blindfolded? I don't crack Piñatas, Pops. Not interested or interesting," she shot back.

Sam re-strategized and offered, "Up to you, but this one's got a fairly steep bounty." She didn't reply, didn't move, or swing her sword. Just long enough for doubt to sneak in through the cracks. Sam saw his opening, and his mannerisms softened. "I also wanted to let you know that Ama's falling apart."

Alaska didn't answer immediately. She kept her focus on the blood-soaked pixel arena stretching out before her and the demons pacing around the edges. Finally, she raised the blade again, her fingers tightening on the sword. "Just fix her, as I showed you."

Sam wasn't having it. "Alaska, I can't keep up with all this tech nonsense. It's probably time to decommission her, maybe sell her for parts and scrap."

Alaska stared into the void, both the real and imaginary ones, where even the pixel demons couldn't pull her out. "Let me think about it," she said. "I'll call you later, okay?"

Sam smiled faintly. "Righty-o," the hologram said, and it blinked out.

The HUD adjusted as the ambient light changed. Alaska lowered her sword, the weight of reality hitting harder than any boss battle. She spoke aloud to the system. "Abacus, how much cash do I have left after that last haul?" Abacus shot out:

GAS. FOOD. LODGING. BIKE REPAIRS. GAMING EXPENSES.
BALANCE: $132.72

Alaska cringed and stared at the number, then at the ashes of the digital battlefield. The real numbers and real monsters infringed on her game and her life. She ordered, "Abacus, resume *Hellblade*."

Abacus beeped, then replied, "You have reached our agreed-upon game time for a twenty-four-hour period. Shutting down, now." The HUD turned off, and the cabin went quiet. Alaska looked around for the source of the voice and considered ripping the speakers out of the wall before settling back into her chair to assess and mainly avoid the decisions looming ahead of her. She picked up her phone, double checked the dwindling numbers on her bank account, and tossed her cell across the room.

11

The Dudes

Ama's private room at the back of The 66 held an unused bed, a chair, a desk, a computer, a drivable micro-car, and a closet for her limited but distinct wardrobe. None of it was necessary for her as a robot, but she had collected and arranged these items over the years to give herself the appearance and 'feel' of a human being.

Much like that of a teenager, she plastered the walls with pictures and posters representing cultures and identities she was trying on for size. Above her desk was a schoolroom-sized map of mainland America, with pin drops, circled areas, and a marker tracing Route 66 from Chicago to the West Coast. One wall featured a mix of musicians who sang about the road, America, and being a human being – the three things she longed to experience but remained beyond her reach. On another wall was a patchwork quilt of images depicting past and present cultural, political, and scientific figures. All were women whose stories she had learned about online, because if she was going to become a human, a human woman, or a human-presenting woman, she needed to draw on a broad range of data points and perspectives beyond her prefab programming.

In one corner sat a trunk full of robot dolls, including 3PO, Data, Battle Angel Alita, G.I. Robot, Robby the Robot, Racheal Nexus-7, Megazord, and B-9 Robot, which she pulled out and played with from time to time, acting out various imaginary scenarios that only she knew about. Nearby, Rock 'Em Sock 'Em Robots, an old toy from the 70s where two miniature plastic robots fight inside a two ft/sq boxing ring, occupied another corner. It was a gift from Alaska and one of the first toys she learned how to play with. Even Sam played with it with her now and then in his rare downtime, on the condition that she not tell anybody about it. He didn't say why. Maybe it was because Ama never lost a single round, so she never pressed him for a reason.

At the back of her room, Ama sat cross-legged on the floor, her mechanical limbs ticking softly as her servos adjusted. Her single remaining arm, resting in her lap like an abandoned tool, flexed just slightly as she watched the old CRT screen in front of her. *Easy Rider*, the iconic '60s boomer counterculture movie, played and crackled through dusty speakers. On the screen, Billy, George, and Captain America were locked in a jail cell – three rebels from a different America, bathed in 16mm color. Captain America leaned into the scene, calm and stoned. "Dude means nice guy. Dude means a regular sort of person."

Ama's face lit up with recognition. "Dude. Nice guy," she softly mimicked, her voice a rough mix of human warmth and machine reverb, then downloaded the meaning and embedded the words into her neural net like sacred code. While she watched the movie, she attempted to hack into federal and international databases on another computer to try to secure a robot license, register a robot, and forge an American travel pass. The movie sound warped, then her head turned. A single red eye blinked, pulsed, and fixed on something. Beyond the walls and perimeter fence of the compound, a slow growl rumbled. It wasn't yet identifiable, but it sounded old, raw, and alive. A V-twin motorcycle engine, all-American and unmistakable, echoed nearby. Ama rose silently. She didn't need to see what was approaching yet, because she already knew that Alaska, her friend and creator, was coming home.

The iron gate slowly creaked open, and Alaska rode in, engine loud and smooth, the sound of her motorcycle resounding through the dust-covered compound like a symphony. She coasted into one of the empty bays and cut the engine, letting the bay wrap around her like an old, familiar blanket. Alaska slung her duffel bag over one shoulder and moved through the shadowed entryway as if she owned the place, which, in some unspoken way, she still did. An artificial Christmas tree stood by the door, crooked and unlit, as if someone had put it up in a hurry. Alaska crouched beside it and deposited two roughly wrapped presents beneath its brittle plastic branches.

A faint whirl sounded from the far side of the room. "Skibidoo." The voice was monotone but warm, as Ama rolled closer on her signature pink skates – a gift from Alaska at a previous Christmas.

Alaska turned and crossed the floor in three quick strides, wrapping Ama in a hug. "You've lost weight," she sighed into Ama's shoulder. Then, pulling back, her eyes zeroed in on the missing arm. "What in the name... happened to you?"

Ama tilted her head, blinking her eyes with artificial calm.

"Your father indicates it's a temporary malfunction."

Alaska fussed and headed toward the workbench. "I'll fix you up in no time." She rummaged through a dented crate labeled SPARE LIMBS—FUNCTIONAL(ISH) and found an arm that matched Ama's remaining one in both size and shade. Standing beside her, she locked it into place with a click and snap of magnets and metal teeth.

"Can I ask you something?" Ama's voice was softer now.

Alaska didn't look up. "Shoot."

"Do you think I will ever be allowed to roam free like a human?" Ama asked.

Alaska paused, and her fingers froze mid-calibration. "I'm not sure, Ama."

Ama looked down at her new arm, flexing the fingers and testing its range of motion.

"I would like to leave Phillip someday and ride across America, just like in the *Easy Rider* movie.

"Why do you want to do that?" asked Alaska.

Ama immediately jumped in enthusiastically. "Dude, to touch the grass: to stand at the base of the Statue of Liberty or Ellis Island and take the American pledge, then travel down the Mississippi River like Huckleberry Finn, hit Route 66, then see the Grand Canyon and the Grand Tetons, and make it to the Pacific Ocean and ride the Ferris wheel on the Santa Monica Pier."

Alaska sighed. "Yeah... that's a tough one. AI laws, tracking, travel restrictions, special passes... It's a whole lotta system, and then there's the ridiculous cost of robot licensing and registration."

Ama processed the data and replied, "I also need to know that if I were to break down outside of our compound, does

America have the spare parts to fix me like you do?"

Alaska nodded and smiled, "Yeah, I'm sure America's got the parts."

"Okay. Just one last question. Is America safe for robots? For someone like me?" Ama asked.

Alaska shook her head from side to side and couldn't answer.

"I would like to know because I researched that in 2015, a hitchhiking robot that relied on the kindness of strangers traveled peacefully across Germany, the Netherlands, and Canada. However, the robot's journey across the US was cut short when it was beheaded, dismembered, and stomped on within hours of arriving in Philadelphia. Is that true, Alaska? Is that true, skibidoo?" asked Ama.

Alaska just shrugged. "It could be."

Ama stood up straighter, rolled her new arm experimentally, then glided to the wall and ripped down a weathered poster:

COPYCAT KILLER – $500000 REWARD

"Risk has been calculated. Will this cover all the costs?" asked Ama.

She handed it over to Alaska, who took it, eyes scanning the details. "That's a pretty big bling."

Ama's eyes glowed faintly. "Do you wanna jam?"

Alaska lit up. "Hell yeah."

Ama's core speaker crackled, then pulsed out the haunting anthem *Pocahontas by AnnenMayKantereit*. Alaska head-banged instinctively at the chorus, her hair whipping, boots thumping in a syncopated rhythm. Ama danced beside her, all sharp angles and servo-smooth groove, her roller skates slicing curves across the concrete.

Sam, hearing the commotion, stepped out of his office and paused at the edge of their fun, smiling and admiring his daughter and her friend. "Mind if I cut in?"

He attempted a few rough, awkward dad dance steps, but Ama raised her newly fixed arm and blocked him. "Three's a cluster buster."

Sam raised his hands in surrender and backed away, chuckling at his futile effort. As the music faded, he stepped forward and pulled Alaska into a brief, clumsy hug. She held him for a moment before pulling away. "When you didn't call, I figured you found an excuse to bail," Sam said, trying to hide his relief.

"You know how I feel about dropping the plot, pops," she reminded him, as if she were still a teenager.

"How long are you staying?" nudged Sam.

Alaska replied, "A couple of days. Maybe three." She walked away and pulled her saddlebag from her bike.

Sam nodded, brushing past the conversation and stepping toward his office. "I'm heading to forensics. Wanna tag along?"

She shook her head instantly. "It's the holidays, Dad. Can you give it a rest already? Besides, I really don't wanna do the cop thing."

Sam stopped and proudly insisted, "Alaska, if I've said it once, I've said it a thousand times, you were first in your class at the academy. You have a knack for this."

Alaska deflated his praise and raised her palm. "I also had a knack for calling my supervisor a kunt and having seizures in the bullpen. Real professional. And poking around cadavers for Christmas was not exactly on my bingo card."

Sam gave a half-shrug. "Suit yourself, but I'm stopping by Sonny's after. Fried fish?"

Alaska placed her saddlebag beside her duffel. "You mean you're stopping by Sonny's for a single malt and ordering takeout from Joey's."

Sam grinned, busted.

Alaska rolled her eyes at his predictable routine, and Ama tilted her head, twirled her finger in the air, and smiled like she understood more than she let on.

12

The Call

Rachel's cell phone rang sharply and suddenly, cracking the quiet kitchen like a plate dropping on tile. Rachel's nerves rattled as she snatched it off the counter. Her voice was hollow when she spoke, as though it had been living underwater. "Yeah?"

Lucia hesitated on the other end of the line, then said quietly, "It's Gemini."

Rachel fell silent. Her face didn't change, but behind her eyes, she crumbled and collapsed.

The phone call ended. Rachel couldn't remember hanging up or the details of their conversation. She could only stagger toward the bathroom, tearing off her clothes as she went, and stumble into the shower, using the wall for support. The faucet squealed when she turned the knob, and rusty water dribbled out, as if it were bleeding from the pipes. No pressure, heat, or relief, just a reluctant trickle from a shower that hadn't worked properly in weeks, if not months.

Rachel stood there naked, grabbed the bar of soap, and began scrubbing compulsively, as if she could peel off everything

− the fear, the rage, the grief, and the name Gemini. She dry-rubbed her skin raw, then turned off the dripping tap and slid down the cold tile. She hit the floor, shuddering in sobs that tore her apart in slow motion, in places she didn't know could break. Her ribs trembled as her hands clenched the soap like a life raft. And the bathroom, with sunlight slicing through the bars of its small window, giving more of an appearance of a psych ward than a sanctuary.

13

The Corpse

Rachel stood next to Lucia outside the medical examiner's sterile observation room, with garish lights buzzing faintly above, casting a cold, clinical, and antiseptic glare over everything. Although both women were used to dressing in their individual, apocalyptic punk styles, they now wore surprisingly plain clothes, which made them feel even more uneasy in an already uncomfortable environment. Their eyes were fixed on the large viewing window in front of them, its glass as thick as you'd find in an aquarium or in front of an all-night liquor store cashier. On the other side, the slab waited under bleak lighting. Gemini's fading blue body lay motionless on it, not quite at peace.

Lucia opened her mouth, but no sound came out; instead, she just nodded. It's the kind of gesture people make when their mind refuses to keep up with what they're seeing. Rachel didn't nod or move at all; she just slowly turned her head. Her eyes, red-rimmed and distant, followed nothing as she stepped away from the window, as if distance might protect her from the truth.

Behind them, the attendant, dressed in a white coat and with a blank expression, reached up and slid the viewing shutter closed. With a dull, mechanical clunk, the slab disappeared.

* * *

The autopsy room hummed with a refrigerated rumble, lit by surgical lights that cast everything in a ghostly white-blue glow. Gemini lay beneath a sheet, center stage on another cold, stainless-steel slab. To one side, Sam stood next to Alaska. Across from them, Wayne Sinclair, a mix of science geek and digital precision, flipped through his tablet. In his forties, with a paunch just starting to show and glasses slipping down his nose – much like the rest of him, his lab coat looked worn and overused. Wayne pulled back the sheet without looking up. "Positive ID. Fingerprints and dental matches. Gemini Moon, confirmed missing person. The autopsy reveals intersex anatomy – differences in sexual development that don't fit typical male or female patterns. Without further genetic testing, I can't determine the exact condition, but the presentation suggests one of several possible intersex variations."

Alaska's gaze was laser-locked on the cross cut on Gemini's forehead, then she reached down and gently lifted Gemini's arm, revealing the faded dolphin-and-moon tattoo curled just beneath the elbow. *"Ayahkwêw,"* she said quietly.

Wayne looked up, confused. "Come again?"

"Two-Spirit," Alaska explained. "It's Cree. Means someone who walks with and between genders."

Wayne gave a suspicious nod. "Right."

Alaska leaned closer, examining the blue hue of Gemini's

skin, now shimmering like river stones under the light. "Why is their skin so blue?"

Wayne offered in his clinical monotone, "The blue skin results from methemoglobinemia – a rare blood disorder. The body can't process oxygen properly, and the low oxygen levels cause that blue discoloration."

Sam raised his eyebrows. "Methemo-what now?"

"Globinemia," Wayne repeated. "The description fits the condition. Also..." He hesitated, glancing at the lower body, "severe genital mutilation."

Sam winced, and Alaska's hand trembled slightly as she made mental notes, but not enough to cause a full tremor.

Wayne handed over the report. "Chloroform saturation. Enough to sink a ship."

"So they were chloroied," Sam affirmed. "And still, no DNA? No blood, spit, or semen?"

"Clean," Wayne clarified, "Like someone meticulously scrubbed them. No matches in any central databases either." Wayne gestured toward Gemini's chest. "Rope burns here. Bite marks near the heart. Deep scratches, too."

Alaska reached out, brushing her fingers against one of the wounds, and asked, "Are those human or animal marks?"

Wayne squinted and explained, "Hard to determine. It could be an animal – a stray dog or coyote that found the body."

The doors whooshed open behind them, and Valerie John-son entered like an unsheathed saber. She was in her late 30s, wearing a black leather skirt and a polished silk shirt that hugged her curves close. Her sky-high heels glided her across the room like a panther on points. When she saw Sam, her face lit up with something that might've been history or heat. "Good to see you again," she charmed.

Sam nodded. "Valerie, this is my daughter, Alaska. Valerie works psychic detail for the department."

Alaska offered up a smile, and Valerie returned it, already tugging latex gloves over her hands. "May I?"

Sam gestured. "Be my guest."

Valerie turned to face Gemini's remains but stopped halfway, in a soundless wave of recognition. She sharply turned her head, struggling to swallow whatever rose in her throat.

Sam peeped it. "You okay?"

She nodded too quickly. "I... That's, ah, I know them."

"You don't have to do this," Sam nudged gently.

Valerie composed herself and declared, "Actually, I do. I insisted on being assigned to this detail." She quickly pressed her hands against Gemini's leg. Her pupils widened, and she glanced upwards. Then her eyes closed, she withdrew inward, and flashes of images surged through her mind:

A body tumbling end over end down an embankment, vanishing into dark water.

A hulking masked shadow watching with a knife, invisible but present.

A terrified, naked child.

A white van peeling away, tires shrieking, and the smell of burnt rubber.

A pink dolphin cutting through the water's surface.

Valerie staggered slightly and caught herself. She took off her gloves, her eyes still clouded with visions.

Sam approached. "What did you see?"

She refocused. "A white van. A shadow I couldn't identify. And a child. Young – probably eight or nine, and a pink dolphin?"

Sam nodded slowly. "Boy or girl?"

She shook her head. "I couldn't tell. I'll get you a sketch."

"Anything else? What about the killer?" Sam asked.

Valerie hesitated. "I couldn't hear the voices − it's hard to break through the killer's mental walls"

"You know, I don't believe in psychics," Wayne scoffed from across the room.

Valerie spun around quickly, walked straight toward him, and placed a hand on his shoulder. "Well, I don't believe in skeptics, so I guess now we're even. Oh, and by the way, your wife is having an affair. Right now. On your couch. You know somebody named Clarence?"

Wayne stared back at her, searching for a clue to see if she was punking him, but she called his bluff and kept a poker face. He shook his head, eyes dropping to the floor, his face going pale, and he stumbled toward the door like a drunk after last call.

Valerie called after him, "Come by for a reading sometime. We'll have some fun!" She turned back to Sam and winked. "I'll get you that sketch."

14

The Whiskey Bar

An hour or so later, the sterile fluorescent lights of the city morgue felt like a distant, blurry nightmare, as Alaska and Sam sat shoulder to shoulder at the counter of Sonny's Whiskey Bar, both of them elbow-deep in a greasy takeout box from Joey's Fish Hut. The bar, Sam's second, and sometimes first home, reflected amber light against brass accents and cracked leather booths. Sam preferred Sonny's over other dives because it mostly played songs with lyrics he didn't understand or required him to think, but always seemed to throw him a lifeline to his next breath. Behind the counter, a worn turntable spun *Dentro Al Cinema by Gianmaria Testa*, highlighting a shrine to all things analog. The walls were lined floor to ceiling with vinyl records, some cracked and sun-faded, while others remained pristine. Liquor bottles stacked on shelves like a stained-glass mural, including Japanese blends, Irish firewater, mezcal, American cheap shots, and eighty-eight kinds of liquid therapy.

Sam sipped his single malt like it was a sacred ritual — a quiet benediction for a man who preferred his ceremonies aged in oak without questions, confessions, or carrying others' guilt. Alaska wiped a smear of fish grease from her cheek with the back of her sleeve, eyes still on her plate as she broke the silence. "So," she suggested casually, "you gonna ask her out?"

Sam paused mid-sip, the glass hovering at his lips, his eyes narrowing. "Ask what?"

"Valerie," she replied, her voice dry and straightforward, as if describing traffic patterns. "Your friend. Looks like she's crushing on you."

He didn't respond, just took another long, contemplative draw from his whiskey, which was more of an answer than anything that could've passed out of his lips.

Alaska leaned in, propping her elbows on the sticky wood of the bar, her eyes playfully twinkling at him. "Dad, you gotta come out from behind your desk. Get back in the game."

Sam snorted, low and dismissive, but the corners of his mouth lifted like he'd caught the scent of amusement. The music buzzed faintly from behind him, Testa still singing about whatever and such. "What do you know about dating?" he countered. "You live like a hermit in the woods."

Alaska grinned, tore off a corner of her fish, and popped it into her mouth before answering. "I know that if a woman likes you, she'll want you to make a move." She chewed and swallowed. "And I know she likes you."

Sam side-eyed her, lifted his glass again, and casually inhaled the whiskey fumes before responding. "What are we now, a psychic?" he asked, taking another slow sip. "She's a little too adventurous for me."

Alaska arched an eyebrow, licking salt from her thumb. "When was the last time you did anything adventurous?"

He didn't even blink. "Packers-Bears. Lambeau Field."

Alaska scrunched her face as if she'd just bitten into a lemon off her plate. "Dad, that was five years ago. And the game was delayed due to the heat and a dust storm."

He shrugged it off with the ease of a man who had made peace with the monotony and melancholic beauty of his sweet routine. "At least they finished, and the Packers won. Besides, we don't have enough in common."

Alaska cocked her head back, incredulously. "Duh! You both hunt psycho killers. You have a lot in common and things to talk about, which is all you really need in a friend," she insisted, while tearing off the last chunk of haddock with her teeth, chewing like it was proof of her point.

Sam leaned back in his seat and nodded to Frankie, the owner-bartender, signaling a silent code for the check, before draining the last drop of scotch like a man clocking out of work. "Yeah," he proclaimed, tapping the rim of his glass against the counter, "and she also moonlights as a dominatrix."

Alaska stopped mid-bite. Silence. Then she choked, coughing into her napkin as laughter and fish bits sputtered out. "Ohhh. Ad-vent-ur-ous." She wiped her mouth, still giggling as her shoulders and belly shook uncontrollably.

Sam smiled, finally cracking his mask just a little, enjoying watching his daughter caught in a rare moment of laughter, even if it was at his expense. He watched adoringly as she demolished the last of her fish and then reached over to finish what was left of his.

He excused himself, stood up, and headed to the restroom. He entered, leaned over the sink, and rolled up his sleeves to wash off the fish oil and salt from his hands. The soap dispenser sputtered, and the faucet squeaked with just enough water to do the trick. He moved closer to the mirror, examined his reflection like a stranger, and took mental notes: a few more lines and less hair. His eyes looked tired, but they weren't entirely shot. "What's she talkin' about..." he muttered, turning off the faucet and drying his hands with a towel. "I got game." He tossed the paper towel into the trash can, missed, and left it there. Then he spun on his heel, pushed through the door, and strolled back into the bar like a man who might still have a few wild cards or oats up his sleeve.

Alaska was already waiting for him at the door. He passed by and nodded in appreciation to Frankie, who was now spinning '*Le Traiettorie Delle Mongolfiere*,' another of *Testa's* mystery ballads that complemented his whiskey-propped, fish-fed, and sweetly curated moment with his daughter, and then they walked out together.

15

The Hacker

Alaska sat beside Ama in her back room at The 66, connecting cables from Ama's data core to a salvaged computer. She bypassed government security protocols and hacked into encrypted case files buried in the system. She flipped the switch, and the mechanical clicks of data scrolled across the screen. Then she turned cautiously and looked over her shoulder like a sleuth, making sure she was still alone as her fingers tapped instructions on the keyboard.

Alaska's eyes stayed fixed on the screen as one autopsy photo after another appeared, showing past victims. Some bodies displayed the same patterns: crescent-shaped bite marks in bruised flesh, scratch lines, and crosses carved into their foreheads. She zoomed in on Taino, her mother, the one who made her stomach clench. Alaska's fingers trembled slightly as she dragged the image of an autopsy photo into focus, along with her memories, time-stamped and tagged in sterile, emotionless font.

Her hand trembled as she toggled between crime scene files and old newspaper clippings filling the screen:

Wife of Cop Killed
Indigenous Leader Murdered
The Roach Not Guilty

Then she clicked on the array of images from her mother's case. She zoomed in, isolating a bite mark along the ribs, deep and rough like an animal or something animalistic had clamped down and gnawed. Below that, raw claw marks raked across the flesh beneath the collarbone.

On another monitor, she pulled up more newspaper clippings, including grainy surveillance shots of 'The Roach' – a man in his forties, sallow and visibly frail. Another popped up of Catholic Brother Di Segni, and the crumbling stone arch of St. Mary's Church. Headlines followed in quick succession and glitched like a broken traffic light:

Local Catholic Brother Murdered by Local Serial Killer
The Roach Convicted of Multiple Murders
Serves Victims in Tacos

The grotesque headlines struck Alaska like an iceberg, causing a brain freeze. Her breath became shallow, and her heart sank as she leaned toward the screen until her forehead nearly touched the glass. She was unaware of the footsteps approaching from the hallway behind her as she cross-referenced the files of her mother, Gemini Moon, Brother DE Signi, and two other victims pulled from the Copycat file – all sharing these various bite marks and scratches.

Sam stepped into the room, still wiping black grease from his hands with a threadbare rag. The moment he saw the image of Taino, his deceased wife, opened and autopsied, he

80

froze, mid-step. The rag slipped from his hand as his voice came out hoarse, guttural, and grief-stricken. "Jesus Christ. What are you doing?"

Alaska ignored him. "I'm looking at Mom's files."

Sam moved quickly across the floor, each step feeling like he was walking through a tar pit of buried memories. "Ama, get them off there." His voice was sharper, and his anger hit like a slap. The monitor blinked dark, and a cold silence fell over the room, sucking the air and life out of it.

Alaska hesitated for a moment, then snapped back, "Ama."

The files flickered back to life. Taino's image reappeared — bloodless skin, lifeless eyes, evidence, all too violent to ignore. "Look at the marks," she insisted, voice sharp. "They match. The same ones on these victims are the same as Mom's."

Sam's face flushed red. "They're scavenger wounds from wild animals. Ama, get these files out of here."

"On five different bodies?" Alaska shot back, louder now, and angrier. The files remained, and Taino's corpse stared out from the screen like a verdict.

Sam took a half-step forward. "Ama." His voice cracked, almost pleading. Ama's head swiveled from side to side, her optical sensors flickering with conflicted programming; her eye lights glitching in anxious indecision, torn between competing commands and loyalties.

Alaska stared at Ama, who wheeled backward and kept the images up. Alaska then slowly turned to face Sam, assessing his role in her life as both her father and a cop. Her voice was steadier now, both calm and deliberate. "You asked for my opinion. So here it is. Gemini Moon, Mom, Brother Di Segni, and these other two guys all share the same wounds. They found Brother Di Segni and Gemini Moon's bodies near or at

St. Mary's; maybe there's a connection."

Sam ran a hand through his hair, leaving a streak of grease in the gray hair at his temple. His shoulders sagged as if gravity had just entered his body. He looked at the screen again, then back at his daughter, her stance rigid with stubborn determination. He knew that look. It was Taino's look. "Alaska, not now," he grumbled and insisted.

But Alaska didn't let up and fired back, "Not this time," she countered, "I came back to spend Christmas with you. I can stay longer if..."

"It's been twenty years." Sam's voice rose sharply, cutting her off, as pain leaked out of his pores. "I pinned four murders on The Roach and his goddamn taco truck, but I couldn't prove he killed your mother. The Roach is in prison, and the case is closed. Besides, all this is what started your seizures."

Alaska's voice sharpened again, baiting him, "The Roach killed Brother Di Segni from St. Mary's. The same place you found Gemini Moon. And they have the same markings as Mom. This case isn't closed, it's cold."

Sam shook his head, his facial muscles jumping out of his cheeks. "We're not reopening The Roach. Period." He turned, stomped away, shoved open the steel door, and disappeared into the depths of the garage, as if the conversation or his old life had never happened.

Alaska leaned back against the desk and crossed her arms. "Short and sweet visit it is, then," she said to no one.

* * *

The shop tools slammed into drawers, and shelves rattled as Sam tore through his workbench, wiping his hands on random tools and stacking parts that didn't need stacking, moving with the cadence of a man trying not to think or feel. Ama rolled up beside him and hovered nearby, her eye lenses pulsing faint blue. "I detect you're doing it again," she calculated in her cadenced, digitized voice.

"Leave it," Sam growled.

Ama tilted away, retreating without another word – if she had a tail, she'd have no doubt tucked it between her legs. Sam leaned on the workbench, hands braced, head bowed. His shoulders heaved once, silently, then collapsed.

* * *

Alaska knelt beside her motorcycle, grime smudging her face. Her hands moved with practiced precision, fingers coated in oil as she wiped the wrench and then twisted the new filter into place with a steady, confident torque. Every movement was familiar: clean, controlled, and deliberate. Sam came out from the workshop with his shoes kicking over gravel and broken bolts, drying his hands on a rag that looked like it had cleaned a hundred engines. He watched her for a second, maybe five, before fessing up, "Okay."

Alaska glanced at him briefly, then reached for the oil cap and turned it three clicks tight. "I don't believe there's any connection," Sam added, his voice monotone, as if he had memorized the words many times before they finally made it past his lips.

"Mm-hmm." She kept working, silently judging his presence.

Sam shifted his weight and let out a sigh, soul-deep and filled with resignation. "But if you help me with the current case..." He paused, and the rest unnerved and grated on him like fingernails scraping across his inner skull. "...we'll take another look at The Roach."

Alaska's hand halted mid-reach for the rag, and she looked up slowly, eyes narrowing as they locked onto him. She scanned his face, searching for a hidden subtext or some conditional clause he hadn't spoken, but found nothing. Just her father, offering a faint thread of trust. She stood, wiping her hands on her jeans, fully facing him now, eye to eye, mano a mano, a ghost of a smile touching her lips. "Okay... dealio."

He nodded once, then pulled a worn leather wallet from his back pocket and took out an old, tarnished badge. He placed it in his daughter's hand without ceremony, and she stared down at it. "Already cleared it with the Captain," Sam said. "Consider yourself deputized."

It was something she hadn't expected or seen in a long time. The weight of the badge sat heavily, as if it was burning a hole in her palm. She ran her thumb over the seal: state-issued, official, **and shiny.** It felt like brushing the surface of an old memory and a new mission.

Alaska clipped the badge to her belt and smiled, but not fully – just a spark shining behind her eyes that hadn't lived there in a long time. She and her dad didn't need to say anything out loud, but their instincts made it clear they were about to jump back into the deep end, together, and without any life jackets, a boat, or a way back to shore. Ama hovered nearby, twirled once on her gimbal, and flashed a string of green lights in a quiet little celebration, acting like a mechanical puppy that had just heard the word treat.

16

The Masks

One wall of the garage was lined with half a dozen monitors, a string of old processors, and newer rigs that Alaska and Ama had assembled using their unorthodox methods. A homemade forensic lab collected everything they needed in one spot: maps that blinked with pin drops, photos of corpses arranged in grim order, timelines, case files, surveillance stills, and a rogue's gallery of the killer's many masks.

Ama sorted through the data as Alaska squinted at the mosaic of the killer's identities. Some were made of simple cloth, while others were crafted from detailed leather or silicone; however, most were 3D printed in latex. Each one staring out with its peculiar shape. Sam traced a finger over the image of a rough burlap mask stitched with human hair and murmured, "He avoids facial recognition by using masks modeled after real-life serial killers, and he's getting bolder. First, Copycat used masks modeled after the Carnival Killer. Then the Bedwetter. Then the Euro Ripper. Then the Twitter Killer. Then the Toy Box Killer. Lately, he's been copying the big names: Bundy. Rader. Dahmer. He went dormant for a few years, but there's recently been an increase in killings bearing his signature. Not sure why."

Sam pointed to several of them sequentially. On one monitor, a grainy image showed a man exiting a Detroit bus station, wearing the grinning latex mask of The Carnival Killer. Another clip from a toll booth camera captured him dressed as The Bedwetter, complete with a blood-splattered raincoat. Then there was the Euro Ripper mask, worn with uncanny confidence at a gas station outside Duluth. All are legends in the horror pantheon, resurrected in leather, plastic, and rubber.

Alaska stepped in for a closer look. "Do we know if Copycat is a he, she, they, or multiple killers?"

Sam shook his head. "No, I just call him he for now. Keep it simple."

"So 'he' likes to play dress-up, is brazen, and flaunts us behind masks. Projection. Identity transfer. Idolization. Craves notoriety," observed Alaska.

Sam nodded in agreement. "Some kind of homage. Like he wants to make varsity."

Alaska thought it over and then said clearly, "A malignant narcissist and psychopath doesn't just want to make varsity; they want to own and outshine it. Wants to consume the entire team or even the idea of a team. That's their cycle and the pathology of cruelty."

Sam and Ama looked at Alaska, then at each other. Sam was proud as a peacock of what Alaska had been studying and of who she was becoming. "Where and when the hell did you learn all that?" poked Sam.

Alaska simply smiled and replied, "From a hermit who lives in the woods."

Sam grinned, touché.

Alaska pressed it further and said, "Ya gotta learn your opps to burn your opps."

Sam raised an eyebrow.

Ama processed Alaska's assessment before replying, "Narcissistic injury cycle. Fluctuates between victim and God-complex, and an overall small-dick flex."

Sam looked at Alaska as if to say, *'Have you been teaching her to talk like that?'*

Alaska just shrugged and responded, "Well, she's not wrong."

Ama didn't register the subtle nuances of human interactions and kept cycling through the faces of victims on the screen.

Sam clicked through each one like flipping through a dark family album. He crossed his arms, thinking as patterns coiled and uncoiled in his mind like cobras, and offered, "Nine are known so far. All experienced genital mutilation. Four, including Gemini Moon, had a cross cut into their forehead, along with teeth and scratch marks on their bodies." Photos flashed: a man in a business suit, slack-jawed and dead-eyed; a young woman with a bleached pixie cut; and a paunchy middle-aged man in gym shorts, his whistle still around his neck. Each name and location lit up underneath.

Sam continued, "A businessman in Chicago. Hairdresser in Madison. A coach in Green Bay. Retired priest in Racine. A schoolteacher just across the border in Sault Ste. Marie. The gymnastics coach and Boy Scout leader are local."

Alaska scanned the screen, her gaze sharp. "Where did the priest work?"

Ama's voice broke the silence, tinny but clear. "Six parishes worldwide." She paused. "Chile. Mexico City. Boston, Munster, Lyon, and St..." Her sentence broke mid-syllable, and the lights inside her casing dimmed and flickered erratically.

Sam looked at her and then at Alaska. "She's been shorting out."

"I'll update her drives," Alaska reassured him. She walked over and slapped Ama across her back as if waking a sleepy night watchman.

Ama buzzed back to life. "... And St. Mary's. Two years."

Alaska's expression changed as the dots started to connect in her mind, and they weren't pretty. "Why a Canadian schoolteacher?" she asked Sam. "Seems reckless, sloppy, even. Breaking pattern, crossing borders, and leaving his territory. That's not like him."

Sam exhaled a breath that was not quite a sigh. "Could be a copycat of the Copycat."

Alaska didn't answer, her eyes fixed on the boards, studying the faces, symbols, and chaos. Somewhere in that tangle of terror, the mystery of her mother's death remained buried. Sam watched her from the edge of the room knowing also that somewhere inside this web, the killer was watching back. That the hunt was starting again, and this time, their past was hunting with them.

17

The Burial Ground

The city's cemetery felt as if it had been ripped from Hecate's dark underworld and dropped into the light of day. Off to one corner, surrounding Gemini Moon's grave, the smell of freshly turned earth hung heavy, damp, and metallic, while crows hunched like prophets on the leaning, nearby head-stones. A young curandera–cantara stood near headstones, strumming a solo guitar and singing a version of *Pink Skies by Zack Bryan.*

Rachel stood at the edge of the grave, her black dress buttoned up, dark sunglasses hiding the full freight train of her grief. On either side, Lucia and Valerie held their silent vigil – a trio carved in stillness and statuesque. Around them, Nick and an informal circle of artists, punks, and goth kids gathered. Mourners with tattoos and cigarette burns on their inner wrists wore leather and lace, torn fishnets and combat boots, spikes and scarves, with black nail polish chipped from trembling hands. They all looked as if they were dressed for both a funeral and a revolution.

Surrounding the inner circle were hundreds of Gemini's

clients from various walks of life: professionals, suits, la-
borers, some dressed as fairies, sea creatures, and dragons,
standing beside moms and dads with kids, aunts and uncles,
and grandparents. Everyone looked like they'd been carrying
the weight of the world and this day for years. Some of the
mourners cried, but most didn't.

Off to the side, keeping to themselves, was a small group of
Indigenous people of unknown origins – possibly from South
America. Near this group, Gemini's spirit lingered, pink and
translucent like moonlight, leaning casually against a tree at
the cemetery's edge. She watched silently, her spectral eyes
more curious than sad, as if she'd seen this all before and
knew what was coming. She observed Rachel step forward,
slip off her sunglasses, and read aloud from Gemini's battered,
sticker-covered book, *Rise Alive and The New Earth.* Her voice
trembled slightly, but she maintained her composure.

*"We have all walked home with our keys between our fingers
and avoided streets with bushes and trees.*
We have all shared our live locations with friends.
We have all made phone calls, both real and fake.
We have all tucked our hair inside our coats.
We have all planned our escape routes and struggled to stay
alive.
And still, we rise."

Lucia nodded to Rachel, stepped forward, and unfolded a
piece of paper. "This is a poem that Gemini wrote that they
asked me to read, should they ever leave us. It's called *What
the River Told Me.*" Lucia gathered herself and recited,

"Don't you dare cry for me.
I am the pink spirit
you catch from the corner

of your grief–blurred eye,
the ripple that says
'I was never just a body.'
When they carry my shell
to the muddy bank,
know that I am already
swimming in the spaces
between your ribs,
in the river water
behind your eyelids.
Death is the cruelest kind of magic.
Trick—
makes you believe
that the magician has disappeared
when really
she just stepped
into a bigger hat.
Listen:
Every seed that falls becomes a tree.
Every woman who gives birth becomes a garden.
Every goodbye becomes the hello you haven't learned to hear
yet."

Lucia started to tear up, her chest shaking, then she sobbed. Valerie quickly leaned over, gave her a comforting hug, took the paper from her hand, and kept going.

"I am not gone.
I am rain.
I am the way water remembers how to laugh,
the way daughters carry their mothers' names
in the curve of their spines.
Stop searching for me in yesterday's river.

I am today's current, tomorrow's rain,
the warmth of every kiss
you will ever give or receive.
The only thing that dies
is the lie
that we were ever
separate
from this wild,
unending
river."

Silence among the gathered mourners, deep and heavy, filled the air after the short and straightforward eulogies. A gentle breeze picked up, blowing strands of hair across tear-streaked faces. The curandera began to play and sing medicine songs, *Sirenita Bobinsana by Orka* and *A Thousand Years by Christina Perri*, as Rachel, Lucia, and Valerie each took a fistful of earth and tossed it into Gemini's grave. The dirt clung and grasped, holding onto memories on the way down, scattering across the pine box, then halted.

From the tree line, Gemini's anime-like, pink spirit blinked once, then stepped backward into the tree bark, melting into it like a swirl of mist into a mirror – fully gone and fully here.

Nick slowly stepped forward from the group and approached Valerie. "Sorry about Gemini. You okay?"

Valerie's voice was barely above a whisper. "I'm still pretty shaken. How are you?"

Nick, unable to find the words, just turned his head from side to side. Lucia leaned forward, wrapped him in a tight hug, and they held for a few breaths before releasing.

He stepped toward Rachel and held her a little tighter and a little longer. Her sunglasses stayed on, but her breath caught just once against his chest. "How are you holding up, Rach?"

Rachel calmly replied, "I'm doing alright, under the circumstances. Have you found a place yet?"

Nick shrugged. "I'm still at my folks'. It feels like I got caught in the middle of a never-ending, passive-aggressive, ping-pong match."

A small smile escaped Rachel's lips, almost involuntarily. "You still got a box at my place."

Nick scratched his head. "I've been meaning to pick that up."

She reached into her coat and handed him a stack of black-and-white postcards featuring Gemini's face on the front, with a memorial date and time scrawled on the back. "Think your band could play the memorial?"

Her request caught Nick off guard. "Yeah. Yeah, of course. Count us in." He hugged her once more, stepped back, and moved toward the edge of the group, where Roland Donner leaned against a crumbling mausoleum, vaping something foul and minty. Roland always looked three beers in, like he'd rolled out of bed drunk and never found the door back, or where he left his life the night before. Beside him stood Yoshima, her sharp facial angles matching a thin, black vinyl coat, her sunglasses hiding a stare and an unemotional mystery.

Nick slapped Roland's hand hard, leaned in for a shoulder bump, and asked, "Rachel wants us to play at Gems' memorial. Think we can get Diego out of the cave?"

Roland shrugged, "Man, I dunno. I've barely seen him since their last, local *Burning Man* gathering. The Burn-head's in pretty deep, might need a crowbar to get him out of there."

Their attention, along with the rest of the mourners, turned to the curandera, who began to sing *Gozar Hasta Que Me Ausente by Paloma Del Cerro*. The song provided a joyful, celebratory counterpoint to their communal grief at the other end of the spectrum. Gemini would have liked that. As if on cue, a couple of hand drummers emerged from the group, and some mourners started to move spontaneously. Some danced, while others amplified the ululating and trilling sounds from the song, as if to proclaim, 'Not today, death, not today.'

Parked across the street under the shade of a wilting elm, Sam watched through the long lens of a weather-beaten Nikon. Alaska sat in the passenger seat, chewing on a pen, her eyes scanning the crowd like a hawk, and was intensely focused on the small group of Indigenous people. Through the long lens, Sam snapped a few photos, capturing faces, gestures, and groupings: turning mourners into evidence, potential leads, or suspects. He lowered the camera and exhaled, "Our Gemini Moon had quite a posse."

Above the cemetery, the light shifted. Wind rolled in, slowly and gritty, dragging a dust shower across the edge of the city and scattering the mourners, as this storm looked heavier than any of them had prepared to fend off or face unprotected. Alaska leaned forward, frowning at the sudden shift in weather. She looked around for the group of Indigenous people, but they had already disappeared. Sam tilted his head out the window, glanced up at the oncoming storm, then quickly turned the ignition and drove away.

Alaska sat quietly, her boots on the dashboard, and gazed out the window. It occurred to her that the only funeral she and her father had ever attended together was her mother's. She only remembered, mostly from pictures and what her grandmother had told her, that people traveled from all over the Americas; there was lots of food, singing, drumming, and storytelling that went on for days during the ceremony held a year after her mother's death, as per Cree tradition. She looked over at her dad, wanting to say something but hesitant to press her luck by scratching at his still scab-covered wounds, which, like hers, have a life of their own. Instead, she just stared out the window, savoring whatever memories of her mother she could still find, and sustained her smile.

18

The Unusual

A haze of sunlight filtered through dusty skylights, casting fractured light across the chaotic clutter of the Creatrix Gallery. Lucia and Rachel were mid-motion, sliding copies of Gemini's book, *Rise Alive and the New Earth*, onto a display shelf. There was reverence in both of their movements, and they both looked up when the bell above the entrance door jingled as it opened.

Boot heels echoed across the gallery's concrete floors as Sam stepped inside with the steady confidence of a cop who'd done this ten times daily before breakfast. His eyes quickly started cataloging the details. Alaska followed just behind, eyes scanning everything with quiet precision: the spray-painted canvases, protest photos, handmade zines, shelves packed with worn books about revolutionaries, hand-poured candles, and patchouli incense that lingered around a sculpture of melted circuit boards in the corner, like an in-house deity.

Lucia straightened up, her expression sharpening like a razor. "Can I help you?" she asked, suspicion already in her voice, while Rachel remained quiet and stoic behind her.

Sam flashed his brass badge, unimpressed by art or attitude. "I'm Detective Morse," he said, nodding to Alaska, "and this is Deputy Rainmaker. We're looking for Lucia Sky."

Lucia smiled, her game face on with all her teeth but none of her warmth. "Sorry, Chad, nobody here by that name."

Sam didn't budge; he just tilted his head slightly, like seasoned cops do when they're giving you a second chance to change your answer. "Someone filed a missing persons report for Gemini Moon from this number. Phone records led us here."

Lucia folded her arms, her eyes unreadable behind thick, geometric frames. "Leave it to La Junta."

Alaska slowly approached, her voice calm but firm. "We just want to ask you a few questions about Gemini Moon. When did you last see them?"

Lucia glanced toward Rachel, then her gaze drifted far away as if she were still searching for the missing Gemini. "At the water protest."

Sam's voice cut in, flat and focused. "Did you see anything unusual?"

Lucia stared back, grimacing, and offered, "You mean end-of-the-world unusual, or the usual unusual?"

Sam gave her a long, studying look and mirrored her. "Usual, unusual."

Lucia shrugged, "Lots of cops and bots. Like always."

Alaska leaned in. "How did you know Gemini?"

Lucia hesitated, then her voice softened with memory. "We met in lockup after a climate sit-in in New York. We were just a couple of kids — fifteen going on infinity."

"New York?" Alaska asked. "They're not from here?"

Lucia chuckled. "Moon? They always said they were from the stars, but I think it was the Bronx or maybe Brazil. They used to talk a lot about their time in the Amazon, so maybe that's it, but I'm really not sure. They moved out here from New York because the thin air triggered their condition. It turned their skin that shade of blue. Kind of like a canary in the climate coal mine, you know?"

Sam took a small notebook from his pocket. "Any enemies you're aware of?"

Lucia's smile disappeared. "All kinds. Gemini was radical with zero to the square root of zero fucks left to give. People hate that kind of freedom."

Behind her, Rachel moved in closer, worry etched into the lines around her mouth. "Have you found anything out?"

Alaska shook her head and replied, retrieving and trying on her trained cop-speak, "We just opened the curtain on this investigation."

Sam focused on Rachel, familiarity flickering in his eyes. "Wait a minute... You're Rachel Lamont, right? From Mischief?"

Rachel gave a tired, half-smile. "Yeah, that's me."

Sam brightened, almost sheepishly. "I catch your show whenever I can. Good work."

"Really?" Rachel's surprise was genuine and fleeting. "Thanks. Listen, why would someone do this?"

Sam tucked his badge away; his weariness was creeping back in. "We're just getting started," he said, reassuringly, and handed her his standard-issue cop card – nothing flashy, just a name, a number, and the promise of long nights ahead. "Call me if you need anything or have any questions."

Alaska drifted toward the counter, drawn to a display of

Gemini's book. The covers were ink-washed in blue and pink, with silver foil stars, and glowed beneath the light. She picked up a copy, opened it, and thumbed through the pages with quiet curiosity. Her brow furrowed as she squinted and looked around the room. "Where do I pay for this?"

Lucia waved a dismissive hand. "It's pay-it-forward, for the next customer. But we don't accept money from first-timers." Alaska studied her for a moment, then nodded. She reached into her hip pouch, pulled out a tobacco prayer tie, slowly waved it in front of the stack of books, and gently placed the tie on the counter.

Alaska looked over at Rachel, then back to Lucia, and asked, "I have another question. In my Cree culture, we have the word Ayahkwêw. It refers to someone who walks with and between genders. Do you know if Gemini identified with that?"

Lucia hesitated, then quietly replied, "Gemini embraced all the pronouns – he, she, they, or anything else that felt right in the moment. One day, she would feel the 'she,' though on another day it could be different entirely, and she would respond to any number of her aliases: We, Moon, Pink, C7 Major, Boto, Amor, or Starfish. Gemini wasn't particular about such things."

Alaska nodded her thanks, then turned to survey the rest of the gallery, which was overflowing with paintings, artifacts, and anarchy spilling out of the brick, as if she were seeing it again for the first time: the main gallery displayed a *'Pussy Riot'* art installation, posters offering workshops on safe protesting, classes in self-defense, courses on growing your own food, and a yoga-meditation schedule plastered on the community bulletin board.

Sam and Alaska left the way they came in, two cops carrying

a little more than they had walked in with. They hopped in the Plymouth, peeled out, and navigated their way through the dusty city. Alaska rode shotgun, Gemini's book open in her lap. Her finger traced and her mouth shaped the words, page after page, chapter by chapter, through the book's eclectic material. Alaska was aware that she was listening to an extraordinarily unique voice. A voice that had already passed beyond the veil. A voice that could also help lead them to the killer, and maybe even the mystery of what happened to her mother. She looked over at her dad, about to share what she was learning, but kept her quiet as they pulled up in front of Gemini's mid-city address.

19

The Healing Sanctuary

Gemini's studio-loft door creaked open reluctantly, its hinges dry with age. The landlord, a doughy man with a permanent scowl and the demeanor of someone who never left the first floor, motioned for Sam and Alaska to enter without stepping through the door frame himself. They entered the studio, focusing on their first and most insightful impressions. The air inside was thick, saturated with turpentine, palo santo, and something sweeter, like childhood. A space built not for profit or praise, but for survival; maybe even for healing and magic.

Sam and Alaska remained still for a long moment, allowing the studio to speak and reveal itself. The main area opened before them like a sanctuary. Paintings lined the walls, bursting with colors that contrasted sharply with the gloomy and dusty city outside: mermaids swimming in sunlit kelp forests, children laughing mid-leap, and dolphins twisting through river dreams. In one corner, sculptures crafted from found metal and glass stood like spirit totems. Above, holographic river turtles spun midair, and whales arched slowly and serenely. The entire ceiling pulsed gently with painted constellations; digital blue light dripped from the stars like rainwater.

Alaska moved first, her boots silent on the paint-splattered floor. She drifted from corner to corner, phone out, documenting everything silently. Her face remained still, but her eyes constantly moved, soaking in the story hidden within the brushstrokes and the beauty. Enlarged photos covered one wall, depicting Indigenous people living along the Amazon and Orinoco river basins: kids holding up finger paintings of rivers, trees, butterflies, dolphins, jaguars, and glitter-streaked suns. Collages of photos showed adults seated in circles, hands clasped or resting on knees, their expressions both wholesome and hopeful.

Alaska stood in awe of the vibrant paintings on one far wall, depicting people living their daily lives through activities such as cooking, hunting, fishing, singing, and boating. The photos were labeled Yanomami, Warao, Kayapo, Shipibo, and many others. On top of a shelf, Alaska saw a small hand-drawn card depicting river dolphins. She opened it, and on the inside it read: *The spiritual is personal, and the personal is political – With love, your boto family.*

She put the card back down and continued looking around the studio.

Sam worked methodically, crouching beside a crate of sketchbooks. Years of investigating crime had taught him to read a room slowly and methodically like a library of books. He stepped to one wall and paused in front of a few flyers half-tucked beneath a cracked seashell-shaped ceramic bowl. He picked them up carefully, recognizing the weight of what he'd found. Bold colors flourished on their thick paper, surrounded by collage cutouts of children and adults of various backgrounds sitting in a circle, holding up hand-painted pictures. Beside them was a neat stack of Gemini's book. Well-read. Used. 'S.A.S.S.', the flyer read. *Sexual Abuse Survivors Support*, and beneath it, a tagline read – *Grow through what you go through.* He turned one of the flyers over; the back was blank except for a hand-drawn, pink dolphin.

Underneath the bowl, he discovered a security safe, slightly hidden behind a hanging cloth. He checked the handle, saw it was locked, so he got up and handed a flyer to Alaska, who took it without a word and flipped it open. Her eyes narrowed as she scanned the contents inside: a mixed collection of amateur paintings of children, forests, rivers, houses, wildflowers, ghouls, and monsters. Then she looked back at the room, not just at the art now, but at the person who'd lived between its lines. The diplomas on the wall confirmed what the space already disclosed: Psychology, Marine Biology, and Art Therapy.

Alaska turned back to Sam and saw the safe that had been revealed. "What's in there?"

Sam looked down at the safe, then turned to her. "It's locked."

Alaska ignored him and bent down to get a closer look. She touched the dial, leaned in to listen, and spun it around twice. She took a breath, then slowly turned the dial clockwise. Click. Then counter-clockwise. Click. Then another clockwise. Click. She hesitated, then turned the handle – it opened. She smiled.

Sam raised his eyebrows. "Let me guess, a hermit taught you that, too?"

Alaska replied, "Don't ask," as she swung open the safe

door. Inside was a single manila envelope. She pulled it out, opened it, and revealed six passports from different countries: Bolivia, Brazil, Colombia, Ecuador, Peru, and Venezuela. She flipped each open to show passport photos of the same Gemini Moon – same blue skin. She stood up and showed them to Sam, who said, "Who the hell owns six passports?"

Alaska shrugged. "James Bond? I'll have Ama run them through their consultants. See what gives."

Alaska stood at the center of everything, the flyer still open in one hand, and the passports beside her. For a long moment, neither of them spoke, taking in the magical studio that buzzed softly around them. The studio wasn't just a sanctuary where someone painted; it was where some wizard, shaman, or 007 fought and won.

20

The Cosplayer

Miles across the city, in a cluttered apartment filled with climate graphs and cosplay gear, Eris Harlow, aka Captain Climate Change, stared at her computer screen. The artifacts of her alter ego were spread out behind her like sleeping bats: a phosphorescent green cape sagged from the closet door, oil-stained blue pants sprawled across a chair, battered tactical boots, a cracked face shield, and gloves with solar panels stitched into the backs, scattered on the floor. Her costume looked less like a cosplay and more like the uniform of someone ready to throw hands with the apocalypse.

The walls and shelves of her apartment were a jumble of contradictions: anime posters and handwritten protest placards, collections of toy samurai figurines, an assortment of stuffed animals, and maps with green markers tracking the planet's changes – highlighting sea-level rise, carbon emissions, and drought zones. California looked like a burn scar, the Midwest was brown and barren, Florida was submerged under ocean-blue ink, Texas was flooded with swollen rivers, thermal imaging revealed the reversal of the Gulf Stream and ocean currents, and graphs charted volcanic eruptions beneath the Antarctic ice sheet.

The swirl of a computer fan hummed like the distant window AC, barely louder than the slow tap-tap-tap of keys under Eris's chipped green fingernails. She sat hunched forward, creeping on Rachel Lamont's social media feeds, which spread open like a buffet: recent reposts, curated stories, and photos of protests, friends, trips, city life, and thirst traps.

Eris leaned back, cracking her spine against her chair like a chiropractor, and reached for her phone. She found a number she had sleuthed online and dialed – one ring, then two.

"Hello?" Rachel answered from the other end.

Eris sat up straighter, her voice tense and controlled. "Hello. Is this Rachel Lamont?"

Rachel paused suspiciously, then answered, "Yes, it is."

Eris quickly responded, "I think I found your wallet."

* * *

The Broken Arrow diner squatted on the edge of one of the city's many forgotten strip malls. It was wedged between a shuttered vape lounge and a pawn shop that hadn't rebooted its neon lights since the last blackout. The light inside the diner was dim and inviting, curling around the long counter, where the purr of old machinery mingled with the jarring sounds of the espresso machine. *Riptide by Vance Joy* bopped out of ceiling-mounted speakers surrounded by paint-chipped walls and potted plants clinging to life. It was the kind of place that tried to keep a 1950s retro-hip vibe, but reeked of overheated circuit boards and overpriced espresso grounds. Still, it pulled a diverse crowd of artists, system busters, hackers, digital nomads, and revolutionaries, not for the quality of the bean, but because it offered free, 'untraceable' Wi-Fi for those who wanted to stay incognito under the radar of their opps — any opp.

Rachel and Eris sat across from each other in a cracked vinyl booth near the back, where the lighting was lowest, and the noise from the counter barely registered. Rachel had pulled her black hoodie low to partially cover her eyes, shadowed by insomnia and the weight of too much doom-scrolling and screen time. She looked like someone who hadn't decided whether she was coming, staying, or going. Eris appeared slightly sharper, but her hair was still matted and messy from the perma-dust, and her jacket still carried the scent of ozone and pepper spray.

An awkward waiter bot rolled up on squeaky wheels, its scratched chrome catching the light. It filled their mugs with sterile precision, steam rising and swirling between the two women like a Van Gogh. Rachel watched the bot roll away, still unsure of the proper etiquette for interacting with robots that served coffee. She never really knew how or if to respond to any of the bots: delivery bots, taxi bots, cop bots, waiter bots, and grocery store self-checkout bots all felt the same to her. Instead, she turned her attention to Eris. "Thanks for bringing me my wallet back. I usually never bring my real ID to protests — must've fallen out of my backpack somehow."

Eris smiled and said, "Yeah, you can never be too careful out there. I've got like twenty different IDs and forged documents for different situations."

Rachel casually fiddled with her wallet, reluctant to check inside so as not to seem mistrustful. However, her curiosity killed her cat, and she checked to see if the twenty-dollar bill was still where she left it. It was, so she pulled it out and slid it across the table. "Coffee's on me. So, do you go to many protests?"

Eris leaned back into her comfort zone, one arm draped over the booth as if she owned it. "Thanks. Every single one. I'm Captain Climate Change. Maybe you've heard of me?"

Rachel tilted her head, then broke into a slow smile. "No way. I see you all the time."

Eris joked, "Yeah, way. Most people don't recognize me when I'm not cosplaying."

Rachel studied her closely, thinking about how many times she'd seen her out there, but they had never formally met. "Wow! How long have you been doing that?"

Eris paused, as if pulling up a magic formula from an archived file, and sipped her coffee: black, no cream or sugar coating. "When I was stationed in Japan a few years back, I realized I hated the military structure, but I liked the gear and uniform. Turns out I like to play dress-up. Cosplay lets me shape-shift into whoever I want to be that day. And without all the bullshit orders and schedules."

Rachel twirled her forefinger in the air. "Like a trickster."

Eris's lips curled, a sly spark of amusement flashing out from behind her eyes. "I suppose." She paused for a moment, then said, "I started watching episodes of your Mischief livestream. Super metal."

Rachel thought it over and offered, "I should have you on the show sometime."

Eris sat up straighter, feeling like Homer, being recruited for a new odyssey. "For real? How did you get into all that, anyway?"

Rachel's grin flattened, turned inwards, and her fingers

now circled the rim of her mug. "Long story short, I lost a girlfriend when I was younger. That shattered my illusions about life, got me interested in human behavior, and led me to pursue a psych degree that ultimately got me nowhere. I figured I'd share what I don't know on a livestream. And surprisingly, people tuned in."

Eris nodded slowly, letting the silence settle between them. "Girlfriend, huh? So you're…"

Rachel's face quickly flushed pink. "Bi-ish, I guess. Depends on the person and the mood."

Eris smiled, slowly and deliberately. "I'd date you."

Rachel shook her head, her cheeks now warming to red. "I'm just getting out of something."

Eris turned up the dial a notch or three. "They tell me I'm one of the best rebounders around… maybe we could hang out sometime… for the plot."

Rachel hesitated, raised her mug again, and brought it to her mouth to hide an expression she hadn't yet decided on. Then she looked over at Eris and met her eyes. A fragrance passed between them like curiosity, recognition, or maybe the start of a double-dog dare. She then dropped her gaze and, with a quiet smile, said, "You have my number."

Eris nodded once, as if she'd just completed a successful recon. Rachel turned away to watch the waiter bot whirl past, appreciating the momentary distraction.

* * *

On the sidewalk outside of the Broken Arrow, Rachel knelt beside her scooter and unlocked it. She stood up, startled to see Eris standing too close behind her.

Eris looked up at the sky and said, "Looks like we've got another dust storm coming in. Can I give you a ride home?

Rachel was already strapping on her helmet. "That's okay, I'm used to riding through it."

Eris hid her disappointment and pointed toward the parking lot. "Are you sure I can put your scooter in the back?"

"That's sweet of you, but maybe another time. Thanks again for bringing me my wallet," Rachel said as she hopped on her scooter and drove away.

Eris watched her go, then called out, "Be careful of the dark forces of the night."

* * *

Rachel's scooter engine buzzed through the darkness, its headlight slicing a narrow trail down the dusty street. She hunched over the handlebars, hoodie pulled up, helmet strapped on, and backpack slung tight across her shoulders. Store LED signs fluttered like broken beacons in the periphery: open, closed, stop, closed, blink, closed, open.

A white van tailed her at a cautious distance – unmarked, predatory, and the sound of its tires rattling over the broken concrete. No headlights or license plate lights, just slow movement, mimicking every turn she made, prowling with quiet patience.

Rachel peeked into her side mirror and clocked the van – too close, and too steady. She yanked the handlebars hard and turned into her apartment complex's driveway, skidding to a stop beside the rusty staircase, quickly muted the engine, and dismounted. She didn't look back, and the weight of unseen eyes pressed between her shoulder blades like invisible daggers. Maybe it was one of those untethered, AWOL delivery bot-drivers, maybe not.

She moved swiftly, keys rattling in her hand, and her boots pounding up the stairs – not running, but not walking either. Halfway up the flight, she stole a glance over her shoulder at the van hesitating at the curb. There was a long pause, then, without warning, it peeled away, its taillights flaring briefly before vanishing into the shadows.

Rachel froze, standing on the stairs, her keys clenched tightly between her fingers. Her breathing was quick and shallow, and she stared into the quiet street long after the van had gone. The sound of coyotes, who increasingly occupied the city to forage for food scraps, rodents, and water, broke the silence. They kept yipping into the night, shifting her out of fawn and freeze mode, as if it were a sign that it was time for her to fight her way back inside.

21

The Wrestler

Back at The 66, Alaska sat next to Ama, who was linked to the computer screens, which quickly began filling with images, but not too congested. Pictures of Gemini's six passports popped up all at once. "Each consultant confirmed – all official. Have located Gemini Moon at the protest," Ama said, her voice calm and methodical.

Gemini's face appeared first, caught mid-shout at the protest, their mouth full of fire. More frames showed Gemini leaving as riot cops moved in like armored insects, and another of them stumbling down Central Avenue, one shoulder cradled and the other hunched. Then, another one of them staggered into a side street and vanished into the city's rib cage. From the other side, someone sped past on a wheelboard, green hair blazing, and a cape trailing behind like a comet tail.

Alaska leaned over Ama's shoulder and examined the images closely. "Any security cameras up that alley?"

Ama processed for a few seconds, emitting a soft click that chattered like skeleton teeth. "No, but a mobile unit on the other side picked up what appears to be 'Copycat' in a white van." New footage populated the screen – the nose of a white van emerging from the alley like a predator from its den.

Sam stood behind them and wiped the sweat off his forehead. "Who the hell is it this time?"

The footage zoomed in, and Ama isolated the driver's face. The image sharpened, then shifted: cross-referencing, pulling files, and digging through the archives of past nightmares. A mugshot appeared on the adjacent screen, and Ama rolled it out. "Subject identified. Juana "La Mataviejitas" Barraza. Former Lucha Libre wrestler. Murdered 16 elderly women and was sentenced to 759 years in prison in Mexico City. She posed as a social worker to gain entry into their homes. Once inside, she would overpower and strangle the women with objects like cords, stethoscopes, or ligatures."

Sam let out a long, tired breath, as if someone were trying to exhale a century of grief. "That's our guy… or gal. False plates again, I take it?"

Ama spoke up like a drill sergeant. "Affirmative. Dark, dusty, and too cloudy for consistent coverage." The screen changed again, glitching slightly, as the white van disappeared from view.

Alaska thought it over and offered, "He's got a pattern – masks for identity concealment, dust storms for cover, always operates at night. At least he's predictable. Now, how about we go check out The Roach?"

Sam didn't answer right away. He just looked at her, as if she were a stranger he'd only just recognised. Then he shook his head slowly and resignedly walked away, carrying the weight of unresolved wounds, unsettled graves, and a decision he wasn't ready to make.

22

The Roach

The concrete block Brankston prison, or 'Angst-Alacatraz,' as it was known among its inmates, squatted against the scorched earth, surrounded by razor wire glinting in the sun, with towers scanning the yard like mechanical vultures. Guards watched from behind metal shades, unmoving and holding sniper rifles – rested and ready.

In the yard below, prisoners drifted like orange-coated ants in sluggish patterns. Some worked out, some shot craps and the shit, others smoked dope and cigs, and a few just stared into the void. Robots patrolled the perimeter with blank optics and tireless motors, their movements mechanical but menacing, efficient, silent, and impossible to bribe.

Sam and Alaska rolled up to the prison's tall metal gate and stopped. Sam recognized the head guard, nodded, and flashed his badge. The guard scanned it and looked at him, then they easily passed through and navigated their way to a pre-assigned parking spot.

They leaned out of the car and walked toward the building, and Sam looked at Alaska. "Remember, stay in the back. If you need to speak, keep it brief, and whatever you do, don't let him know who you are."

Alaska stayed silent, focusing on what was ahead. Sam tapped her on the shoulder to get her attention. "Capech?"

Alaska refocused and replied, "Capech."

The heavy steel interior prison door groaned open automatically and scraped the floor, its hydraulics squawking like the dead awakened from a coma. They stepped inside and walked down the narrow, oppressive corridor; its white, claustrophobic walls stained with the oily fingerprints of time. Harsh overhead lights buzzed, casting a sickly, greenish, cold tint that made everyone look as if they were already halfway in the grave.

A sleek, humanoid guard bot, its face a blank matte-chrome panel, stood sentry at the entrance to the solitary visitor's cell. With a press of its wrist, it disengaged the magnetic lock, and Sam and Alaska entered the room as if they were descending into a crypt or catacomb.

The Roach was already there, shackled to a steel table bolted to the floor. Now rail-thin with a wiry frame, his body was all elbows and bone. A metal device connected to his throat, linking a hose to an oxygen tank that sat beside him on the floor. His skin was yellow − evidence of illness that had ravaged his liver and lungs. Much more deathly than the newspaper photos from a decade earlier, his eyes gleamed with mischief and madness, like a rat that'd made peace with the trap. Roach saw Sam and called out through his grating, muffled throat device, "Mooorrseeee. You old dog, did you bring it?"

Sam pulled a bent cigarette from his shirt pocket and placed it on the table, fulfilling his part of their pre-arranged bargain, along with his own form of protection against the abyss. Roach grabbed it and grunted, "Since I got the cancer, they recommend that I don't smoke. But hell, it's gotta be God's last great addiction."

"I'd argue coffee is." Sam struck a flame with his Zippo, the scent of butane briefly cutting through the stench of bleach, steel, and creep.

Roach leaned in, with his chronic twitch and neck tic giving the impression that something was trying to escape or enter his body – maybe his soul. He sucked on the cigarette for salvation and exhaled with a shudder. "What's the difference between a hippo and a Zippo?" He grinned, pausing for his punchline. "One's heavy, and the other's a little lighter."

Sam didn't bite – he just stared at him with a cold, camouflaged face. "Now tell me again how you killed Brother Di Segni?"

Roach's voice turned musical and staccato, almost like German techno DJ on MDMA. "Strung him up. Snap, crackle, popcorn." Alaska shot Sam a look, a mix of disgust and disbelief. Roach peeped it and leaned back, smacking his lips. "It was easy breezy. But not as easy as McDermott. My only regret was not chopping up Di Segni into cutlets and tasting him. I've always wondered if Di Segni would have been as delicious as McDermott. I mean, with hot sauce in a corn tortilla? McDermott was a delicacy."

Alaska's eyes darted to Sam, then back to Roach, trying to gauge the depth of his depravity, and finding no bottom. Not one to be an extra or background player, she tapped her wrist device. Crime scene photos animated of Brother Di Segni hanging from a rafter and a cross carved into his forehead. "What kind of knot did you use?" she asked.

"What kind of question is that?" Roach took another long, slow drag, the ember flaring off his handcuffs.

Alaska looked up from the photos and pointed out matter-of-factly. "There are all kinds. Slip knots. Sailor knots. Square knots. Hangmen."

"It was a knot-knot." Roach laughed at his joke like a man who'd never played with pain that wasn't someone else's.

Alaska didn't flinch. "And your other victims? The mutilation? The chopping? The missing parts? What was that all about?"

Roach whinnied, "It just takes over, and I had a roach coach to run. You animal rights snowflake-woke-flakes took away all my meat. What was I supposed to do? Make vegan tacos? A man's gotta grind." Roach laughed out of nowhere. "Oh, my God. Grind, get it? A man's gotta grind. Fucking hilarious! I still got it, Moorseee, I still got it."

Alaska brought it back down to reality and pointed out the discord. "You discarded their genitals."

Roach shrugged it off as if she'd just complained about soup seasoning. "What are you, a sicko? Nobody wants to eat-eat those."

Alaska tried a different tactic. "Do you know a Gemini Moon?"

That made Roach pause; then he grinned again. "What's with all the questions? Morse, you didn't tell me you brought a game show host."

Alaska's mouth tightened. "I said, do you know a Gemini Moon?"

Roach smacked the table, making a fake buzzer sound. "*Ennh!* What is 'I-do-not-know-a-Gemini-Moon' for forty points?" He took another long inhale and exhaled, acknowledging to himself that he still had his wit, quick as spit.

Sam interjected, "We're looking for a connection to a body that washed up near St. Mary's."

Roach's eye twitched slightly as he pulled out an old dagger. "I thought the only body you cared about was the one that washed ashore at your cabin."

Alaska turned away, lowered her head, and muttered to herself. "Piece of shit."

Roach leaned forward now, his eyes sharp as he studied her like a safe or a soul in need of cracking. "Morse, you didn't introduce me to your partner." He snickered, "She looks familiar. Oh, wait, I see it now. She's a little Pocahontas, but she's got those cocky eyes of yours. He turned to Alaska. "You're the kid, aren't you? From the cabin. When that big bad wolf hurt your mommy?" Firing back at Sam, "Is this your runt?"

Sam's face turned cold and hard. "That's enough." Alaska's hand trembled at her side, curling it into a fist.

Roach clocked her hand, and his face lit up with cruel joy. "Did you feel scared, little girl?"

Alaska bent forward, ready to strike, and Roach grinned. "You wanna kill me, don't you? How's that feel? I know your Daddy, the big bad serial killer hunter, wanted to kill me, too. Everyone's afraid of him. But everyone's got a blind spot. Right, Morse?"

Sam reached out and caught Alaska by the arm before she did something they couldn't walk back from. "We're done here." He pulled her toward the exit, steady but firm, her rage simmering underneath her breath.

Roach shouted after them in a rotten, sing-song-metal voice and tugged at his chains. "Come on, Mooorrseeee. You used to have a sense of humor!" He took the last, long drag from his cigarette, eyes fluttering shut, shivering like he'd just taken communion or ejaculated.

* * *

The car door slammed shut like a gunshot, and Alaska dropped into the passenger seat, fuming, her teeth clenched so tightly it looked like they might crack bone. Sam slid in behind the wheel, calm, but wound tight as an unspun top beneath the surface. He turned the engine over and pulled away, hoping that the road and time would ease the tension. The Brankston prison walls hung low in the background as they drove off. Alaska didn't waste any time. "If he didn't kill Mom, how the hell did he know I was in our cabin?"

Sam kept his eyes on the road, both hands steady on the wheel – more to control himself than the Plymouth. "He rage-baited you, and you fell for it. I told you to stay in the back and not let him know who you are."

Alaska grinned, mostly to herself, and looked out the window. "I'm sorry, I missed the part where that was still relevant. I said, if he didn't kill Mom, how did he know I was in our cabin?"

Sam shook his head from side to side and huffed, "He's just messing with your head, and he's got a license to print lies. That's generally what he does."

Alaska turned to face him. "He's a liar, sure. But he didn't even recognize the noose on Di Segni; he didn't know it was a hangman's knot, even though I practically gave him the cheat code. That's specific."

Sam raised an eyebrow, surprised by what she knew.

She saw it and reminded him, "He's a liar, and he's cannibalistic."

Sam fired back. "So was Dahmer. So was that sick fuck in Japan — The Kobe Cannibal."

Alaska, now exasperated, turned back to the window, watching the landscape bleed by with its broken fences, dead brush, and rusted road signs pointing to places that no longer existed. She readied herself for a duel and launched in, "Roach's insanity plea said he felt possessed. Said something took over, made him wanna kill and eat something."

Sam stated, point-blank, "Yup. He's one fry short of a Happy Meal."

Alaska insisted, "What about the voices in his head?"

Sam tried reasoning with her, "Schizophrenia. Auditory hallucinations. You've seen the psych reports; they're practically textbook."

She remained silent, stewing over her thoughts, then offered, "Maybe. Maybe Roach was possessed." She pulled out Gemini's folded S.A.S.S. flyer. "Maybe by something that looks like one of these." She showed him the image of the hand-drawn creature, all twisted limbs, empty ribs, and dark, primal eyes.

Sam glanced at it and shook his head. "I'll consider anything with a rap sheet, fingerprints, DNA, history of trauma, or child abuse."

Alaska looked over, reloaded, and challenged his eyes and logic. "Did Mom ever talk to you about something called the Wetiko?"

Sam brushed it off. "Of course!"

"What if it was a Wetiko?" Alaska pushed back.

"I'm not chasing myths." Sam exhaled a sound that was

halfway between a laugh and a grunt.

Alaska stayed shielded, silent, and sulky, then rallied her offense. "Mom told me... "

Sam cut her off and countered, "I didn't bring you here to chase your mother's old stories and superstitions."

Alaska was stunned. "They weren't her superstitions; they were her beliefs. There's a difference. And so what you're saying is, you believe in psychics, but not the spirit world?"

"Psychics can point to actual evidence." Sam planted his hand on the dashboard.

Alaska raised the flyer in front of him, pointing to the image again. "So psychic visions are fine, but the spirit world is nonsense?"

Sam shook his head and defended, "I prefer hard facts over strong opinions, Alaska. Things that stand up in court."

She scoffed, raising her palm, and mimicked a southern Louisiana lawyer's voice. "Your honor, ladies and gentlemen of the jury, I present Exhibit A — the further proof of my father's willful ignorance."

Sam was brief and direct, "Just drop it."

Alaska, never one to surrender last word rights, looked out her window and quietly grunted, "I said what I said."

The car rolled forward, heavy with unspoken grievances. They sat, trapped in the thick silence that only comes between two people who are experts at hurting each other. Neither spoke. The silence cut deep — too deep to force either of them to throw in the towel and break it.

23

The Burn-Head

On the outskirts of the city, the steady whir of skateboard wheels rolled over the decaying suburban street. Nick and Roland, who had last seen each other at Gemini's funeral, glided down the block, weaving lazy arcs around potholes with precision and purpose. They rolled past a crumbling, cement-block fence and stopped in front of a sagging house, its siding sun-bleached and faded. They stepped off their boards and headed for the basement door, sneakers crunching over the chipped walkway. Roland pounded on the door frame, his knuckles smacking the hollow wood. No answer. "Yo! Burn-Head, are you dead?"

Nick, annoyed by the silence, tapped the door with his skateboard. "Come on, we know you're in there."

A glow pulsed from the room's only light source: a computer screen, glimmering with the haze of a video game. Diego 'Burn-Head' Towais, late twenties, sat like a wax figure. His thin, gray skin pallid under the basement heat. His eyes looked like two sinkholes of paranoia and fatigue, as though he hadn't seen the sun since his last pilgrimage to the *Burning*

Man Festival – a now monthly occasion taking place wherever Burner's could gather in the now-everywhere-dust. The knock echoed through the basement and his head, but not enough to make him move, blink, or think.

Roland slammed his fist again, this time harder. The wood creaked under the abuse. "We got a gig coming up!" Still no response, just the sound of wind rushing through the gutters and the low courtship call of cicadas in the barren yard.

Nick surveyed the window, looking for a crack in the curtain, then turned to Roland. "Should we come back?"

Roland answered, annoyed, "I can't keep dragging his sorry ass to the ER every time he chokes down a handful of downers and fucks around with molly-crystal combos."

Nick fished a postcard from his jacket, squatted, and slid it under the door with a flick of his wrist. The card scraped and flipped across the carpet like a wayward leaf. Diego stared at it, then slowly reached down; his fingers trembling as he picked it up. He stood, stiff and unsure, and peeling back the edge of the curtain just enough to glimpse daylight, which blinded him, causing him to slam the curtains shut.

His friends were already walking away, heading back toward the sidewalk with their skateboards, but without any promise of a band in hand. Yoshima, Roland's friend and skateboard novice, arrived late and hung out by the curb, arms crossed, quietly scanning the neighborhood. Nick looked over at her. "Yoshima seems rad. What happened to Cindy?

Roland drew a long drag from his extra-strength vape, his eyes already glazing red. "She stopped listening. Now that you're single again, you can take her for a spin if you like." Roland scratched the back of his neck. "In fact, why don't we go back to my place and have a threesome?"

Nick shook his head. "What gives with you and your three-ways?"

Roland pulled deeper from his vape, exhaled something foul, and smugly shrugged. "I just like human contact, man."

The two dropped their boards with a clack and stepped on, ready to roll. Nick shook his head and deflected, "Nah, I'm good to go. Besides, I gotta go play Saint Nic. Let me know if you hear anything from Burn-Head." He pushed off and disappeared down the block, wheels carving a lazy swirl around the corner. Roland watched him go, pulled again on his vape, then glanced back at the house, but missed the basement window curtain flapping, just once, then nothing.

24

The Forest

Except during the Christmas season, the downtown parking lot was usually vacant, but now it was stacked shoulder-high with blue spruce and white pine Christmas trees. Ranging from five to ten feet long, the seasonal merchant had twined, corralled, and huddled in formations – for easy customer access.

Nick arrived later than he wanted with the band's van, hoping to find one that was still plush, or at least not sad and needle-less. He walked up and down the rows, AirPods in, listening to *These Days by Nico*, a melancholic, heartbreak song that, combined with the holidays and tree shopping, created a dangerous, lethal cocktail of existential angst for most. Still, for Nick, it only added more fuel to his songwriting fire. Barely paying attention to his surroundings, he turned a corner in one aisle and bumped into Valerie. She was instructing Forest, her middle-aged, focused assistant, on which tree to pull from the pile. "No, not that one, the longer one underneath."

Nick quietly approached Valerie from behind and stood

beside her without her noticing. He nudged her and said, "That looks like a fine tree."

Valerie turned to him, smiled, and replied, "Oh, hey. Yeah, it's that time of year again. And Merry Christmas!" They each leaned in for a hug as Forest pulled out the long, plump tree from the pile.

"Yeah, Merry Christmas! Ya know, it's not Christmas without a real tree and Santa doing his chimney drops," answered Nick. He immediately wondered if those word combos were maybe even a Christmas song, which he had never actually tried to write.

Valerie glanced around the lot. "You see one you like?"

"I'm actually picking this up for Rachel; no doubt she'll want a picture-perfect one," replied Nick, with a sly, knowing grin spreading across his face.

Valerie smiled and placed her hand on his shoulder, "That's really nice of you to do that for her. Rach said you were staying with your parents for a while. All good?"

Nick replied, "I am, just not for the holidays. We've got relatives coming in from out of town, and it's filling up from couch to crib. I might ride this one out in the van."

Valerie studied him, then offered, "Well, you can stay at my place for Christmas Eve. I've got plenty of room."

Nick wavered from side to side and said, "Yeah, I don't know."

Valerie put her index finger up to her lips and made a ssshhh sound. "I have a pet peeve about friends being alone at Christmas. Just send me a text first," She didn't wait for his response, turned and walked away, with Forest shouldering the tree behind her.

Nick smiled, scratched some gravel with his foot, as *Stick*

Season by Noah Kahan weaved through his AirPods. The song gave him a little spring and pep in his step. This Christmas might have had some 'Fa La La' and tinsel left on it after all. He walked around and surveyed the lot, looking for the postcard tree. Whether his face would be back in that picture, he couldn't say.

25

The Christmas Tree

Rachel creaked open her apartment door; the weight behind her ribs was barely hidden behind a strained smile. Nick stumbled in, wrestling with the Christmas tree wrapped in twine and awkwardness. She held the door open. "Thanks for your help. I needed some normal right now."

Nick steadied the tree. "Where do you want it?"

Rachel, already walking toward the fridge, called back over her shoulder, "The usual spot. You want a beer?"

"Is that a trick question?" Nick dropped the tree into a rusted stand by the corner window and looked around. The living room was quiet. It was the kind of quiet that used to mean perfect peace and now felt as if it had slipped between the pillows like a coin into the cracks of the couch.

Rachel handed him a beer, and they clinked their bottles. She pressed play on her Christmas music playlist, which randomly played *2000 Miles by The Pretenders* over a montage of tree decorating activities: lights unraveling in snarled loops, hands fumbling with ornaments, tinsel sprinkling on the tree and everywhere, boxes cracking open like photo albums, then out came garland and chipped snow globes.

Nick climbed a chair with all the grace of a tipsy reindeer and crowned the star on top of the tree. Rachel switched the lights, resurrected the tree, and smiled at its familiar glow and aura. Still, their personal revival of happiness didn't quite hit the usual mark in their hearts – neither hers nor his.

So they switched to plan B and found themselves drinking their second, maybe third beer, along with an equal number of vodka shots. Then, in the last box, forgotten on the top shelf of the closet, sat Snowy – a fluff-covered, two-foot-tall robotic French poodle. Rachel pulled it out and handed it to Nick, who cradled it like it were a miniature ship anchored in the harbor of his old life. He then called out, "Snowwwyyyy."

Nick flipped the switch on its belly, and the Christmas ornament-dog bot buzzed, blinked, and barked with a voice like a horny elf. "Meeerrrryyyy Christmas!" The little ball of electrons sprinted forward, spinning like a mutt on magic mushrooms before crashing face-first into the wall. Sparks of cheer fizzled as Snowy toppled over, shaking once before giving up.

Nick reminisced, "We got him what, seven years ago?"

"Eight. Eight years ago," Rachel corrected him, trying to resist that habit without much success, then walked toward the balcony. Nick followed her outside, and they leaned on the railing, their eyes scanning the neon-lit skyline and the dust drifting through the night clouds. Rachel pondered, "You know, sometimes when I try really hard, I imagine the dust as snowflakes. God, I miss how they used to float and fall, each one like its own little angel." She shut her eyes and stuck out her tongue like a kid pretending it still mattered. Nick followed suit, a little or a lot drunk, a little or a lot lost, wobbling as he copied her tongue ballet.

Rachel opened her eyes, shrugged like she'd just lost something small and precious, and looked over at Nick. "Are you okay to drive?"

Nick pulled his tongue in like an embarrassed, clumsy child and followed Rachel back inside, dragging the night and the wannabe snowflakes with them. Nick, still wobbly, steadied himself by grabbing hold of the hanging punching bag and trying to hide his condition. "I'm ah, I don't, ah... "

Rachel sized him up and down. "Stay on the couch tonight and... "

Nick let go of the punching bag, waved his hands in the air, and reached for his old, rehearsed lines. "I know, I know. Keep the cupboards closed. Don't drink the milk outta the toilet, I mean carton. Seat up when peeing, and down when done. And that toilet paper thingy."

Rachel smirked at his all-too-familiar performance. "Okay, you remembered."

"Oh, I remember lots of things," slurred Nick, as he stepped closer and touched her cheek. Rachel blushed and removed his hand. He moved in for a kiss, and she held him back, but he tried again. This time, she kissed him and their tongues jousted, medieval style. She took off his shirt. He unbuttoned her blouse and unhooked her bra. She unbuckled his belt and unzipped his fly.

Snowy briefly came back to life, tail wiggling and eyes blinking, but just as quickly went limp and died again.

Rachel noticed, and that was all it took. "We can't do this." She backed off and pulled her blouse over her bare shoulders.

Nick put his hand on his forehead, trying to calm his nerves and bluish balls. "Come on, Rach. It's Christmas."

"Not to be a Grinch... but my mood's not in the mood." She walked away, disappeared into the bedroom, and shut the door with a soft finality.

Nick stood in the wreckage of their almost re-flame and looked over at the poodle bot sprawled out like the corpse of his new enemy combatant. "Thanks for nothing, pal." He grabbed his shirt and buttoned it up, then buckled his pants and zipped them over what remained of his shriveled pride and prick. He walked out, closing the door behind him like a tattered bookend. He stepped outside, took a deep breath, and prepared to sleep it off on the newly scattered pine needles of the van floor. He opened the side door, crawled inside, and thought to himself, *'If baby Jesus could handle a day in the hay, surely he could survive a night in the needles.'*

26

The Night Stalker

The next morning, back at The 66, Alaska sat hunched over the desk, scanning the computer monitor and stopping at a photo of Richard Ramirez, aka the Los Angeles 'Night Stalker'. His gaunt face, greasy hair, and eyes looked like they'd seen Hell and sent selfies back. She zoomed in on them to reveal pupils looking like dark caverns, staring back like a curse. Sam approached from behind, muffling his footsteps against the concrete, and quietly watched her for a moment. Then, he broke the silence, asking, "Why are you looking at Ramirez?"

Alaska stayed focused on her research and didn't turn around. Her eyes reflected what was on the screen, intense and burning. "Look at his eyes. You can't tell me something wasn't possessing him."

Sam exhaled his weariness. "He was a sociopath and sadist, like all the rest."

Alaska pointed to his face. "Maybe the psychosis... maybe it acts like some kind of portal. Opens the door for something else to get in."

Sam shook his head, the way someone does when they're

trying to swallow a scream. "Alaska, where are you heading with all this?"

She paused, then turned to him, with her eyes full of mystery and vagueness. "I don't know." She pushed back from the desk, stood, and crossed the room, driven by an instinct.

Sam called after her, "Where are you going?"

Alaska quickly grabbed her helmet and kept moving. "Grandma's." The door slammed shut behind her, leaving Sam alone with Ramirez's stare still beaming on the screen, as if this particular killer, although dead, was still out there hunting.

27

The Grandmother

Alaska's motorcycle speakers played *La Oscuridad y la luz by Cielo y Tierra*, and her tires chewed through the debris and grime of one of the city's many forgotten quarters. She leaned into a dusty wind tunnel, her eyes scanning the ruins of what used to be a semi-functioning neighborhood: burnt-out shops, boarded-up tenements, and graffiti that looked like it had lost multiple, spray-paint pissing contests. Military helicopters passed overhead – the third sweep this week. 'Training exercises,' they called them. Her grandmother called them 'Turbulent winds' in Cree.

She pulled up in front of a weathered apartment complex that sagged under its anonymous history, with bricks stained with rust, dust, and neglect. It was the kind of place where some recently dead people probably still paid rent, or owed it. Alaska inserted her key into the metal security door, warped from years of brutal summers and delinquent tenants. She swung it open and began her climb up the stairs, past an elevator that had been frozen between floors a decade ago and now sat abandoned. She moved down the corridor, the floorboards creaking under the weight of her boots scuffing over the torn linoleum, stopped at 4A, raised her fist to knock, and heard through the door, "It's open."

Alaska entered slowly, and the warmth touched her like a spring morning's mist, mingled with air that smelled of sweetgrass, lavender soap, and cookies. Around the room, pottery bowls and figures shaped by hands that remembered stories, lined every surface. Dreamcatchers swayed gently above doorways, and beaded tapestries hung beside oil paintings of mountains, rivers, and bears. Her grandmother's used-weathered crossbow and a quiver of feathered arrows stood sentry on the far wall, and a curtain rippled gently in the draft coming through the only remaining window that the landlord had not painted shut. Everything was rooted in the same, familiar order, including Kokum – her grandmother, who insisted that the only way she would ever vacate her sanctuary was by being carried out in a wooden box.

Kokum stood at the sink, her sleeves rolled up, with her hands submerged in soapy water. Her long, braided silver hair spiraled down her back like a strand of moonlight. She didn't turn when Alaska entered; she didn't need to, as her presence and awareness filled the four corners of the room and beyond.

Alaska stepped closer and felt her aura ripple and expand at once, a reaction her grandmother always had on her whenever she got near. She crossed the room, wrapped her arms gently around her grandma, and buried her cheek against her shoulder. Alaska's heart sang, "Kokum," who turned, kissed her on the forehead, picked up a plate of freshly baked cookies, and placed it on the kitchen table without a word. Alaska slowly sat down in a chair, and her arm trembled as she reached for a cookie. The tremor was barely visible, but it was there, like a buried memory struggling to make itself known.

Kokum noticed. "You still got those shaky-shivers, dear?"

Alaska nodded, her eyes avoiding her grandmother's. She instead focused on her cookie, tasting the delicious, secret recipe, still soft and sweet in the warm center. Alaska took a breath, steadied herself, and looked up at her Kokum, quietly asking, "Do you still miss Mom?"

Her grandmother comforted her, "Every day, sweetheart. Every day." Her reassurance filled the room, gentle but somewhat intangible, like something her granddaughter couldn't quite hold onto.

Alaska swallowed the lump rising in her throat as her voice cracked, opening up the past. "Sometimes I miss, I just miss having a family and friends."

Kokum's weathered eyes softened as she turned her full attention to her granddaughter. "I understand, but I am your family. And so is your father. The water is our cousin. The trees are our aunts. The crow is our uncle. The butterflies, our brothers. The bear, our sisters. The earth is our mother, the sky is our father, the sun is our grandfather, and the moon is our Kokum. All our ancestors: below, above, beside, behind, before, and in front of you — are our relatives and friends. Always."

Alaska looked down at the table, feeling the weight carried in so few words, although she was only slightly more comforted. "So much has been lost. I want to discover more about who I am." She blinked back tears and pulled out a tobacco prayer tie. It was roughly bundled but carefully knotted, and she handed it across the table as an offering of respect. Kokum accepted it with a knowing smile, her slow nod a gesture of gratitude for the traditional honor.

They slipped into their Cree language, words delicate yet powerful, shaped by generations and the rhythm of the earth itself. Its cadence curled around the room: soft, circular, and alive. Her Kokum instructed, "Nothing is ever really lost. Keep learning our language. You know our grammar has no gender; it's just alive or less alive – things with a soul or things without one. Know our language, and you know yourself and the world."

Alaska leaned in. "And our culture?"

Kokum smiled. "Our culture? Although there are many shades of the rainbow, there's only one culture. The one born of love, appreciation of beauty, respect for diversity and dignity, and the knowledge that all life is interconnected and stitched together. Everything else? Smoke and mirrors, child."

Alaska reached into her bag and pulled out Gemini's folded *S.A.S.S.* flyer. She chewed slowly, letting the words melt with the cookie in her mouth. "I want to ask you about the Wetiko."

Kokum dried her hands with a dish towel, slowly and deliberately. "What about it?"

Alaska opened and smoothed out the folder, setting it in front of her Kokum, revealing a few drawings of monsters and creatures. She hesitated and pointed to the drawings. "I want to know if this is a Weitko?"

Kokum chuckled softly. "*Little Red Riding Hood.* Just fairy tales from the old days. Long gone now."

Alaska fully straightened the flyer, revealing the image of one particular creature staring back at them from the page: bone-thin, fanged, and hungry-eyed. Her frustration prickled under her skin, and she asked, "Grandma, I want to know if they're real?"

Kokum deflected, "As I said, just old stories. Long gone now. Best left alone."

Alaska's body tensed up. "If there's something you know that I don't."

Kokum's face darkened, just for a second, as a memory moved behind her eyes. "Just an old 'Once upon a time.' Now, have some more cookies, dear." Her grandmother pushed the plate toward her, and Alaska stared at it before relenting. She reached for another cookie, biting down hard, even as the answers she sought were out of reach. She watched her grandmother, whose eyes drifted toward the window, where the wind had suddenly shifted, bringing with it another wave of dust. Somewhere in the distance, a crow called out. Kokum said nothing. She sat there, drying her hands like the world wasn't shifting beneath their feet.

28

The Fetish Arts

Caminos de Alcanfor by Darío Poletti played hypnotically from the speakers in the fetish arts loft where a middle-aged woman hung naked from the ceiling, wrapped tight in Japanese Shibari bondage rope. Her eyes glazed, and her face contorted and fluctuated somewhere between pain and pleasure. Her businesswoman's mask was smeared away by sweat and mascara, as a feather teased the arch of her foot. "Oh God!!!" she screamed, as her feet were tickled to the point of what surely felt like death.

Valerie, dressed head to toe in a black vinyl catsuit, leaned in and mischievously whispered in the woman's ear, "Nobody up there's going to help you down here." Her deep, blood-red, polished fingernails lightly scraped down the woman's spine, causing her face to twist and her eyes to roll as she moaned and simultaneously choked back laughter. The experience was both mind-numbing and body-enlivening, which was the woman's preferred kink, and what she paid and yearned for.

In the corner, her assistant, 'Forest The Gimp,' hooded and

obedient, stood on duty, holding a bouquet of leather straps like he was an over-proud French florist. Valerie pointed, and he dutifully handed her a strap that she tapped on the woman's inner thighs, which spread in anticipation.

* * *

Bullwinkle, Pt.II by The Centaurians drifted from Sam's Plymouth speaker as he rolled leisurely through downtown, passing storefronts that popped pink tubes and red bulbs, offering every promised and fleeting pleasure. He drove past rows of porn galleries, dive bars, massage parlors, and a retro theater. Junkies staggered up to dealers to arrange their fix, next to a zealous preacher standing on the corner, peddling and thumping his particular version of the Bible to any passerby who would either stop or not stop to listen. He was the kind of preacher who, if Jesus Christ himself had walked up and tapped him on the shoulder, he would no doubt try to convert him to Christianity.

Sam entered a narrow alley lined with dumpsters overflowing with abandoned dreams and discarded demons; in stark contrast to the music and laughter spilling out of open windows that filled the street. He drove past a lively and busy health clinic offering free services and a well-decorated retirement home for healthcare workers. He slowed down, spotted a light buzzing over a solitary door with a metal sign, marked – JOAN OF ARCADE. He parked, turned off the engine, and stepped onto the sidewalk. Sam looked up at the two-story, reclaimed warehouse building, then over each shoulder down the alley for privacy, and out of habit to check for anything suspicious or a tail. He pressed the buzzer next to the security door, and a slow, melodic, Russian-accented voice of Forest came through the speaker. "Easy Peasy."

Sam looked around, slightly embarrassed, then leaned on the buzzer and repeated the code word, "Lemon Squeezy?" The buzzer buzzed, unlocking the door. He swung it open, entered, and climbed up the extra-wide, creaky, wooden stairs.

The client, now dressed in a crisp navy business suit, straightened her hair in the mirror and then walked toward the loft door. Forest, still hooded, held it open and silently handed her a freshly clipped rose as she passed by, then returned to his private room, located down the hallway at the far end of the loft.

The client nodded politely to Sam as she walked past him on her way out. Her heels dangled from one hand like a nunchuck, since she was too tired and her feet were too sensitive to wear them. She walked gingerly down the hallway in an unplanned 'walk of shame' with her dignity only partly restored – another one of her more favored erogenous zones.

Valerie greeted Sam with a smile. "Come on in, we're just finishing up. Make yourself at home and pour yourself a drink, and I'll have a glass of white while you're at it." She pointed to the bar tucked in the corner in front of the floor-to-ceiling windows, large enough to see out, but private enough that you couldn't see in. A one-eyed tabby named Scrappy, because that is what she did when she was out prowling the hood, relaxed on the windowsill.

Sam walked toward the bar. "Was that Senator Gordon?"

Valerie turned around and responded with the discretion her profession required, "That's confidential, but you'd be surprised. I mostly get members of Congress, Wall Street power brokers, Silicon Valley tech-bros, technocrats, crypto-heads, surgeons, judges, professional types, and religious zealots of all kinds. I even once had an Ambassador to France here; he was a big fan of rope and ice-cold butter. Another time, a Guru came from the Himalayas; he wanted to prove that he had transcended all physical pain and his mortal body – he failed. Her voice trailed off as she listed various kinks from anonymous clients – the only way she actually remembered and cataloged them.

As she turned toward the central kitchen and walked away, Sam called after her, "I've never really asked you about your clients. What's their angle?"

Valerie stopped in her tracks, turned back, and said point-blank, "Power. People with worldly power eventually get tired of wielding it and want someone they can voluntarily hand it over to. They're also sometimes just looking for high-end fun." She turned, kept walking, and her voice casually joked as she entered the kitchen. "I bring the fun."

Sam stepped behind the bar, poured himself a whiskey and a glass of Chardonnay from the fridge, then paused to survey the space: a mix of boudoir, lifestyle luxury statement, and BDSM-fetish arts haven. The main social space tried to be festive. It was sporadically adorned with holiday decorations: tinsel hung beside whips, red and green lights lazily blinked around steel beams and bondage racks, a ceramic Santa grinned on a shelf next to a bottle of lube, and a Christmas tree, still fresh and newly decorated with various fetish-styled ornaments and toys.

Holiday cheer, dungeon-style.

Sam surveyed the area around the bar. The building's permits, consisting of a business license, an adult entertainment permit, private club registration, and 'Historical building preservation' status, were a work of art – stacked on the wall like a protective charm. He eyed a creepy centerpiece on the bar: a mason jar half-filled with a cloudy fluid, and inside, something pinkish and absurd floated lazily. A Sharpie label on the bottle read: R. SPECK. He lifted the jar and saw a severed breast, wrinkled and bloated like a drowned jellyfish. He studied it the way he examined anything related to killers, with his curiosity and encyclopedic mind, which his line of work insisted on. He knew the history of Richard Speck – the killer who, in a fit of alcoholic rage, broke into a nurses' dorm on a murder spree, killing all but one nurse who hid under the bed. He occasionally thought about that nurse and her narrow escape, connecting it to his protective feelings about his daughter's narrow escapes, but rarely brought it up to anyone, including himself.

Valerie stepped out of the kitchen area, carrying a bowl of freshly cut strawberries and mango slices. "Careful. That fluid's flammable," she warned, setting the bowl at the edge of the bar.

Sam moved the flame slightly away from the glass and asked, "Where'd you get this?"

Valerie casually picked up her wine. "The coroner who did Speck's autopsy was a collector, and it ended up on the black market. I'm still searching for the other one."

Sam, always the detective, asked straight up, "Why? What do you want it for?"

Valerie took a sip of her well-deserved, wind-down wine. "My aunt was one of his victims... call it ancestral closure."

Sam studied her, watching the flames dance in the glass like it now meant something. He looked over at the bowl of fruit, but his stomach, though used to eating in the presence of dead things, declined to eat, and he thought out loud. "Strange that a killer grew breasts in prison."

Valerie shrugged it off, "Not strange, it's simply supply and demand. He smuggled in hormones and became someone's bitch, or booty buddy, in exchange for protection. Nature adapts."

Sam turned up the questioning, exercising his next favorite pastime after the whiskey he sipped from his glass. "How can you be so matter-of-fact after what he... or she did?"

Valerie turned to him, eyes deep purple and penetrating. "In my line of work, the first thing to go is a judgmental attitude."

Sam followed up quickly, "And the second?"

"Boundaries. And the third is comfort zones. I've never been too comfortable with my comfort zones." She held his stare and looked right through him. He nodded slowly, getting it and her, as Valerie reached across the counter and handed him the drawing of the eight-year-old child. The lines were sharp, clean, and precise. "Here's the sketch my friend created. It's fairly accurate," she claimed.

Sam gave it a quick once-over. "Thanks." Sam glanced again at her wall of permits, then back to Valerie. "They sure got you permitted up the wazoo."

Valerie smiled. "There are a few things I've learned about the agents of the regime. They always crash out the hookup websites wherever they gather for their conventions, they conceal their kinks by pointing out everyone else's, and it turns out authoritarians love dungeons, they just don't want anyone else to have them. The inspector who comes by monthly to 'verify compliance' expects a hefty bribe and a session on the rack. I give it to him, and then I give it to him.

He told me the last time that a bot was replacing his job. I don't know if I'll have to bribe it, or if they have kinks they'll want to play out. You know, it's only a matter of time before the bots take over my gig. We're starting to see fetish studios pop up, run by Dom bots, and the 'techno-garghs' have directed most of their resources to AI sex and porn simulations. Come to think of it, if the bots ever develop kinks of their own, we might all be in trouble."

Sam stared at her, took a sip of whisky, one longer than usual. "That sounds crazy."

"Maybe, but I've been called crazy my entire life. You want to know what crazy is? Crazy is just someone who sees too early and speaks or acts too soon." Valerie stepped in close and turned her back to him. "Would you mind?" Sam reached up, fingers brushing her spine, as he pulled down the zipper of her catsuit. She peeled herself free of the tight vinyl, hips swaying, shoulder blades flexing beneath a geisha tattoo that danced as she moved. A geisha, still, poised, and eternally graceful on a field of inked skin slick with sweat, covering the full length of her back. "Don't mind the sweat," cautioned Valerie, giving more tongue than cheek.

Sam blushed and brushed it off. "It's not a problem."

She drifted into the bedroom, peeling off her vinyl as she walked away, tossing it on the dresser as she sauntered past. Sam's eyes followed her through the open door, and he saw an altar of Goddesses: stone, gold, and obsidian. They watched over her as she crossed the room bare and unbothered, selecting a silk robe from the closet with ceremonial ease, and slipped it on. Sam tracked her movements while pretending not to look, but not entirely succeeding. He reached out, "I wanted to ask you something."

She stepped out of the bedroom, all casual and cool, her robe clinging to her damp body. "I'll talk about anything, just as long as we agree not to talk about the heat."

Sam grinned and turned his attention to the drawing of the child. "What did you mean by that it's hard to penetrate the killer's mental walls?"

Valerie responded from her well-earned, learned experience. "Some people carry trauma like plate armor. Layer after layer. Emotional, mental, psychic, and ancestral. You try to reach them, and it's like screaming or swimming through concrete. Nothing gets in, and nothing gets out. Sometimes the only way to build a bridge is through their flesh." She moved closer with a rhythmic step; the space between them became friction-close.

Sam observed her nonchalantly. "You have such an unusual gift."

Valerie smiled and said in a low, raspy voice, "You and I are a lot alike, Sam. We both see better in and through the dark." She breathed closer, her voice like a raspberry-scented breeze. "Can I top up your drink?"

Sam checked his watch. "How about a rain check?"

She nodded, touched his hand, and in that touch, a flash of a vision:

Sam kissed her, hungry.

Sam on top of her, bed sheets tangled.

Her hands were cuffed to the headboard.

Both naked and lost in primal hunger and animal instincts.

Valerie blinked, and her professional mask slipped back into place. "Rain check it is." Sam handed over his empty glass, and she took it, grazing his cheek with a courtesy kiss, just enough to linger, but not enough to stay. He smiled it off,

tucked the drawing of the child into his pocket, then turned
for the door and walked out.

29

The Museum of Modern Murder

The reserved, single-story brick building crouched like a poor man's mausoleum, squeezed between a burned-out liquor store and a loan shark's lair. The MUSEUM OF MODERN MURDER sign was nailed into the plaster, above the steel-framed door with a glass pane painted black. Sam hit the rust-bitten buzzer with a knuckle, his eyes scanning the shadows to his left and right, then looked up at the security camera. Alaska stood beside him, taking in the buildings' sadly strung Christmas lights, with their missing bulbs and syncopated blinks. "So, this guy's an expert?" she asked.

Sam was deep in thought about the history of murder on the other side of the door, then pulled himself back to the surface. "He knows a thing or two about a thing or two."

Alaska glanced at his face and squinted. "Looks like you've got a little lipstick on your cheek."

Sam wiped it off with the back of his hand and studied the smudge, pretending to be surprised. "I musta have cut myself shaving."

Alaska looked at him sideways and was about to say something 'cheeky,' but was interrupted by a faint buzzer from inside the building. The lock clicked, and the door creaked open. Dustin stood in the doorway, like the curator of a Halloween haunted house; his smile was lopsided, and his eyes gleamed with the 24-hour caffeinated enthusiasm of a seasoned professional. He wore a velvet blazer over a graphic tee that read – H.H. HOLMES WAS FRAMED, and felt much more relaxed in his private museum than he did when he was out promoting his wares with media engagements. He grinned and sang, "Merry Christmas, maestro," and invited them in.

Sam and Alaska walked past him, and Sam nodded, "Likewise, this is my daughter, Deputy Alaska Rainmaker. Alaska, meet Dustin Guidry."

Dustin's brows jumped, and he gave a little bow. "Deputy? The ornament doesn't fall too far from the Christmas tree."

Alaska gave him a polite head tilt, but her eyes were already darting around the room – enthralled. The interior felt like stepping into a reliquary crafted by Jack the Ripper. Black-and-white mugshots and crime scene polaroids, each image a face shrouded in blood and infamy, lined the walls. Artifacts from human nightmares were boxed and tagged behind glass: Bundy's tire iron, a knife from Zodiac, a plaster mold of Ed Gein's belt buckle, Christmas and birthday cards sent and received by various serial killers throughout history. Floor to ceiling, shelf to shelf, the place pulsed with the stench of killer paraphernalia and memorabilia, and something sour and stale beneath the floorboards.

Sam looked around. "How's business?"

Dustin rubbed his thumb and forefinger together. "Boomin'. Just sold one of my Gacy clown paintings."

Sam was surprised. "You didn't."

Alaska's eyes widened. "Wait, you had a John Wayne Gacy?"

Dustin replied nonchalantly, "Still got three more in the hallway."

Alaska was now gushing like a serial-killer fangirl. "Whoa."

Dustin pointed down the narrow corridor lined with atrocities masquerading as art. "They're behind bars, pardon the pun." Alaska didn't hang around for further niceties and wandered toward them, pulled by the curiosity tugging at her heels. Dustin moved to the counter, grabbed a bottle of whiskey from his private stash, poured two glasses, mixed in some eggnog, and handed one to Sam. "How goes the hunt?"

Sam accepted the glass, tipped it for a cheer, and took a sip. "Same shit, different shovel."

Dustin offered his version of holiday cheer. "I got a new one for you. How many narcissists does it take to screw in a light bulb? They don't – they convince everyone else that darkness is the new light."

Sam gave him a deadpan look that could freeze time, then pulled out his latest one for the 'who's going to crack first, gunfight.' "How many narcissists does it take to screw in a light bulb? None, they use gaslighting."

Dustin kept his stare blank, then cracked a smile, and then laughed.

Sam was glad to see that Dustin was the first one to break again, and he followed the banter with a more genuine tone. "I heard you on that Mischief livestream. Well done." Dustin, unsure how to receive or trust a compliment, just raised his glass and took another sip. Back to the business he was there for, Sam cut to the chase. "Listen, I wanted to ask you about The Roach. You once said you didn't think he killed Brother

Di Segni. Why?"

Dustin's tone shifted, less sideshow and more scholarly. "Because 'Taco' had a style that was ritualistic and methodical. He wouldn't just hang someone up and leave 'em clean. He'd always dismember them and carve 'em up for the taco truck. If anything, Taco was consistent as nacho sauce on a cold night in November. Di Segni was the wrong profile, the wrong scene, and didn't match his other victims."

Sam pressed him further. "Maybe Di Segni was just the wrong guy, at the wrong place, at the wrong time?"

Dustin held his position. "Nah. Taco didn't do sloppy, even his chaos was calculated."

Sam nodded slowly, taking it in. "Have you ever heard of someone who might have one of Richard Speck's... breasts?"

Dustin casually replied, "A local collector has one. I tried buying it once for ten grand, but they refused to part with it."

Sam tossed back more of his whiskey and nog. "Ten grand seems a little steep."

Dustin laid out the numbers like a tax accountant. "That's the going rate for a dead killer's tit. Some collectors never part with their pieces, no matter the offer. Some items only increase in value – better returns than the stock market."

Alaska reappeared, eyes wide and fixed on a painting nailed to a splintered beam. It showed a creature, hairless and bone-thin, with hollow eyes and a ravenous hunger. Fangs glinted beneath a snarling mouth, looking starved of soul. She stepped closer, her fingertips brushing the frame. "Is this a Wetiko?"

Dustin's face shifted again as he adopted his salesman face. "Sure is, but it's not for sale. It's an original, made by a real shaman."

She pulled out Gemini's S.A.S.S. flyer, unfolded it, held it out, and pointed to one of the drawings. "Ever seen one like this?"

Dustin's expression changed from surprise to seriousness. He nodded and turned to a shelf, "Let me show you something." Sam rolled his eyes in the background while Dustin rummaged through a cluttered bookshelf. He ran his fingers over rows of manila folders and stacks of true crime biographies with cracked spines until he found what he was after and pulled it out. He blew dust off the cover and laid it open on the counter. Inside were clippings, century-old newsprint, yellowed and brittle. Headlines in uneven type revealed:

Man Becomes Beast

Northern Family Slain and Demon of the Pines Strikes Again.

The folder contained blurry photos, ancient ink, and hand-drawn sketches of creatures. He handed them to Alaska one by one. "These are all old reports of the Wetiko from the 1800s. Back then, that's how people explained psychotic serial killers through stories of pathology, and hungry spirits wearing human skin. Some of them had this Wetiko possession. Have you ever heard of it?"

Alaska stood taller and straighter. "Yeah, it's one of the ways my ancestors explained the dark, spirited, and cruel-hearted ones – cannibals, psychos, greedy beings, and murderers." Alaska looked over the images. "It's like our cultural version of psychopathology."

Dustin turned to Sam, then back to Alaska. There was respect in his gaze now. "You know your stuff."

Alaska deflected the compliment, "Can I borrow these?"

"Take 'em, for as long as you need." Dustin nodded.

Sam exhaled, annoyed. Alaska peeped it and shrugged. "My dad thinks it's all superstition."

Dustin side-eyed Sam. "Sometimes, superstitions tell you more about what you're lookin' at than fingerprints and footprints."

Alaska looked at Sam, smiled again, but wider this time, then stared at both of them and said, "How many serial killers does it take to screw in a light bulb? Two...." She took her time to deadpan between the two of them, then went for the jugular. "....One to screw it in the light bulb, and one to make a lampshade out of skin." Sam and Dustin deadpanned her, looked at each other, and then both cracked up. Alaska mic-dropped, deadpanned them back, picked up the Wetiko folder, nodded to Dustin, then calmly walked toward the door and out.

Dustin glanced over at Sam, gave him a thumbs up, and offered, "You got yourself a real spitfire there. Well done." Sam grinned, shrugged, and tilted his head, as if to say, *'You don't know the half of it.'* He concealed his greater pride, placed the empty whiskey glass on the counter, nodded his head in appreciation, and followed Alaska out.

Sam and Alaska crossed the parking lot, their footsteps crunching over the gravel, as they left the dark, eerie museum behind. Alaska flipped through the yellowed pages about the Wetiko. Her eyes scanned some of the old Cree-referenced text, her mouth moving slightly as she read about shadows of hunger and greed that devour people from within, or without. She stopped and looked over at Sam. "Says here it's up to a medicine person to defeat a Wetiko. If he can't do it alone, he relies on his wife, a group of women, or dresses up as a woman to access his feminine power." She smirked and asked, "Dad, are you willing to wear a dress?"

Sam stopped beside the Plymouth and turned to her with that worn, crooked smile that had seen more graves than birthdays. "First of all, I'm not a medicine person. That was your mother's wheelhouse and is your grandmother's domain. Second, I'd prance down Main Street in a goddamn tutu if it meant catching this son of a bitch."

Alaska laughed. For a moment, tenderness passed between them, perhaps a recognition of her bloodline and their blood bond. He smiled, nodded once, climbed into his car, and she mounted her bike. Their engines roared to life at the same time, and they drove off, leaving more questions than answers behind. But they both knew they were in the questions business, answers being something you could neither control nor predict, usually arriving on their own terms and with their own consequences.

30

The Amazon

Ama sat cross-legged on her battered office chair, her computer open and the *Easy Rider* film playing in front of her. Onscreen, the three men sat around a campfire: George, Billy, and Captain America. Ama leaned in, eyes sharp, dialed in like a sniper. Her lips moved silently, syncing with the scene on screen:

George/Ama. "Oh, no. What you represent to them is freedom."

Billy/Ama. "What the hell's wrong with freedom? That's what it's all about."

She hit pause, and the screen froze on Captain America's eyes as she sat back in the chair, arms folded, and analyzing all the possible meanings of these words, as they related to America. She started up her road trip playlist and listened to *Born To Be Wild by Steppenwolf*, *Born To Run by Bruce Springsteen*, and *On Ira by Zaz*, while she reviewed and charted road maps of America. She continued her online research into alternative avenues to gain access to and/or legal status for the land outside of Phillip. These included sponsorship, political asylum, and studying the escape strategies of escapees such as those from Alcatraz, as well as those of Timothy Leary, John Dillinger, and Assata Shakur.

Sam worked diligently in his office, sorting through pieces of the mismatched, scattered puzzle, while Alaska sat at the cluttered workbench in the garage, half-focused on playing *Hellblade* on her wrist device. Her fingers moved, but her mind wandered over the table around her: a chaos of broken tech guts, busted drives, and a mess of yellowed Wetiko clippings, laid out like pieces of a scrambled riddle that felt more like her scrambled mind.

Alaska thought about the 'not-for-sale' Wetiko drawing by a shaman that she had seen at the Murder Museum and turned her attention to Gemini's book. She picked it up, flipped through, and honed in on Gemini's understanding of the role of the Shaman or Medicine Person. Her finger traced the page, mouth shaping wor**ds: Spec**i*fic healing roles, training, and responsibilities vary significantly across cultures, and some groups have multiple types of spiritual practitioners with different specialties. The role and responsibilities can vary considerably between communities, even within the same ethnic group. Many tribes and nations use terms like 'Medicine Man/Woman (English)', 'Chaman or Curendaro/Curendera (Spanish)', or 'Pajé (Portuguese).*

Alaska read about the Amazon, which Gemini had a strong and sustained interest in. The very Amazon itself was filled with a constant symphony of sounds from its diverse wildlife – as if in a continuous state of storytelling, singing, and cele-bration. Gemini described this experience as the 'relentless hum' of the jungles, rainforests, and rivers that sounded like *Sunrise Over The Ucayali River by Shipibo Shamans*, which she located and played from her streamer.

Alaska learned about the pink river dolphin, known as a boto in Portuguese and a bufeo in Spanish, which holds deep spiritual importance throughout many Amazonian cultures. There were stories in Gemini's book about the boto's role as a messenger between the visible and invisible worlds, transforming to deliver prophetic dreams and healing visions, with the pink dolphin serving as a bridge between aquatic and terrestrial, as well as human and non-human, realms of healing and transformation.

Additionally, since dolphins are considered ancient, they are the mammals that have remained in the water. Meanwhile, their human cousins evolved on land, and they love human children as if they were their own. They communicate telepathically with each other, both within various dolphin species and across different species, below and above the waters. There were many stories and dolphin medicine healers from around the world and throughout history, such as those in Hawaii, New Zealand, Australia, and the inspiring Torovim Dolphin Medicine legends of the Tongva in Southern California.

Alaska thought about visiting the Amazon someday. She also wished she could have met Gemini and felt the rare emotion of envy for those who did. She was unaware that she had drifted into a well-deserved nap while reading about these beautiful people and creatures of the Amazon, and she dreamed of songs, rivers, and the pink dolphins.

Ama's road trip music bounced out of her room and interrupted Alaska's sleep — a concept that, even though Alaska had tried to explain it to her six ways from Sunday, Ama still had not caught its drift. Alaska begrudgingly opened her eyes, still dreaming about what she had learned in Gemini's book. She surveyed the still chaotic riddle on the table and chose her wrist device and the digital dream-fight she could navigate.

Ama rolled into the garage with the stiff grace of someone trying to pretend they were human, and getting closer every day. She quickly turned her attention to Alaska. "Question, Alaska. The campfire scene at the end of *Easy Rider*, where Captain America says to Billy, 'We blew it.' What does he mean by that? Blew what?"

Alaska didn't look up, keeping her eyes on her wrist screen. "I dunno. Screwed everything up."

Ama moved closer, her voice curious and almost reverent. "Oh, I bet you if I were a human being, I could fix it. Actually, I think I want to be a real human."

Alaska finally paused the game, and her expression softened with a kind of tired affection. "So do I, Ama. So do I. What would you do if you were a 'real' human being?"

Ama lit up – the thought alone triggered an internal fire in her hard drive. "Dude, I would feel all the feels. Pain. Anger. Love. Compassion. Wonder. And I would be all fire and breezy just like Captain America, I'd invent everything needed for everything, and I'd march on Selma, Alabama with Coretta Scott King and Martin Luther King Jr."

Alaska thought about telling her that the Kings were dead, but she had already tried to explain, like sleep, the concept of death to Ama many times, with little success. Instead, she replied, "You can be anything you want to be."

Ama tilted her head, studying her face like a child looking for the truth behind a bedtime story. "Alaska, can robots dream?"

Alaska thought about both the question and Ama, wondering whether her programming, primarily designed for clerical and detective tasks, had been tampered with. If Ama had hacked her way out of it, or if she ever truly had any programming at all. "I don't know... sure."

Ama spun around once on her roller skates. "For realz? Can I be Cree like you, your mother, and your grandparents? And also be like Captain America? Can I do that, Alaska?"

Alaska smiled and held up a hippy peace sign with her two fingers. "You do you, skibidoo."

Ama blinked, processing the information. "Oh, okay. If that's true, could you ask those Panther folks to spring me like they did with Assata Shakur, 'cause this place is slowing my roll and I'm really feeling the urge to bust out of here."

Alaska just looked at her and thought, *'What the hell have I created?'*

"And another question," asked Ama. "Do you prefer scrolling and playing video games over playing with me?

The guilt landed sharply and suddenly. Alaska looked up, then scanned her wrist, pressed play, and *Come and Get Your Love by Redbone* blared out over the garage speakers. She stood up and sashayed over to the tree; the plastic squat thing her dad had now decorated with speed and spare LED lights. She shrugged at the tree and her dad's efforts, saw that he had added a present for her, grabbed Ama's wrapped box underneath, and danced back across the room. "Here." She handed it over.

Ama tore and hacked through the paper as if it were data encryption. Her eyes shone with delight when she saw what was inside. "Ten terabytes of RAM?! Put it in, put it in!"

Alaska waved her hand. "Turn around for a second. Let's blow your mind to smithereens."

Ama followed her instructions, as Alaska grabbed her tools and gently powered her down. Ama's head dropped like a wilting flower. Alaska worked fast, hands steady, and with no hesitation. The door creaked open behind her, and Sam walked in holding the sketch of the child, creased, smudged, and too real. He interrupted, "Ama."

Alaska raised her hand to stop him. "Just a second." She inserted the new RAM, secured the panel, and then pressed the reboot button. A hum of life, a flicker of code, Ama's head jerked up, her eyes flashed bright, and she started to move quickly, smoothly, and almost humanly.

Sam stepped closer. "Are you awake?"

Ama spun around in circles. "Oh yeah, dude. I'm super awake."

Sam held out the sketch of the child. "Okay, run this sketch through the database. Check foster care and juvie. See what pops up." Ama grabbed the sketch, twirled it, then spun in circles on her roller skates, dancing around the room like a juiced-up ballerina. She stopped when she noticed her rusted, micro-toy car, jumped in, threw it into drive, and sped through the compound, leaving Sam and Alaska in her dust.

31

The Hunt, The Hunter, and The Hunted

The air reeked of metal, mold, and something fouler – a mixture of old blood and burnt plastic. A cocktail blend of *A Message To Pretty by The Rising Storm* and *Coconut by Harry Nilsson* played simultaneously on opposite cellar speakers sitting next to stacks of photocopied crime scene photos scattered across the table. Each one captured the hollow, dead gaze of The Roach and all his terrible lunacy and legacy. His face, bloated and lifeless in one, grinning smug in another, now slowly rotated on a computer monitor, rendering a digital reconstruction. Beside the monitor, a 3D printer hummed with cold precision, its nozzle gliding back and forth, printing something with a palpable sense of menace. Bit by bit, the machine birthed a new face, a skin-tight mask of The Roach reborn in silicone and synthetic flesh.

The killer swayed and danced from side to side, watching reverently as the mask finished printing. He lifted it carefully, like cradling a newborn, and ran his fingers along its contours: eyelids, lips, and the sick curve of its smirk. He pulled the mask over his head with a snap, then turned to the wall, where a photocopy of Rachel stared back at him – her face was soft, captured mid-laugh, and wearing the innocence of someone unaware she was being tracked. He brushed her cheek with his thumb, slow and intimate, like he already owned her. Then he pinned her photo beside another of Gemini Moon, part of his growing collection of targets, grabbed his forged travel pass to match his forged identity, and walked up and out of the cellar, one creaky-creepy step at a time.

* * *

A white van rolled through the city like a steel predator in hunting gear. Behind the wheel, the killer wore the freshly minted, tight-fitting Roach mask. The mouth didn't move, but the eyes were alive with the hunt. He drove with purpose past dusty scenes of neon motels, boarded-up buildings, coyotes, junkies, and girls with too much makeup and nowhere else to go. He watched them through the windshield like a jackal behind glass, thinking about how easy it would be to pick one, or all of them off: the coyotes, the junkies, or the girls.

* * *

The glow from the livestream lighting made the room feel intimate, like a confessional without pretense or a priest. Rachel sat behind her mic, wearing a snug headset, fingers casually toying with a half-empty coffee mug. The show's theme song faded out, and her voice flowed out smoothly and steadily, like she'd done hundreds of times before and still had fuel to spare. "Hello, I'm Rachel Lamont, and you're listening to Mischief. Today, I'm with my friend and activist Lucia Sky.

Lucia sat opposite her host, dressed in equal parts glam-punk and prophet. Her eyes and mind were sharp. "Thanks for having me on."

Rachel smiled at her friend. "For our listeners' benefit, you're a New Yorker, a performance artist, gender-queer activist, climate champion, and co-curator of the Creatrix Gallery. How do you find time for all of this?"

Lucia answered in a way that could break your heart and your worldview in a single sentence: "I make time for what I love." Her words sprinkled and settled into the air like fairy dust.

Rachel sipped her 'comfort coffee' that had gone cold an hour ago. "Well, you're one of the most passionate people I know. In honor of our friend Gemini, today we're going to talk about some of the cultural roots of personal violence in America."

Lucia tilted her head back and gazed up at the ceiling. "You know, I thought about whether this was the right timing for this, but I know Gemini wouldn't want us to stay silent. If anything, Gem's legacy is that the louder the mouth, the better. Gemini used to say, 'They want us isolated, afraid, and silent. So we gather, we speak, and we love. That's resistance.' As for the cultural roots of personal violence, we could start by talking about authoritarian domination and power over systems of control that are programmed and repurposed in our country and around the world to shame, diminish, and abuse human beings through our political, religious, and interpersonal relationships. Domination, power-over, authoritarianism, easily being America's greatest perversion.

I grew up Boricua in New York. You learn early what it means to belong to a country that owns your island but won't claim your people. That's not ancient history. That's the electric bill."

* * *

Sam sat hunched in his metal chair, which he had spent more years sleeping in than in his bed. Screens crackled around him: surveillance stills, autopsy photos, and old maps. Rachel's voice drifted from a dusty computer in the corner of his office. He let it play as background noise, turning it into an unintentional, comforting gospel. "Ah, yes, power over culture is one, kinky bitch. My French relatives have never understood Americans. For instance, they don't know why, if things are so bad and nobody sets something on fire, how do you expect to fix it?"

Sam smiled at her irreverent attitude, cracked his neck, and ran a thumb over a photo of the sketch. The kid's eyes were wide and much too old, and had too much story for his face. Lucia's voice interrupted his focus. "I think Americans prefer to live with the comfort of our known insecurities, rather than our still unknown possibilities and promise of freedom.

* * *

Rachel let out a soft laugh that carried both exhaustion and agreement, then topped off her cup with more caffeine than she actually needed. The mic captured everything, including her breath and a hint of irony itching in her voice. "I think you just described my life."

Lucia chuckled. "Yeah, our toxic system can create a whole snake pit of emotional anxieties, trauma bonds, triggers, projection, inadequacy, and hyper-aggressivity. I believe violence toward others can be a misguided attempt to over-compensate for the mess inside, the one we all seem to be hell-bent on avoiding."

Rachel stared at her coffee, as if it were a muse that might talk back, her voice dropping to a tone people use when they're scared or sure they're right. "I wonder if that's what incels are all about?"

Lucia was hitting her stride and responded, "Perhaps. Involuntary celibacy driven by loneliness, emotional inse-curities, over-compliance, and hooked on algorithms and digital cosplay. All the usual suspects, which reinforce self and group image, Ai-porn addiction, repressed rage, and an extreme mistrust of women and men. There are also gradients and levels to it, like the black pill incels who represent the terminally nihilistic and existential angst-ridden, where the only power option is destruction and annihilation of everything."

Rachel processed her insight and offered, "Sounds like a dose of puberty gone south."

Lucia smiled and spoke softly as if she knew from personal experience. "It's not easy being a boy or young man in the diminishing, fear-based, dominating system either, whether in this country or another. It can, in fact, be soul-crushing. An incel, regardless of the type or subgroup, is essentially just a sensitive boy. The secret that nobody talks about is that boys and men tend to be more sensitive or yin on the inside than other genders, no matter how much their posturing and overcompensation may hide or pretend otherwise." They sat quietly for a moment in that shared silence, the kind that says, *'We're diving deep now.'*

* * *

The white van idled at the edge of the alley's throat, cloaked in shadows and grime, like something discarded and intentionally forgotten. Steam curled upward from a nearby vent, drifting in slow tendrils across the windshield. The killer, his face hidden beneath the tight-fitting Roach mask, sat utterly still, one gloved hand resting on the steering wheel, the other cupping an audio sampling device retrofitted into an untraceable radio receiver.

Rachel's voice echoed through the van's speakers, sharp and cutting through the dark like a knife coated in sweet honey. "Maybe they'd like to be in sexual relationships, have lovers and partners, but they can take rejection extremely personally." The Roach mask stayed still, with only the eyes behind it, glassy and blinking, zeroing in on the crosshairs of the conversation.

* * *

Lucia nodded thoughtfully, her fingers pressed to her chin, as Rachel's phone rang with a dial-up ringtone. She grabbed it, pushed the line, and her voice shifted into pro-mode. "Looks like we have our first caller. Hello, this is Mischief. You're on the air."

A moment of silence, then a voice came through, nervous and tentative, like a kid at the edge of a cliff or going through puberty. "Yes, hello. Thank you for taking my call. I'm wondering if your guest believes that the Copycat Killer fits the incel profile?"

Lucia leaned into the mic, voice calm but precise, the kind that could untangle knots in the belly of a whale if needed. "Cousin. He's in the ballpark, but not all incels are necessarily violent."

There was a pause, and you could hear the caller's breath catch. When he spoke again, his voice was slower, almost apologetic. "Good to know. I kinda get nervous around girls, get angry and depressed for no reason, and am not sure what to do. Okay, umm. That's all." The line clicked, silent.

* * *

The killer stayed still, his breath behind the mask shallow and measured. The voice on the radio, the boy, and the ache behind his words floated in the van like a vapor trail. He tilted his head slightly, trying to memorize it. *'Not all incels are necessarily violent.'*

* * *

The sketch of the child trembled slightly in Sam's fingers, more from what it implied than from his grip, while the phone buzzed through the livestream in the background. "Looks like we have another caller. Hello, this is Mischief. You're on the air."

Then a long silence.

Sam paused, his eyes still locked on the sketch, but his ears were with Rachel, who reached out for a response. "Hello? Hello?" Still nothing, just dead air.

* * *

A deliberate, gloved hand reached into a tangle of electrical wires and switches, flipping the main breaker of the building's basement electrical panel with surgical precision. The lights in Rachel's building went out at once, like a patient suddenly taken off life support.

* * *

Darkness swallowed Rachel's apartment whole; the buzzing of the light bulbs and electronics faded into silence. Rachel handed Lucia a candle, then lit one herself, its flame casting silhouettes across the room. As she moved to the apartment's light switches and flicked them, only the faint crackle of wax and wick guided her from room to dark room.

* * *

Sam looked over and noticed that the livestream had gone dark and silent. He sat up, then got to his feet, emerging from the office with his gut instinct, his eyes hard and already knowing. "Ama, get me Rachel Lamont's address." He looked toward Alaska. "You wanna go for a ride?"

Alaska nodded and was already on her feet before she could say, "Yes."

* * *

Rachel heard a soft, casual knock at the door, as if someone were asking for a cup of sugar or a candle. She walked toward it, holding a candle in her hand, looked through the peephole, and carefully opened it as far as the chain door guard would allow. Roach stood there, his mask and skin indistinguishable in the low light, carrying a flashlight and a worn tool bag. He pointed to a fake ID pinned to his shirt pocket. "I'm from maintenance. I've come to check your power outage."

Rachel looked him up and down, quickly scanned his badge and tool bag. "Oh great, thanks," she said, then unhooked the chain and opened the door.

Roach stepped inside and surveyed the room. "I'll check the box. It could just be a breaker or a fuse."

Rachel moved aside and gestured. "It's in the kitchen."

He walked past her like he'd done this before, moving like a man with a plan and a timeline. He found the fuse box, set his bag down, unzipped it slowly, then pulled out a rope, tape, a rag, and a dark-glass bottle filled with chloroform. He soaked the rag, concealed it in his hand, turned back toward the living room, and eased up to Rachel. "The fuse seems to be okay."

His hand squeezed the rag concealed behind his back, ready to strike, when Lucia called out, "What's that smell?" She emerged from the bathroom, candle in hand, and her face half-lit like a guardian from some old, forgotten myth.

Roach froze, but quickly shifted gears. "Power could've tripped the gas regulator. I'll check it out." He nodded, slipped past them again, opened the door, and stepped into the hallway.

He returned to the basement breaker, where his hand lingered for a moment, as if it wasn't quite ready to let go of the dark. He flipped the switch, and the lights snapped back on in the building, which to him felt like an irritating, overblown neighbor's Christmas display. He exited through the basement bulkhead and crept back to the van.

Roach sat behind the wheel, breathing in irritated, shallow, ragged gasps. He attached a voice modulator to his phone and watched the window of Rachel's apartment. The livestream on the van's speaker crackled to life, and Rachel was the first to speak. "Looks like we had ourselves a little power outage."

Lucia covered her flank like a loyal, battle-worthy wing woman. "Maybe Mercury's in retrograde."

Rachel bantered back, "Yeah, when isn't it?"

Roach cracked a smile at the joke, picked up his burner phone, and dialed.

* * *

Rachel leaned into the mic. "It looks like we have another caller. Hello, this is Mischief, you're on the air."

The voice on the other end sounded like something caked in mud, twisted through a carburetor, and then sharpened with a diamond cutter. "Incels are pussies. They don't have the balls to do what I do."

Rachel's voice stiffened. "Excuse me?"

Roach ramped it up and demanded, "Do you want the left or the right?"

Lucia interjected, "What? Who is this?"

Roach repeated himself, more annoyed now, "The left or the right?"

Rachel shifted from host to investigator. "Nick? Is this you? Is this some kinda joke?"

"Oh, you think I'm a joke? I bet you think I have issues," growled Roach.

Rachel looked over at Lucia, both equally puzzled, then

leaned back into the microphone. "Is this a prank? Who is this?"

* * *

Sam pressed harder on the gas, and Alaska's eyes were locked on the livestream, listening to every syllable and nuance. Roach's voice emanated from the Plymouth speaker. "I'll give you a clue. It starts with a "c" and ends with a "cat."

Rachel stepped into her French-boss-bitch mode and shot back, "Are you sure it doesn't begin with a 'c' and end with an 'unt?"

Alaska looked over at Sam. They both nodded their heads and smirked as if to say, *'That was a good one.'*

Roach mimicked a laugh. "Ha, Ha, very funny. Do you know what happened to the last person who mocked me and told me I had issues?... Right. Your friend didn't suffer too much. Just kidding. I lit that Moon-bitch, up just like your Christmas tree."

Sam pressed the pedal, pushing to 85 MPH – the old car's limit.

* * *

Now, rattled, Rachel stood, walked to the window, and looked out. "You bastard," then pivoted back to the livestream booth.

* * *

Roach sat there, watching her silhouette slowly move away, the light behind her making her an easy target, had he ever decided to lower himself to amateur status by using a gun. He pressed the phone to his lips one last time. "So, which titty do you want me to cut off first? The left or the right?" Then silence on the line, before continuing to toy with her like a cat with a cornered mouse. "Eenie-meenie-miney-mo! The left one's got to go. Now stop doing this fucking show!"

* * *

The livestream went dead, and Sam's car screeched to a stop on the opposite side of the street from Roach, who ducked low, his eyes scanning the mirrors.

* * *

Rachel sat next to Lucia on the couch, while Sam leaned forward, opposite them, on a borrowed kitchen chair. The tension and faint echo from the replayed livestream filled the space between them. Sam hit pause, and Roach's recorded voice cut out before he spoke. "Any disgruntled boyfriends, or anybody you know who'd want to hurt you?"

Rachel looked down and tugged at a loose thread on her sleeve. "There's Nick, but... he wouldn't hurt a flea."

From the window, Alaska stood and watched a shadow peel away from the curb – an unmarked van melting into the night like it knew it had overstayed its welcome. She turned back to Rachel. "We'll put an extra security detail around your building," Alaska said, then stepped closer. "This might be too personal, but I've been reading Gemini's book. I keep thinking about how she described your mutual friend, Mia. We both have seizures. Do you know if hers ever stopped?"

Rachel glanced at Lucia, looked down, then back at Alaska. "I don't think so. I'm not sure."

Alaska sensed the tension between the two of them. "Do you mind if I ask how Mia died?"

Rachel hesitated. "Uhm... suicide."

"I'm sorry to hear that." Alaska exhaled.

Rachel stood and crossed the room to a bookshelf cluttered with old zines, memoirs, and diaries too precious to lend, but she pulled one out anyway. It was the kind of book that had been cried on more than once, with worn edges and dog-eared pages. She handed it to Alaska. "This is Mia's diary. I can lend it to you if you want. There's a lot there that's not in Gemini's book."

Alaska took it carefully, as if it might fall apart in her hands. "Thank you. I'll get it back to you."

Sam stood up and nodded at Rachel. No cop clichés, just the look you give someone who's been through it. He looked at Alaska, tilted his head toward the door, and signaled that it was time to wrap it up. They quietly left, shutting the door behind them.

* * *

Sam gripped the wheel of his unmarked Plymouth like it owed him money, or at least a shot of whiskey. Alaska sat in the passenger seat, scanning traffic with her cop-activated eyes, sharpened by years as a bounty hunter beyond the city's limits. On the dash, Ama's digital face flickered to life, cold and efficient, and played back Roach's recorded voice. "Do you know what happened to the last person who mocked me and told me I had issues?" His voice slithered and crawled out of the speakers, distorted and inhuman.

Ama interjected. "He's using an off-the-shelf voice modulator that can replicate any language, gender, accent, or frequency – untraceable and impossible to reverse engineer."

Sam slammed the heel of his palm against the steering wheel. "Dammit."

* * *

Rachel drew a deep breath and said, "I'll be fine. I just need some space right now." Lucia didn't argue. She knew that tone of voice when people say "space"; they're just barely holding on, but she let her go and left anyway.

* * *

Sam's phone lit up with a text message. With a quick look, the tight line of his jaw relaxed. He let out a breath and cracked a rare, crooked smile as they pulled up in front of The 66 and came to a halt. "I'm gonna drop you here."

Alaska raised an eyebrow. "Where are you headed?"

Sam didn't answer immediately. He just stared out through the dusty windshield like he was seeing something that wasn't there yet. "I gotta cash a check." He left his words hanging as Alaska stepped out and shut the door with a clunk behind her. Sam peeled off into the night, tail lights fading into another one of the city's shifting dust storms.

32

The Feathers

Rachel unrolled her yoga mat, but the only thing she could offer her sporadic practice was to lie down and fall asleep in Savasana. She woke up later, unsure how long she had been 'practicing', and went to the fridge; it was empty except for a plastic container of extra-cold pasta, the sauce half-congealed, but Rachel forked it into her mouth anyway, chewing like it was fuel instead of food. While she ate, she scrolled through her phone and called the number. "Nick, just seeing if you're around?" No answer, silence, just the dull click of the end of her call.

She took a sip from a warm cup of chocolate-cacao. It tasted flat. Maybe because she had drowned gallons of it trying to maintain her balance and her vibe. Even the most potent methylxanthine bliss compounds in the most organic, fair-trade cacao had lost their edge and effectiveness. They no longer managed to find or activate her hidden and latent joy states. She finished the rest of the cacao anyway, hoping for the best, but kinda wished she had chosen a cup of java instead.

Then, a video request lit up her phone screen from Captain Climate Change. Rachel answered, and Eris popped up. "I heard the caller on your show. Thought I'd check in. You okay? Want some company?"

* * *

Eris stood by the bookshelf tucked in the corner of Rachel's apartment. She was a figure of soft seduction in leather shorts, a corset bustier, and a feathered jacket that looked like it was made of fire. A black fedora shadowed her eyes as she sipped wine delicately, as if it were her last ounce of oxygen. She turned on Rachel's shelf speaker and Bluetoothed *Picture of You by Chappell Roan* from her phone, then faced the kitchen. "You sure got a lot of books about phobias. I think cosplay helps me with my fears, too."

Rachel entered with another bottle of red and refilled Eris's glass. "For real? What are you afraid of?"

Eris didn't hesitate and said, "Open spaces, closed spaces, heights, crowds, and random things that seem to come and go of their own volition. I think dressing up helps me feel safe and gives me the courage to do life."

Rachel confessed, "I feel ya. I'm afraid of spiders."

Eris peered down at the hardwood. "There's one right now."

Rachel's face flashed into high alert. 'What?! Where?" She froze, then practically levitated into Eris's arms. Their bodies collided in an accidental embrace charged with more than just friendship.

Eris looked down again and smiled. "Oopsies, it's just a dust ball." Rachel focused her eyes on the floor, but her body didn't move. Eris leaned in, and Rachel looked up and paused for a heartbeat, then kissed her. They stumbled into the bedroom, shadows colliding, breath sharp, and hands fumbling and urgent. Their clothes hit the floor, and feathers spiraled through the air, landing like the wreckage from exotic, plucked peacocks.

33

The Eighth Wonder

The Joan of Arcade loft door creaked open, and there Valerie stood, all sharp cheekbones and sultry shadows, wrapped in silk. Her eyes scanned Sam like she was looking at a forbidden, smoky flavor of a 'cured' man she couldn't wait to tap, then she stepped aside without a word.

Sam prowled in, dust still clinging to his shirt like a second or third skin. Valerie reached up and touched his cheek, unbuttoned his shirt with a slow, deliberate flick, then tore the rest open, like she was gutting a promise. He grabbed her shoulders and pressed her against the wall. Her robe fell to the floor, revealing nothing underneath but heat and hurry, and what to him looked like the world's eighth wonder. She climbed up on him like the first rungs of a fire escape, lips crashing into his with a violence that blurred the line between lust and lethal. She yanked at his belt, unfastened his pants, and let them hit the hardwood with the sound of *who the fuck needs these.* Sam gripped her hair like the mane of an unbridled Andalusian, and bit into her neck like his name began with Count. She gasped, ached, and arched into him with an impulse that screamed, *'fuck me, love me, or kill me – or all three.'*

He then spun her around, pulled her into her bedroom, fell short of the bed, folded her onto the Persian rug, and pinned her on her back with the weight of every previously unacted urge firing between them. Her nails scratched and carved lines down his spine, raw and rough. There was no music and no mercy, just sweat, breath, and the beautiful violence of two people aiming to fuck the pain out of their bones – intent on succeeding, or at least dying while trying. If there was an act as ravaging and enrapturing as *'Fucking your woman to God,'* then surely that was it.

Love to Love You Baby by Donna Summer may or may not have played out of her bedroom speaker, or it might have just been the sound rising from her body and the memory of her body's pleasure. Valerie didn't care either way, nor did the ecstatic Goddesses who expressed themselves in the moment through the arch of her spine, the deepening of her breath, and the curling of her toes.

34

The Doppelgänger

The morning light slanted through the curtains, soft but uninvited, casting perfect bars across Rachel's tangled sheets. She blinked herself awake and saw Eris standing at the window, wearing one of her wigs and her AirPods, listening to *Copycat by Billie Eilish*, her telescope aimed like a sniper rifle, tracking movements across the street. She was wrapped in the strange stillness of someone watching a world that was also unaware of being observed. Eris felt Rachel waking up behind her and lowered the volume on her AirPods. "Interesting neighbors. Any one of them could be the Copycat. Ya know, if I ever caught that guy, I'd slay him with one swipe." She sliced the telescope through the air like a bayonet, laughing softly to herself.

Rachel raised her head from the pillow. "Is that my wig and outfit?" The outfit, a mash-up of blond curls, vintage leather, and leopard print, was unmistakably Rachel's.

Eris turned slowly, a grin twitching at the corners of her lips, and confessed, "I found these in your closet. I hope you don't mind."

Rachel tried to play it off, but something about the scene made her cringe and feel unsettled. She looked down and saw that her right leg was still tied to the bedpost with a silk scarf from last night's rumble. Eris crouched, slid a hand into her boot, and pulled out a slender dagger: small, ornate, and very real. Her eyes met Rachel's. A pause. Then, she leaned in and sliced the scarf clean with a practiced flick, the blade disappearing like a card trick, back into her boot.

Rachel sat up quicker and straighter than usual, her breath shallow and thin, while Eris smiled at her like nothing was out of place and asked, "What do you want to do today, babe? I know! We can dress up, get a mani-pedi, or take a train to New York. I can get us some travel passes and I think my points will cover us both."

Rachel stalled and concealed both her skin and nerves that shivered beneath the sheets. "Umm... I don't like trains. And the water's running again for shower day. Can we catch up later?"

Eris stood there for a moment too long, then nodded, her smile faltering just slightly. "Oh. Okay." She peeled the wig from her head, set it gently on the nightstand, and went back to looking at the neighbors through the telescope. Rachel watched her, eyes squinting just a bit, suddenly unsure of where last night had ended and what exactly she'd let in, or cat or bird, she'd let out.

35

The Gunslingers

Alaska stepped into the prison cell, her boots scratching like sandpaper on the prison floor. The security bot hovered near the door, silent but tracking her every move. Roach sat shackled to a steel table, his wrists in iron cuffs, throat-hose connected to his tank, and his mouth somewhere between a smirk and a snarl. "Where's your Daddy, Deputy?"

Alaska didn't answer.

Roach tried a different tactic and charmed, "Ya know, Pocahontas, I have to say that when we first met, you had me at hello."

Alaska ignored him again, pulled a cigarette from her pocket, and placed it on the table, just out of his reach. Roach strained, but the chains held, and his eyes crawled over her. "You're too cruel for school."

Alaska pulled a length of rope from her back belt loop. "Show me the knot you used on Di Segni."

Roach sighed as if it bored him. "Not with the knots again." She tossed the rope on the table. Roach stared at her, picked it up, tied something, and threw it back.

"Sorry, chief, that's not the knot," Alaska insisted.

Roach fired back, "Of course it is."

Alaska pulled out a picture of the noose around Di Segni's neck and showed it to him. "The math ain't mathing. You didn't kill Brother Di Segni."

Roach shrugged his shoulders. "We've gotta smarty pants here."

Alaska moved further into interrogation mode. "Is there a reason why you confessed to something you didn't do?"

Roach blew her off and chuckled dry, and guttural, like a man chewing on his lung phlegm. "My only regret's not getting to him first. Confessing was the next best thing. Kinda like sloppy seconds, but it'll do."

"Why's that?" she cut him off.

He leaned back, his mask slipping slightly, and his eyes glinted. "Because he was a kiddie raper."

Alaska kept the pressure on. "How do you know that?

Roach responded, smugly, "I just do. Now, about your mommy. Did you hear her pleading?"

Alaska just stared at him, her eyes deflecting his arrows, as Roach continued to unleash his sharpened knives of cruelty. "Next to the sound of a saw cutting through bone, pleading is my fave."

Alaska turned to the security bot. "Leave us alone for a minute." The bot hesitated, ran its data processor, then exited. Alaska moved toward Roach and stood over him. "How do you know Di Segni was a raper?"

He looked up at her, silence serving as his defense. Alaska insisted, "I said, how do you know he raped children?" He remained poker-faced, so she pulled out Gemini's *S.A.S.S.* flyer, unfolded it to reveal a creature, a blurred shape drawn in trauma and ink, and showed it to him. "Have you ever seen something like this?" Roach stared at it. Not at the image, but through it. Then his eyes settled on Alaska, with a fire old and bitter boiling beneath his gaze.

Alaska reached for the cigarette on the table and pulled a lighter from her pocket. "Alright, so did Di Segni rape you?" His eyes shifted to those of a hurt little boy, so she twisted the knife deeper. "He stuck it in you, didn't he?"

Roach's body started to shake as she lit the cigarette, inhaled, and exhaled out the corner of her mouth. "Who else knows?" He looked at her like he would axe-bury her if he could, as she blew smoke toward him. "Did you cry or did you like it?" Roach stayed defiant, yearning for the cigarette, as his face started glitching. Alaska pressed, full court. "You liked it, didn't you? Did he make you plead? Is that why you like that sound?"

Roach stared at her, trembled, and then peed his pants. Alaska blew more smoke in his face and extended the cigarette to him. "Help me to help you. Just tell me who else knew about Di Segni?" He reached for the cigarette, but she quickly pulled it away..

Roach bit hard on his lip. "Keppler... Brian Keppler. Now just gimme the goddamn smoke!" His volume of venom startled Alaska, and she dropped the cigarette on the table. He grabbed it, pulled it to his mouth, and smoked it fiendishly. Alaska reached forward to take it back, but her hand, then her arm, began to shake.

She stepped back, reached into her pocket for her medica-tion, and opened the bottle. However, it rattled and slipped through her fingers, landing on the table. Roach grabbed the bottle, tossed it across the room, and the pills spilled across the floor like broken teeth. Dazed, Alaska's eyes clouded, and she stumbled toward the pills. Her whole body trembled as she searched for her lifeline, fell to the ground, bit her jacket, as her tremors intensified.

Roach observed her, took a drag of his cigarette, inhaled, and blew calm, smoke rings in her direction. He smiled as his neck twitched, as if something was trying to escape from his arteries. He stubbed out the last of the cigarette, yanked on the chain looped to the top of the table, unhinged the legs, and set himself free. He walked across his cell, dragging his oxygen tank behind him, and stood above Alaska to whisper in an eerily quiet voice, "As I said before, it just kinda takes over... allow me to introduce you to my two friends."

His eyes turned coal-black, his face contorted, and his skin paled. Alaska clenched her teeth as saliva foamed from her mouth, while Roach appeared in and out of her vision. He leaned over and straddled her. "Pain...and...fury," he whispered, wiping his finger through her saliva, tasting it, then tracing his finger down her neck and through her cleavage. He leaned in close, smelled her hair, and bit hard on his lip, which dripped blood onto her cheek, then whispered, "Poor, poor, pitiful pearl — ain't no fun when the rabbit's go the gun, huh?"

Alaska lost consciousness entirely, her anime-like spirit disassociated, and hovered above her body, and drifted away into a memory that could have lasted a few seconds or an eternity:

Taino and the young Alaska stood still in the meadow, observing the forest. Its trees, once serene, now twisted into silhouettes, clawing at the sky. The forest floor seemed to vibrate with something dark and ancient. Above, a coven of crows exploded from the trees, cawing as a warning. Near the edge of a forest, at the far end of the meadow, a real bear appeared – massive and silent. Its ears twitched as it turned to face the woods, then it rose on its hind legs. It let out a deep growl followed by a vicious snarl, then bolted, crashing through the tree line. The forest gave way to the loud sounds of a territorial battle: flesh hitting flesh, claws against hide, and branches cracking and thundering to the ground.

Taino and Alaska leaned in to listen to the whimpering and snarling roar of the bear. "Mama," Alaska gasped, staring at the tree line, "Bear is in trouble."

She hesitated before taking a step toward the forest, her small hand reaching out, but Taino grabbed her arm. "Get inside," she ordered, cold and fierce. "Quickly."

Alaska knew not to argue and ran, her bare feet slapping the wooden steps, arms pumping as she dropped her berry basket and hurled herself through the open door into the cabin's shelter. Taino followed, slamming the door behind her. She threw the bolt, latched the lock, then turned to her daughter and demanded, "Get in the closet."

Alaska hesitated. "Why, mama? Is it the Wetiko?"

Taino's face paled and tightened. "Just go." Alaska's stomach turned cold and knotted with fear. She ran to the hall closet, pulled open the narrow door, wedged herself inside, then curled up and clutched her knees to her chest.

Taino moved through the cabin, shuttering the last of the windows. Her movements were swift but not rushed – precise, like she'd done this before. The crunching of footsteps outside wasn't animal – it seemed slower, and its breathing was a grating rasp. A dragging rhythm scraped the trees and pounded on the meadow floor, then stepped onto the front porch, which creaked.

Alaska heard the door blast open, followed by the sound of glass shattering and a lamp crashing to the floor. Then:

A GROWL, guttural and sick.

A SCREAM, piercing and inhuman.

A STRUGGLE, scratching and kicking.

A SOB, deep and unending.

A SILENCE.

Alaska sat alone in the dark closet, frozen and unsure whether to breathe or blink. Her small body started to tremble violently, and she clung to the shelves as her limbs shook uncontrollably. Her breath caught in her throat, signaling the beginning of her first tremor and seizure. Her eyes rolled back, foam slipping from the corners of her mouth, while her arms jerked and her spine arched violently, dragging her mind along with it.

A second version of Alaska, translucent and flickering, peeled away from her physical body. An ethereal, pale-blue version of her girl-self, outlined like an anime spirit, hovered above her convulsing body, watching.

Young Alaska's vision blurred and faded into a fog, both curious and confused, as her attention shifted toward the door and she listened to the footsteps dragging across the floorboards. The steps were near, moving down the hallway, the wood creaking beneath each slow, heavy step. The sound of breath licked against the closet door – deep, ragged, and starving. The spirit of Alaska remained floating above her body in the closet, caught between worlds, bearing witness.

From that perspective in the prison cell, Alaska's spirit saw a hairless, bone-thin, dark entity emerge from Roach. Outside the cell, the security bot heard the commotion, looked through the security door window, saw Roach grabbing at Alaska's breasts, and a *'Danger-Danger'* signal flashed across its eye screen. The robot swung open the door and tasered Roach, who let out a piercing yell, fell over, and hit the ground next to Alaska. Silence settled as the dark entity merged with Roach and then disappeared back into his body, coiling around his spine.

36

The Dreamers

Sam lay in the tangled bed sheets beside Valerie, one arm cradled beneath her head, the other lazily draped across her stomach. Her skin felt warm, her breath steady, and her hair was still wild and messy from last night's rapture. *A Warmer Shoulder by Mary Lattimore* rippled softly from the bedroom speakers, as Sam stared at the ceiling, trying to stay awake, then glanced at her. "What do you want?"

Valerie pressed her hand against his thigh. "Right now? I want seconds."

Sam laughed, belly-low and ragged from last night and too many late nights. "No. Your dream. What's your dream?'

She tilted her head, eyes squinting like she was hearing a question she'd never been asked before, and reached for an answer from somewhere unknown or distant. "My dream? I wanna stop staring into the dark, and I wanna take a trip to Tahiti before it sinks under the sea."

Sam smiled at the idea. "Tahiti sounds like fun! Anything else?"

"That... and I wish every disembodied, vapid-souled human

being would either find the courage to heal themselves or launch themselves, along with their blowhard propaganda podcasts, to Mars and leave the rest of us the fuck alone," she mused.

Sam laughed again, but quietly this time. There was a tired weight to her words that carried a buried, yet recycled hope, and her eyes sparkled as she whispered, "What about you?"

He mulled it over, then replied, "I want to make sure my daughter's alright... close the book on this guy... and get the hell out of Dodge."

She reached up, her fingers tracing his chest, slowly and tenderly. His body tensed, then relaxed in a rare moment of peace. "Anything else?" she probed gently.

He considered the possibilities. "I'd like to see the Packers play and win again at Lambeau Field. And some rain or snow would be nice."

She nodded and smiled at his ideas of happiness. Then, Sam's phone dinged, breaking their bond. He reached for it, but his arm yanked back and stopped mid-move. Metal clinked as he turned to see a handcuff wrapped tightly around his wrist, linked to the bed frame. Valerie smiled like a cat that had eaten the canary and its feathers. She plucked the key off the nightstand, leaned over, and unlocked the cuffs like a pro, because she was one. He rolled over and winced: his back was scratched with red lines from her fingernails, a road map of the night that neither of them had entirely survived. He grabbed the phone. At one look, his face suddenly changed. "Damn. I gotta go."

37

The Pink Slip

Alaska sat on the stained leather couch in the compound's central bay, rocking back and forth with her fists clenched in her lap and her eyes locked on a computer monitor. Sam replayed the footage from her encounter with The Roach at the prison. There was no sound, only the cold, sterile image of her writhing on the floor, Roach hovering, and the robot intervening.

"Show me this thing you say you saw," Sam asked calmly, barely concealing his impatience. He rewound the playback: Roach knocking the pills away. Alaska hitting the floor, the seizure, Roach mounting her, the robot bursting in and tasering him to the ground. The whole damn thing on loop: creepy, brutal, and undeniable. No creature, no shadow, and no proof.

Alaska dared him boldly, "I know what I saw."

Sam seethed, "Nonsense. What the hell were you doing in there alone?"

Alaska's voice caught in her throat, her knees bounced, and her heart pounded. "I was just trying to find out if he killed

Mom."

Sam shook his head, "Without backup? Without security? What were you thinking?"

She turned away, her lip trembling, and her fingers twitched like live wires. Sam noticed her fingers. "I'm taking you off the case."

Alaska stared at him angrily. "What?"

Sam stepped toward her and pointed at the monitor. "If security hadn't come in when it did..."

Alaska gathered herself and stood up. "I can handle myself. And I found out Brother Di Segni raped Roach. And a man named Brian Keppler knew about it." Sam's body tightened, but he said nothing. Alaska pointed to the tape. "It's all connected."

He glanced again at the tape for less than a second. "I don't care."

Alaska insisted, "That sounds like a *you* problem. I heard what I heard. A scream. It was the same sound I listened to the night Mom died."

Sam shook his head in disbelief, "You're off the case."

Alaska challenged him, angrily, "I didn't realize it was your call."

Sam lost his patience. "It's absolutely my call."

Alaska shot back, "I was doing my job..."

....and then Sam's temper flared, full fire. "Your job? Your job is to stay alive!"

Alaska went for the jugular — cut and kill. "Maybe if you'd done your job, Mom would still be alive."

It hit him like a punch to the throat, but she didn't wait for his response; she just turned and stormed out, mumbling, "Sucks to be you," under her breath with all her rage and grief barely corralled, and left him standing there – shaken.

* * *

Alaska hastily threw her belongings into her saddlebags, her movements sharp and hurried. Ama hovered nearby, holding out her duffel bag, and asked, "When will you be back?"

Alaska grabbed the duffel and continued packing her things. "I won't."

Ama moved closer. "Oh. I feel sad. I will miss you skibidoo."

Alaska hopped on her bike and stared at Ama. "No, you don't, Ama. You don't feel anything. You're just a computer, a robot. Remember that." Ama didn't budge. She just stood there, her eyes blinking different colors.

Sam burst out of the garage just in time to see Alaska rev her engine and gun it through the gate, spitting *The Way I Am by Eminem* at full volume out of her speakers, although the rap could have just as easily shot out of her muffler. Dust kicked up behind her like a trail of tears, but he didn't call out or chase after her. He just watched his girl vanish down the road, his silence louder than the abyss he teetered on.

Sam turned and staggered through the yard like a man carrying the wreckage of his own life. He kicked over a mannequin, sent a lamp crashing across the gravel, picked up a rock, and threw it at the shooting target, missing. Then he entered his workroom and steadied his numbness by placing his hands on the workbench.

Ama rolled up and stood nearby, silently observing and waiting, as Sam leaned further onto his bench and confessed to the sweat on his forehead, "My wife wanted a cappuccino. We had two percent. We had half-and-half, but I wanted to get her oat milk. I wanted to make it just the way she liked it, with the little swirls and the chocolate sprinkles." He wiped his face with the back of his hand and continued, "She said 'Don't bother,' but I insisted. I said I'd be right back." He shook his head from side to side and blurted, "Fuck. Fuck oat milk!"

Ama slowly moved closer to him. She reached out a hand and mimicked Alaska by rocking back and forth, like she was trying to understand what grief looked like – or how to hold it.

Sam straightened up, stared at the workshop wall, then his eyes darted around as he maneuvered quickly through the room, rummaging through jars and emptying their contents. He turned over boxes and looked under crates. He ran his hand blindly across the tops of the shelves. He got down on his knees and shone a flashlight under the benches. He peered inside toolboxes filled with random screws and bolts, then kicked over muffler parts in a final act of desperation.

And there it lay, under an old rusted pipe, the remaining half of a cigarette butt. Probably eight or nine years old, from what Sam could tell at first glance. He kneeled and delicately picked it up, as if it were some kind of fragile parchment or a Dead Sea Scroll. He squeezed the butt between his fingers to see if it was still firm enough to handle a flame and momentarily dull his pain. It was, so he rolled it over in his palms, then pinched the filter between his thumb and forefinger, and brought it to his lips. He took a long inhale, smiled, shrugged his shoulders, reached into his pocket, and pulled out his Zippo. He lit the flame and brought it toward his mouth, holding it a few inches from the already burnt end. He tilted the lighter toward it, but hesitated when he saw Ama staring at him through the flame.

She didn't or wouldn't look away.

He lowered and snapped his Zippo shut, then watched her, noticing him standing there with the remnants of the cigarette dangling from his lips. He shook his head side to side, plucked the butt, and tossed it into the half-full cup of coffee sitting on the bench. Ama kept looking at him, her eyes flashing colors. She didn't understand what he'd almost done. But she'd stopped it anyway.

* * *

A scratchy version of *Goodbye Porkpie Hat by Charlie Mingus* spun on the turntable as Sam sat slouched in his chair, battle weary, and nursing a hangover that hadn't yet happened. His eyes tracked the walls of his office: photographs, notes, and red thread told a story no one wanted to see, hear, or read about. Even he was sick of it, maybe from it, or most likely of himself.

The images stared back at him: The Roach's grotesque mugshot. The Gothic spire of St. Mary's. Gemini Moon's name scrawled in bold Sharpie. It was all there, a psychotic scrapbook of pain, and a place where he also retreated to avoid his own. He flicked his Zippo open and shut, the metallic clink echoing, offering none of the usual anticipated, antiseptic comfort.

Ama rolled in, carrying a small green-wrapped box in her mechanical hands. "It has your name on it."

Sam didn't look up. "What is it?"

Ama placed it on his desk, watched him closely, and offered, "Same thing she gets you every year. I calculated you could use an early shot of Christmas." She raised her hands in the air and mimed punching. "I wasn't able to get you anything this year, but if you ever want to 'Rock 'em Sock 'em,' you know where to find me."

Sam kept a smile in check, grabbed the green box, peeled back the paper, and spotted the familiar bottle of single malt. He poured a shot into a chipped, used glass and swallowed it in a fiery gulp. He quickly poured another, then leaned forward, resting his elbows on the desk, and surveyed the chaos like a battlefield commander who had seen all the fallen. He muttered to himself, "St. Mary."

Ama perked up. "Sam?"

"What do you have on a Brian Keppler?" he asked. Although technically bankrupt on paper, Sam was back in business.

Ama's optics vibrated, and the computer screen buzzed to life, filling with digital grime. "Did five years for possession of child pornography. Former custodian at St. Mary's. The police report is in your email."

Sam stared up at her, amazed by how quickly she processed data after the insertion of her new Godzilla-fuck-bites of RAM, or whatever it was called. He refocused and riffled through the clutter on his desk like a grave robber until he found what he was looking for – Gemini's flyer. He opened it and examined the childlike drawings of the monster. "Did Gemini Moon go to St. Mary's?"

She drew out the data and replied, "No."

Sam kept piecing things together and looked at an autopsy photo of his wife. "The Roach had scratch scars on his body. Right?"

"Yes," Ama confirmed.

Sam exhaled, "And we checked for DNA under Taino's fingernails?"

"Affirmative," responded Ama. "The results were incon-clusive."

Sam decided, "Okay... technology has evolved. Order a nano-spectrometer DNA test for my wife. Run it against the old samples. See what the dirt gives." He stood up, the chair squeaking under his weight, and he watched the footage again on the main screen: Alaska convulsing, Roach straddling her, the robot storming in. His gaze shifted between that and the hand-drawn nightmares in Gemini's flyer. "Find me an address for Keppler." Ama glided out of the room, wheels humming on the concrete, but Sam stopped her. "And Ama..."

Halfway through the door, she paused and spun around. "Yes?"

Sam softened, "Thanks!"

She cocked her head like a golden retriever, as if considering how to receive gratitude. The best she could come up with was some detective facts. "Sherlock Holmes once said, 'When you have eliminated the impossible, whatever remains, however improbable, must be the truth.'"

Sam chuckled, a tired sound emerging from the bottom of his throat, and watched her roll away. He opened the flyer again, flipped it to the drawings of the creature, with its jagged silhouette, hollow eyes, and bony ribs. His fingers traced the lines as if he were trying to read Braille for the hearing-impaired.

The security footage kept looping in front of him. He drained the malt whiskey from his glass again and picked up his phone, dialing a number. "Hey, Val. I'm wondering if you can take a look at some footage for me, see if you can spot anything unusual." After a pause, he replied, "Okay, I'll transfer it now." He hung up his phone and stared at the computer screen **as if it** might finally be worth something by coughing up some answers that lay beyond his seven thousand questions. He pressed a few buttons on the keyboard, hit send, then walked out, feeling renewed and fueled by the dull glow of habitual obsession.

He hopped into the Plymouth and drove past Ama, who watched him silently as he went through the gate, which closed behind him. She tilted her head down, her body swaying from side to side like a grounded teenager as she nudged the gravel beneath her feet. She looked up, saw her micro-car, jumped in, threw it in drive, spun doughnuts in the yard, crashing into things while playing *Fast Car by Tracy Chapman* out of her little car's speaker.

38

The Boiler Room

Sam walked down the first-floor hallway of a partially abandoned office building, scanning the faded signs of long-closed
businesses. He reached the last door labeled BASEMENT,
opened it, and descended the metal stairs one slow crunch at
a time. He approached a heavy door marked BOILER ROOM,
wiped the sweat from his brow with a worn handkerchief,
and knocked two firm raps – the kind that said he wasn't
leaving. The door creaked open. Standing there was Brian
Keppler, a man in his seventies, with foggy glass eyes and hair
resembling a wiry bird's nest. A hermit dressed in old flannel
and conspiracy theories, he whispered from the dark, barely
muting a growl, "Who are you?"

Sam flashed his badge. "Detective Morse. Are you Brian
Keppler?"

"Return to sender," squeaked Keppler, and started to close
the door.

Sam stopped it with his boot, steel toe meeting steel frame.
"I need some answers to a couple of questions."

Keppler cracked the door, and his smile widened slightly.

His pupils twitched and scanned Sam like a lie detector on legs. "Lee Harvey Oswald didn't act alone, the Twin Towers were an inside psy-op, and we never landed on the moon.

Sam looked him up and down. "Never been to the moon myself. Can you tell me what you know about Brother Di Segni?"

Keppler responded, dryly, "Not my circus, not my monkeys."

"Does the housing authority know you're living down here?" tested Sam.

Keppler rolled his eyes like he was rewinding a tape that had gone sour past its expiration date. "I told you guys this years ago."

Sam raised his eyebrows. "Did you see anything sketchy going on with him?"

Keppler snorted, "What didn't I see?" He paused, then spat out the rest. "I recorded some of it. I was gonna take it to the authorities, but they came to me first. Kicked in my door, grabbed my hard drives, edited the tapes, and slapped on a fabricated kiddie porn charge. I was collateral damage."

Sam pressed him, "They set you up? Who are they?"

Keppler stared at him as if to say, *'You've got to be fucking kidding me.'* He then shook his head from side to side. "Let's just say, when dirty cops, priests, politicians, and prosecutors share a mattress, you don't walk away clean. You get screwed from angles you didn't even know you had."

Sam glanced behind him and lowered his voice. "Who shut it down, the diocese? The feds?

"The higher-ups. The way higher-ups who protect predators because the predators donate to the right campaigns, or become and are the campaign."

Sam had the same appetite for conspiracy theories as he had for superstitions and long-shot lottery tickets, so he brought it back down to the point, unfolded the drawing, holding up the sketch of a wide-eyed child. "You recognize this kid?"

Keppler didn't move; he just looked at the paper like it hurt. "They all looked the same."

Sam pushed him further and asked, "What about Jared Reed – The Roach, did Brother Di Segni get to him?"

Keppler smiled, but there was nothing warm about it. It was the grin of a man who knew too much and regretted every second of it. "Sorry, Alice. I've already been down this rabbit hole." He shut the door with finality and left Sam standing by the gloom of the boiler room and the stink of truth.

Sam stared at the metal slab door and muttered to himself. "He's right. Oswald didn't act alone; he used a Mannlicher-Carcano rifle." He turned, climbed the stairs back up into the light, but still carried the shadows of Hades with him. He stepped back outside, sank into his Plymouth, and drove away, making a hard right through a yellow light that was closer to red, tires kicking up the recently fallen dust. His eyes stayed on the road, but his mind wasn't there. It was buried somewhere in the world's rot, with its names known only by their muffled screams.

39

The Citizen

Ama sat in her room, plugged into a computer, dreaming and downloading another 'road trip' song to add to her catalog of beats she hoped to use outside The 66 someday. As usual, she was studying for her U.S. citizenship application and wanted to be prepared in case she ever got the chance to leave Phillip, immigrate to America, and take the test. Alaska never had the heart to tell her that robots couldn't be citizens, and the chances of her ever making it out of the compound someday were slim, so she let it slide – no harm, no foul.

Ama was fully cognizant that when applying for U.S. citizenship, applicants must pass a naturalization test that includes several parts designed to ensure new citizens understand basic American civic principles, history, and their duties as citizens. There were the typical questions, such as: name one branch of government, name three of the thirteen original States, who was the first President, and what ocean is on the West Coast? There were also questions about the constitution.

Although she wasn't programmed to fail, she carried an ace in the hole with all the answers and computations stored in her hard drive. Ama didn't want to take any chances should the opportunity arise, so she studied hard and relentlessly. She considered herself quite the constitutional expert by now, knowing it by heart and tracking all Supreme Court decisions that impacted the ever-changing rules. She also saw herself as a scholar on the Declaration of Independence and could recite its various drafts and amendments. However, she still wanted to ask Alaska what Thomas Jefferson meant in a letter to the king, included in the Declaration of Independence, when he described Indigenous people of America as merciless Indian savages, and discussed assimilating them.

Ama wondered who these savages truly were. Would she be expected to defeat them? Was Alaska one, her mother one, and her grandparents? And if so, did that make her one, too? Who was this English King? And what exactly was assimilation? Did she need to assimilate, erase her memory, or could she remain true to herself? And what would that even involve? Calculating all this gave her the equivalent of a robotic migraine, making her system glitch and overheat, so she shifted her focus to her language studies. Proficiency in speaking, writing, and reading English was also part of the naturalization test, and this was easily her weakest area, particularly when it came to the use of slang and words that continuously rose from the streets.

She couldn't risk any surprises and was constantly researching the meanings of recently observed American words and slogans on a language tutorial bot. Ama keyed in the words, "Fuck oat milk!" Then, "What does fuck mean?"

The language bot spoke up: "Fuck is an extremely versatile word in the English language. A profanity that often refers to the act of sexual intercourse, but is also commonly used as an intensifier, to assert boundaries, or to convey disdain, such as "I don't give a fuck!" Would you like to learn some phrases?"

Ama responded, "Yes."

The bot instructed, "Repeat with me."

Bot/Ama - "Fuck it."

Bot/Ama - "What the fuck?"

Bot/Ama - "Holy fuck!"

Bot/Ama - "Go fuck yourself. "

Bot/Ama - "Look, there goes all my fucks."

Bot/Ama - "Are you fucking with me?"

Bot/Ama - "Stop fucking around."

Bot/Ama - "He's fucked."

Bot/Ama - "I don't give a fuck."

The language bot finished its lesson, and Ama got up from her chair, remembering what Alaska had said about not remaining sedentary for too long, as it could cause her joints to cease from the dust and render her immobile. So she tightened up her roller skates, commanded *Americano by 10cm* to play on her chest speaker, and rolled off through the compound, bibbidy-bobitty-bopping like she does.

Ama's eyes blinked red, interrupting her 'fitness routine', as Sam's voice spoke into her processor. "Ama, give me a list of everyone who's worked at and every child who attended St. Mary's."

Ama didn't stop and roll over to Sam's office like she usually did. Maybe it was because she was learning to multitask, or maybe she was just tired of working for the man and being oh-so available 24/7, or maybe because she had some of that 'fuck that' juice running through her circuits, so she kept on dancing and called out, "How far back?" Her rammed-up voice was still smooth and synthetic, but loud and sharp enough to cut through the 'big-boss-man's' brain fog.

Sam made the calculations in his head and called back, "Start at forty years. Also, get me any police reports of sexual abuse crimes at St. Mary's."

Ama beeped softly, then called back, "Righty-o, Roger Rabbit," already working and scraping together the skeleton bones of the buried past. She just kept on dancing, like someone who had decided she was the main character and was done pretending otherwise.

40

The Bear Dance

Alaska, still fuming, stomped across her cabin floor, dropped the duffel on the worn-out couch with a dull thump. She unstrung it, turned it upside down, and out spilled her past and present: torn notebooks, sheathed Bowie knife, flint, first aid kit, wrapped gauze, a new box of seizure pills, folded flannel shirts, sandals, a windbreaker, one pair of spare jeans, Mia's Diary, the *S.A.S.S.* flyer, and a small yellow box with a frayed ribbon.

She stepped into the kitchen, brewed some coffee, and walked back into the living room, pushed her personal items aside, and plopped herself onto the couch, where she hummed, hawed, and hated. Her hand shook as she sipped her coffee and stared out at nothing, as if she were a Shaolin Master of dissociation.

After what could have been five minutes or five hours, she looked down and saw Mia's diary, on loan from Rachel. She picked it up, opened and scanned it, looking for any clues or experiences about seizures that might help her to finally wean herself off these *'fucking pills and the system,'* which in her mind were interchangeable opps.

Her fingers trembled over the yellowed pages as she read about Mia's experiences with seizures – almost the same as hers, but there was no remedy offered or in sight. She read another page:

"He's such a narcissist – the manipulation, gaslighting, and ghosting. He makes everything about himself and can never admit a mistake. Nobody believes me, because he can be so persuasive when it suits him. I want to leave, but I'm scared of what could happen. The stress, the yelling, and the fighting can't be good for the baby, plus there's also the climate and the heat."

Alaska flipped more pages and read: *"I know he didn't like that I tattooed a cross on my belly, but I didn't particularly like everything he did either."* Alaska lingered on those words, and she thought maybe that had to do with that Copycat cross, but closed the diary because she'd already *'crashed out'* with *'enough of all that'* already.

She put it back down on the couch, and if she hadn't promised to return it, out of frustration, she probably would have flung it across the room. She could feel the start of another seizure coming on, and her hands and arms began to shake. She rubbed her thumb over her forefinger and looked at the new box of 'city pills,' but she didn't want to take one. She had learned from countless tremors that rocking back and forth could sometimes reduce the shaking. She white-knuckled it, clenched her fist, bit into her hand enough to draw blood, and moved as if wailing at a wall. Her teeth clenched, her hand turned white, and her face reddened as her anger began to surface and seep out.

She withdrew her teeth from her hand, and as though she were spitting nails, her anger and rage rapidly burst out of her belly and through her mouth. Quiet and slow at first, "Fuck it!... Fuck it!... Fuck crosses!... Fuck killers!... Fuck cities!... Fuck America!... Fuck Canada!... Fuck Wales!" Then faster and louder. "Fuck my father!... Fuck the cops!... Fuck the opps!... Fuck boxes!... Fuck copycats!... Fuck The Roach!... Fuck white people!... Fuck English!" Then, frenzied, "Fuck people!... Fuck humans!... Fuck everyone!... Fuck everything!"

After about ten minutes of rewind-ranting, her tremors, shaking, and rage settled all at once, like a locomotive chugging and slowing into a vacant, foggy station. She found herself breathing heavily, and her body was hot all the way to the bones. She collapsed on the floor, her forehead planted into her knees, sweat dripping from every pore, feverish. She cried out to Abacus, her voice scratchy and barely audible, *Snow Patrol.... Don't Give In,* one of Alaska's go-to songs, she leaned on to get through these episodes. The song lifted out of the cabin's speakers. She knew if she could hear it, she could make it.

It might have been another five minutes or five hours before she finally raised her head, crawled back onto the couch, tilted her head back, and closed her eyes for a moment to digest her experience and reorient herself. She looked over and picked up the yellow box sitting lonely at the far end of the couch. She held it delicately, as if it might break in her hands, and unfolded the note taped to it, her fingers testing her dexterity as she read:

I know how much you like anime, so I hacked the system and downloaded every one that has ever been made. Love, Ama.

Alaska cracked a sad and sentimental smile and looked inside the box. Nestled in padding was a chip card. She held it up to the cabin light, watching it catch the golden glow of the sun like something sacred. She rubbed it between her fingers, as someone might handle a photograph of an ancestor or a lucky coin, then inserted the thumb drive into the computer, instructing, "Abacus, play *Princess Mononoke.*" The Japanese anime sprang to life on the wall screen. Alaska had watched *Princess Mononoke* on endless repeat as a child, knowing all the words and scenes by heart, but it had been years since she last saw it.

The screen flicked on, and the glow from the anime bathed the room in soft, muted light. Alaska sat and watched intently, following it to the part where Moro, a wolf spirit carved from shades of shadow and light, appeared and spoke to Ashitaka, a brave young warrior shaped of honor and steel. Moro explained to Ashitaka. "I caught her human parents defiling my forest. They threw their baby at my feet as they ran away. Instead of eating her, I raised her as my own. Now my poor, ugly, beautiful daughter is neither human nor wolf."

One of Alaska's sweet favorite comfort zones was multi-tasking, drifting, and learning, so she picked up the Earth Traditions book from the coffee table. She opened it to the Bear Medicine chapter, where she had left off, and toggled her focus between *Princess Mononoke* and the words on the page, watching. At the same time, she read:

Mythologists consider humanity's connection to the bear and bear medicine among the earliest recorded myths in human history. Archaeologists discovered a cave and uncovered a cave bear's skull, positioned on a stone table with femurs in its eye sockets. It was a 30,000-year-old shrine-like setting, indicating an early, possibly the earliest, form of ritual and myth-making. In ancient times, the bear was one of the ways early humans connected with themselves, the natural world, and the supernatural realms.

In both ancient and many modern Indigenous and Earth-based cultures, the bear is regarded as a family member and kin. To early humans, the bear appeared to combine the spirit of both the 'familial' and the 'other.' To them, it looked like an upright 'nature human' with similar features, such as hands, fingers, faces, child-rearing instincts, fierceness, foraging skills, hibernation habits, and cave dwellings.

Alaska looked back up at the anime to catch one of her favorite parts in *Princess Mononoke:* The Nightwalker, a 300-foot-tall, luminous deer-god, slowly wandered through the forest. Men in bearskins peeked out from behind a log. One man in a bearskin declared, "At last, the Nightwalker! Quick, come and look!"

The Nightwalker continued to move through the forest, and another Bearskin man complained, "That's why we've been sitting in the stinking bear skins."

The third Bearskin man warned, "Don't look, you'll go blind!"

The screen filled with the first Bearskin Man, who scolded them, "And you call yourselves hunters!"

Alaska nodded and said, "Yes, I do," just like she remembered doing as a child, then went back to reading: *Mankind's relationship with the bear is woven throughout human history and cultures across the Americas, the Arctic, Europe, ancient Greece, Africa, the Himalayas, Asia, and the islands. Many of these traditions persist to this day and are active in places like North and South America, Finland, Romania, and Japan, among others.*

Alaska continued to watch *Princess Mononoke* to the end, all the while shifting her attention back and forth between the anime and world bear medicine traditions and practices, along with how bears have become deeply embedded in human culture as symbols of comfort, wilderness, strength, and childhood innocence across virtually every form of media and storytelling tradition.

Alaska finished sorting through the rest of her road kit, then returned to the cabin door, looked out at the meadow and forest before stepping outside. The wind was dry and gentle, rustling the tall meadow grass like whispers from before time. Alaska trudged through it, her boots kicking up the scent of earth and grass. The ancient oak loomed ahead at the forest edge; its branches stretched out like plush-feathered wings. She moved over to a moss-covered circle of ancestral stone slabs, hidden at the tree's trunk, and crouched before one of them: Taino Rainmaker, faintly etched into a weathered slab. She gently and reverently brushed the dirt off her mother's name. From her pouch, she pulled a pinch of tobacco, lifted it to the gray sky as a sacred offering and a gesture of communion, and placed it on the ground. "Mama, are you there?"

The breeze responded, not with words, but with a rustle, a hush that stirred the oaks' branches like someone breathing and reaching out. Tears streamed down Alaska's face effortlessly, and a thin line of blood traced her inner thigh, a clear mark of her womanhood. Near a log, her eyes fixed on a cluster of loose moss and flowering vines curling around them like winged serpents. She knelt, placed tobacco on the ground, and instinctively reached out to pick them. Then she dug into the dirt around these plants with her fingernails, gently pulling out various roots.

For just a second, they appeared at the corner of her vision. Elves. Not like fairy tale creatures, but Nature Spirits emerging directly from beneath the forest: anime-like with vast, translucent, ancient eyes. She didn't approach them; she just nodded, gathered the plants, tucked them into her pouch, and when she looked up, the Spirit beings had disappeared.

* * *

Alaska returned inside, pulled out the wild plants from her pouch, crushed them carefully, and stirred them into a steaming pot of water. She sat on the couch, lit a sage bundle, passed it over the brew, drank deeply, poured the liquid over her head and hair, rubbed it into her skin, closed her eyes, took a deep breath, and gradually slipped into an expanded dreamscape:

Alaska sat on the lake's shore, water gently and coldly lapping against the rocks. Hovering just above the lake was Taino, translucent and beating a hand drum in sync with the earth's steady heartbeat. She sang a long-forgotten, simple children's bear song that she used to sing to Alaska as a child, slowly and rhythmically.

Maskwa, maskwa, tânispî?
(Bear, bear, how are you?)
Maskwa, maskwa, sipâ kîya
(Bear, bear, you are strong)
Maskwa, maskwa, miyowâsin!
(Bear, bear, it's good!)
Hây hây hây Kisakihitinân Maskwa
(Hey, hey, hey, we love you, bear)

Alaska's dreamworld started to fade into animation with edges softening and colors sharpening. Taino floated over to Alaska, arms wide as if reaching for the sky. She whispered, "Maskwa, the great bear, is our ancestor. She is your Manito. Her spirit is *your medicine. Walk with a bear, and she will guide and protect you."* Then just as quickly, Taino's form melted into bear fur and muscle, and then disappeared into the lake's deep, dark water.*

Alaska's eyes snapped open from the dream vision, and she rose to cross the room to where the old chest sat beneath her grandparents' pictures. With trembling fingers, she lifted the chest lid and traced the coarse bear skin inside. She plucked a hair and held it close, examining its thick texture. Then, pulling the skin over her shoulders, she caught her reflection in the window and saw something primal staring back. She stepped outside, under a sky bleeding its sunset, and began to dance in the bear skin. She danced freely, and her mother's bear song ignited her spirit. Her hands moved like claws, mimicking a bear gently playing with butterflies. She bent low, scooping the air as if fishing for salmon in a rushing river. Dropping to all fours, she rose on her 'hind 'legs, spinning and weaving in the fading light.

As the sun sank lower, painting the clouds red and gold, she lit and circled a crackling campfire. Lights twinkled at the forest's edge, transforming into ethereal bears, spirits born from flame and embers, joining her dance. The embers floated upward, dissolving into the night's black canvas of stars, rearranging to reveal the celestial Great Bear-Ursa Major constellation or Ojiiganang in her Cree language – watching over her with the eyes of the cosmos itself.

* * *

The next morning, Alaska sat on the couch, sipping her coffee, and feeling more rested and still coming down from the previous night's exhilarating experience. Ceremony?

Initiation? Dance? Dream? She still wasn't sure what it was, or how it fit into who she was. She flipped through the Earth Tradition book and returned to the section on the bears for any insight it could offer:

She read about the nine bears that had become extinct, whether by nature's hand or man's. The deep sorrow in her chest easily turned to anger over the loss of all these bear species that had gone extinct, which now felt like an extended family to her.

She read that the Atlas bears of North East Africa had been hunted to extinction because they were used to fight the gladiators in the Colosseum of Rome. These bears, along with lions, tigers, elephants, rhinos, leopards, and more, were hunted and killed for entertainment. She could feel her pain, their pain, and the start of a seizure rising in her body, but she was determined to keep reading. She thought to herself, *'If she can't feel, what was the point of even being alive?'* She used her finger to guide her across the pages, speaking out loud the parts that drew her attention,

She learned that many modern religions choose to build their first temples over traditional bear medicine ceremonial sites, whether in the Americas, Asia, Greece, Ireland, Germany, or Russia. In many cases, groups and cultures that honored the bear, bear ancestors, and bear worship were wiped out or conquered by dominant religious forces and colonial empires. She read about bear baiting, as a form of 'Godly' entertainment during the medieval and Renaissance periods. This led to centuries of cruel spectacles where bears were chained and attacked by dogs for public entertainment and gambling.

Alaska's blood boiled, and her body started to shake again

as she learned about all the cruelty, cages, and circuses that bears endured and continue to endure at the hands of humans. All of the hunting and slaughter of the bears for trophies, their organs, or scientific research.

She learned about a one-year-old bear in China called the Rainbow Bear, which recently chewed off its own paw over three days after it got caught in a snare. Alaska looked down at her hand and could feel her fingers start to curl over, burning with agony, as if she was experiencing some kind of phantom or referred pain. She glanced at her Bowie knife, quickly grabbed and unsheathed it, considering the idea of cutting off her own hand – the pain, now shooting up her arm, was that intense. She raised her knife, sliced it down between her outstretched fingers, and drove it into the wooden coffee table with a thud.

Alaska had felt pain, anger, and rage many times before, but never had she wanted, outside of playing video games, to kill, for real. She wanted to kill anyone or anything that had ever been cruel to a bear. She wanted to end the circuses and the cages, the traps and the trappers, the gamblers and gladiators, the trophy hunters and organ extractors, the land eaters and earth destroyers, the colonizers and their cultures, their rites and religions, all the human beings and civilizations that had wiped out, crushed, betrayed, or threatened the bear, the peoples of the bear, children of the Earth, and Mother Earth herself.

Her tremors, which had been in her arms, suddenly intensified in her legs. As if pulled by a force greater than her own, she reached for her knife from the table, pressed her other hand against the back of the couch, and pushed herself off upright. Her legs and body were weak and unsteady as she shakily walked towards the cabin door, managing to find and say, "Abacus, play *Rock Your World by Chubby Cree*."

The song blasted out of the speakers as she stumbled down the stairs. She used her Bowie knife to cut into her clothes and rip away all the fabric piece by piece, even cutting and drawing some of her own blood in a frenzy. By the time she reached the meadow, she was naked, bloody, trembling, and screaming, "I'm going to kill you, kill you, kill you!" She repeated it over and over, louder and louder. Delirious, sweating, and furious, she pressed her feet firmly into the ground and stood ten toes down. She was ready to face whatever darkness, dark spirit, Wetiko, or horror might still be lurking within the forest and beyond. She steadied herself, planted her Bowie into the dirt by her feet, took three deep breaths, and charged into the woods – barefoot, bleeding, and buck naked.

She broke through the real and imagined forest barrier, ran down the remnants of a trail head, toes on dirt and stones. She vaulted over fallen logs, circled jagged boulders, and splashed through a cool, narrow stream. The forest closed in around her, dense and whispering, pulling her deeper. She stopped at an ancient cedar grove, raised her fists, and shadowboxed the rough bark; Her strikes were sharp – palm and elbow snapping like controlled lightning. She scratched, then patted the pine trunks, bit into twigs, urinated on a log, and spun around, circling like a predator marking its territory.

She bolted up the hill, lungs on fire, until she reached a plateau bathed in morning light. She stood naked to herself and the world, dropped to her knees, closed her eyes, and found that power spot inside her body and bones. Then it happened. She raised her arms in the air, hands extending like claws, as a roar wrenched out of her belly – so fierce and raw that it shook the ground beneath her legs, the ground beneath that, and beneath that again. Her endless roar ripped through the woods as both the sun and her spirit clawed higher and higher into the endless sky.

After a long silence, what echoed back to her was the sound, "*ahkasipiskân-maskwa-maskihkiy.*"

* * *

Back at the cabin, she quickly showered, patched her knife wounds, dressed, grabbed Mia's Diary and Earth Traditions, and stuffed both books into her duffel, along with her other belongings. Helmet in hand, she stepped outside, closing the door behind her with sharp renewed determination. She kick-started her bike and headed straight for America, with *Natural by Imagine Dragons, Turtle Island by Renee Christine, Tomorrow by Tyrell Bird, When We Remain by Samantha Crain, DNA by Darla Daniels, Wolf by First Aid Kit, Shapeshifter (Feat. Tia Wood) Snotty Nose Rez kids*, and *Indigenous Awakens by Alkimizta* roaring from her speakers, like fierce, refreshing winds.

41

The Serial Killer, Killer

Rachel stood in front of a cracked bathroom mirror in her increasingly quiet apartment, dabbing concealer under her eyes. The routine served more as armor than vanity. Her phone dinged, and she tapped the screen; Eris's face appeared in the glass. A burst of manic energy in a candy-colored hoodie, grinning like a storm of chaos barely contained, and called out, "Bonjour, mon amour! Is everything okay? You wanna go to the cosplay fashion show tomorrow night? I got a new costume, I call it, Serial Killer Killer!" Eris spun around, revealing a blood-splattered cape stitched with the acronym SKK across the back.

Rachel forced a smile, polite but thinning around the edges. "Cool. I'm sorry, but I won't be able to make that. It's my friend's memorial."

Eris blinked, the bounce in her voice softening just enough to replay, "Oh. Okay. Maybe we can meet up after or later this week?"

Rachel hesitated, her fingers still moving the eyeliner. She didn't owe anyone anything, but she also knew how quickly the wrong kind of kindness could turn into a burden and obligation. "That's sweet. But I don't think I'm ready for anything serious."

Eris barely hid her disappointment. "... Oh. Okay. That's cool."

Rachel tried to soften the blow. "You're super sweet. I'm sure I'll see you around." She hung up before the silence grew even more awkward. The screen went black, and Rachel returned to the mirror, where her faux-smile dissipated and disappeared.

* * *

Eris put down her phone and froze in a cramped studio filled with weaponry and plans for the apocalypse. Mounted knives, swords, and cosplay trophies lined the walls. Plushie animal hats to cover her head and red sequins for blood sat in the corners. Suddenly, she howled, wild and wordless, and hurled a knife across the room. It thunked into a painted target nailed to the wall, dead center between two others already stuck in the foam board. She stared at the knife, breathing as hard as if she'd run a mile or ten, or was about to. Then she pressed play on her music app, and *Beggin' by Maneskin* growled through her wall speakers, inspiring her to dance wildly around her room.

<h1 style="text-align:center">42</h1>

<h1 style="text-align:center">The Entities</h1>

Sam examined the computer screens, covered with faces in religious costumes – men and women who'd preached salvation but left ruin and wreckage in their wake. Ama's voice came from overhead, crisp and clear, "There are no police records available regarding child abuse at St. Mary's. However, these are the files of the associated members."

Sam scanned the rogues' gallery of Brothers and Sisters; smiles frozen in time, framed in the black-and-white certainty of old ID photos and faded files. "Where are they now?"

Ama displayed the data. "Mostly disappeared."

Sam refocused, his fingers twitching near the lighter in his pocket. "What do you mean, disappeared?"

Ama pulled up an image of the fire-damaged church. "Everything burned."

Sam thought to himself, '*Of course, always a fire of some sort,*' and ordered, "Check the Archdiocese. See if you can access their database."

"I found old records of lawsuits against the diocese, and a list of restricted and reassigned members," Ama responded immediately, listing the facts as images of church Brothers and Sisters appeared on the screen.

Sam looked over at her, "Ama, what in the hell are you actually on?"

Ama's whole body shook with delight. "This new RAM has me jazzed." The screen blinked again, loading another wave of images: mugshots, court photos, grainy scans of newspaper clippings:

Pedophile Priests Imprisoned
$10 Million Lawsuit Settled in Silence

Sam curled his hand tighter around the sketch of the eight-year-old kid. "Who are you?" he grunted. He held the drawing up to Ama's nearest optic sensor like he was daring her to give it a name. "Have you had any luck with this?"

Ama turned her head from side to side and replied, "Negative."

Sam insisted, "Then cross-reference with anyone who attended St. Mary's. Yearbooks, neighborhood records, and old social media archives. That face belongs to somebody."

A chime rang out, and Valerie appeared beside the prison footage on the computer monitor. She looked like she hadn't slept in days, but she smiled anyway. "I checked the video together with a few clairvoyant friends. There's something there, Sam. We've never seen an entity as dark as this before."

Sam leaned in, eyes fixed, and asked, "An entity? Are you talking about possession?"

Valerie shrugged, "Maybe. It's similar to a Buddhist Preta, also known as a Hungry Ghost. Or a Dybbuk in Jewish folklore. Some cultures call it a Succubus, Incubus, or Jezebel spirit.

The Hindus call it Rakshasa, Asura, or Bhuta − a spirit that tries to drain light and life-force energy from others. The old alchemists believed it could be reptilian, vampiric, or parasitical in origin, feeding off fear, control, and cruelty toward the innocent. It appeared for just an instance, then 'poof', gone."

Sam remained silent, thoughtful, attempting to expand his frameworks and beliefs, but still glitching.

Valerie, recognizing that reading through the veil was her domain, waited patiently, then said, "But Sam, before you disappear, I need a date for tomorrow night. You want to come out for a drink?"

Sam didn't answer right away. He looked at the photo of Brother Di Segni, then at the sketch, then at the burn pattern from the St. Mary's fire, and finally at the prison cell and for some invisible entity-thingy. He clicked open the lid of his Zippo. "Sure, just send me the details."

43

The Q Bar

The marquee above The Q Bar flashed:

Gemini Moon's Memorial

Through the doors of the crowded steampunk joint, gears and bodies swayed against the sticky haze of sweat and cheap liquor. The crowd moved beneath brass goggles and corsets, lost in the electric fusion of grief and ecstasy. Off in one corner, a group of friends surrounded Rachel, who turned sharply, catching Nick's eye across the room. He smiled, and she returned it, a fleeting scent of something that might have been hope. At another table, Valerie and Sam sipped their drinks, their faces shadowed by the dim lighting.

The spotlight shifted to center stage, and Lucia stepped up, her voice opening up the room. "In honor of Gemini, I want to sing a song an old drag queen taught us; a little something we sang to pass the nights when we first met in a New York jail cell long ago. We sang it every time we found ourselves behind bars, since, which was more times than I care to count or remember."

The backup band kicked in, gritty and ragged, and Lucia delivered an upbeat, sassy version of *Rise Up by The Parachute Club,* a rebellious anthem from the '80s. After Lucia's inspiring rendition, she followed up with *Rebel Without A Pause by Public Enemy* and *Rebel Rebel by David Bowie.* Then, a few more bands, spoken word poetry recitals, and spontaneous eulogies took the stage. The crowd erupted louder with each performance as the night went on, and the more they sang, danced, and drank, the more it helped fill the impossible void that Gemini had left behind in their lives.

Rachel stepped out into the slightly cooler night air, feeling the weight of the memorial lingering in her chest, like a three-day fever. Nick followed her outside and quickly closed the gap between them. "Rach, you gonna stick around for our set?"

Rachel looked at him, avoiding his eyes. "I'm tired. I think I'm gonna head out early."

Nick's eyes narrowed, trying to read any familiar body language. "You alright?"

She looked away. "I think he called me... during my livestream. The cops even showed up," the sentence trailing off.

"What're you talking about?" Nick quizzed delicately.

Rachel pointed out the obvious, "Copycat."

Nick's face tightened. "You sure?"

"I don't know. I just..." Rachel swayed from side to side.

Nick saw an opening. "Want me to swing by later?"

She hesitated, torn, as Roland burst out of the club, carrying two freshly poured pints. "You coming back or what? We're about to go on. Oh, hey, Rachel." She glanced at them, then turned and walked off, leaving Nick standing still, with his gaze burning after her. Roland turned to him. "What's her problem?" Nick shot Roland a glare sharp enough, under different circumstances, to sever a friendship, then they hurried back inside.

Nick and Roland's punked-up version of *Fairytale of New York by The Pogues (Rapalje Version)* poured into the night, ragged and melancholic. Rachel could hear it playing from a distance as she walked down the dark sidewalk – lonely and unraveling. She passed two homeless men wearing tilted Santa Claus hats, slumped on the curb, sharing a bottle of dollar store port as if their sorrows depended on it. Behind her, a shimmering, translucent pink light appeared on the street – Gemini Moon's spirit, quietly watching over her, protectively. Rachel sensed a presence, but didn't look back, and as quickly as she had appeared, Gemini's spirit swam back through the veil.

The Fairytale of New York continued to echo through the bar's thick smoke, matching the crowd's mood, which felt, in part, like a ragged Christmas hymn. Nick, at the piano, leaned in close to the keys, his voice melancholic, singing from the depths of his Irish ancestors. Diego, who made it out of his cave, sleeves rolled up in a battered Packers jersey, smashed out the drums. Bassie, the bass player nodded his head like a bobble, fingers slapping deep and steady, and Roland played sideman guitar.

The song spilled through the dressing room door, like a distant lament under the chatter of the crowd. Lucia stood between Valerie and Sam, the night's magic still clinging to her like precious perfume. Valerie's eyes shone with pride as she looked at Lucia. "You ate tonight."

Sam tipped and cheered what remained of his drink. "Well done."

Lucia cracked a smile. "Thanks, Big Brother."

Valerie laughed, raising her glass. "Raise 'em! To a wonderful night for our beautiful Gemini."

Glasses clinked, the warmth of the moment folding them in close. Lucia leaned forward and hugged Valerie tightly, whispering, "Thanks for coming tonight. I'd love to see you for a reading sometime. Maybe kick start my love life."

Valerie let go of the hug. "Sure, anytime."

Lucia fumbled with her phone, frustration evident in her eyes. "My phone's just as broken as my bank. I need your number again. Here, write it on this." She plucked a used matchbook from a bowl and handed it to Valerie, along with a pen. Valerie scribbled her number on the inside of the flap and returned the matches with a smile. Lucia kissed her on the cheek, gentle and quick. "Have a nice night." Sam nodded, then left with Valerie as the evening's celebration carried on, delicate and electric.

44

The Ride or Die

Loveland by Milky Chance played lightly on the garage speakers as Valerie strolled through The 66, taking it all in with sharp curiosity. Her fingers brushed the frame of a weathered photo of Taino, fierce and beautiful, etched in black-and-white. She drifted to another picture, one of Sam and Alaska, grease-smudged, with their heads bent over a stubborn motorcycle. She stepped toward Ama, standing silently and statue-still. Valerie reached out and poked her arm, but she remained motionless.

Sam came in, carrying drinks, passing one to Valerie, who received it gracefully. "Quite a place you've got. Where'd you get the robot?"

Sam looked over at Ama. "Mostly Alaska's doing. She built Ama after her mom passed away. Alaska's a bit of a tech-savant; I just helped fit some parts together." Ama's eyes flicked open, Sam peeped it, and signaled to her silently that it was time for her to skedaddle. Without a sound, Ama rolled out the back door and retreated into her room.

Valerie turned her attention back to Sam. "You know

what you said about wanting to get out of Dodge? Were you serious?"

"Sure as shooting." He warmed up.

Valerie tasted her drink. Yum! "I've been thinking about it too. Maybe make a break for it and hit the road sometime, like Bonnie and Clyde."

He raised his eyebrows, surprised. "For real? Sounds like lots of fun, also sounds like lots of funds."

Valerie dismissed his concerns. "Yeah. Money's just a construct. Besides, I've spent my whole life saving and investing. Joan of Arcade started with a one-room fetish-arts studio. I worked my way up to the loft I'm in now, eventually bought the building, then the entire block. I like being unbothered, and wanted to make sure I kept the speculators, imitators, and haters at bay. Now I basically do what I want, when I want."

Sam was impressed. "That's good, because it can be pretty rough out there."

"You know what's rough? My grandmother raised me. I was eight years old and found her curled up on the floor after they told her that Speck had killed her daughter, my aunt Jose. Even rougher was trying to lift my grandmother off that same floor for fifteen years until I buried her," she recounted, testing the temperature for how vulnerable and honest she could be.

Sam's eyes softened, and he asked, "That's what kept you here?"

Valerie considered her reply. "That, and you know that health clinic and retirement next to my place? I fund and keep those doors open. Or should I say my clients do? I extract a pound of their flesh and turn it into healing and support for others who wouldn't get it otherwise, kinda like a pain-or-pleasure tax. I also enjoy having lots of fun, along with the never-ending work of defusing psychos. I've got more than a few clients teetering on your side of the ledger, ya know. And you?"

Sam just said, "I like to finish what I start."

Valerie took another sip of her drink and mused. "Whoever fights monsters should see to it that in the process he does not become a monster… "

"… And if you gaze long enough into an abyss, the abyss will gaze back into you.' Fredrick Nietzsche," followed Sam, completing the quote.

Valerie smiled, her eyes drifted back to the photo of Taino, and the unspoken tension still lingering there. "Do you think it'll ever be over?"

Sam felt the weight of her question and understood the pain she was hinting at. "I don't know. But what I do know is that Bonnie and Clyde were outlaws. They didn't make it."

Valerie's eyes lit up. "I know, but I like to think they had one helluva time trying."

Sam smiled and looked her directly in the eye. "You know, I've seen and been in a lot of situations, and there's a lot less road out in front of me than there used to be. I'm pretty sure there are plenty of more recent models floating around."

Valerie kept his gaze. "There are, but most of the rides either stall before they can pull it out of park, or get easily spooked by wide open roads or one's less traveled."

Sam grinned, grabbed her by the hips, lifted her onto the table, and locked her lips.

* * *

The morning sun shone outside the compound door as Valerie moved toward the gate to catch her taxi bot just before she stepped into the light beyond the wall. She turned back and smiled. Sam waved, then walked back to his office and the comfort zone of its scattered puzzle pieces. He placed one hand on the edge of the desk, the other gripping a faded photo of the blackened and scorched ruins of what had once been St. Mary's. He called out, "Hey, Ama, how did St. Mary's burn down?"

The holographic display on the desk blinked to life, revealing timestamped images of Diego Towais: a cigarette in one hand and a can of gas in the other, a mugshot, and social media posts of him playing drums and drinking in punk-rock dive bars.

45

The Arsonist

Sam pulled up in front of Diego's house, parked, and got out. He walked through the yard, littered with beer cans and sagging bushes, and onto the porch, which was made of rotting wood and rusted nails, every step threatening to buckle under his weight. Sam knocked once: sharp and deliberate. A second later, the door's steel slot shhhk-ed open. A narrow slice of Diego's mother's face peeked through, her eyes a cocktail of piss and vinegar. "What do you want?"

Sam adjusted his gaze. "Is Diego home?"

The slot slammed shut. "Diego! It's a deadbeat friend of yours!"

Sam muttered under his breath, dry as gunpowder, "She's a piece of work."

From behind the door, a voice growled back, "I heard that, asshole!"

The door creaked open, revealing Diego in nothing but sagging boxer shorts, a tattoo of a flaming skull visible on his chest. His hair was chaotic, and his eyes half-sane, squinting against the sunlight. He recalled, "That was an epic show last night!" Then he looked up to see Sam standing there. "Who the hell are you?"

Sam flashed his badge. "Detective Morse. I want to ask you about St. Mary's."

Diego squinted again, wiping crusted stuff from the corner of his mouth. "I already did my time."

Sam nodded. "Yeah, I know. What I don't get is why you did it?'

Diego leaned against the door frame, which supported both him and his hangover. "I like watching things burn, okay!"

Sam held his stare. "Including Brother Di Segni?" That name hit, knocking the grin from Diego's face. Sam held his position. "We've got some reports that he –"

Diego knew the drill. "That he liked little boys."

The voice of his mother rose from inside the house, slicing through the tension like a torch through tar. "Your burrito is ready!"

Diego looked Sam up and down, a shadow of shame and guilt buried behind his bloodshot eyes. "Sorry, man, I can't help you." He slowly shut the door, though he wanted to slam it, but didn't dare.

Sam stayed on the porch a moment longer, scanning the yard, the scorched wounds behind Diego's eyes lingering in his mind like an unreadable crossword clue or misplaced Tetris block.

46

The Wisp

Roach stood barefoot in his prison cell. He was shirtless, ribs like blades, and his skin was as gray as a drowned man's eyes. He had just ripped the hose from his throat and left it discarded near the oxygen tank in the corner, and was hunched over a dented bucket, filling it with his piss. He finished off with a casual, prolonged shake and mumbled to himself, "It's graduation day." He then howled out loud, a sound like broken glass rattling in a paper bag – unnerving and grating. Without warning, he punched himself in the face, flesh on bone, the slap echoing off the concrete walls.

"Hey! Cut that out!" he yelled, then added, "Stop being a pussy."

He turned, talking to himself again in a different voice, as if he were caught in a fun house mirror. "Who's calling who a pussy?"

He slammed his shoulder against the wall, and blood trickled from his temple. He scratched his scalp fiercely, then bit into his bottom lip until it burst, and a line of red spit hit the floor. "I'm getting us out! They think they got us, but they don't! They don't!"

He tipped the metal can, warm piss flooded the floor, and a golden tide circled his bare feet. His eyes rolled back, and his laughter turned into screams. "They won't be happy! I'm telling!"

"To hell with them! They never loved us anyway!" His right hand twisted, fingers digging into his cheek, forcing his head against the wall again.

The other hand flailed in protest. "No! Stop it!" Panic surged through him like a poison, and he called out, "Help me! Somebody help me! Help!!"

The reinforced security door burst open. A security bot stormed in, stopped, and quickly processed a risk and threat assessment:

Erratic Danger Caution

Roach lunged toward the bot, slipped on the spilled urine, and fell hard. Yet he still scrambled toward the bot, screaming and skittering like a cockroach on crack. The robot deployed its taser, sparks flew, and the cell filled with the snap-hiss of electricity. Roach convulsed, and both man and machine collapsed, smoking and glitching into an eerie stillness. The bot fried and froze first. The Roach's charred flesh twitched once more, and a thin wisp of something not-quite-smoke nor shadow rose from his chest, rippling with dark malice. Formless and translucent, it watched its dead, fried former host for a moment, then slid upward, slipped into the vent, and vanished.

47

The Thumbs

Sam stepped out of his office, his boots skidding across the concrete floor and leaving faint scuff marks from the street dust still clinging to the soles. "Ama," he said, not slowing down, "our short list just got shorter and longer. I want a surveillance warrant on Diego Towais."

Ama dinged, "Affirmative," but didn't get to work right away because she was sitting in her room, busy looking at and responding to emails on the compound's mainframe computer. She came across two of them and wasn't sure how to process them, how to tell Sam, or if she should say anything to him at all. Her eyes drifted toward the open bay doors, where the familiar sound of a motorcycle rolled in like distant thunder, but she remained frozen, staring at the computer.

Alaska rolled through the gate and dismounted. She walked straight into the compound and zeroed in on Sam. Her voice was flat, but something raw buzzed just beneath the surface as she pulled out and read from Mia's diary. "I know he didn't like the cross on my belly."

Sam remained silent, registering what he had just heard,

then called out to Ama and ordered, "Pull up the files on Mia Amato." He walked toward his office, followed by Alaska. The file was already on the computer screen when they arrived. Mia's face appeared on the screen, lifeless and framed in grainy gray scale. Next came the autopsy photos of scars on her abdomen, faint but deliberate – a tattooed cross, carved by an unsteady hand. Alaska zoomed in on the image. There it was, raised skin in the shape of a crucifix, jagged, puckered, and primitive.

Alaska pointed to the screen. "It's crude, but you can see it." The video panned across fresh scar tissue on her wrists, her thighs, and her arms – a telltale map of pain over the years. Alaska continued, "She was married to Roland Donner."

Ama rolled into the office slowly and sullenly, carrying a computer printout.

Sam immediately turned to her. "Get me the address."

Ama just stood there, frozen and unresponsive.

Sam looked at her, then at Alaska. He then took charge, walking over, raising his arm to slap her on the back, and kick-start her. "We don't have time for this."

Ama slowly raised her arm and extended the printout. Sam took it from her, read down the page, his brow furrowing, and his face whitening as he did. Alaska peeped it. "What is it?" Sam didn't respond, so Alaska impatiently repeated, "What is it? What does it say?"

Sam slowly looked up from the printout, but remained silent.

Alaska stared at him with a sense of apprehension. "What?"

His silence continued, he swallowed, then finally revealed, "The Roach is dead."

Alaska blinked once, her face showing no change, but her

fingers curled slightly around the edge of her pockets. "What? How?"

Sam scratched his head, informing her, "He attacked a prison bot. Got himself electrocuted."

Alaska looked at him. "Well... Alright, then that's that. " She glanced over at Ama, "Ama, give us the address."

Neither Ama nor Sam moved or said anything. Frustrated, Alaska's eyes darted back and forth between them, "What gives with the two of you?"

Sam looked at Ama, then back to Alaska, "While you were gone, we ran a new nano DNA test on your mother."

Alaska shrugged her shoulders. "Yeah, so?"

Sam took a deep breath and admitted, "We found some DNA under her fingernails. It matched with The Roach."

Alaska just stared at him.

Sam stepped forward and whispered, "Alaska."

She quickly raised her palm to stop him. "Don't," she commanded.

Ama slowly rolled over, but was stopped in her tracks by Alaska's other hand. Alaska teared up and ran out the door, leaving Sam and Ama staring after her, then at each other. Ama leaned to follow her, but Sam raised his arm to block her. "Just let her be."

About an hour later, or less, Sam went to find her and discovered her at the far end of the compound, curled up against the wall between an old shed and a rusted-out Chevy. Sam knew where to look for her. It was the same place she had always gone since she was a child, whenever she had an emotional outburst or needed to settle down after a seizure. However, this time was different – the crevice cut deeper, and the wound was wider. He was often reassured after talking with her grandmother to give Alaska both space and time, however much she needed. Time and space, being Alaska's primary comfort zone and love language, across all areas of her life.

And so that's what he did.

Sam would check on her, sometimes finding her lying down, curled up, or sitting up. She never looked at him during the following days, even when he left a blanket and pillow, or strapped a tarp between the Chevy and the shed to shield her from the dust and the sounds of the coyotes, which seemed to be circling the compound even closer.

Sometimes he would hear her cry out in the night, which sounded more like a howl, and every time it broke his heart in equal parts, if not more. Sam was not immune to night sweats and terrors of his own, which crept into his dream world on their own accord. He would often awake startled by nightmares, sometimes with a scream, unable to tell if the cry was his or from the shifting nightmare figures who filled his life. Most likely, his night screams, Alaska's night howls, and the coyote yelps ricocheted off each other and the walls of the compound. Still, neither of them, including Ama, could truly grasp or calculate what it all meant.

During the daytime, Sam quietly brought and left fresh water and plates of food for Alaska at the edge of her makeshift shelter. Most of it was left untouched: little nibbles off chicken, a bite out of an apple, partially eaten chocolate cake, or a half-drained glass of water.

Even Ama helped out by wheeling over a computer, controller, and her headset, leaving them there in case she wanted to battle with Senua. At one point, Ama dropped off some of her toy robots and Rock'em Sock'em boxers, along with a note that said, "You can choose red or blue," referring to the color of the two miniature plastic robots.

Sam mainly wandered around the shop, cleaning up and fixing nothing in particular. He never entered his office, and doing any detective work was out of the question; it felt absurd to him, and highly uncomfortable. When he went out again the next morning to deliver some breakfast and pick up another mostly untouched dinner, Alaska was sitting up, eyes closed, rubbing her thumbs over her forefingers, with her back leaning against the compound wall. As he dropped off the food, picked up the plate, turned, and walked away, he heard Alaska say matter-of-factly, "I heard you in the middle of the night."

Sam stopped, standing still.

Alaska kept her gaze and continued. "Grandma said that Mom was never happier than when she was with you."

The words, both an echo from his past and a flame to his heart, stopped his breath in its tracks. His chest rose and fell, and he sighed once. The moment presented him with the choice to keep walking back to the building or to turn around. He chose the latter, and did so slowly and carefully. Alaska stared at him, measuring his movement and response, and Sam quietly nodded, acknowledging what she said, and replied, "You know, sometimes when you're thinking hard about something, or when you're upset, you rub your thumb over your forefinger, just like you're doing now. Your mother used to do the same thing with you when you were fussy. She'd take your tiny hand in hers and rub it with her thumb. She called it 'magical ancestral healing thumb.' Said it could fix anything – scraped knees, bad dreams, the hiccups. You'd go from screaming to this perfect calm, just staring up at her face. I never told you that's where it came from. I thought it might hurt you too much to know. But watching you do it now, it's like she's still here somehow, still trying to comfort you through something she taught your hands to remember."

Alaska mostly cried as she stared closely at her thumbs rubbing her forefingers, as if she was experiencing it for the first time – feeling her mother's presence weave through her thumbs, fingers, blood, and bones. She steadied herself, wiping away the rivers of tears flowing down her cheeks with the back of her shirt. She looked down at her thumbs again, then back up at her father.

Sam held back a smile, paused for a moment, nodded, and muttered a word he hadn't heard or said in a very, long time, "Hiraeth."

Alaska asked, "What does that mean?"

"It's Welsh for longing. For home. The grief and the joy, and the trees."

Alaska thought about all of her ancestors and wondered if *'her mother and grandparents had been from Wales, she would have resonated more with those folks over there, in the same way that if her mother and grandparents were from the moon, she would feel closer to a moonbeam.'* She gradually steadied herself and responded, "Ask Ama to get the address. I'll be in shortly."

Sam patiently observed her, then whispered, "You don't have to do this."

"I insist that you put me on this detail," Alaska firmly replied.

Sam quietly turned away, and walked back to the compound's office. Whatever was waiting there for them wasn't going to solve itself.

48

The Repo Man

The Plymouth glided through the fractured arteries of the city, heading toward the slightly less bleak suburbs. They passed by store mannequins displaying their latest 'dust wear', and Alaska distracted herself by tracking the drones buzzing overhead and the civil bots roaming the streets. The suburbs flashed by in a blur of brown grass and abandoned strip malls, and Sam turned into a neighborhood of uniform single-story bungalows – some restored, but most boarded up and left on read for another day. He pulled up to Roland's address and slowed the car to a stop, then looked over at Alaska. They both got out, methodically.

They moved up the driveway through a maze of repossessed cars, a tow truck, half-gutted, chrome-plated delivery bots, and droids in partial disassembly, staring at them through lifeless lenses. They walked past a sagging inflatable Santa Claus left to melt in the heat, and Reindeer motors clicked in staccato loops, resting on what remained of the lawn.

The garage door was just open enough to spill out a sliver of torchlight. Yoshima emerged from the depths of the garage, wiping a wrench with a rag and wearing oil-smudged coveralls. Sam caught a glint of light speckling across her eyes, moving too fast to see unless you were trained to notice. "Hello," she said politely. "Can I help you?"

Sam stepped forward and flashed his badge. "Police Department. We're looking for Roland Donner."

She pointed to a Ford inside the garage. "He's working."

From beneath a chassis, Roland slid out on a wheeled creeper, grease staining his arms like ink blots. "What's going on, babe?" Sam walked over and handed him his card. Roland flipped it over as if it were a parking ticket. "Wow. What's this about?"

Sam began, "We've got a few questions about St. Mary's and Brother Di Segni."

Roland stood up straight, wiped his hands on a rag, and cracked his knuckles as Yoshima quietly stepped aside. "Do you mean Salty Sack Di Segni?" Roland smirked. "Everyone knew not to be alone with him, if you know what I mean."

Sam's voice stayed steady. "Why's that?"

Roland held back his laugh. "He was a little too touchy-feely."

Alaska stepped forward. "Ever heard of a Brian Keppler?"

Roland reached for a bottle of water. "Yeah. That creepy janitor who got fired for kiddie porn."

Sam pressed him further, "How do you know Diego Towais?"

Roland paused, attempting to conceal his anger, but failed. "Leave Diego alone, he's already been through it."

Alaska didn't back off. "We've also got a few questions about your first wife."

"Mia?" Roland squinted with incredulity. "That was ten

years ago. Listen, I've got work to do."

He turned away, but Sam looked at Yoshima up and down, had a hunch, and called after him, "You know it's a steep fine, even jail time for harboring an illegal."

Roland sharply turned back and deflected. "She has her papers."

Alaska took a deep breath and stepped forward. "I want to ask you something personal. Did your wife have a miscarriage before she died?"

Roland stared at her like a blade had slipped between his ribs. "It's nunya business," and squeezed the water bottle in his hand.

Sam intervened, "Mr. Donner, we… "

"My wife killed herself," Roland snapped. "And now you want to bring up her miscarriage from ten goddamn years ago?"

Alaska didn't budge. "We understand. We need to know, were there complications?"

Roland sighed, his eyes distant. "Yeah. We lost a baby. It sucked." He turned back toward the car he was working on. "Now, unless you've got something relevant, I've got a transmission to swap out."

Sam's voice was quieter now, meant to disarm him. "Do you know why Mia had a scar in the shape of a cross on her belly?"

Roland didn't look back. "She was a cutter. It was her way of honoring the baby. I disagreed, but it was her body."

Sam nodded once. "Thanks for your time." Sam and Alaska walked off, and Roland watched them closely, lit his vape, and exhaled, as if trying to forget the conversation and his resurfaced memories.

Alaska climbed into the passenger seat, and Sam slid behind the wheel, his eyes still on the house. "You think his bark has any bite?" she asked.

"It's a toss-up." Sam replied. "However, most abuse, child, spouse, or otherwise, is enacted by someone the victim knows in their immediate circle: friends, family, neighbors, employers, or significant others. When it comes to a partner's miscarriage or abortion, it can be a game-changer for men. It can trigger guilt, substance abuse, and violence."

Alaska shook her head slowly. "Why is it that some men always use pain they'll never understand as an excuse to explode over something that isn't theirs, or they can't control?"

Sam had no further answers, questions, or insights, so he started the car and pulled away.

Roland drew on his vape and tracked the car as it drove down the street through a haze of cherry-scented mist. He walked over to Yoshima, still chewing on the bitter taste of old memories. "How many times," he insisted, "have I told you not to go near anyone without your sunglasses on? I'm not a fan of people knowing what you are."

Yoshima turned to him, her head tilted like a curious parrot. "And what am I?"

Roland hesitated, then reached out and pulled her in for a kiss, his hands gripping her like something he might lose. "You are..." he whispered against her lips, "... you are my girlfriend." He slowly released her. "I'll be back later, just take care of everything around her for me," he said, then hopped into one of his restored, vintage cars and drove off.

49

The Ghost

Dierdre Clark, all pierced lips, combat boots, and inked fingers, stood behind the recycled glass counter of the Creatrix Gallery, thumbing a vape pen like a miniature emotional support plant. Rachel was tense, her head wrapped in a scarf that still smelled like last night's worry. "She hasn't returned any of my calls or texts since the memorial, and I was supposed to meet her an hour ago for our Sunday brunch," her voice flared through the air like a match strike.

"Lucia's usually here to open up." Dierdre inhaled and exhaled her vape.

Rachel looked at her phone, then back at Dierdre. "Did you leave the Memorial together?"

Dierdre shook her head from side to side. "Nah. I cut out early."

Rachel's silence stretched like a tightrope. Dierdre looked up, eyes scanning Rachel's face with sympathy. "Maybe she went out last night. Sometimes she doesn't make it in 'til later after a night out."

"Right... Thanks. Have Lucia call me when she makes it

in." Rachel turned and left, the gallery door squeaking closed behind her, leaving it up to chance and the street to swallow or cure her anxiety.

50

The Permafrost

The knocks on Rachel's apartment door were soft but rhythmic. Four quick taps followed by two slow ones, then silence before repeating, resembling a secret code from someone she knew, and a playful nod to 420–marijuana. She opened the door to find Nick standing there: her past-time lover, part-time ex, and full-time enigma. She looked him over, observing him slouched in a dusty hoodie, unshaven, smelling faintly of eight days without a shower and rehearsal rooms. "What are you doing here?" she asked over *Frosty by Bebe Stockwell* playing in the background.

Nick stepped inside, pushing past her hesitation and privacy. "Forgot to pick up my box of stuff." He noticed her hard eyes, and his smile faltered as he asked, "You alright?"

Rachel pointed to the box by the closet. "Have you heard from Lucia?"

"Not since Gem's party." He crouched to grab his cardboard box, its edges frayed and an anarchist sticker peeling off the side. A protest sign leaned beside it, bold letters shouting into the void:

FRACK OFF – GASHOLES

Rachel hovered near the doorway like she was still guarding it. "I was supposed to meet her this morning, and she hasn't responded to my calls and texts."

"Chill, Rach, she's probably still out having a good time." He stood, trying to summon that grin that once charmed her, but it didn't quite land past her worry. "Listen, I gotta go. We're taking the band out to play a few gigs. A club promoter showed up at Gem's and said they had last-minute cancellations he needed to fill, and secured us a travel pass." He raised his fist in the air and grinned. "Fortune favors the brave and a break for the band."

Rachel raised her eyebrows and asked, "Right now?"

Nick opened his box. "Tomorrow. I'm crashing at Val's tonight. My parents and relatives are driving me nuts."

Her expression sank, and she sourly asked, "You're just gonna leave on Christmas Eve?"

"You're the one who asked me to," he reminded her. He looked inside the box and pulled out Snowy, the plush android-dog, with its scratched metallic coat and loyal eyes. "Here, you should keep Snowy," and placed him in her hands.

Rachel held Snowy for a moment, then offered him back to Nick. "You can have him."

Nick raised his palms in the air, refusing the offer. "Rach... I got him for you. For us."

"And I'm giving him back to you," Rachel insisted, pushing him toward his hands.

He looked down at the dog bot, then stepped back, shook his head, and still refused.

Rachel turned away, still clutching Snowy, and asked,

"What about Lucia?"

Nick tried to deflect the conversation. "It's not her first rodeo."

"What if..." Rachel fidgeted with Snowy.

Nick shrugged. "What if what?"

Rachel turned back to him. "What if it's Copycat?"

"Rach, you're paranoid. She's probably just out having some fun." Nick ran his hand over his eye and scratched, hoping to relieve himself of the itch and the conversation.

Rachel crossed her arms to shield her vulnerability. "I'm just worried about her."

"That's the problem with you, Rach. You catastrophise too much," Nick insisted, trying to defuse her, but accidentally setting off a time bomb instead.

Rachel's face reddened. "The problem with me? You touring around in some 'wanna be woke-broke punk band' that can't support me or even the idea of having kids was the problem."

Nick put on his rarely-used, rusty reasoning hat. "I thought you didn't want to do the kid thing 'cause of the permafrost thing? Look, I'm working on a new song. I know it's going to be a hit and fix everything."

Rachel grew frustrated and snapped. "Oh, please, just stop. Your problem is you spend too much time with your head in the clouds."

Nick shook his head, refusing to accept what she was saying, then deflecting, "You spending all your free time protesting the end of the freaking world, instead of working on us, is the problem!"

Rachel pushed back. "No, that's not it. The point is, I want to feel safe; the permafrost is melting, and it is a catastrophe.

There are now mosquitoes in Iceland for the first time in history, and the Christmas Island Shrew just went extinct."

"The Christmas Island, what now?" Nick looked at her like they were both losing their minds.

"The tiny shrew, it's like a little mouse that just went extinct. It's gone, erased." Rachel teared up.

Nick took a step towards her.

She put out her hands, took a step back, and shook her head. "I don't want to open Christmas presents in my bikini, and it's been years of playing an on-again, off-again broken record with you, which is the point. We're done, done! Just take the goddamn dog!" She thrust Snowy at him, but it dropped on the floor.

Nick looked at it, then at Rachel, and slowly backed out of the apartment, the box and another missed shot in hand, then closed the door behind him. Sparks flew out of Snowy. "M-merry... Chri..." Its ears sparked, and smoke rose, creating a cremation effect from its seams. Rachel dropped to her knees, lifted Snowy, cradling it for a moment, before flinging it across the room. It bounced off the wall and fell in a shower of sparks and burning wires, next to Nick's mainly unused protest sign that he also left behind.

If there were a place called loneliness and abandonment, this was it. Gemini, Lucia, and now Nick, and even the broken dog lying at her feet. The Christmas Carol played on in the background.

Outside, Eris watched Nick leave Rachel's apartment building from behind a dry, thirsty arborvitae, crouching in the shadows, as both a ninja and a hurt girl. While she tracked him, her face stormed with jealousy, her shoulders tensed, and her nervous system registered more fight than freeze.

Eris silently watched Nick disappear down the street, then she slipped into the side alley of the apartment. She pulled at the back door of the building. It was locked, so she tugged again. Still locked. Behind her, she heard steady footsteps as a security guard stepped out from the building's skeletal perimeter. "Put your hands on your head," he ordered.

Eris froze, the tone of the voice stopping in her tracks. She stared ahead, muscles tense, then slowly raised her arms, allowing the neck of her SKK cape to fall down her back. Her mind raced; her eyes darted from side to side, scanning for exits and weighing her chances. She pointed down the alley to draw the guard's attention, then kicked his gun out of his hands, slipped behind him, and climbed over a neighbor's wall.

Back in her apartment, Rachel scanned the room for a lifeline – anything. She spotted her phone lying on the floor near the coffee table, crawled over, picked it up, and opened her music app to the playlist titled:

HEARTBREAK HOTEL – THE GREATEST HURTS

She lay down on her back, hesitated before pressing play, knowing she was playing Russian Roulette – whatever songs randomly popped up could wound or end her. When she heard the first chords of *Favorite Crime by Olivia Rodrigo* echo through her empty apartment, she closed her eyes and sank into the music and all the feels.

Some of the greatest hurts that followed were *River by Joni Mitchell, Somewhere in the Middle by Sam Scherdel, Body To Body by Siibii & Aysanabee, Wild Horses by The Rolling Stone, Melody Noir by Patrick Watson, You Want It Darker by Leonard*

Cohen, The Dark End of the Street by The Commitments, The Door by Teddy Swims, Aunque es de Noche by Enrique Morente, Trova De Amor by Manuelcha Prado, Bang Bang by Nancy Sinatra, I'm So Lonesome I Could Cry by Cowboy Junkies, Send In The Clowns by Judi Dench and David Kernan, A Good Year For The Roses by Elvis Costello and The Attractions, When The Roses Bloom by Billy Bragg, Wilco, Turn Me by Norah Jones, On Rising by Lhasha, Take on Me by a-ha, I Still Set a Place For You by Nina Blaze, If I Ain't Got You by Alicia Keys, I Try by Macy Gray, Try by Blue Rodeo, That's All I Wanted From You by Jalen Ngonda, Pictures of You by The Cure, Besame Mucho by Cesaria Evora. La Complicidad by Perota Chingo, and Killing Me Softly by Roberta Flack, which, well, killed her softly.

Rachel knew she was entering dangerous territory when the French songs and their troubadours of love's sorrow showed up as though lined in a perfectly positioned firing squad. The only thing missing was a blindfold, an offer of a last cigarette, or rights, before they unloaded their Gatling guns in slow motion, just to make it count. *Quelqu'un M'a Dit by Carla Bruni, Voilà by Barbara Pravi, Ne Me Quitte Pas by Nina Simone, Je L'aime à Mourir by Francis Cabrel,* and *Sonatine by Chilla.*

After those bullets, to end whatever remained of a pulse, the jazz songs flowed in like river tears: *There Is No Greater Love by Miles Davis, Heartbeat by Charles Leclerc and Sofiane Pamart, Chet Baker's Born to Be Blue,* and *Weather Report's A Remark You Made,* bled through her room before she was startled back from her shattering with *It's A Heart Ache by Bonnie Tyler.* She found a reason to breathe again when *You Haven't seen the Last of Me by Cher* elevated out of the living room speakers.

Rachel opened her eyes, knowing she was still alive. She knew because she was still bleeding – the taste of her own heart-blood still lingering in her mouth and memory. She was French after all. It was her right and her birthright to love-bleed, so she slowly rolled over, got back up, and headed for the shower, hoping that today, of all days, there would be water.

51

The Gentlemen's Club

The Galore Gentlemen's Club throbbed with synthetic bass and flashing red neon bar lights. The air reeked of spent paychecks, dry ice, sex, sweat, and burnt ozone from the faulty cooling grid overhead. Holographic dancers shimmered on poles above the stage, their pixelated edges glimmering like naked skin, while the projections moved in and out of sync. Nick sat alone at a small table near the edge of the stage, nursing a half-empty *'I'm so over Rachel'* drink. He stared at the real, human dancer up front as she moved, topless, bored, and barely trying. A strobe light flashed against her skin, trying to keep pace with the thumping of *Sweet Disposition by The Temper Trap*, teasing out of the sound system.

Roland stammered up and plopped into the seat next to him. He was all swagger and smirk, with his index finger wrapped in a makeshift bandage. Nick glanced at it and asked, "What the hell happened to you?"

"Shitty guitar strings," Roland mumbled, flexing his bravado. "Snapped mid-solo, and bit back hard." He pulled out his vape, inhaled deeply, and exhaled a putrid cloud.

Nick quickly turned his head and covered his nose. "What the hell is that?"

"Glory, man. Glory." Roland's eyes reddened, and he laughed.

Nick turned his focus to the stage and snorted, "All set for tomorrow?"

Roland nodded, his lust drifting toward the waitress. "We'll scoop the boys early, and Yoshima's gonna roadie for us; she's a tiny thing, but fierce as a firecracker." The waitress passed by, and without missing a beat, Roland reached out and grabbed a generous fistful of her ass like it was his constitutional right or duty.

She spun around with dagger-eyes and snapped, "Hands off, asshole!" then slapped him hard enough to rattle teeth and turn heads.

Roland just laughed, rubbing his jaw, as he watched her storm off.

Nick winced and leaned in, his voice awkward and embar-rassed. "Brah, the juice ain't worth the squeeze."

Roland grinned unapologetically and kept his eyes on the ass of the waitress as she disappeared into the club. "Just checking the oil. Gotta see what's under the hood, right?"

Nick pretended not to hear him and glanced toward the bar, where he saw the manager lean over and whisper something to the bouncer, who looked like he kept shovels in his trunk.

Trouble.

Nick threw back the rest of his 'Rye and Rachel' and turned to Roland. "Let's get out of here. Now." They slid out of their seats and quickly made their way out through the back exit.

They turned the corner, and Roland declared, "Fuck that place, let's go to Lillie's instead."

"I'm going to head over to Valerie's," Nick replied.

Roland grinned. "That sounds like fun. I'll call a cab."

Nick looked at him to see if he was serious and whether he should invite him. "I'll have to check with her first," he said as he pulled out his phone and sent a text.

52

The Safe Word

Valerie answered the loft door in silk shorts and a tank top, her hair pinned carelessly as she'd just rolled out of an unbothered bath. "Hey," Nick gestured, holding up a gift-wrapped bottle of vodka. "Thanks for letting me crash and for allowing us to have a quick nightcap. You wanna join?"

Valerie's eyes skimmed over both of them, and she responded, "No, I'm good. Thanks."

Nick shrugged, headed toward the minibar, and made himself at home. At the same time, Roland lingered by the doorway, his eyes catching something beside Valerie's designer leather suitcase – a black leather riding crop with a solid brass handle. He picked it up, sat on the couch, and smirked, "So... you into horses now?"

Valerie crossed the room in three slow steps, her expression calm and stern. She swiftly removed the crop from his hand like an annoyed lioness. "Clients only."

Roland side-eyed her. "Clients?"

The bottle made a satisfying crack as Nick opened it, pouring two generous shots, and answered for her. "Val's into fetish."

Valerie added, coolly, "And fun. You like fun, Roland?"

Roland pulled on his vape, then licked his lips, exhaling, "What's your fun rate?"

Valerie looked down at his shoes. "You can't afford it."

Roland responded, "Try me."

"Five hundred an hour for locals. Fifteen hundred International, twenty thousand for the one-percenters, plus ten percent donation to the health clinic next door," she said flatly.

Roland hesitated, then balked. "What makes you think you're worth that much?"

Valerie stood taller, her eyes dismissive. "What makes you think I'm not?"

Roland grinned, "I guess I could use a little social interaction. What can I get for Two-fifty?"

"My boredom." She turned and walked toward the kitchen.

Roland looked over at Nick, who shrugged, then called out to Valerie, "You're a mean one, mista Grinch."

Valerie stopped, paused, exhaled, then turned around, examined him, and peeped that his height was on the shorter side. "You have the confidence of a much taller boy. Have you been naughty or nice?"

He searched for the correct answer, glanced at Nick, then back at Valerie, and shrugged, "Both?"

Valerie stared at him, assessing the level of bullshit he was delivering or whether she was in the mood for it. "Thirty minutes. That's it," she replied, while checking the clock behind the bar.

Roland pulled out his phone, found 'Joan of Arcade' on Cash App, tapped a command, and pressed send.

Valerie strapped on her stilettos – the only prop she ever actually needed. Her phone dinged on the side table. She picked it up, saw the transaction, and nodded once, instructing, "No drugs." She strode over, snatched his vape, turned it off before he could exhale, and stared him down like a pistol-carrying bandit. "So, are you into pain or pleasure?" she teased.

Roland leaned back on the couch, arms wide, and chewed on his lower lip. "Same difference."

She arched an eyebrow. "Is that so?"

Roland reached for the crop again, but Valerie yanked it away and pressed him back onto the couch with a sudden, swift motion. "Pain, it is." She turned and opened her case, and a collection of gear spilled out: cuffs, wax, straps, clamps, sterilized ball gags available in various colors and sizes – all instruments of fine design, pedigree, and promise of the right or maybe wrong kind of adventure.

Nick stood stiff near the bar, drink in hand, eyes darting between Valerie and Roland, and asked, "Are you sure about this?"

"Don't worry, pal." Roland grinned like a man who'd already made peace with his bad decision and tugged off his shirt. "This is my jam."

Valerie adopted a thick German-Berlin accent, and she buckled a cuff to Roland's wrist. "Any hard limits?"

Roland shrugged. "Let's play it by ear. I'm a wing-it kinda guy."

Valerie held back a smile. "Ground rules: Ropes, straps, wax, whips are green-lit: no blades or blood. The safe word is pineapple. Say it, and the fun stops. Got it?"

He nodded. "Bring it!'

The first thwack of the crop was playful. Roland flinched but hid it behind his cocky grin. "Ooohh... that's all you got?"

She responded with an even sharper crack. A welt instantly appeared on his leg. He winced and sucked in air. "Ouch."

Valerie's eyes sparkled. "Found your glee spot, Roland boy?"

Roland sneered, "Sorry, babe, you don't have the balls."

Valerie's next strike hit hard on his chest, already welting. Nick, still at the bar, shifted and mumbled, uncomfortably, "This is getting kinda intense."

"Stay out of it," Valerie snapped. She stepped forward, raising her stiletto heel, and gingerly pressed it on Roland's crotch. His grin returned until she pushed harder, then even harder. "You like that?" she whispered, seductively.

He grimaced, teeth clenched, groaning – not entirely in pain and not entirely out of it. She repeated, "I said, do you like that?"

"Y-yes," Roland croaked.

Valerie tapped her crop against his knee. "Yes, Mistress Valerie."

Roland nodded obediently and panted, "Yes, Mistress Valerie." Valerie leaned forward, heel still grinding his crotch, then stomped once. His body curled inward, trembling, gasping, as his fist pumped the air. "Damn," he wheezed. "You're good. Nick, send her a grand, I'm good for it."

Nick just stared at him, then at Valerie, who nodded. Nick picked up his phone, dinged the money on his app, then gazed at his bottle of vodka, assessing whether he had enough to carry him through the night or the rest of his life.

* * *

A few hours later, the sound of *Bad Guy by Billie Eilish* seeped through hidden speakers in one of the interior dungeons. A violet light above the door pulsed slowly, signaling that a scene was still in session. Roland and Nick were tied face-to-face, arms above their heads, naked, their welted backs gleaming with sweat, painted in patterns resembling an early Jackson Pollack. Valerie sat in a high-backed chair, her crop draped across her lap like a scepter. She watched them silently, sipping from a crystal glass filled with lemon sparkling water.

Nick groaned and gritted his teeth. "What the hell did you get us into?"

Roland grinned, despite the pain. "You consented, pal. Could've used that safe word."

Nick shook his head slowly, his shoulders trembling from strain, making Roland throw his head back like a hyena and laugh uncontrollably, its sound echoing off the dungeon walls like something freed too late.

53

The Intruder

The city filtered gray light through the Plymouth's windshield, still dusty from last night's storm. Sam drove with one hand on the wheel and the other holding a paper cup of fresh coffee from his favorite morning breakfast run — two pancake specials from Jerry's, the only decent breakfast place still open on Christmas. *Llorar by La lom* played over the car speakers, and he thought about how long it had been since he had spent Christmas with his daughter, and was looking forward to surprising her with an early breakfast.

As he drove back through the city, a soft chime echoed from the dashboard; Ama blinked to life on the monitor. "Patrol encountered a female suspect attempting to break into Rachel Lamont's apartment. Non-lethal force authorized. The subject fled."

Sam straightened in his seat and directed, "Show me."

Footage from the security guard's body cam showing a pale-skinned face with combat-cropped hair appeared on the screen. Sam leaned in and asked, "What's her story?"

Ama's voice was clinical, "Eris Harlow. Two years in

juvenile detention. Multiple foster homes. Served four years in the army – honorable discharge. Admitted to a mental health facility after discharge. PTSD from combat stress. Diagnosed with dissociative identity disorder. She believes she's some kind of superhero."

Footage continued to play from a security body cam, first-person and shaky. The security guard approached Eris in a dim alleyway. "I said, put your hands on your head."

Eris obeyed, eyes wide but steady. "Please, you don't understand. She's in danger."

"Turn around, slowly," cautioned the security guard.

Eris pointed and stared past the guard, as if she were seeing something miles away, then moved quickly, precisely, and inhumanly. She pivoted, kicked the guard's weapon free, caught the wall with both hands, and scaled up like it was instinct, then flew over the rooftop, gone before the guard's gun even hit the ground.

Sam whistled low. "How the hell did she do that?"

The video shifted, and patrol lights lit the alley in sporadic flashes.

Ama continued, "Enhanced conditioning. She's an ex-black ops. There's also footage of her at the protest where Gemini Moon was abducted." A new video played: Eris on a wheelboard cutting through the crowd at the protest, her cape and telescope in hand. She zoomed past Gemini before they disappeared into the crowd. Ama returned to the dash. "Officers knocked on her apartment. She escaped through the window, leaving behind tactical masks, gear, and a full psych profile on Rachel Lamont."

Sam's forehead furrowed, and he clenched his teeth. "Put out an APB. I want her brought in alive. No hero bullshit."

* * *

Rachel swayed in tight, nervous circles, listening to *The Rising Tide by Mia Doi Todd* on her AirPods, which wrapped around her apartment, swirling with her pools of anxiety. Her cell rang, she lowered the music, tapped her screen, and Sam's face lit up on a video call. "Just checking in. We got a report that someone tried to break into your building."

"I'm okay," she said quickly, brushing hair from her face. "But... there's something else. It's about my friend Lucia. She disappeared after the memorial at the Q Bar and didn't show up for our meeting yesterday."

Sam tightened his grip on the wheel and reassured her, "We'll look into it. Promise."

Rachel nodded once and disconnected.

Ama appeared instantly, her digital face lighting up the dashboard monitor. "New report. They found another body."

Sam didn't react at first. He just stared out the window and sighed. "Pull the Q Bar footage and the guest list. Gimme a full scrape. Also, input my coordinates to the crime scene, ask Alaska if she wants to meet me there, and tell her I brought her some breakfast." He reached for his coffee. It was empty. He shook the cup like it owed him answers or his sanity, then tossed it into the back seat, where a couple of hundred others lay like a scattered shrine to the bean, his motivation, and his life.

54

The Inferno

Police radios squawked from patrol cars, voices blending with Christmas carols coming from nearby robot-run shops that never close. The Christmas-themed police tape printed in patterns of reindeer and snowmen sagged like a tired, weary kite, fluttering in the wind's annoying dust. Sam and Alaska arrived at the same time, ducked beneath it, their boots echoing off the concrete sidewalk as they entered the building and moved toward the damp boiler room. They pushed through the stench of old oil and the blood-filled bones of the boiler room. Emergency lights cast a harsh red glow on the walls, which bounced off damp pipes and rusted valves, while first responders moved with methodical urgency, like ants after a colony collapse.

Headlamps flashed, medical scanners blinked, and someone coughed into their mask. Captain 'Carly', still in the battered suit from the Gemini crime scene, with the same hangdog eyes, stepped forward from behind a utility pipe. His silver beard caught the light as he muttered, "Can't even get a goddamn break for Christmas, Sam," he murmured, rubbing the back of his neck. "My wife's pissed. Says if I miss one more holiday with her and the kids, she's filing for replacement rights." Then his eyes shifted to Alaska, and a soft grin spread across his face. "Well, I'll be, Alaska, been a minute."

Alaska nodded and extended her hand. "Good to see you, Captain." No genuine warmth, but the respect was mutual. Alaska looked around, reading the room like she would when playing a video game, before pretending to put on a metal suit and wield a sword.

Sam's eyes fixed on the partially covered body slumped near the broken burner, stiff and lifeless. "Christ, it never stops. I just talked to this guy last week."

Carly followed his gaze. "Dead for about a day, give or take. The cleaning lady said she came to exchange their annual holiday gift, and found him like this. Imagine that."

Sam crouched down, examined the curve of the tarp, then looked back at Carly and asked, "Copycat?"

Carly hesitated, then replied, "Don't know yet. But, you're gonna want to see the back room."

Alaska and Sam followed him through a small, rust-bitten door. The smell of candle wax and mildew seeped into their skin, and a single bulb swung overhead, casting a sickly yellow cone of light. The room felt claustrophobic, with no windows or ventilation – only a makeshift altar, stacks of old theology books, and a cot that hadn't seen a clean sheet in years. In one corner, *Alice*, a stop-motion dark-fairy-tale film by *Jan Švankmajer,* played on a loop on an old TV.

A conspiracy theorist's wet dream covered the walls: threads, pins, and holy faces torn from forgotten parishes. Lines drawn in twine and grease pencil stretched between schools, churches, missions, and monasteries. At the center:

266

the Vatican. Surrounding it: a pyramid of faces. Priests. Brothers. Nuns. Labeled, dated, and cross-referenced. Some had Xs, and others had question marks. They formed a pyramid that stared back, their faces full of guilt and secrecy. Lines extended from these to dozens of faces and names from the upper echelons of the social matrix: local and foreign politicians, bankers, stockbrokers, royals, and celebrities.

Alaska silently moved to a wall covered with photographs. Some were black-and-white, and a few were surveillance stills. She reached up and tapped one. "Sister Judith Fish- burn."

Sam stepped closer. "The Canadian schoolteacher."

Alaska pointed out another. "Father Brian Jones, the retired priest from Milwaukee. It looks like they changed their names." She touched another photo labeled Brother Chet Burdock. "Who's he?"

Sam shook his head, pulled out his phone, and subvocalized. "Ama, give me everything on Chet Burdock, St. Mary's."

Ama's soft chime acknowledged his request.

Alaska kept scanning. On the opposite wall, a massive collage of headlines screamed in muted horror:

· *37 million adult survivors of child sexual abuse living in the US today: Time Magazine*

· *Pedophile Pastors of Pennsylvania Convicted: New York Times*

· *Mormon Church faces 91 new child sexual abuse lawsuits in 26 California counties – Floodlit*

· *'Sugarcane – Academy Award-nominated Documentary exposes abuse of Native children in Canadian schools: PBS*

· *4,000 US Roman Catholic priests accused of sex abuse.*

· *3 of the US's biggest religious denominations are in turmoil over sex abuse. PBS*

• Boy Scouts of America $2.5 Billion settlement for 82000 sexual abuse survivors: Reuters

• Survivors of sexual abuse by nuns want greater visibility for their claims: NPR

• So, Let's Talk About Republicans and Sex Crimes: Slate

• National Southern Baptist leaders release a previously secret list of accused sexual abusers: NPR.

• Churches, Synagogues, and other religious organizations purchase insurance known as abuse and molestation liability to protect themselves from lawsuits.

• The President was alerted by the DOJ that his name appears in the files: The New York Times.

• One in Four Girls and One in Thirteen Boys sexually abused in the US: Time Magazine.

Alaska interrupted the seemingly endless list and turned to Sam. "You're right. It never stops."

Sam looked at the collage. "A fish rots from the head."

"It also rots from the inside out," observed Alaska.

Ama popped up on Sam's phone. "Brother Chet Burdock. The church transferred him back to the Vatican from St. Mary's. They found his body in the Piazza San Pietro with a cross cut on Burdock's forehead. His body had scratches and bite marks, and his testicles had been cut off and stuffed down his throat."

Sam recoiled, his stomach churned at the thought of it, and he took a step back, darting his eyes to each wall of maps, charts, and pictures. "It could be a ring," he mused. "Someone targeting a ring, or some kinda vigilante, or both."

Alaska stepped toward a cork board near the altar. Her eyes found Gemini Moon's face in a photo, surrounded by a handful of men and women. She reached into her pocket and pulled out a folded *S.A.S.S.* flyer. A few of the grainy faces matched. "Maybe Copycat was in one of Gemini's survivor groups."

Sam was already speaking into the device. "Ama, subpoena Gemini's client files. I want everything. Mental health records, group rosters, now."

"Copy that, and the Q Bar intel just came through," Ama replied.

Carly stepped closer and gave a signal for coffee by tilting his hand to his mouth.

Sam turned to Alaska. "We're going next door for some coffee to talk this through. You wanna come?"

"I'm going to look around for a bit," Alaska replied. "I'll catch up with you later."

Sam nodded and walked out with the Captain, while Alaska gloved up and crouched beside Keppler's body, his neck torn and covered with scratch marks, his jaw frozen in a final rictus. She scanned the room, and her eyes caught something on the door frame: gouges, four of them, scratched deep into the wood. She followed the trail downward to a single claw lying behind a wooden crate on the floor: a one-inch-long talon, serrated like bone, still covered in what looked like dried blood. Alaska's inner voice whispered, *"Are those human or animal marks?"*

The coroner's voice from Gemini's autopsy echoed in her memory: *"Hard to determine. It could be an animal – a dog or coyote that found the body."*

Alaska reached into her side pouch, pulled out a pinch of tobacco, and laid it on the floor beside the claw in a quiet ritual for protection. She extended her hand, and as her fingers brushed the claw, her arm trembled, a twitch that originated in her tendons and climbed to her shoulder. She clenched her fist to stabilize her arm, then trapped the claw and placed it in the pouch. She squeezed her fist tightly again, as if trying to hold back the sensation of something that had just attempted to move through her.

55

The Buzz

Buzz was the kind of place that used to be a novelty but was now the norm. The lengthy, narrow 24-hour espresso cafe felt like it was a cross between a hospital waiting room and the middle lane of the German Autobahn. With its sterile, green walls dotted with a handful of AI-designed nature posters, Buzz wasn't designed for sitting and staying, but rather moving and leaving. There were quick line-ups on any given day for customers who came for the twenty-one flavors of espresso, automated robots who served it up fast and without plastered-on smiles, and a polished counter stacked with brewing and grinding machines. The brewing and grinding perfectly matched the pace of the java junkies who usually frequented Buzz, but today were absent due to the holiday.

Five server bots hovered and mulled around the mainly empty cafe, hesitant and not programmed to truly handle the Christmas lull. Sam and Carly were equally jittery in the presence of peace, along with the infusion of their second, triple espresso, they nursed as they sat by the window.

Carly looked out at the empty street, then back at Sam. "There's not much you can do about what we saw in that boiler room, Sam."

Sam raised his eyebrow and replied, "What do you mean, not much we can do? It's all mapped out. Plain as the nose on your face."

"I never told you this, 'cause you never needed to know, but now you do. Years ago, when I was making my way up the detective ranks, I was working on the same threads of that case that you saw in the back," recounted Carly as he tapped his fingertips on the table.

"You mean the one where Keppler was the fall guy," replied Sam.

Surprise rolled across Carly's eyes. "How did you know about that?

"I never needed to tell you that I knew, but now I do," bantered Sam.

Carly leaned back in his plastic chair, designed to be uncomfortable. "I was working that case with Captain Marlen, do you remember him?"

Sam took another sip from his espresso fuel. "Of course, he was the GOAT. I always wanted a chance to work with him – too bad about that heart attack, you know?"

"Yes, no," Carly quickly answered.

"What do you mean, yes, no?" Sam said, his detective whiskers perking up.

Carly hesitated for a breath before offering, "Yes, he was legendary, and no, he didn't die of a heart attack."

Sam just looked at him, his silence indicating an opening for Carly to continue.

Carly looked over at the bored, calcifying robots, then out

the window, then back to Sam. "Let's just say, a couple of suits dropped by once upon a time and hung me on the horns of a dilemma. It was pretty clear. 'Stop looking into this, find a fall guy, or you'll end up like Marlen.' It's no accident that you saw that boiler room; now you know what I've been carrying. What it doesn't show is that the ring has rings. They were using those kids for themselves, then pimping them out, trafficking, selling, and disposing of them when necessary. Parties, power, and pedophiles are a dangerous mix. Every time we got close, we got squeezed out."

Sam shrugged. "So that's that, then?"

Carly scratched and wiped a bead of sweat from his forehead. "No, that's not that, Sam. In about ten minutes, five unmarked vans will arrive in front of that building, along with backup vehicles and drone support. Twenty-five guys in beige hazmats are going to go in there and scrub that place clean, sprinkle it with so much perfume you could take it out on a date."

Sam pulled out his phone and typed, 'You still at the boiler room?' and pressed send. He looked back at Carly, stared at him, and answered, "Alright."

"No, Sam, it's not alright. I don't know what you did, or who did what, or why we found Keppler's face flat on the floor, but they're pulling the plug," Carly pointed out.

"What do you mean by pulling the plug?" quizzed Sam, his voice and nerves now irritated.

Carly sighed, "I mean, it's over."

"How over?" asked Sam.

"Over, over. The case is closed. They'll find someone to pin it on. Cut off funding for the department, offer a leave of absence, revoke travel passes, scramble access to communications and intel – over.”

Sam looked at the 'no' response from Alaska in his text, then at the remaining espresso in his cup, trying to read it like tea leaves. “I see.”

Carly leaned in. “No, you don't see, Sam. Things have changed since you and I started; there are snakes in the grass you don't want to step on or piss off. They have eyes that can see you blink from outer space and ears that can hear you fart in the woods from as far away as Fiji. Since we walked out of that building, they've sent me a message. They said your robot. What's her name, Ama? She's been hacking into places she has no business – Interpol, government records, and the DOJ. Your bot will be classified as a national security threat. They're confiscating, most likely melting her down and turning her into a manhole cover or a lamp post.”

Sam stared out the window. “Is there anything you can do about any of this?”

Carly withheld his grief. “I got an early pension coming up. I like fly fishing, margaritas, a marriage I'd like to keep, and a gallbladder that I don't. Health insurance, ya know. I can probably buy you another day, two max. I would suggest you chuck it in the fuck it bucket and use whatever time you have to pack things up, disappear for a while, take a vacation – you've earned it. You still got that cabin in Canada?”

Sam waited and watched the bots spin around the shop, then nodded his head. He threw back the last of his espresso, stood up, reached for his belt, unclipped his badge, and set it down on the table.

Carly looked slightly surprised. “What's this?”

Sam blurted out, “Something that used to mean something.” He walked past him, out the door, and into the empty street , shadowed with his own doubt.

56

The Scar

Alaska stepped inside Kokum's apartment, slowly closing the door behind her. The room carried the familiar scent of sweetgrass and cookies, and *Beauty by Delbert Blackhorse* played softly from the transistor radio, which was half-buried under prayer ribbons and scattered jewelry beads. Kokum sat at her small wooden table, regal and unmoved, her hands resting over a chipped porcelain plate. Without a word, she slid a batch of still-warm Christmas cookies across the table.

Alaska remained standing. "I didn't come for the cookies," she said in her Cree language, then unfolded a square of cloth and laid it on the table to reveal the claw, still slick with an oily sheen.

Kokum's eyes didn't move, and Alaska's voice grew more assertive. "What can you tell me about this?"

Kokum gave her a guarded, fortress-like look and remained silent.

Alaska unzipped her bag and spread out several images of the Wetiko – etched renderings, charcoal, and ink sketches. Kokum's body shifted slightly. Her hands clenched and her knuckles whitened under the table. She looked at the images, then looked away. Alaska again pointed at the claw. "Is this from a Wetiko?" she asked, louder and sharper this time, as if forcing the words might make the truth cough.

Kokum's silence filled the room like sage smoke. Alaska reached into her pouch and placed a small tobacco tie in front of her grandmother, more like an all-in poker bet than a respectful offering. Then she pulled a tattered copy of Earth Traditions from her satchel, flipping it open to the torn chapter. "Why is the section on the Wetiko ripped out?" she demanded. "Where are the pages?"

A long breath escaped Kokum's lips. Resigned, she reached into a kitchen drawer and slid out a thin folder with yellowed pages torn from the original book. She handed them over, reluctantly. "They're shapeshifters," Kokum acquiesced. "Wetikos can be born... or made. A human can rot from the inside out, or get infected and possessed from the outside in."

Alaska flipped through the brittle pages, finding old wood-cut illustrations of creatures with eyes like voids, hollow bellies, and claws like the one on the table. "How many are there?"

"No one knows," Kokum explained. "They are distorted shadows and move in shadows, cloaked not just from sight, but from our belief. Whether alone or in groups, a Wetiko wears many masks, and can remain invisible even to themselves." She stared at the claw again. "The elders told us that the first of these long-clawed ones arrived on the boats, wearing black robes, and the ones with the metal and wool hats. As is our custom, we welcomed them as guests into our home, but then they disturbed and stole our land, decimated our people, and our way of life. We've never seen Wetikos like these before. They mimic the light within human beings, but their souls are dead inside, so they have to feed off and cannibalize the souls and the light of others, especially the children."

Alaska scanned the pages and images of puritans, pilgrims, pirates, priests, and profiteers, then swallowed a steel coil tightening in her chest, and delicately asked, "Did one of them kill my mother?"

Kokum, dreading to answer the question she had avoided for twenty years, wrestled with herself and replied, "Your mother tried to protect you."

Alaska's face turned a deep red, and she repeated, "Did-a-Wetiko-kill-her?"

Kokum paused, her gaze cracking like glacial ice breaking beneath her feet. Her silence stretched long and fragile. Then, she nodded regretfully.

Alaska stood taller, her voice steady and measured, "Then how do I capture or defeat it?"

Kokum stared out the window, searching for a response, then turned back to Alaska. "We were just children then. My sister was seven, and I was nine. We were given numbers and called by them. I was number 88, and my sister, your great auntie Niska, was number 89. Although our family tried to hide us in the woods, the government agents found us and took us away to the boarding school, to the poison ivy league indoctrination and genocide camp, as we've since called it out.

The nuns, priests, churches, and their government sponsors were cutters. They severed our language, our hair, our families, our cultures, our lands, and they cut many children off from their own lives. They punished us if we refused any of the cuts. They would cut long rubber straps from old tires and beat or whip us with them. They made the older children beat the younger ones. When it came time for me to be one of the older ones, I refused to beat the younger ones, so they beat me even more."

Alaska looked down at the claw on the table, and then back at her grandmother, encouraging her to continue.

Kokum took a moment, then exhaled. "Sometimes they would cut the leaves of poison ivy and rub them on our skin. When our wounds were open and raw, they made us take steaming hot water baths mixed with salt. And both the nuns and the priests would sexually abuse the boys and the girls. Sometimes the girls got pregnant, and they got rid of the babies."

Alaska's jaw and fists clenched; her reflex was to hit and punch something, but she kept her breath moving and her eyes locked on her grandmother.

Kokum recounted, "They forced us to sit in their church chairs every morning, and for six hours on Sunday. We had to go to the priest afterwards to confess our sins, but we had to make them up because we didn't have any. We were all just children, and we stuck together. We would laugh together, speak our languages in private, and play outside in the winter snow. We would lie down in fresh snow and wave our arms up and down, leaving the imprint of angels. Sometimes we would draw a large circle on the snow, and some of us would stand at the four corners – East, South, West, and North, just like we did back home. Some of us would run through the forest to see the moon and stars. Some ran away to find their way home, while others were caught, brought back, and beaten. Some of us found our way home, but others got lost or died in the wilderness and the freezing snow."

Alaska reached across the table, lit some sage, and let it burn in her grandmother's bowl – cloaking both of them in clarity and a field of solidarity and protection.

Kokum looked back out through the window, as though it were a source for her well of memories. "In the springtime, they let us pick berries in the meadows, but they punished us if they caught us eating a single berry, and we were not allowed to eat any of the berries we brought back to the kitchen. Still, some of us would eat the berries one at a time, hide them in our cheeks, and savor them until they melted. They were yummy.

Because the nuns and the priests wore these long black robes, we used to call them 'the black bears.' But we were just children, and maybe that's the only way we could understand their predatory nature. The truth is, the bear would never have harmed us like these Wetikos, and even the bears would have shared their berries with us."

Alaska teared up; her hands and arms started to shake.

Kokum picked up the claw, her own fingers trembling as she turned it in the light. "They're increasingly mutating," she said. "Fusing with human traits. Learning us. Mimicking us. If no one stops them," her voice trailed off, then she added, "they could consume everything, even Mother Earth herself."

Alaska sat and settled down in front of her grandmother. "Mutating?" Alaska's eyes narrowed, and she reached out, rubbing her thumb on Kokum's hand. "Grandma, how do we stop them? All of them?"

Kokum looked down, as if searching for and drawing a response from her ancestors. "They are terrified of light or being seen. You can sometimes dissolve them with intense, fiery light, but it's hit-or-miss. Their hearts are ice, even when their eyes seem warm. You kill the body or host with fire – an arrow to its frozen heart. But it's real power? You have to defeat it in the spirit world. You have to see through them and outlast their masks."

Alaska's face tightened. "Why didn't you tell me any of this before?"

"Because you weren't ready," Kokum said, her tone grave. "There are no shortcuts. Knowing all of this too early could have destroyed you."

Alaska sat back in her chair, her eyes darkening, and asked, "And how am I ready now? I don't know anything about the spirit world."

"You've been preparing for this moment your whole life," Kokum gestured. "You've used your instincts to follow your path – you've danced with our bear ancestors, felt their sorrow, held and expressed their dark rage, and also the sorrow and rage of Mother Earth herself. You've ascended to the highest light of joy, can descend into the depths of the darkest darkness, and have woven all the colors in between. You are and always have been our ancestors' *âhkasipiskân-maskwa-maskihkiy*."

Alaska's lips parted, and she whispered, "Rainbow bear medicine."

Kokum nodded, slid the plate of cookies across the table, and Alaska took one. "Yes, our bear relatives live on the outskirts of our community to protect the most vulnerable among us. And of all our animal relatives, the bear spends the most time in deep hibernation looking into its own heart, which helps it to see into the hearts of others, including your own."

Alaska raised the cookie to her mouth, but decided not to bite into it. "What does this have to do with the Wetiko?"

Kokum's eyes grew deadly serious. "Although your rainbow bear medicine journey has helped you heal your heart, the Wetiko will try to trick you by playing on any unhealed pain remaining within you. You mustn't give your power over to what has hurt you, expect or want it to change in any way, for you to heal and regain your power. The only way to defeat a Wetiko is from your scar, not your wound, and it can only destroy if it can distract you."

Alaska looked at the claw again. "So where do I find this?"

"Take the talon to someone who can see past the veil," Kokum instructed. "Someone who walks between worlds. And listen. Our ancestors – they're ready. They'll help you become who you already are, and Alaska, you are here to help them and us as well."

Alaska rubbed the cookie between her fingers and asked, "And who am I?"

"That's for you to decide," Kokum said, smiling faintly. "But this I know, you cannot alter your fate. However, you can rise to meet it if you choose."

Alaska's eyes lit up. "That's from *Princess Mononoke*."

Kokum smiled, shrugged, and said nothing. Alaska nodded, took a bite of the cookie, grabbed a few more, and tucked them into her pocket. She reached for the claw, delicately, as if it might bite, since it was still warm with clarity, carrying both poison and purpose. Her hand trembled just for a second before she re-wrapped it and sealed it back in her pouch. Then, without ceremony, she stood up, lifted the crossbow from the wall, and slung a quiver of arrows over her back.

Kokum called out to her, "Wait." Alaska turned around,

and her Kokum reached into a drawer, pulling out a small, sealed jar. "Take this with you, and dip your arrows in it. This medicine contains the sap of the pine, which will catch fire when ignited, and the sap of Jewelweed, a plant that grows near Poison Ivy. Nature always provides a complementary remedy, or *Pisâskwan* and the Jewelweed will break through any poisonous layer or shield of a Wetiko. Our ancestors of the Pine and the spirit of the Jewelweed will help you. Also, you never got to meet your grandfather, Archie, but he sometimes visits me in a dream, or when I am cooking or crafting. He told me to tell you 'rat-tat-tat-tat,' and that you would know what it means."

Alaska smiled.

Kokum paused, then leaned forward, "Know you are strong, like your grandfather. He used to say, in his own words, 'Everybody loves to poke the bear, but don't nobody want to fight... that mother fucker for real!'"

Alaska paused, then placed a tobacco prayer tie in her grandmother's hand, took the jar from her, turned, and stepped into the light bleeding through the door.

Kokum watched her leave, reached for a cookie, took a bite, and smiled, while *Boarding Schools by Lyla June* and *Lee Moquino*, and *How Much You Mean to Me by The Bearhead Sisters* played defiantly on her transistor radio.

57

The Smoke Signals

Now untethered and with a greater urgency, Sam passed Ama on the way to his office and said to her, "Keep an eye on Interpol, Homeland Security, and the DOJ. Hack your way in until you make them your little bitch, and if you detect any movement towards Phillip, let me know." Ama knew the order to hack, froze on the 'little bitch' command, but nodded and blinked her eyes in agreement anyway.

Sam quickly leaned over the computer monitor in his office, filtering through security footage from Gemini's memorial at the Q Bar, shown in digital frames: strobes of neon, bodies grinding to the rhythm, drunk laughter, and neo-punk bands. He scrubbed through the footage like a surgeon peeling back skin, searching for the tumor beneath.

There, Lucia, weaving and swirling through the crowd like a Dervish. She danced with Roland, light on her feet. Then she broke away, kissed Diego on the cheek, leaned in close, and whispered something private. A moment later, she slid onto a barstool beside Nick, radiating easy confidence and poised grace.

Sam refocused, froze the frame, and zoomed in. "Ama," he inquired, his voice steady. "I saw this guy at the funeral, and he played the memorial with Towais and Donner. What do we have on him?"

Ama's voice emerged from the wall console, calm and omnipresent. "Nick Durrell. Attended St. Mary's. Current residence is seven blocks from Gordon Dent, a confirmed Copycat victim." Photos flickered on-screen. DMV. School yearbook. Funeral pictures. The faces matched and lined up like checkers on a board. Sam leaned back, sipped his coffee, and flicked his Zippo – still searching for a reason for it all.

58

The Morning After

Nick woke up alone, tangled in sweat-soaked, dark sheets in the corner of Valerie's dungeon, which reeked of latex, kink, and expensive perfume. His pupils contracted against the soft light slanting through red curtains, and he looked toward the foot of the bed, where a riding crop lay next to a ball gag, discarded like evidence from an adventure he didn't expect, but took the red pill anyway. He sat up, touched the welts across his back and ass, and his fingers trembled slightly. "What the hell...?" he wondered, scrambling for his memory and clothes while trying not to look at himself in the mirror – half-naked, branded, and more confused than ashamed. He ran his hand through his hair, turned to the mirror, and declared, "Merry Christmas, champ!" He scribbled a note for Valerie and stuck it on the mirror, then he quickly dressed, opened the door, and left.

59

The Stalker

Back at Rachel's apartment, the sun filtered through the Christmas morning dust like a torch. Rachel sat alone on the living room floor, drinking coffee, scrolling through her phone, and replying to a few familiar, 'Merry Christmas' texts. In the background, *The Cat Carol by Bruce Evans* played for the ninth time on repeat. She thought about Jonesy, her ginger cat, which had vanished the year before, and although unfounded, she had never really stopped blaming the coyotes for its disappearance. She looked at the unopened presents resting lonely under the tree: a few from distant relatives, none from her parents, whose differing political views prevented peace from passing between their respective lips and ears, and one from her brother, whom she only stayed in touch with through the remaining thread of their annual gift exchange. Another one was from Nick because old habits die hard, and the last one – a ribbon-wrapped box from Lucia.

Without Snowy around or operational to keep Rachel company, the thought of opening them alone or even touching them made her nerves growl. She took the last sip of her coffee, put on her shoes, picked up Nick's FRACK OFF poster he had left behind, and walked toward the door. It was giving 'definitely desperate' vibes. She justified it to herself, saying she liked clean breaks, throwing out protest signs made her stomach churn, and she could ask Valerie about Lucia's absence. So she marched out that door carrying the protest sign that could have easily said:

LONELY AND STILL IN LOVE

Christmas mornings alone can make you crash out and act out of pocket like that. Rachel hurriedly stepped out, hoodie half-zipped, keys already in her hand. She didn't see Eris until she was nearly on top of her, in her sleek black ninja cape with the SKK insignia, and her shoulder-harnessed speaker rig. "Hey, Rachel," Eris whispered.

Rachel spun around, startled. "Jesus, Eris. What are you doing here?"

Eris peeped Rachel's protest sign. "Are we protesting today? I didn't hear about it."

Rachel lowered the sign behind her back and dismissed her, "No, I have things to take care of."

Eris's eyes widened and became glassy, her voice steady. "Oh. Well, your life is in danger."

"What?" Rachel blinked.

Eris pointed to the sky. "Dark forces of the night."

"Dark forces of what?" Rachel almost laughed.

"I'm here to protect you," Eris warned, pointing to her SKK insignia.

Rachel looked at her incredulously. "I don't need your protection."

Eris stuttered, "Rachel."

"What?" Rachel barked impatiently.

Without warning, Eris leaned in for a hug, her lips parting, and she reached out.

Rachel shoved her back. "This is too much." She stammered, turned, stormed to her scooter, kicked it into gear, and drove off.

Eris watched her leave, her face shifting from confusion to rage. She bit into her forearm hard, then howled into the morning sky, "Too much? I'm not too much?" She dropped her wheelboard, spun *Black Is Black by Los Bravos* from her speaker, then launched after Rachel, following her from a distance through the barren, dusty streets.

60

The Roadie

Yoshima was on her hands and knees, cleaning the kitchen floor in Roland's bungalow. She had a daily list of tasks to complete, along with preparing meals and ordering groceries. Roland was very particular about everything and insisted that it be done correctly, to his specifications.

While she was leaning in and cleaning the back of the oven, the wisp-entity that had escaped from The Roach's body and his prison cell vent slipped quietly and unnoticed down through the flue pipe into the oven. Whether it was the first available host or matched Yoshima's overall vibe and aura, or that of her environment, the wisp seeped into the back of her neck and wrapped itself inside her along the length of her back.

Yoshima couldn't detect if she had accidentally left the gas on while scrubbing or if she had hit her head on the oven's roof, but she experienced the wisp possession like a jolt of electricity. Her body shook briefly before settling as she retreated from the stove and kept cleaning the kitchen.

Yoshima obsessively vacuumed Roland's living room, wobbling slightly, banging into the furniture, and knocking things over. *Who Put The Bomb by Jaakko Eino Kalevi* played on the living room's sound system, but still sounded like a drone note behind her vacuum's hum.

Out in the garage, Nick hauled the last of the musical instruments into the back of the battered road trip van. The clank of metal on metal echoed in the stillness. He sensed a shift of weight behind him and turned around. "Wow, Yoshima." His voice cracked. "You scared the hell out of me." She just stood there with a blank stare, her face unreadable. "What kind of roadie are you? I thought you were gonna help out," he challenged her.

"I haven't received new instructions," she replied in a monotone, sleepy voice.

Nick cocked his head sideways and remarked, "Do you ever do anything without someone telling you to?"

"I simply follow directions," she responded flatly.

Nick stepped toward her, his eyes flirting with curiosity, maybe attraction. He reached out slowly, his fingertips brushed her cheek, and then down the side of her neck.

"You do not have permission," she ordered, and in one smooth motion, Yoshima seized his left arm, twisted, and broke his elbow.

Nick screamed, "Bloody hell!" and crumpled to his knees. Yoshima's face showed no reaction. No anger or triumph, just cold, precise efficiency.

<h1 style="text-align:center">61</h1>

<h1 style="text-align:center">The Russian Sub</h1>

Forest sat alone in his private dungeon cell at the far end of the labyrinth-like hallway that housed various private rooms of Joan Of Arcade, curated for kink and role play: the teacher/student room with a desk, pointer, and blackboard for those who enjoyed after-school punishment scenarios; the doctor-nurse office with white coats, tools, stethoscopes, and clip boards hanging on the wall hooks for the naughty nurse and misbehaving patient types; a religious-themed room complete with alters, confessionals, and candles for all those fetishes to find a home to play out, along with a collection of themed pleasure and pain rooms equipped with floggers, canes, straps, cages, racks, tables, and pillories – the whole 'shebang'.

Forest was Valerie's loyal and obedient submissive for nearly ten years now – a role akin to an Alfred to Batman, but with more of an edge. He didn't just hand over his time and power lightly; both he and Valerie regarded their consensual arrangement thoughtfully, respecting each other's boundaries while enjoying their shared activities. Forest was

292

a workhorse, handling all the daily administrative duties of the Arcade, including scheduling, bookkeeping, responding to emails, and ensuring the premises stayed spotless and germ-free. With black belts in jujitsu and karate, he also handled security and acted as a bodyguard, prepared to intervene if anything went wrong or if Valerie was threatened. Such incidents were rare, and he handled them diplomatically, resorting to force only when absolutely necessary.

Like all submissives and servants, Forest held his own unique position of power, as he could decide both his yeses and nos for limits and hard limits related to the roles, power dynamics, and kinks he was willing to explore with Valerie and/or her clients when needed. Today was his day off; his sub and security services were not required, so Forest spent Christmas morning alone in his cage. His preferred way of resting in sub-space was sitting on a pillow, locked in his cage, hooded and masked, with one hand cuffed to the cage bar. In his other hand, Forest was reading *Metro 2033*, a dystopian novel by Russian author Dmitry Glukhovsky. One storyline involved the "dark attacks," telepathic assaults from a mysterious, evolved humanoid species called the Dark Ones. Their attempts at communication overwhelm the human mind, causing intense hallucinations, paranoia, and eventually madness, perceived by humans as violent, unprovoked attacks.

Forest inhaled Russian novels as a soothing escape into darkness. He had read many works by the renowned Soviet-Russian writers, including Leo Tolstoy, Fyodor Dostoevsky, Ivan Turgenev, Nikolai Gogol, and Anton Chekhov, as well as their contemporaries such as Lyudmila Ulitskaya, Vladimir Sorokin, Victor Pelevin, Guzel Yakhina, and Aleksey Ivanov.

Forest had even managed to earn his Master's Degree in Russian Literature online on his days off.

If he were honest with himself, Forest's most authentic kink was exploring the dark passages and insights within the minds of his country's writers. Mostly, his daily life served as a means to an end so that he could stay connected to the Russian spirit and soul as often as possible. He appreciated being around other darkened, enlightened, creative-minded types who could handle it and relate. He knew Valerie could, and had witnessed her in both her personal and professional life, skillfully navigating and transforming all shades of darkness – alchemizing pain or pleasure into power and self-empowerment, like no one else. To him, she was both a queen of the underworld and a queen of the heavens, seamlessly balancing and merging the two. She also volunteered to help the detectives catch some seriously batshit-crazy individuals and cared for the local community's health, making her a hero or heroine in his mind.

Forest also spoke Russian fluently, his native language, and was proficient in German, Mandarin, Arabic, Farsi, French, and Spanish – all of which proved helpful when the high-rollers and oligarchs came to town, seeking Valerie's expertise and services. These clients tipped generously, which is what kept him flush, but he really did not need the money, having adopted a zen-minimalist lifestyle. He sent most of his earnings back to his parents, who were now refugees of the latest war. It was the least he could do, having narrowly escaped the draft himself and fled the country for America and its promised land.

He looked up at the security monitor hanging above his desk in the room that served as his dark sanctuary and office.

Nothing visible on the security cameras placed in the hallway, living area, or outside on the street. He smiled, knowing that all was well; it was Christmas, his Mistress was safe and happy, and he returned to his novel, reading and re-entering the mysterious darkened soul that uniquely resided there, and within him.

Outside Forest's private, dark cave, the daylight streaming through Valerie's loft windows was too bright for how Roland's skull felt. He blinked hard, trying to chase the haze from his eyes and to relieve the weight of an endorphin hangover pressing him down on the leather couch, limbs heavy and breath thick with the residue of last night's after-thrill-after-party. Across the loft, Valerie moved as if she owned the air, dressed in nothing too soft or revealing. Her presence was a mix of silk and steel, appearing as a mirage to Roland, who rubbed his temples and peeled his tongue from the roof of his mouth. "Where's Nick?" Roland croaked, his voice still sandpapered by sleep.

"You just missed him," she answered, not bothering to look at him. "He went to load up for your road trip."

Roland sat up too fast. The sudden jolt brought bile to his throat, and he muttered, "He went to my place?"

Valerie shrugged and replied matter-of-factly, "Yeah."

"Ah, shit," he cursed, holding his head and nervous system together with both hands.

Her brow arched. "What?"

"Nothing," he lied, already dialing his phone. He stood, one bare foot still half in a sneaker, waiting for the call to connect. "Yoshima? Hhheeeyyy, did Nick go by there?" A pause, then he squinted his eyes. "Say what now? Oh, that's, yeah, unfortunate. I'll be home soon." He ended the call, found his vape, and took a long drag as if trying to make everything go away.. As he laced up his shoes, his eyes honed in on Valerie. "How come you weren't down to bang me last night?"

She didn't slow her roll and said, "I don't entertain clients. Point. Blank. Period."

Roland smirked. "Come now, you don't like dick? I figure that your last name is Johnson, you're built for this," pointing to his crotch.

Valerie turned around and looked him in the eyes, glanced toward where he pointed, smirked, then back to his eyes, and singed him with, "I already have a man."

Roland looked down, all his bravado bleeding into the floor, as Valerie walked away without waiting for a rebuttal and disappeared into the next room.

A loud knock on the loft door startled Roland. He got up, cracked it open to see Rachel standing there, her eyes sharp with determination, her helmet in one hand and a protest poster in the other. "What are you doing here?" she asked.

He smiled like it hurt, and replied, "Little going-away party, party!''

"Is Nick here?" she asked, looking past him.

"You just missed him." Roland's smirk turned dismissive.

"Where's Valerie?" she asserted.

Roland snapped and pointed his fingers. "In the back."

Rachel moved to enter, but Roland blocked her with a laid-back swagger. She pushed past him, and he made a half-hearted attempt to stop her with his arm, more petulant than forceful. "What are you doing?" she demanded and swatted his arm with a glare intense enough to draw blood. He stepped aside and raised his hands in mock surrender.

Valerie reappeared, brushing her hair behind her ear, casual but attentive. "Oh, hey!"

Rachel didn't hesitate and asked, "Have you seen Lucia?"

Valerie's expression shifted, and she replied curiously, "No. What's going on?"

"She went MIA after the memorial." Rachel's throat tightened. "She didn't show up to our brunch yesterday, and hasn't returned my calls or texts."

Valerie, now with greater concern, exclaimed, "You're kidding."

Rachel shook her head, explaining, "I talked to the cops. Someone even tried to break into my apartment yesterday."

Valerie's voice softened. "Are you okay?"

Rachel nodded, but her eyes betrayed her, growing more distant, caught somewhere between rage and fear.

Valerie could see through it, pointed toward the kitchen, trying to recalibrate the room's vibe, and invited, "I made some breakfast. You guys should eat."

Roland grabbed his jacket, refusing, "I gotta bounce."

Valerie stepped close to him, picked up her crop, and lightly tapped the end of it against his thigh. Not hard, but not soft, either. "Roland," she insisted with a smile that carried both pain and seduction in equal measure. "Stay for breakfast."

Roland paused, swallowed, and looked at her like a moth might gaze at a flame and still willingly walk in. "I could do a bowl of Cheerios."

Rachel shot them a look, part amused and part disturbed, as if she'd wandered into an after-party in a glitched dimension or timeline.

62

The Footage

Sam sat at his desk, gazing at the computer, scrolling through feeds and profiles, and isolating images of Nick, Diego, Roland, and Eris frozen on separate monitors like mugshots still waiting to confess. Next to him, Ama worked silently, parsing data from digitized yearbooks and scrubbing pixels to find a face that matched the sketch of the young boy.

Sam clicked, zeroing in on the Q Bar footage and rewinding to the moment Diego left. The kid glanced over his shoulder, pulled his hoodie tighter, then slipped into the night as if he were being followed. Sam split the footage, comparing interior feeds with parking lot cameras. Cars peeled off one by one. He caught Nick, alone in his van, pulling out like he had somewhere urgent to go or to forget. Then came Roland — swaggering with a woman Sam couldn't quite identify. She moved like she was half drunk. Roland's voice from his interrogation at his house floated up from memory: "*Yeah, that was the creepy janitor who got canned for kiddie porn.*"

Sam leaned back in his chair. "Ama, keep looking for the child. I'm gonna check something out. And Ama, take care of yourself. If anything moves on Phillip while I'm gone, let me know." Ama just blinked her eyes as Sam stood up, grabbed his keys, and headed out the door, while the computer monitors kept running behind him, spilling out more digital clues and questions.

* * *

Sam pulled his Plymouth into Roland's cluttered driveway. He parked, checked his phone, saw the battery was at 3%, then plugged it into the charger before stepping out of the car. His eyes scanned the quiet street behind his dark sunglasses, noting no movement, no cars, and no pedestrians. He walked to the front door and rapped twice. When there was no response, he circled the house, boots crunching over broken pavers and cigarette butts, and checked the windows. Most were coated in grime or had yellowed blinds drawn tight, but a back window revealed light, and possibly something moving in the hallway.

His phone buzzed in the car just as he reached for the side gate. Ama's avatar lit up the dashboard screen, her voice clipped and urgent. "Sam, we have a match." The static crackled, then the monitor split: a surveillance sketch rendered in digital charcoal beside a faded yearbook photo. The same angular jaw, same haunted eyes, only younger, and less corrupted by time. "Interpol confirmed Italian and Canadian tourist visas," Ama inserted. Still no response, so she called out to him again, "Sam? Sam?"

The empty car remained silent.

63

The Matches

Roland lounged at the breakfast bar, nursing a half-bowl of soggy cereal like nothing was out of place. Across from him, Rachel pushed her eggs around the plate, her eyes downcast, her thoughts darker than the burnt turkey bacon she tried to eat, but couldn't. Valerie leaned against the counter, rolling a joint with casual precision. Her painted nails shimmered like cat claws, and she smiled, "Anyone got a light?"

Roland dug into his pocket, pulled out a crumpled pack of matches, and tossed them to her. "Here."

Valerie caught them, lit the joint, inhaled, and her fingers fidgeted with the pack of matches. She turned them over, and her number, scribbled in violet ink, was visible from the inside flap. She froze, lifting her gaze with a laser-sharp focus, directly at Roland. "Did you have fun at the Q Bar the other night?"

She passed the joint to Roland, who took a hit and exhaled slowly, smoke curling around his lips. "Oh yeah, it was savage! Just like old times."

Valerie nonchalantly asked, "You see Lucia after the show?"

Roland took another drag, exhaled, and responded through his nasal cavity, "Nah. I dipped early."

Valerie's jaw clenched slightly, showing her concern. "Oh really?" she questioned, holding up the matches like a courtroom exhibit, and exclaimed, "Then where did you get these?"

Roland mumbled, staring at them through his stoned eyes, "They look like Q Bar matches."

"No, these matches. They're the ones that I gave Lucia before I left. My number's on them," she asserted.

He took another drag, awkwardly meeting Rachel's unforgiving glare.

"Roland," Rachel cut in sharply, like a scalpel. "Did you see Lucia at the end of the night?"

"No," he muttered, too quickly.

Valerie stepped closer and demanded, "Then who gave you these?"

Roland kept his composure with a stoic, blank stare, but his eyes blinked around the edges. He scratched his neck, coughed into his fist, and finally offered, "I don't remember. I probably asked her for a light. Yeah, that must've been it."

* * *

The purr of Alaska's motorcycle broke the usually quiet Christmas morning as she pulled up outside the Joan of Arcade. She dismounted in full bounty hunter mode: a Bowie knife strapped to her outer thigh, a lasso looped and clipped to her other hip, and her mental armor dialed up, then walked toward the building.

On the opposite side of the street, Eris scaled up a fire escape, crouched on a rooftop behind a rusted vent, and muttered to herself, eyes wide and glassy. "I'm not too much. Why'd she say that?" She unstrapped her speaker harness, set it on the vent, raised her battered telescope to her eye, and scanned the skyline. The opposite building came into focus, window by window and frame by frame, until she found Rachel, Valerie, and Roland standing in the living area.

She lowered the scope, trembling with a quiet kind of rage – the kind that burned beneath her skin without light or promise of relief. "I will protect her," she whispered to herself, "from the dark forces of the night."

Eris zeroed in on Alaska, a possible threat, walking up the street, then brought her scope and attention back up to the loft.

* * *

Valerie sat still, her fingers instinctively rubbing the worn pack of matches like a genie coaxing a message from a bottle. Her pupils dilated and her breath shallowed, locking her vision on a place beyond the room:

A flash of cold concrete and copper pipes sweating in the dark.

Lucia's eyes were wide with terror, gagging screams echoing in her throat.

The killer was leaning over her.

The sterile glow of a single dangling bulb.

Valerie's hand trembled, dropping the matches to the floor, and she looked over at Roland, her voice clearer from what she'd seen, and insisted, "Roland... where's Lucia?"

Rachel stepped forward, her voice strained with suspicion. "What did you do?"

Roland scoffed, his calm facade cracking under the surface. "I really don't like your vibes right now. You've been messing with me my whole damn life."

Rachel nervously glanced at Valerie.

"You're the one who let Mia go drinking that night," Roland continued. "You're the reason she lost the baby."

"What in the fuck are you talking about?" Rachel demanded, stunned.

"Our baby was supposed to fix everything. I was gonna be a dad." His voice shook, with grief and bitter venom.

Rachel took a step closer and insisted, "Roland, what did you do?"

Roland's face contorted, "What did I do? Mia's the one who killed herself."

Valerie's voice sliced in, and demanded, "Roland, where's Lucia?" He glared at her but stayed silent, so she stepped forward, with fire in her eyes. "Where is she, Roland?"

Roland's lips curled into a crooked smirk, and he shot back, "Come on, Val. It was just a party. I told her the vodka was in the pantry." His tone darkened considerably. "But our boy Luke had to go open the cellar door instead. Dumbass faggot with tits!"

Rachel cracked and lunged at him, fists pounding against his chest. Roland barely budged, then flung her aside like a paper doll, and she hit the floor with a grunt. Then Roland's body jerked, muscles seizing, his head twitched, and his eyes burned darker.

* * *

From inside his cell, Forest was engrossed in reading the lines

303

of *Metro 2033*, where *Khan*, a philosophical and mysterious figure, offers a blunt summary of humanity's flaws to the protagonist, Artyom: *"You reap what you sow, Artyom. Force answers force, war breeds war, and death only brings death. To break this vicious circle, one must do more than just act without any thought or doubt."* He looked up from his novel and saw in the security monitor that something in the loft was very, very wrong. He shouted, but his face was masked and muzzled. He quickly dropped his book, tugged on his cuff – and was trapped. He pressed the full weight of his back against the cage bars and launched both his legs and feet against the cage door. He kicked once, twice, and on the third kick, the door cracked open. He yanked on his cuff again, clawing his hand tight, trying to squeeze his knuckles through its metal grip.

Nothing but white, numbing pain and the first chafing of blood. He then grabbed the chain with his free hand to see if it would break the cuff or bend the bar by pulling with all his full force. He was caught in a battle between the bar, cuff, and his bleeding knuckles. Sweating and feverish, he looked back up at the security camera to see the fight still ongoing and yanked on the bar again – still unbending, cuffs unbroken, and knuckles still raw and scraped. He squeezed the cuff tighter and began rotating it in a circular sawing motion, cutting into his flesh and drawing blood.

* * *

From the opposite roof, Eris saw Rachel being shoved, lowered her telescope, and her mouth opened in shock; confusion crawled across her face. Her eyes darted left, then right, like she was trying to make sense of a plot that she walked into mid-movie. "Shit," she panted, "shit, shit, shit..." She turned away from the ledge, pacing the rooftop, unsure whether to jump, scream, or fly.

On the street below, Alaska approached the door of Joan of Arcade and rang the buzzer. When there was no answer, she looked over both shoulders, pulled out her knife, slid it along the lock, swung open the door, and stepped inside.

* * *

Back at Roland's house, Sam edged open the side door of the garage, his grip firm on the gun in his holster. He looked around and saw a faint light seeping from beneath the far door, partially hidden by shelves. He glanced over both shoulders, then stepped into the garage, closing the door quietly behind him. His phone vibrated on the seat of the Plymouth. Unanswered. Ama's voice crackled from the dashboard, urgency layered beneath her code. "Sam... where are you? Sam?" Her image glitched, then faded away.

* * *

Alaska stalked down the building's hallway, nearing the door of Valerie's loft. Her phone rang, and she answered without looking. Ama's voice came through, quickly and urgently, declaring, "Roland Donner is the match for Copycat."

Alaska calmly responded, "Ama, how do you know that?"

"Because we matched him with the sketch of the boy, along with Interpol visas to Canada and Italy at the same time as the two murders. Sam's at his house, but he's not answering. He might be in trouble, and I'm going over there now," replied

Ama.

Alaska stopped her cold and insisted, "Ama, stay put. You can not leave The 66."

"Yes, I can," Ama declared and disconnected without another word.

Alaska quickly turned on her heel and headed back the way she came in.

64

The Battles and The Braves

Valerie's breakfast table had become a chessboard battlefield. Rachel's stare burned into Roland, but it was Valerie who made the first move. She quickly reached for a shelf, grabbed a miniature ceramic Santa Claus, and smashed it against his face. The porcelain shattered, and Roland reeled as Rachel picked up a steak knife, lunged, and drove it through his hand. Roland howled and stumbled backward, dragging the blade with him, as Valerie and Rachel ran for the door. Roland looked up, pulled out the knife, ran, and leaped over the couch like a gazelle, grabbing Rachel's wrist before she could unlock the door. Valerie then picked up a fork and stabbed him in the back. He didn't cry out; he just grimaced, yanked, and tossed it and both of them to the floor.

Scrappy, the tabby, rested quietly on her cat perch, observing and waiting.

* * *

Ama paced the compound yard, stopping and starting, then

sat down in a chair to lace up her roller skates. She clicked the circuit, and the heavy compound gate opened, allowing her to roll out into the dusty daylight. From down the alley, a battered old truck clanged as a junk man tossed rusted metal into the back. The side of the truck read:

MANNY'S METAL AND SCRAPS

He looked up at Ama, leered, and called out, "Hey there, sweetie."

As Ama had never been outside of the compound, she replied in a way that was both curious and cordial, "Skibidoo. Who are you, skibidoo?"

"Do you need a lift? I can take you wherever you need to go?" the man whispered.

Ama stopped, scanned the decal on the side of the truck, noticed a pair of robotic legs kicking and flailing from the back of the truck, then looked back at the man. She slowly processed the data. He stepped toward her as if trying to corral a stray cat, and Ama raised her palm, signaling to him to stop. He didn't, so she powered up her processor and let it rip at full volume. "Fuck. Fuck you. Mother fucking fuck!"

It startled both of them, and he backed off. Ama turned and rolled back to the compound, opening and closing the gate behind her. She grabbed a mini-drone from the garage's charging bay, keyed in a command, and launched it into the air, where it buzzed upwards, disappearing over the wall.

* * *

Sam eased open Roland's basement cellar door. Its hinges

squeaked with rusted metal as a damp, earthy stench hit him, filled with mildew, rot, and a putrid smell fermenting below. The stairwell descended into a grim underworld, walls lined with shelves of mason jars, each containing something too grotesque to be called anatomical: fingers, eyes, and maybe a child's ear floating in amber fluid.

He stepped onto the cool cellar floor, heard a muffled groan coming from the back, and cautiously followed it. He peered around a pillar and saw Lucia, strapped to a stained wooden table, bruised, with her eyelids fluttering, and her breath shallow. Blood had dried along her temple in spidering rivulets, her wrists and ankles were bound tight with electrical cable, and duct tape gagged her mouth. "Hang on," Sam shouted, his voice winding tight, as he peeled the tape free and unwound the electrical cable.

Although barely conscious, Lucia gasped, eyes widening in terror. Her gaze shot past him, trying to scream, but croaked out instead, "Bbbeeehind...!"

Sam spun as a shadow appeared and lunged; Yoshima surgically whipped a looped electrical cord toward his neck. He ducked instinctively, the cable slicing through the air, and slammed his shoulder into her midsection, driving her back against a concrete beam with a sickening crack.

Lucia pushed herself off the table and crawled toward the stairs. Behind her, Yoshima staggered upright, almost serene as she assumed a fighting stance toward Sam: legs planted, eyes unblinking and samurai-like.

"Not today!" Sam grunted, glaring at her and matching her stance.

Yoshima moved and kicked first, swiping his leg, and he hit the floor hard, flipped by the sheer precision of her sweep.

She straddled him in an instant, her hands wrapping around his throat, while her expression remained eerily calm. Sam managed to knee her in the ribs, rolling them both into the wall, slammed her head onto the floor, but she barely blinked, kicked him off, and rose like a machine – rebooting herself.

Sam rolled onto his feet and punched her across the jaw. He cringed and grabbed his shattered, broken knuckles. Yoshima tilted her head, slowly, like an animal studying its prey, then smiled and showed him her teeth: extended canines, gleaming ivory with surgical precision, spliced, sharpened, and weaponized. She grabbed a knife off the bench, and it glinted as she slashed downward like a maniacal sushi chef. Sam weaved, but took the blade across his forearm, which gushed blood, causing him to stagger backward, scanning for another escape around Yoshima.

None.

* * *

Valerie rolled and reached for her leather satchel, grabbed a bullwhip, snapped it through the air with a crack, and it coiled around Roland's wrist. She pulled at it, but he pulled harder and yanked her toward him with ease. His hand gripped her throat, squeezing until her legs buckled, and he hurled her across the room. Seeing Valerie in trouble, Scrappy leapt off its cat perch, landed claws on Roland's back, and dragged southward, leaving bloody tracks. Roland screamed but easily tossed that *'little bastard'* aside.

Rachel grabbed her protest poster and plunged toward him, adopting a boxer's stance – one first raised and the other ready to strike with her weaponized poster. She shifted to track Valerie on her flank, who crawled back and reached into her bag again, her fingers finding her cold steel, spiked spindle. Valerie surged forward, stabbing him in the chest and slicing him from his nipple to his navel. He screamed and doubled over, and Rachel seized the moment to drive her knee into his crotch, collapsing him to his knees, and slicing the top of his head with the poster stick.

Roland rolled and rose, yanked the spindle from his chest, bit it in half, and flung it aside. Blood oozed between his fingers, bringing them to his mouth, licking them, then biting down on his lip, hard, blood trailing down his chin. His face shifted, and his skin drained to a pale, almost ashen hue, as his pupils dilated, his joints cracked, and his body contorted, as if something beneath the surface was trying to break free. Rachel grabbed the discarded, bloody knife from the floor and held it in between them, trembling.

* * *

Eris panicked, lowered her telescope, and crouched low on the edge of the building. She spotted a tension cable stretched between rooftops, a makeshift line across the void. She reached for it, tested the tension, and it quivered in her hand. It wasn't built for humans, or even choice, but she gripped it anyway and began her crawl across.

On the street below, Alaska stepped back onto her bike and gunned the engine forward. A glint caught her eye above her, and she looked up to see Eris dangling. The cable whined, the bolts buckled, wrenching from their building anchors. "Shit!" Alaska shouted.

Eris screamed as the line snapped. She swung wildly

through the air, crashing through the Arcade's second-story window in a hail of glass and steel. The window exploded inward, startling Rachel, Valerie, and Roland, while Eris bounced off the shattered window frame and fell to the street below. Roland hesitated just long enough to turn toward the window. Rachel moved first and lunged, but Roland tackled her, and both of them hit the floor. The knife skittered away, clattering under the couch. Valerie scrambled to her feet, face streaked with sweat and blood, but Roland reached the knife first. He picked it up and faced both of them, now trapped.

* * *

Alaska dismounted and sprinted toward the broken body slumped on the concrete street. Eris, her face pale and her lip split, lifted a trembling, broken arm and pointed upward. "Rachel..." she rasped, breath catching in her throat. "Dark forces of the night." Alaska's eyes moved to the shattered window above, adrenaline burning through her veins, and she quickly ran back toward the door of the Joan of Arcade, cracked it open, and leapt up the stairs.

* * *

Lucia crawled out of Roland's garage door, stood up, gasping, the daylight glaring in her eyes like a slap. She paused on the driveway, clutching her ribs, her eyes fixed on Sam's car. She turned and stomped back into the garage, blood in her mouth and revenge fueling her bones. Garden tools lined the walls like surgical instruments. Lucia's eyes scanned the selection: a rake, a shovel, and a hoe, until she spotted the machete. Old, rusted, but solid. She grabbed it, her grip tightening around the worn handle − something older than muscle memory, older than her, settling into her palms as if it had always been there. Her bisabuela's hands in the cane fields. Her abuela's stories on the stoop. Dale, she whispered. And descended back down the cellar steps.

Outside, Ama's drone and her eyes on the scene, hovered silently, its red eye blinking as it slipped through the garage doorway and past Lucia into the cellar below. From the drone's view, Yoshima's blade sliced through the air, catching Sam off guard and slamming him against the damp concrete wall. He dropped to the floor, dazed.

Lucia stepped onto the cellar floor, her scream sliced through the shadows − machete raised. She brought it down across Yoshima's shoulder. Sparks erupted: no blood, just metal, wiring, and the cold shimmer of circuitry.

"What da fuck... " Sam muttered.

"Wepa − a robo-kunt? Oh, hell to the no," Lucia snarled.

Yoshima spun, and Lucia swung again, her blade carving into Yoshima's synthetic skin, sparks cascading across her chest. The android staggered but quickly recovered, back-handing Lucia across the room, who crumbled against a stack of wooden crates.

From her computer screen, Ama watched the chaos and reacted like someone in a fight − rooting, ducking, grimacing, and shadow boxing Rock 'em Sock 'em style. She saw metal claws extend out of Yoshima's hands, reach down, yank the blade from her chest, raise it overhead, and survey the room − hunting for Sam.

"Hey, Frosty!" Sam called out from the shadows, holding up a mason jar filled with floating, milky eyeballs. He smashed the lid against a concrete beam and hurled the jar and its contents at Yoshima. The fluid soaked her as the eyeballs bounced like wet marbles across the floor. Sam struck his Zippo; the flame bloomed, then he tossed the lighter, and it tumbled through the air, as though in slow motion.

Yoshima's eyes tracked the Zippo as it struck her chest and ignited. She let out a mechanical howl as fire devoured her synthetic body. Blinded, she stumbled backward and slammed into shelves filled with jars. They shattered in a chain reaction of flames. POP! POP! POP!

Lucia scrambled to Sam's side, looked at his broken hand, slung his arm around her shoulder, and together, they climbed the stairs and burst through the firestorm. Behind them, the drone caught fire mid-hover, spiraled out of control, and crashed into the flames.

The flames licked the walls of the cellar stairway as Sam and Lucia stumbled through the smoke-filled garage entrance, coughing and leaning on each other. The heat pressed against them and surged them forward. They stopped when they heard a knocking sound echoing from the van parked in the back of the garage. Sam moved first, kicking the latch with a grunt. The back doors creaked open, revealing Nick, bound with twisted cords, his arm mangled, and bruises covering his body. "Jesus," Sam muttered, reaching in and pulling him out. He and Lucia dragged Nick into the yard, as sirens wailed from the distance, blending with the low moan of wind whipping dust across the lawn.

* * *

Back at the Arcade, Roland looked around, his pupils turning into black moons. He chewed his lip raw, blood dripping down his chin. His fingers curled like talons around the knife, pointed the blade at the women, and growled deep in his throat. "Eenie... meenie... miney..."

Bam! The loft door burst open.

Alaska stepped through like an assassin, eyes sharp, ready to pounce, and calmly commanded, "Drop the weapon!" Roland grabbed Rachel by the neck, dragged her in front of him as a human shield, and pressed the blade to her throat. He smiled like a man with nothing to lose.

"I said drop it!" Alaska repeated.

The dungeon door swung open behind them. Forest, still masked, lurched through, tangled in leather, one hand gnawed away and bleeding to the bone. "Stop right there!" Alaska barked, drawing her Bowie like a lightning bolt, ready to strike.

Valerie waved frantically. "Don't. Get down, Forest!" He slowly crouched and kneeled to the ground, bleeding out, but battle-ready..

Roland used the distraction to drag Rachel toward the bedroom door.

"Let her go!" Alaska commanded.

Roland glanced around once more, grinned like a bastard, and smirked, "Pineapple." Then he shoved Rachel toward Alaska, slammed the door behind him, and jammed a dresser against it. He rushed to the window, kicked it open, and jumped onto the fire escape.

Alaska burst through the door, sprinted to the open window, caught a glimpse of Roland as he hit the bottom rung, leaped, and landed on the pavement. She pulled her lasso but had no room to spring it, so instead she leapt onto the fire escape and descended, while Roland bolted down the alley.

Eris limped around the corner with a bruised face and blood-stained SKK cape, spotting Roland. She paused to steady herself before pulling a sharp Japanese Shuriken from her hip pouch and throwing it. A scream tore from Roland's mouth. "Fucken A!" He stopped, staring at the shuriken sticking out of his ass like a dart.

"Banzai!" Eris howled.

Roland yanked the shuriken free and threw it back. It struck Eris in the chest, and she gasped, falling like a marionette with cut strings. Alaska ran past her, eyes locked on Roland, who ripped a nearby rider off his motorcycle, tossed him aside, hopped on, and rode away. Alaska launched her Bowie knife end over end; it landed in the spokes, and they kicked it back out. Then she slung her lasso, which landed over his head and around his chest with a snap. Roland wobbled but stayed upright, dragging Alaska along the ground for half a block before she let go. Roland regained control of his bike after Alaska's weight at the end of the rope was released, flung loose from his shoulder, and he careened forward down the street.

Alaska ran back and mounted her bike one-handed, her com unit flaring. "I'm on Donner," she instructed Ama. "Track me, and send an ambulance to my location." Alaska tore after Donner, and behind her, Rachel dropped to her knees beside Eris, who gasped through blood-soaked lips. She held her close, surrounded by a rising and swirling dust bowl that howled above and around them.

* * *

Sam left Lucia and Nick on the lawn, hurried to his car, and opened the door. Before slipping inside, he turned to Lucia, who stood firm with Nick in front of the now-burning house. "Hey, Big Sister," he shouted, a grin spreading across his face, and gave a thumbs-up in appreciation.

Lucia nodded as Sam climbed in and floored it in reverse. Ama's face appeared on the dashboard monitor, slightly distorted by the comms interference. "Alaska's in pursuit of Roland Donner, sending coordinates," she dictated, urgently. The car's tires screeched against the concrete as Sam ripped through the oncoming dust shower and down the street.

65

The Lighthouse

Alaska tore through the choking city streets on her motorcycle, her eyes locked ahead, tracking Roland. Her engine screamed past a pair of robot construction workers who dove out of her way as she hit a plank, angled off a dump truck, and launched into the air. She landed hard, parallel with Roland's motorcycle, its sleek frame flashing in and out of the dust like a silver ghost. He veered left down a side street, past an empty market. Alaska stayed close on his trail, ducking low to avoid the empty fruit carts and swirling past the street debris. A delivery bot truck suddenly appeared out of nowhere, and she swerved, skidding into an alley, then widened her turn to reconnect. She caught sight of him again as he exited the city limits, a gray blur carving a path forward, and Alaska shifted gears, following him at full throttle.

Alaska pursued him through the barren, open fields, tracking him to a lake and the city's only remaining reservoir, which was sealed off by 16-foot electric fences and patrolled by security bots. She rolled up to the slightly open gate, passed through, and saw the head of a robot lying next to its mechanical body, tucked behind the guard booth. She followed a trail of blood to the water's edge and came across Roland's motorcycle flipped on its side at the base of a decommissioned lighthouse.

Alaska rolled up, dismounted, drew the crossbow from her saddle bag, and moved quickly, following drops of blood up the spiraling, lighthouse staircase.

The lighthouse terrace was initially empty, dust swirling across the concrete as she stepped into the open with her crossbow raised. She surveyed possible exits or hiding spots, then turned to see Roland emerging from behind the tower. His face was gaunt and pale, looking like a hollow man barely wearing his skin.

"Roland Donner," Alaska demanded firmly, aiming steadily. "Hands where I can see them."

He stepped forward without blinking. "Go ahead," he insisted, "you'd be doing me a solid."

"I know what happened at St. Mary's," she asserted, with a calm, firm voice.

"You don't know shit." His voice cracked.

"I know about Di Segni and the rings," Alaska replied, holding his gaze.

Roland took a step closer. "They all took turns, and now it's mine."

Alaska raised her crossbow, her finger brushing the trigger. "Stand down," she warned.

Roland's voice twisted and cried out, "I made them pay for what they did to me, to Diego, and the others," then lunged toward Alaska.

Thwunk! The arrow burrowed deep in his shoulder. He staggered, but didn't fall. Roland's bones cracked, and his hollow and empty rib cage elongated. His jaw split, fangs pushing through. Claws erupted from his fingertips as his eyes turned black and bottomless.

Thwunk! Another arrow hit him in the gut.

He grinned, bloody and broken, and bit off a piece of his lip.

Alaska raised her voice, cold steel. "I said stand down." She reloaded a pre-dipped arrow and lit it.

Roland rose, monstrous now, charging in full-Wetiko mode.

Thwunk! The flaming bolt struck his heart, and Roland shrieked, fell backwards, then tumbled over the edge of the lighthouse, limbs flailing like broken branches.

Alaska carefully moved to the edge, looked down, and saw his crumbled corpse lying motionless. She let out a sound that resembled relief and gazed out over the lake.

A scratching noise came from the base of the lighthouse, causing her to look down and see a pale, emaciated creature: hairless, fanged, and clawed — rising silently along the side of the lighthouse. Its black eyes locked onto hers, hovered for a moment, then slipped past her like a wisp of smoke and disappeared under the lighthouse tower door.

Alaska quickly followed, pulled the locked wooden door, and raised her boot to kick it open. Then she slowly crept up the old spiral staircase. She heard another scratching sound coming from the top of the stairs. She paused, raised her crossbow, then climbed again. As she neared the top, she heard a child sobbing. She then turned the final step, and there, huddled in the corner, was Alaska's younger self. "Mommy shouldn't hurt like that," the girl whispered. "I'm scared. Why won't Daddy come back? Doesn't he love us?"

Alaska froze and slowly lowered her weapon.

"Please hold me," the child begged.

Alaska crouched down, opened her arms, and moved toward her. But as she neared, the image of her younger self flickered and became distorted. Her grandmother Kokum's voice echoed in her head. *"It will try to trick you... play on any unhealed pain. You must fight from your scar, not your wound."* Alaska stopped and stepped back, shaking. Her vision blurred. She fumbled for her pills in her pocket, but she remembered she had left them at the cabin, and froze in panic. She heard Kokum's voice again. *"Our ancestors will help you."*

Alaska closed her eyes and sang the children's bear song softly into the dark:

Maskwa, maskwa, tânispî?

(Bear, bear, how are you?)

Maskwa, maskwa, sipâ kîya

(Bear, bear, you are strong)

Maskwa, maskwa, miyowâsin!

(Bear, bear, it's good!)

Hây hây hây Kisakihitinân Maskwa

(Hey, hey, hey, we love you, bear)

As she sang, her spirit lifted and left her body. From above, she watched the child transform into the Wetiko, its eyes widening, its form recoiling, then launching towards the lighthouse window. Alaska's spirit chased after it, grabbing its leg, and they tumbled down the roof, crashing into the lake below with a splash.

Beneath the water, the battle raged. The Wetiko clawed, bit, and dragged Alaska into the depths, slicing and bleeding her Light as they cascaded further to the bottom.

Kokum's voice echoed once more in her heart. *"Become all of who you are."*

Alaska expanded and transformed into a massive and powerful Bear Spirit. She roared, lifted the Wetiko, and smashed it against a wall of rocks. The Wetiko stabilized, mutated, and multiplied. Everywhere Alaska looked, another Weitko charged at her, biting, chewing, and clawing at her Bear Light. There must have been ten thousand Wetikos, wearing masks from across all the human bloodlines and timelines, attacking her nonstop. Masks of envy, jealousy, cruelty, betrayal, greed, scarcity, doubt, deception, unprocessed pain and trauma, helplessness, despair, control, hatred, and vengeance: all mixing and shapeshifting into chaotic, distorted, and fragmented human forms.

Monstrous claws and fangs sliced her throat, pinning her Bear Spirit against the jagged lakebed – feeding, cannibaliz-ing, and devouring her weakening Light.

Her Bear Spirit could neither see nor sense her way in the dark. The darkness was everywhere, and it was nipping, siphoning, and swallowing her life-force. She cried out, "Help me. Help my *Senua* and *Ashitaka*. Abacus, Ama. Help me Maskwa, help me Mom and Dad, help me ancestors, help me Kokum and Moshum. Help me trees, help me whale people, help me wind and fire, help me Mother Earth."

She felt their presence. All she could see and sense was silence, death, and stagnation – hers and everything else's.

On her last breath of Light, her Bear Spirit heard a whistling sound coming from the water. She couldn't tell if it was coming from above, below, or behind her. The sound grew louder, and she could make out a song composed of clicks and whistles. It wasn't from her ancestors, but it was familiar. As the sound grew louder, a pink light began to drift in a wide area around her. She could now see the shapes and sizes of the Wetiko, and their millions of layered masks, which had been closing in on and consuming her. The pink light spiraled around her, getting closer and closer, corralling and drawing all the masks of the Wetiko back into the center, forming a shrinking, unified entity.

As the dark entity shrank, her Bear Light stabilized and grew stronger.

And as her Bear Light grew and expanded, the Weitko again shrank smaller and smaller, revealing itself for what it was behind all its masks – fear and the illusion of fear, separation and the illusion of separation.

Alaska's Bear Spirit Light reached out and grabbed the Wetiko with her claws, opened her jaws wide, and swallowed the Wetiko whole.

From the surrounding water, she could see familiar spirit faces. They were the faces of the South American Indigenous friends of Gemini who appeared at her funeral, singing *Waco-maya*, the healing water song by *Yawanawa Saiti Kaya*.

As they sang, a bubble slowly emerged from her Bear Spirits' mouth, then another, and then another one – each filled with all the colors of rainbow fractals spanning from the deepest darkness to the brightest Light. The bubbles floated outward, filling the water in every direction, bubbling up from her mouth. Inside each bubble were children of the new Earth.

From around her Bear Spirit, the pink light retracted its spiral into a single shape resembling a pink dolphin. It turned and swam away, dissolving into the water along with the full spectrum of the rainbow that now permeated the water. As it did, Alaska's Bear Spirit glowed brighter and grew larger, transforming into the rainbow bubble itself, and floated upward.

Above her, Sam drove up in front of the lighthouse, got out, saw Roland's body crumpled on the rocks, and ran into the lighthouse. He quickly went up the stairs, scouted the empty platform, saw the open door to the tower, and hurried to the top, where he saw Alaska's limp body. He moved swiftly to cradle her. "Hang in there, baby," he cried desperately.

From above the water, Sam's voice called out, "Alaska! Alaska!"

Her Bear Spirit pivoted, transformed again, and Alaska's spirit emerged whole, floating and swimming upward. Her body gasped on the tower floor, as her spirit merged back into her bones, she opened her eyes, and whispered, "It... it was real. pink light." Sam nodded, held her tighter, and looked out the open lighthouse window where the wind had stilled, and the dust had settled — for the first time in a long, long time, a silent rain fell clean and clear.

66

The Easy Riders

Ama sat in her back room, watching her screen. Easy Rider flickered across the TV. And Captain America leaned and asked George, "You got a helmet?"

Ama nodded solemnly.

George responded, "Oh! Oh, I got a helmet. I got a beauty."

Alaska strapped the last bag onto her bike and called out from the yard, "Ama! You coming or what?" Ama heard her, but kept her attention on her movie.

Sam stepped out of the garage, his hand wrapped in a cast, walked across the yard slowly and thoughtfully, carrying a small gift-wrapped box that he had pulled from under the tree. He handed it to Alaska, saying, "You forgot something, kiddo."

Alaska tilted her head. "What's this?" She unwrapped it to reveal her mother's beaded bear pendant, edges dulled with time. "Mom's," she sighed.

Sam nodded, eyes damp, and reminisced, "She wore it beautifully. I was going to wait until your day to give it to you. But, I don't have time for time anymore."

Alaska slipped it around her neck, hands trembling. She then took hold of her dad's bandaged hand in her palm and gently rubbed it with her thumb. They simply looked at each other for the longest time. Sam smiled and asked, "You got your pills?"

She shook her head. "Not gonna need 'em. Or this." She released his hand, pulled the old deputy badge from her belt, and placed it in his good hand.

Sam shrugged. "If you say so." His voice cracked, and he recovered with, "I transferred your money to your account, and your travel passes, registration, licenses, and ID chips are on record. You'll call me from the road?"

"Of course," Alaska assured.

Ama stepped out wearing her Easy Rider jacket and a patchwork of rebellion. Alaska eyed her intently. "You ready?"

Ama lit up. "Really? I get to go?"

"You got a helmet?" asked Alaska.

Ama grinned and held up her vintage football helmet. "Oh! Oh, I got a helmet. I got a beauty, and my playlist," pointing to the hard drive buried into her hip. She glanced at Sam. "You coming too, skibidoo?"

Sam chuckled, "Nah. I've got a few things to handle."

Ama bowed dramatically and declared, "You shall be missed."

He smiled back. "You too, dude."

Sam watched as they rolled through the gate and out of the compound, while Ama played *Passenger by Iggy Pop* from her chest speaker.

Sam wasn't exactly sure where they were headed; all he knew was that his daughter was safe, and Ama was finally getting her wish to leave the compound and see America, and maybe even become an American someday.

67

The Files

Sam slowly drove along Roland's street and parked along the curb, down the block from his driveway. A few police cruisers, forensic vans, and drones hovered above. Crews milled about, coming in and out of the garage and through the front door. Sam got out of his car, walked up the street, and approached the two security bots. They scanned him and flashed 'access denied.' Sam contemplated which one to kneecap first, but before he could do anything he would regret, Carly stepped out of the garage and called out, "He's with me." The bots turned to the Captain, then back to Sam and signaled him through. He walked past the deflated Santa Claus and Reindeer motors that had seized in the dust, and past printing machines, computers, and cabinets, arranged on tarps on the driveway.

He passed and nodded to the crew carrying boxes and carts filled with melted masks, broken bottles, body parts, IDs, costumes, weapons, knives, a machete, rope, cassettes, burner phones, bottles of chloroform, and a half-melted 'robo kunt.' One of the rookies whispered, "Hey General," as he passed, unsure whether he was allowed to call him that or

328

even talk to him. Sam nodded to them and greeted Carly, who waved him into the garage.

Carly guided him over to a table, pointing out the partially melted Roach mask. "He copied Taco." Sam half-huffed, shook his head, but didn't say anything else.

Carly picked up and opened some paper folders – revealing files, plans, maps, photographs, and newspaper clippings inside. "It looks like our Copy Cat was the one who strung up Brother Di Segni. My guess is it was his first kill. Maybe some sort of a sacrifice." Carly pointed to a smoke-covered bottle. "This is the only one that we found that was still intact. Word on the street is you were looking for it. I don't know why, but it's yours if you want it."

Sam picked it up, smudged the layer of smoke off the bottle, and saw what looked like a floating breast soaking in formaldehyde, and whispered, "Speck."

Carly nodded. "Also, I can't be certain, but I'm pretty sure our Copy Cat took out Keppler."

Sam was still examining the bottle. "What makes you say that?"

Carly ducked his head outside the garage to check for surveillance drones, turned back, reached into his jacket pocket, and pulled out an envelope. "Keppler sent these to him a while back, maybe as some kind of insurance policy for himself or both of them. Copy Cat was, if anything, a master of tying up loose ends and not leaving a trail."

He handed the envelope to Sam, who opened it, peeled through the contents, which included photographs and a flash drive, and stared at them for a moment. "Is this who I think it is?"

Carly nodded his head.

Sam kept flipping through the contents. "How do you know if they're not fake?"

Carl pulled out his phone and showed him the screen. "It's unmistakable. The paper stock matches the time frame, and the metadata checks out on the flash drive."

"Where did you find this?" Sam asked.

Carly shrugged. "In the cellar. It's as creepy as Krueger down there. One of the guys said he saw a pinkish light shining in the crawl space. He followed it in and found the envelope tucked above one of the beams. As soon as he pulled it out, everything went pitch black. He scrambled and ran out, and has refused to go back in."

Sam closed the envelope. "What does this have to do with me?"

Carly looked down at the ground, reaching for his words. "You know, when I used to be able to go fly fishing before everything went to shit; you cast for weeks and sometimes you'd catch something, but most of the time you don't. Sometimes you pull one in, but you've got to let go because it's not big enough, even though there's no guarantee you'll ever catch another one. And sometimes, whether through patience or providence, that river delivers one that is beyond your dreams. You might set the hook, but it's still a crap shoot to get it in the net." He looked up at Sam.

Sam glanced around the garage, then back at Carly, "What if there's a bigger fish?"

"There's always a bigger fish, but there's not always a bigger net," Carly quietly replied.

Sam tucked the envelope in his pocket, grabbed the bottle, turned, and walked out of the garage.

Carly called out, "Hey, General."

Sam stopped and turned around. Carly pulled his hand out of his pocket and threw Sam's Zippo through the air. "Happy New Year!"

Sam caught it, smiled, and clicked it. Damaged, broken, burnt, but still offered up a flame.

* * *

Sam sat in the booth opposite Rachel at the back of the Broken Arrow cafe. Between them sat an in-house laptop. Rachel pulled the flash drive out and handed it back to Sam, who said, "Are you sure this can't be traced?"

Rachel smiled. "It's been scrubbed clean. Nobody's tracked back here."

Sam scanned the Broken Arrow cafe again, then nodded to Rachel, who pressed send.

68

The Outlaws

Valerie sat at the kitchen table at the Joan of Arcade, drinking her morning coffee across from Forest, who was looking bomb in a freshly pressed suit. He flexed his new robotic hand, which wa**s shiny and new,** and he examined its clever design. "You know it was Udo Kier, the renowned Germa**n actor, who onc**e said, *'People never understand what friendship is. I'll tell you what a friendship is to me. Friendship to me is, if my friends need my little finger to live, I'm going to have it cut off. I'm going to the hospital, they cut off my finger, and maybe I have a gold finger instead, and I become famous. But I still give it to my friend.'"*

Valerie smiled and slid a passport across the table.

Forest opened them and said, "Demetri Yuri, I like that name. I still don't know how you managed to get me new papers, an identity, and a passage on a cargo ship?"

Valerie grinned. "I have friends in high and low places, in all the places."

Forest smiled back and replied, "You know I don't want to go, but my mother is kinda losing her memory, and my father, well, he's getting on in age."

Valerie nodded and slid an open laptop across the table. He looked at the screen and said, "This is too much, I can't accept this money."

Valerie held up her hand and pointed around the room. "Nonsense. You helped me build all this from scratch."

Forest looked out the window and recounted, "*Doctor Zhivago by Boris Pasternak* is an epic tale about the effects of the Russian Revolution of 1917 and its aftermath on a bourgeois family. In the novel, Dr. Zhivago offers a compelling perspective on what deserves true loyalty when he says, *"How many things in the world deserve our loyalty? Very few indeed. I think one should be loyal to immortality, which is another word for life, a stronger word for it."*

Valerie smiled and thought about how she would miss him and all the Russian tales he would entertain and amuse her with. Forest turned back from the window, closed the computer, and placed it, along with his passport and cargo pass, in his briefcase. The loft buzzer rang. They looked toward the door, then back at each other, and grinned.

Sam stood on the street, and Forest opened the door for him. Sam looked him up and down, and at his new robotic hand. Forest nodded, then glanced at his bandaged hand. They considered a handshake, but given the circumstances, let it slide as Sam passed him and stepped inside. Forest looked down the street, hailed a robo cab, got in, and drove away — heading back to his homeland.

* * *

Valerie opened the loft door and beamed as she let Sam in, who immediately handed her a brown paper bag. She looked inside and pulled out a mason jar and its other breast belonging to Speck. She stared at it and melted. Taped to the jar was an envelope; she opened it and saw a plane ticket. "Tahiti?" she whispered, her eyes glassy. "Why are we going through Toronto?"

Sam replied, "I can get us out of here through a back way."

Valerie reached over to cup his cheek. For a moment, their world softened, right as rain. Sam quietly clicked the Zippo open and shut in his pocket, signaling – here we go, again. He looked down at her packed bags. "Are you all set?"

"Yes, just a sec." She walked over to the bar, placed the Speck bottle next to the other one, lit a stick of incense, and offered a silent prayer.

69

The Livestream 2.0

Love & Revolution – Cinnamon Version by Seun Kuti, a pulsing new theme song from Rachel's livestream, faded as she leaned into her microphone, her voice smooth yet sharp. "It's great to have Lucia Sky back on Mischief. Today, we're talking about dating and finding love in these ever-changing times. To help give it a vibe, we'll be playing some music, and we've cracked open a bottle of red while we spill the tea.

Lucia grinned and spoke into her mic. "Thanks for having me back."

"Your dating style has always inspired me. Got any hot tips, takes, or tea?" inquired Rachel.

Lucia smiled, "Here's one. Just because something is covered in syrup doesn't mean it's a pancake, waffle, or sundae. I've also always wondered? Does life smoke a cigarette after it screws you, or does it just sneak out the back door in the morning?"

Rachel cackled.

Lucia went on, "I've dated men and women, before and after I became myself. Want to know which is easier?"

* * *

On a random city street, Eris zipped by on her wheelboard, with a cast on her leg and an arm, a new red cape flowing behind her, marked with the name BANZAI. Earbuds in, listening intently to the livestream.

"Which?" asked Rachel.

Lucia spoke in a slow, sassy voice. "Bubble baths, pinot, candles, and underwater vibrators are all easier. But if it's love you want, sometimes ya gotta get out of the tub, dry yourself off, and get at 'em."

Eris smiled, raised her fist, mouthed the word "Banzai," and sped off down the street.

* * *

Nick drove the band's van with his arm propped in an 'L' cast on the van's windowsill, listening to the livestream on the speaker. Rachel chimed in, "Everyone seems to be looking for the one. How do you know if you've found the one, one?

Lucia responded, "That's the hundred-thousand-dollar question, but I would say just find someone who's fifty-one percent good and compatible, and go with that."

Rachel leaned forward. "Why fifty-one percent?"

Lucia continued, "If you're looking for perfection, just get a pet, plant, or stare at an algorithm and its shiny objects, but if you are looking to bond with an actual blood and guts, finite, fallible, and imperfect human being, then just follow Route 51, and see where it takes you from there."

Rachel added quietly, "A human being. Ugh, oh yeah, those things."

Nick grinned ear to ear, knowing he was answering the call of the wild and his renewed dream. Diego tapped the dashboard in rhythm beside him, his Packers jersey half-buttoned up, and Bassey lounged in the back, smoke curling from another, newly lit jay. The bumper speaker on the back of the van read:

DON'T GIVE UP YOUR DAYDREAMS

* * *

Mischief played on his dashboard monitor as Sam drove his Plymouth along the back roads, one hand on the steering wheel and the other nursing his cup of coffee with his ban-daged, knuckle-broken hand. Valerie snuggled in close, her arm wrapped around his shoulder, and a smile beaming across her lips.

Rachel suggested, "I know my French ancestors would call me a traitor for this, but sometimes I just don't know if love is worth it. Ya feel?"

Lucia's voice came through clearly on his speaker. "Love can be hard, but it is always, always worth it, chérie. The truth of life is that love and humans can get messy – people can heartbreak, whether through dispute, ditching, divorce, or death." She paused, then added: "Sex is cool and all, but there's nothing quite like fucking the system."

* * *

Back in the livestream booth, Lucia opened Gemini's book to a dog-eared page. "Gemini quoted Elizabeth Kubler-Ross

337

in her book, which I think slays. It says here, *"The reality is that you will grieve forever. You will not 'get over' the loss of a loved one; you will learn to live with it. You will heal, and you will rebuild yourself around the loss you have suffered. You will be whole again, but you will never be the same. Nor should you be the same, nor would you want to.'"*

Rachel took a sip of her wine and leaned into her mic. "Ah, Gemini. I can't even. Let's dedicate the first song to Gem. It's called *Pink Moon by Nick Drake.* Enjoy!"

As if summoning her spirit, Gemini Moon appeared and shimmered near Rachel and Lucia in the corner of the living room. They saw her clearly and smiled at Gemini, at he, she, they, we, Moon, Pink, C7 Major, Boto, Amor, or Starfish. Gemini smiled back, shimmered for a few moments, then turned into a pink dolphin spirit and swam out the window, leaving a trail of pink light, joy, and mystery in her wake. Rachel and Lucia stood up, walked to the window, and watched her swim out of the city in slow, circular motions, losing sight of her in the light of the sun. They smiled at Gemini, then at each other.

Rachel and Lucia sat back in their chairs, topped up their wine glasses, and cracked open another bottle as they bantered back and forth, uncovering and dissecting some common-sense secrets of love and dating in these changing times, interspersed with a selection of music. *Painted Silhouettes by Quantic, Doo Wop (That Thing) by Ms. Lauryn Hill, No Diggity by Blackstreet, Dr. Dre, Turn Your Lights Down Low by Bob Marley & The Wailers, All of You by Billie Holiday & Cole Porter, Dance With Me by Nouvelle Vague, Je Veux by Zaz, Time On her Side by Future Islands, We Are The People by Empire Of The Sun, Young Folks by Peter Bjorn, and Somewhere*

Else by Federico Aubele.

70

The Bear Ancestors

Sam never did get a call from Alaska on her road trip, but he was happy to receive some texts with photos attached. He also got a few old-fashioned postcards, which nobody seems to send or receive anymore. Although it took him some time to figure out how to use the printer, he printed the text images and pinned them next to the postcards on the wall of their Tahitian cabin, since he liked to see everything out in front of him.

• Pictures of one or both of them beside trees, rivers, dogs, cats, older adults, children, trucks, and other robots they met along the way.

• A photo of Ama sitting at Kokum's kitchen table with the caption: Ama loves Grandma's home.

• Photos of the two of them together at Pipestone Quarry.

• Another text of theirs at an inter-tribal Powwow dance. "Ama got me to dance." :)

• One of them standing proud at the Adena-Serpent Mound in Ohio.

• Multiple pictures and captions of them at various Phillips

66 Gas stations, along with notes like, "Ama wanted to see who was home," and "Ama likes our home better."

· One on a fairy boat in front of the Statue of Liberty, with Ama holding up a pretend torch, and a new Turtle Island passport Alaska had made for her. Alaska even mentioned that she gave her a one-on-one citizenship test to be granted citizenship to Turtle Island and America, where she aced the exam that included the history of the people and the land she was living with, within, and a part of.

· There was another photo with a note attached, showing the two of them alone on a bridge in Selma, which said, "I told Ama that Coretta and Martin couldn't make it, but she wanted to march anyway."

· There were other pictures of them visiting zoos, parks, nightclubs, and sitting in fancy cafes. The last one was of them throwing beads on Bourbon Street, during Mardi Gras, with a note that said, "Ama's learning French, wants to be called Mustang Sidecar Sally from here on," and "Heading back to the cabin for a break before heading westward. LOVE YA POPS, Alaska and Sally."

Sam mainly avoided the news and turned off the technology. A few weeks later, a small envelope arrived in the post – no return address, just a Museum of Modern Murder stamp in the corner. Inside were two newspaper clippings: one about the White House Press Secretary denying the legitimacy of images of the President in compromising positions with minors, and another reporting the President had suffered a cardiac event and was on sabbatical in critical condition. On the back of the second clipping, in Dustin's unmistakable handwriting:

"How many humans does it take to screw in a light bulb? One – he holds it up and expects the planet to revolve around him."

Sam read it twice, chuckled, and clicked the Zippo once. He pinned it on the wall next to Alaska's postcards.

* * *

Alaska carved along a ribbon of open road, the engine's growl humming to music requests from Ama's road trip playlist, because she was feeling all the freedom feels: *Green Onions by Booker T. & the M.G.s, De Camino a La Vereda by Buena Vista Social Club, Beautiful People by SuperHeavy, Everyday People by Sly & THe Family Stone, On & On by Erykah Badu, Freedom by Waldeck, Joy Malcolm, Flying High by Slackwax, Colors by Black Pumas, Follow The Rainbow by Clinton Fearon, 7 Seconds by Youssou N'Dour, Ma Mama by Gerald Toto, Ventura Highway by America, Take Me Home, Country Road by John Denver, NDN KARS– Remix by The Halluci Nation,Road Drum by Mozart Gabriel, Cree Healing Song 1 by Cecile Moosomin, Peyote Healing by Robbie Robertson, Verdell Primeaux, Johnny Mike, Stand Up(From Harriet) by Cynthia Erivo, Universo de Amor by Herbert Quinteros, Bohr by Balquis, El Cielo by Radio Citizen & Bajika, El Mundo Llora by Green Valley, Spirit Bird by Xavier Rudd, My Silver Lining by First Aid Kit, Ride by Lana Del Re, Wild In The Streets by Garland Jeffery,* and *Send Me On My Way by Rusted Root.*

Ama, or 'Mustang Sidecar Sally,' tapped the seat to the rhythm of the music, wearing her old-fashioned football helmet painted with stars and stripes, and an American flag and Turtle Island cape flapping in the breeze. She looked to her right and could have sworn that she and Alaska passed three riders: Billy, George, and Captain America – *los tres bandidos de Easy Rider.* Sally waved as they passed because maybe they were there, and maybe they weren't.

Alaska's motorcycle rolled beside the river, down the dirt road, and pulled up to the cabin, and dismounted. Sally immediately jumped out, looked around, and ran-wobbled toward the edge of the lake, where she picked up a flat stone and skipped it over the water, joy-lights sparking in her eyes.

Alaska watched her for a while, then unpacked her bags and dropped them in the cabin. She stepped back outside, wandered into the meadow, placed a tobacco offering on the ground, and gathered wildflowers. From the treeline, a massive mama bear crossed with two cubs. The bear stood, met Alaska's gaze, then lowered itself, turning into the woods without showing fear. Alaska smiled, walked back toward the cabin, gathering wood along the way.

Alaska re-entered the cabin, placed the wood in the fire-place, lit it, peeled the crime scene photos off the walls, and tossed them in. Smoke curled up the chimney like an exorcism. She contemplated the moment, but not any longer, preferring that the fire take care of the rest. On the empty wall, she hung a framed photo: a younger version of herself nestled between her parents. Beneath it, she placed a vase with wildflowers from the meadow, then walked over, sat down at the kitchen table, and made herself a cup of coffee. She asked Abacus to play *My Mother's Mother by Sara Diamond*, looked outside the window in wonder when she saw Sally dancing under the open sky, then falling, getting back up, and Alaska thought that Sally was maybe even dreaming.

Alaska took another sip of her coffee and observed her fingers grow and extend into bear claws. She studied them, knowing that they were now part of her. She rubbed her thumbs across them, and as she did, her claws shifted through different colors of the rainbow. She instinctively dragged them beneath her chin, down her throat, carving five lines into her flesh and blood – an etched tattoo representing her own Cree markings of initiation, medicine, and ancestors. Blood and all.

As quickly as her rainbow claws appeared, they retreated into her fingers.

Then Alaska looked out the window again and saw her mother and ancestors appearing as bear-shaped spirits dancing over the lake, while the Children's Bear Spirit song whispered in the breeze.

Alaska smiled.

She

was

home.

Hiraeth.

71

The Epilogue

And what about our friend, Gemini Moon? Whatever became of he, she, they, we, Moon, Pink, C7 Major, Boto, Amor, or Starfish?

It has been told by those who speak of such things that in the murky depths of the Amazon and Orinoco River basins, where ancient trees whisper secrets to rushing waters, a familiar pink glow has returned home. Gemini Moon's spirit, transformed into the ethereal dolphin that briefly appeared in the northern waters of Turtle Island, has found her way back to the vast network of Amazonian currents found throughout much of the Amazon and Orinoco river basins in Bolivia, Brazil, Colombia, Ecuador, Guyana, Peru, and Venezuela, where her kind have swum for thousands of years. A place filled with stories where boto shamans journey between different tribal territories, carrying messages and sacred objects, attending inter-tribal gatherings, and sharing knowledge of river navigation, fishing techniques, plant medicines, and seasonal changes.

A place where boto spirits, at the request of the beautiful

Amazon river and forests, transform into 'blue-skinned' dolphin-humans. These beings can travel vast distances overnight, moving through both aquatic and terrestrial realms to connect to distant communities, and appear during meaningful ceremonial exchanges as initiators and protectors.

Gemini's rose-colored essence now shimmers alongside the legendary boto pink dolphins of the Rio Negro and Rio Solimões, her presence adding a new voice to their ancient chorus of clicks, whistles, and songs that carry the wisdom of both forest and of the chocolate-brown waters.

To this day, the Indigenous communities along the Amazonian riverbanks speak in hushed, reverent tones of the new arrival — a pink dolphin whose spirit carries the memory of distant struggles and hard-won victories. They call her Luna de Gemela, Lua Gêmea, Killa Mellizo, or Jasy Joaju, but to name a few of their names in the hundreds of Indigenous languages spoken throughout the Amazon.

Unlike her companions who have always known only the Amazon's embrace, they say Gemini Moon speaks of stamped passports, of concrete cities and dust storms, of eclectic music and beats like *Heroes by David Bowie*, of protests and art, of revolution and rebellion, of fallen governments and fallen Presidents, of northern ancient knowledge and modern science, of robots and digital screens, of friends and family, of clients and teachers, of trauma and healing, of her besties Rachel and Lucia, of Alaska — her initiated rainbow bear spirit sister, of a world where water is not always seen as sacred and voices are not always heard.

To this day, medicine people, shamans, chamans, Pajés, and curandero/as, recognize Gemini with her white top hat, as a weaving rainbow bridge-spirit: one who bears the pain and hope of multiple worlds, teaching both humans and dolphins, the eagle and the condor, the South and the North, the East and the West, Heaven and Earth, that healing can flow from the most unexpected sources.

They say her clicks sound different from the others — more urgent, more purposeful, as if she still carries the revolutionary fire that once burned in her human heart. They say that when children fall ill in the riverside villages, their mothers now leave offerings of traditional flowers, children's drawings and toys, and sometimes even small pieces of electronic wire and devices at the water's edge, somehow understanding that this particular encantado/a responds to the prayers of both the modern world and the ancient ones.

These days, Gemini Moon appears to wayward travelers not only as a guide back to safety, but as a reminder that identity itself is as fluid as the rivers she now calls home — that transformation is not death but evolution, and that some spirits are too vast and necessary to be contained by a single form, culture, tradition, or lifetime. In the eternal rhythm of the Amazon and Mother Earth, where magic and reality dance together in perpetual twilight, where all life co-creates a symphonic and relentless chorus, Gemini Moon has found her truest home: not just as human or dolphin, but as pure spirit, forever swimming between worlds, singing the songs and inspiring the dreams of those who refuse to be silent or silenced.

And so today, the everywhere, everyday people gather and sing songs from or inspired by the Amazon and South America, such as *Dautibiua by Amazon Ensemble, I Will Purify by Ayahuasca Icaros, Pink Dolphins by Bird Tribe &Deva Runa,*

Aldeia Samaúma – Tsoî Hêpîti Kito Kito Tarifa by Aliança Noke Koî, De Ushuaia a La Quiaca by Gustavo Santaolalla, Cuñaq by Curawaka, Cuatro

Vientos by Danit, Lunita J.Pool Remix by J. Pool, Danit, Agua de estrellas by Orka, Amanecer Andino by Grupo Aymara, Oso Blanco by Freedom Café, Manuel Villaescusa, Norbi Pan, Amin Varkonyi, Koka Kintucha by Manuelcha Prado, Carnaval de Tambobamba by Jaime Guardia, Tonguere by Iskukua, Onde o Jaguar Espreita by Advan Haschi, Bambeo Koyo Granda by Bonobo &Innov Gnawa, Ayahuasca by NTO, Agüita Del Equilibrio by Alejandro y Maria Laura, Icaro For Wisdom And Love by Shipibo Shamans, Herlinda Augustin Fernandez.

And on, and on, and on.

THE END

72

The Music Playlist

Here are all the songs that are in italics in the novel, listed in order from beginning to end.

Qobuz Playlist

Maskwa Novel

Spotify Playlist

Qobuz Maskwa Playlist
  Maskwa Novel
  Spotify Maskwa Playlist

Currently, all 167 songs are available on Spotify and 156 on Qobuz.

Also, feel free to stream the tracks in the playlist below on your preferred platform.

More songs will appear in future editions, and/or check back on www.Divergencies.com

Rise Up by The Parachute Club is only available on YouTube.

The Children Bear song is fictitious. The author encourages you to hear your own version, create a children's bear song of your own in any language, dialect, rhythm, or tune. And sing and share it with children, others, or your own inner child. Additionally, the author encourages readers to create and sing children's songs about various aspects of nature, such as whales, bees, water, trees, flowers, mountains, and more.

PlAYLIST

Disco Inferno by The Trammps

Can't Hold Us Macklemore Ryan Lewis

Gone Surfing by Sixteen Wheelers

Rudolph The Red-Nosed Reindeer by Sound Haven

This Is America by Childish Gambino

Riot by Three Days Grace

We've Got The Power by Sunny Luwe

Cáncer by Bad Bunny

Aguila y Condor by Arthur Mena

Who Says That's Not American by Raye Zaragoza

Save It For Later by Eddie Vedder

Bandit by Juice WRLD (feat. YoungBoy Never Broke Again)

Young Americans by David Bowie

Hellhound on My Trail by Robert Johnson

A Good Day to Fight the System by Shungudzo

Pocahontas by AnnenMayKantereit
Dentro Al Cinema by Gianmaria Testa
Le Traiettorie Delle Mongolfiere by Gianmaria Testa
Pink Skies by Zach Bryan
Sirenita Bobinsana by Orka
A Thousand Years by Christina Perri
Gozar Hasta Que Me Ausente by Paloma Del Cerro
Riptide by Vance Joy
These Days by Nico
Stick Season by Noah Kahan
2000 Miles by The Pretenders
La Oscuridad y la luz Cielo y Tierra
Caminos de Alcanfor by Darío Poletti
Bullwinkle Pt II by The Centaurians
Sunrise Over The Ucayali River Shipibo Shamans
Born To Be Wild by Steppenwolf
Born To Run by Bruce Springsteen
On Ira by Zaz
Come and Get Your Love by Redbone
A Message To Pretty by The Rising Storm
Coconut by Harry Nissen
Picture of You by Chappell Roan
Love To Love You Baby by Donna Summer
Copycat Billie by Eilish
The Warmer Shoulder by Mary Lattimore
The Way I Am Eminem
Goodbye Porkpie Hat by Charlie Mingus
Fast Car by Tracy Chapman
Americano 10cm
Don't Give In by Snow Patrol
Children's Bear Song*

Rock Your World by Chubby Cree
Natural by Imagine Dragons
Turtle Island by Renee Christine
Tomorrow by Tyrell Bird
When We Remain by Samantha Crain
DNA by Darla Daniels
Wolf By First Aid Kit
Shapeshifter by Snotty Nose Rez Kids
Indigenous Awakens by Alkimizta
Beggin' by Maneskin
Rise Up by The Parachute Club*
Rebel Without a Pause by Public Enemy
Rebel Rebel by David Bowie
Fairytale of New York by The Pogues
Loveland by Milky Chance
Frosty by Babe Stockwell
Favorite Crime by Olivia Rodrigo
River by Joni Mitchell
Somewhere in the Middle by Sam Scherdel
Body To Body by Siibii, Aysanabee
Wild Horses by The Rolling Stones
Melody Noir by Patrick Watson
You Want It Darker by Leonard Cohen
The Dark End of The Street by The Commitments
The Door by Teddy Simms
Aunque es de Noche by Enrique Morente
Trova De Amor by Manuelcha Prado
Bang Bang by Nancy Sinatra
I'm So Lonesome I Could Cry by Cowboy Junkies
Send in The Clowns by Judi Dench & David Kernan
Good Year For The Roses by Elvis Costello and The Attrac-

tions

When The Roses Bloom by Billy Bragg, Wilco
Turn Me On by Norah Jones
Rising by Lhasha
Take on Me by a-ha
A Still Set a Place For You by Nina Blaze
If I Ain't Got You by Alicia Keys
I Try by Macy Gray
Try by Blue Rodeo
That's All I Wanted From You by Jalen Ngonda
Pictures of You by The Cure
Besame Mucho by Ceasaria Evora
La Complicidad by Perota Chingo
Killing Me Softly with His Song by Roberta Flack
Quelqu'un M'a Dit by Carla Bruni
Voilà by Barbara Pravi
Ne Me Quitte Pas by Nina Simone
Je L'aime à Mourir by Francis Cabrel
Sonatine by Chilla and Sofiane Pamart
There Is No Greater Love by Miles Davis
Heartbeat by Charles Leclerc and Sofiane Pamart
Born to Be Blue by Chet Baker
A Remark You Made by Weather Report
It's A Heartache by Bonnie Tyler
Haven't Seen The Last Of Me by Cher
Sweet Disposition by The Temper Trap
Bad Guy by Billie Eilish
Llorar by La Lom
The Rising Tide by Mia Doi Todd
Beauty by Delbert Blackhorse
Boarding Schools by Lyla June and Lee Moquino

How Much You Mean To Me by The Bearhead Sisters
The Cat Carol by Bruce Evans
Black Is Black by Los Bravos
Who Put The Bomb by Jaakko Eino Kalevi
Children's Bear Song*
Wacomaya by Yawanawa, Saiti Kaya
Passenger by Iggy Pop
Love & Revolution—Cinnamon Version by Seun Kuti
Pink Moon by Nick Drake
Painting Silhouettes by Quantic
Doo Wop (That Thing) by Ms. Lauryn Hill
No Diggity by Blackstreet, Dr. Dre
Turn Your Lights Down Low by Bob Marley & The Wailers
All of You by Billie Holiday, Cole Porter
Dance With Me by Nouvelle Vague
Je Veux by Zaz
Time On Her Side by Future Islands
We Are The People by Empire Of The Sun
Young Folks by Peter Bjorn
Somewhere Else by Federico Aubele
Green Onions by Booker T. & the M.G.s
De Camino a La Vereda by Buena Vista Social Club
Beautiful People by SuperHeavy
Everyday People by Sly & The Family Stone
On & On by Erykah Badu
Freedom by Waldeck, Joy Malcolm
Flying High by Slackwax
Colors by Black Pumas
Follow The Rainbow by Clinton Fearon
7 Seconds by Youssou N'Dour
Ma Mama by Gerald Toto

Ventura Highway by America
Take Me Home, Country Road by John Denver
NDN Kars - Remix by The Halluci Nation, Keith Secola
Road Drum by Mozart Gabriel
Cree Healing Song 1 by Cecile Moosomin
Peyote Healing by Robbie Robertson, Verdell Primeaux, Johnny Mike
Stand Up(From Harriet) by Cynthia Erivo
Universo de Amor by Herbert Quinteros
Bohr by Balquis
El Cielo by Radio Citizen, Bajika
El Mundo Llora by Green Valley
Spirit Bird by Xavier Rudd
My Silver Lining by First Aid Kit
Ride by Lana Del Rey
Wild In The Streets by Garland Jeffery
Send Me On My Way by Rusted Root
My Mother's Mother by Sara Diamond
Heroes by David Bowie
Dautibiua by Amazon Ensemble
I Will Purify by Ayahuasca Icaros
Pink Dolphins by Bird Tribe, Deva Runa
Aldeia Samaúma - Tsoî Hêpîti Kito Kito Tarifa by Aliança Noke Koî
De Ushuaia a La Quiaca by Gustavo Santaolalla
Cuñaq by Curawaka ·
Lunita J.Pool Remix by J. Pool, Danit
Cuatro Vientos by Danit
Agua de estrellas by Orka ·
Amanecer Andino by Grupo Aymara
Oso Blanco by Freedom Café, Manuel Villaescusa, Norbi Pan,

Amin Varkonyi ·
   Koka Kintucha by Manuelcha Prado
   Carnaval de Tambobamba by Jaime Guardia
   Corazon de Rubi by El Buho, Minuk
   Tonguere by Iskukua
   Onde o Jaguar Espreita by Advan Haschi
   Bambeo Koyo Granda by Bonobo, Innov Gnawa
   Ayahuasca by NTO
   Agüita Del Equilibrio by Alejandro y Maria Laura
   Icaro For Wisdom And Love by Shipibo Shamans, Herlinda
Augustin Fernandez

73

References and Notes

Here are all the references to books, files, anime, and other media, along with cultural and spiritual traditions in the Maskwa bibliography.

BOOKS AND LITERATURE

Winnie-the-Pooh by A. A. Milne

Rise Alive and the New Earth by Gemini Moon (fictional)

Earth Traditions (fictional book with Bear Medicine chapter)

Mia's Diary (fictional)

Metro 2033 by Dmitry Glukhovsky.

Works by Leo Tolstoy. Works by Fyodor Dostoevsky. Works by Ivan Turgenev. Works by Nikolai Gogol. Works by Anton Chekhov. Works by Lyudmila Ulitskaya. Works by Vladimir Sorokin. Works by Victor Pelevin. Works by Guzel Yakhina. Works by Aleksey Ivanov—Doctor Zhivago by Boris Pasternak.

Poetry - What the River Told Me by Johnny Cole

Poetry by Shel Silverstein (quoted: "My skin is kind of sort of brownish...")

Quote by Elizabeth Kubler-Ross on grief.

Quote by Jiddu Krishnamurti: "It's no measure of health to be well adjusted to a profoundly sick society."

FILMS AND ANIME

Princess Mononoke (Japanese anime)

Easy Rider (1960s film)

Hellblade (video game)

Alice (stop motion film by Jan Švankmajer)

FICTIONAL FILES AND DOCUMENTS

S.A.S.S. flyers (Sexual Abuse Survivors Support)

Various police files and crime scene reports

Copycat Killer files. St. Mary's Church records.

Gemini's client files.

Various passport documents.

Brian Keppler files.

The Roach case files.

NEWS SOURCES

Time Magazine. New York Times. Reuters. PBS. NPR. Slate. Floodlit.

CREE / SPIRITUAL/ HEALING ARTS

Cree language and cultural practices.

Wetiko mythology (Cree and Ojibwe spiritual concepts)

Bear Medicine traditions.

Amazon Indigenous cultures (Yanomami, Warao, Arawak, Ye'kuana, etc.)

Boto Medicine of the Amazon River Basins

Torovim Dolphin Medicine of the Tongva people (Southern California)

Two-Spirit identity (Indigenous concept)

Shiburi (Fetish Arts)

CHARACTERS CREATIVE WORKS

Mischief - Rachel's livestream show

Museum of Modern Murder (Dustin's collection)
Various protest art and zines
AMA'S TURTLE ISLAND CITIZENSHIP TEST
Here are some of the thousands of questions Ama was asked about Native American/Indigenous history, cultures, traditions, systems, and leaders, which may help provide an introductory foundation for understanding the Indigenous peoples of Turtle Island and the Americas.

1. What was the geographic range of Indigenous territories, and how do they span diverse environments from Arctic tundra to tropical regions?

2. What are the various Indigenous names for North America, such as Turtle Island, and what do these names reveal about different tribal cosmologies, creation stories, and relationships to the land?"

3. What were the major Native American trade networks that connected North, Central, and South America before European contact, and what goods, ideas, and technologies flowed through these routes?

4. What is the oldest continuously inhabited settlement in North America, and what does Acoma Pueblo's 1,000+ year history reveal about the sophistication and permanence of Indigenous civilizations?

5. What evidence exists of Norse/Viking contact with Indigenous peoples around 1000 CE in areas like Newfoundland, and how does this predate Columbus by 500 years?

6. What was the approximate Indigenous population of the Americas before European contact 500 years ago, and what is it today?

7. How many distinct tribes/nations existed in North

America at the time of European contact, and how many federally recognized tribes exist today?" What does federal recognition mean?

8. How did the earlier suppression of Indigenous European peoples (Celts, Sami, various tribal cultures) by expanding empires create the cultural and psychological patterns that were later applied to the colonization of Indigenous peoples in the Americas?

9. How did the Spanish Inquisition's methods (including torture) for suppressing 'heretics,' Indigenous European peoples, Jews, Muslims, and traditional healers, become the blueprint for the systematic oppression and forced conversion of Indigenous peoples in the Americas and elsewhere?

10. What are some of the ways that this blueprint impacted Native American populations and ways of life?

11. What accounts from Christopher Columbus's contemporaries and his own writings document his men's sexual abuse of Indigenous women and girls, which is now understood as child sex abuse, rape, and sex trafficking.

12. What evidence exists of cannibalism practiced by European colonists, such as during the 'Starving Time' at Jamestown (1609-1610), and how does this contrast with the stereotypes Europeans used to justify their treatment of Indigenous peoples?"

13. Who was Chief Powhatan of the Opechancanough, and how did he use diplomacy and military strategy to navigate the colonists at Jamestown?

14. How did the Haudenosaunee (Six Nations/Iroquois) Confederacy's Great Law of Peace influence the structure and principles of the U.S. Constitution?

15. What does it mean when people say that Native Ameri-

cans are both citizens of their tribes and of the United States?

16. What is tribal sovereignty, and how does it function within the U.S. federal system today?

17. Approximately how many treaties did the U.S. government make with Native American tribes, and what does the historical record show about how many of these treaties were broken or violated by the United States?

18. What was the significance of the Treaty of Fort Laramie (1851 and 1868), and why were these treaties repeatedly broken?

19. What was the Indian Reorganization Act of 1934, and how did it change federal Indian policy?

20. What was the Indian Removal Act of 1830, and how did it lead to the Trail of Tears?

21. What are treaty rights, and why do they remain legally binding today?

22. What was the purpose and impact of the Indian boarding school system, including schools like Carlisle?

23. How many boarding schools were in operation in Canada and the United States? How many children went through them? When was the last one shut down?

24. What effects did boarding schools have on Indigenous peoples, their cultures, and their mental health? What effects did boarding schools have on the current and future generations?

25. What are the current challenges facing Native American communities (poverty, health, education, land rights)?

26. What was the American Indian Movement (AIM), and what were the key goals and impacts of actions like the occupation of Alcatraz (1969–1971), the Trail of Broken Treaties (1972), and the Wounded Knee occupation (1973)?

27. How do traditional Native American concepts of land Stewardship/ownership differ from European-American property concepts?

28. What is the Doctrine of Discovery? Who wrote it, when, and why? What effect has it had and continues to have on the people of the Americas?

29. What effect did and does slavery and indentured servitude have on the survivors of these systems, and on the Americas?

30. How have some of these systems, mindsets, and structural pillars changed, and how have they remained the same?

31. How do clan systems and kinship structures function in various Native American societies?

32. How do matrilineal kinship systems function in Indigenous societies like the Haudenosaunee (Iroquois), Cherokee, and Hopi, and what roles do women play in political leadership, spiritual authority, and cultural transmission in these communities?

33. What are the purposes and protocols of traditional Native American spiritual practices such as vision quests, sweat lodge ceremonies, fasting, and the use of sacred plants like sage, cedar, sweetgrass, and tobacco?"

34. What are some major Native American spiritual beliefs and practices, and how do they connect to the natural world?

35. What is the significance of powwows, and how do they serve Native communities today?

36. What is the spiritual and cultural significance of the buffalo/bison to Plains tribes, and how did its near-extinction impact Native American ways of life?

37. What is the Sun Dance ceremony? Why is it considered

the most sacred ritual among many Plains tribes, and how did this ceremony survive government prohibition to continue as a vital spiritual practice today?"

38. Who was White Buffalo Calf Woman in Lakota tradition, and what sacred practices and teachings did she bring to the people?

39. How did the Blackfoot Nation's traditional understanding of self-actualization and community wellness influence psychologist Abraham Maslow's hierarchy of needs theory?

40. What was Chief Sitting Bull's role in defending Lakota sovereignty, his leadership during the Battle of the Little Bighorn, and how did his resistance to forced assimilation and his tragic assassination make him a symbol of Indigenous resistance worldwide?

41. What contributions did Sequoyah make to Cherokee culture and literacy?

42. Who was Wilma Mankiller, and what did she achieve as a tribal leader?

43. What was Tecumseh's vision for Native American unity and resistance?

44. How did Sacagawea contribute to the Lewis and Clark expedition?

45. Who was Louis Riel, and what did he do to help establish a provisional government, negotiate for Métis land rights, and become a symbol of Indigenous rights in Canada?

46. What contributions did Lakota medicine man John (Fire) Lame Deer make to preserving and sharing Indigenous wisdom, and how did his teachings about the sacred and modern Indigenous identity influence both Native and non-Native communities?"

47. What is the Heyoka tradition in Lakota culture? How

did medicine men like John Lame Deer embody this sacred contrarian role, and what spiritual purpose does the Heyoka serve in maintaining balance and teaching wisdom?

48. Who was Black Elk, what was the significance of his Great Vision received as a child, and how did his teachings in 'Black Elk Speaks' influence both Indigenous spiritual revival and non-Native understanding of Lakota spirituality?

49. Who is Leonard Peltier? What were the circumstances surrounding his conviction for killing two FBI agents in 1975, and why has his case become an international symbol of injustice against Indigenous peoples?

50. What teachings has Aleut/Unangan elder Larry Merculieff shared about the rise of feminine wisdom, the importance of deep listening, and Indigenous perspectives on healing global crises? How does he flip the narrative from anti-colonial to pro Earth-based and Indigenous values?

51. Who was Jon Smith, the Cree holy clown medicine man, and what effect did he have on Richard Pochinko in helping to create a renaissance in clowning, theater, and the arts in Canada?

52. What impact did the Cree elders and medicine carriers, Paula Shirt and Vern Harper, have on the rejuvenation and restoration of First Nation traditions and rights in Canada?

53. What are the major Indigenous prophecies, such as the Hopi Prophecy, the Seven Fires Prophecy of the Anishinaabe, and other prophetic traditions, and how do these ancient teachings relate to contemporary global challenges and spiritual renewal?

54. What are the prophecies and teachings associated with figures like Quetzalcoatl/Kukulkan in Mesoamerica and similar spiritual teachers who were said to have traveled

throughout the Americas, and how do different Indigenous nations describe the promised return of these wisdom keepers?

55. What is the Prophecy of the Condor and the Eagle, and how does it describe the relationship between Indigenous peoples of North, Central, and South America and the potential for global transformation?

56. What role do star beings and celestial origins play in Indigenous cosmologies, particularly connections to star systems like the Pleiades, Sirius, Lyra, and Andromeda, etc, and how do these star teachings relate to Indigenous understanding of human origins and spiritual guidance?

57. Who was the last reigning Queen in the Kingdom of Hawaii? When did her reign end, and why?

58. What role do oral traditions play in preserving Native American history and knowledge?

59. What role does deep listening play in Indigenous decision-making processes and conflict resolution, and how does this differ from Western communication styles?

60. How do some Indigenous languages like Cree demonstrate a non-binary understanding of gender through their linguistic structures, and what does this reveal about Indigenous concepts of identity and relationships?

CREE LANGUAGES

Cree languages do not use gender in the way European languages do. This is a fundamental and beautiful aspect of Cree linguistic structure. The primary difference lies between animate/inanimate distinctions and classification. It is one of the most profound differences between Cree and European language structures, reflecting fundamentally different ways of understanding the world and the relationships between beings.

Animate vs. Inanimate Classification

Animate (wiyasiwêwin - "having life/soul"). Things classified as animate are considered to possess spirit, consciousness, or life force. This includes: All humans (regardless of biological sex). All animals. Many plants (especially medicines, sacred plants). Natural forces (wind, thunder, lightning). Sacred objects (pipes, drums, bundles).Celestial bodies (sun, moon, stars). Some geological features (certain rocks, mountains). Spirits and supernatural beings.Many tools and objects with spiritual significance

Inanimate (miskotêwin - "without life/soul") Things without spirit or consciousness: Most everyday objects. Some plants (particularly those not used medicinally). Many manufactured items. Abstract concepts. Some natural phenomena.

Linguistic Implications: is within the verb conjugations. Verbs change based on whether their subject/object is animate or inanimate:

Animate: "wâpamêw" (s/he sees them/it-animate)

Inanimate: "wâpahtam" (s/he sees it-inanimate)

Pronouns wiya - s/he (for all animate beings, regardless of sex). awa - this one (animate) ôma - this (inanimate).

No Gendered Language. There is no "he/she" distinction based on biological sex. There are no gendered articles (like "la/le" in French). There are no gendered adjective endings. The same pronoun "wiya" refers to a man, woman, bear, thunder being, etc.

Cultural Significance. This linguistic structure reflects deep Cree philosophical beliefs: spiritual equality, where all animate beings (humans, animals, spirits, and sacred objects) are grammatically treated as equals, reflecting the belief that all possess spirit and deserve respect.

Fluid Gender Concepts. Without linguistic gender constraints, Cree culture traditionally had more fluid concepts of gender roles and identity. People could move between social roles more freely.

Relationship to Medicine Work. In medical and shamanic contexts, this is especially important: medicinal plants are animate (they possess a spirit that can help or harm). Sacred objects are animate (they have power and consciousness). The same pronoun refers to a human healer and a bear spirit teacher – examples in the Medicine Context. Maskwa (bear) is animate - "wiya" (s/he) teaches medicine. Mitêw (shaman) is animate - "wiya" (s/he) heals people. Pîpî (ceremonial pipe) is animate - "wiya" (s/he/it) carries prayers. Maskihkiy (medicine plant) is animate - "wiya" (s/he/it) provides healing. Modern Implications: This linguistic structure means that traditional Cree speakers don't automatically assign gender assumptions. The focus is on spiritual essence rather than biological categories. The same term refers to medicine people of any gender, and sacred relationships transcend human gender concepts.

A valuable explanation of these ideas can be found in this seven-minute video lecture by Thomson Highway at the Canadian Literature Centre. (Cree elder, teacher, composer, and writer). He unpacks the differences between Western world views (as reflected in their languages) vs the Cree worldview as reflected in his language, as it relates to the body, genders, the masculine, feminine, God/Goddess, 'the Garden of Eden', the trickster, and the sacredness of Mother Earth. While Western languages generally describe the world in terms of dual gender (masculine or feminine), in his language, everything is defined as either having or not having a soul, or as alive or not alive.

SHAMAN - CHAMAN- MEDICINE PERSON - CURANDERO/A - PAJÉ'

The word 'shaman' itself comes from the Tunguso-Manchurian (or Manchu-Tungus) language of Northern Asia, specifically the Evenki word šamán or saman. It was borrowed into Russian and then into Western European languages in the late 17th century. The word is believed to derive from a root meaning "to know" or "to heat oneself," referring to the inspired trance state of the spiritual practitioner. The term is linked to the idea of "knowing" or "one who knows," reflecting the shaman's role in gaining spiritual insight or carrying wisdom.

It can also refer to the fever-like trance state of the shaman, suggesting 'to burn up', 'to heat oneself', 'to alchemise' or 'cook one's gifts.' It means 'The keeper of the fire.' Fire, both symbolically and literally, is the source of life, which brings warmth to all the various aspects of life and creation. As such, with small and great gifts come small and significant respon-sibilities. A shaman can carry a responsibility for keeping and tending the medicine fire within self, the community, the collective, and on Mother Earth. He, she, or they can act very much as an alchemical forger, weaver and bridge builder, integrating the aligned middle and 'in between' realms of the diverse expressions of our lives: our animal and human natures, human and divine selves, masculine and feminine energies, shadow and light dualities, rational and irrational behaviors, empathetic and narcissistic masks, victim and perpetrator tendencies, conscious and unconscious patterns, fears and ferocious inclinations, foolish and practical impulses, potential and potentialized gifts, unhealed and healed psyche, grief and joy tending, underworld and upperworld voyages, dark soul nights and illuminating rebirths, life and death cycles, past and future leanings, separate and 'other' connected, self and collective service, social and cultural complexities, and navigating a path within and outside of the our human species, Mother Earth, and the stars, as well as between what is known and the very mystery itself.

Many Indigenous people have specific meanings beyond "shaman" and can refer to different types of spiritual practitioners, healers, or religious specialists within their cultures. Many of these terms translate more accurately as 'one who knows,' 'wise person,' or 'keeper of power,' rather than 'shaman.' Some terms translate more accurately as 'holy person,' 'one who has power,' or 'keeper of sacred knowledge.'

Indigenous terms often carry much more specific meanings than shaman, and are related to particular types of spiritual practice, healing knowledge, or ceremonial responsibilities. It is central to understanding all these roles that they describe and connect to the mysterious spiritual power that flows through all existence. Some of these include:

Plant/Herb Specialists, Sweetgrass Keepers, Coming of Age Ceremonialists, Divinators and Prophets, River Keepers, Water Spirit Mediums, Word Revealers, OracleWater/River Medicine, Pipe Carriers, Bundle Holders, Plant spirit healers, Traditional massage healers, Dream Specialists, and Bone Setters. A broader perspective of medicine carriers can include craftsmen/women, singers, artists, dancers, scientists, alchemists, chefs, yogis, meditators, energy healers, death doulas, martial artists, change-makers, inventors, creatives, pioneers, visionaries, parents and grandparents, midwives, astronomers, and record keepers, among many others.

One aspect of a Medicine Person, Shaman, Pajé, or Curendera/o is their spirit animals or allies, such as the lion, jaguar, wolf, whale, and birds like the eagle, condor, and hummingbird. There is no limit to what could be considered an ally or spirit helper: all human beings, all ancestors, plants, rivers, rocks, mountains, caves, angels, volcanos, along with air, fire, water, wind, Every thing that a human being can experience with the five senses and beyond: a mandala, a rock, a wound, a piece of art, a building, the trees, spirit guides, the clouds, animals, all children and elders, an entire group or tribe of people. The stars, the moon, the sun, and what some call the beautiful ball of blue wonder, Gaia, Pachamama, or the Queen of the Buddha. The very Earth itself - all of life, in fact, sacred and medicine. A Medicine.

Understandably, all this initiation and transformation can be quite demanding on one's energy, time, psyche, and overall well-being. It's one of the reasons why in many of the ancient cultures, when a shaman would walk through their community to scout the young people for a potential apprentice, knowing of the demands of the shamanic gig on the shaman's life, and preferring a more stable path, the young people would turn away and pretend not to see the shaman looking their way. Invariably, the shaman would locate and tap the shoulder of the one hiding behind a tree, or the one who has taken sick, or talking to fairies, or discovering someone who, in some way, just doesn't fit in. Whether nudged by an elder shaman or by the inner shaman within our own lives when we experience some form of deep hiding, trauma triggers, spirit communing with self or another, or no longer fitting into our current life structures, we can all either repress or choose the call of shamanic initiation of becoming and serving all the unique gifts and capacities of who we are. We are all autonomous, free-willed choice makers like that.

I am often asked who or what a good shaman is to work with, and I usually respond that you are —and everyone is. I perceive everyone as an extraordinarily gifted shaman with unique healing powers, teachings, and potentialities. Every human being is simultaneously innocent, unhealed, and in the process of healing. The only real task or invitation of a shaman, like any being, is to become more of who you are, discover and give your gifts, and to love increasingly more today than yesterday. It is never done or complete –only eternal.

Fundamentally, if you are a human or any being, at some point your spirit shoots out of the mystery into a body or form, undergoing all kinds of experiences and initiations, before shooting your spirit out, leaving some bones or dust behind, and dissolving back into mystery again. I mean, how incredible, how magical, how mysterious and shamanic is that? Quite masterful, really, and a gift that very few beings of the universe, the one-song, have experienced.

Many tribes and tribal nations use "Medicine Man/Woman" as the English translation for their traditional leaders. Still, the indigenous terms often carry much more specific meanings related to particular types of spiritual practice, healing knowledge, or ceremonial responsibilities. Some terms translate more accurately as "holy person," "one who has power," or "keeper of sacred knowledge."

The following is a brief list of names of Medicine people from the Americas and around the world. More to illustrate the breadth and scope of healers from various cultures than the multiple names or their interpretations. Additionally, I list them because in many situations, they were/are the first to be targeted and brutalized by empirical, homogeneous systems of power and control. Many of these individuals lost their lives simply for their gifts, leadership roles, and support of their families and communities. I share these names/titles/roles out of respect and honor.

THE LANDS OF THE CONDOR (SOUTH AMERICA)

Here's a partial list of what Shamans, Chamans, Medicine People, and Curanderos/as they are called across South American cultures, with both English and indigenous-language terms where available.

Shipibo: Onanya (Plant Spirit Healer), Meraya (Master Shaman). Kayapó: Wayangá (Shaman), Benadjwyre (Medicine Person). Yanomami: Shapori (Shaman), Hekura (Spirit Medium). Xingu Peoples: Pajé (Shaman), Kumu (Sacred Leader). Guaraní: Pajé, Karaí (Sacred Person). Terena: Pajé, Koixomuneti (Medicine Person). Shipibo-Konibo: Onanya, Muraya (Master Healer). Ashuar: Wishin (Shaman), Uwishin (Powerful Shaman). Machiguenga: Seripigari (Shaman), Curandero. Aguaruna: Wishin (Shaman), Iwishin (Vision Shaman). Cocama: Pajé, Curandero. Achuar: Wishin, Uwishin (Master Shaman). Huitoto: Mambeador (Coca Priest), Curandero. Kofán: Curaca (Shaman), Dau'su (Medicine Person). Inga: Yachak (Knower), Curandero. Embera: Jaibaná (Shaman), Curandero. Shuar: Uwishin (Shaman), Wishin (Healer) Achuar: Wishin, Uwishin. Cofán: Curaca, Curandero. Siona: Curandero, Yajé-ero (Ayahuasca Shaman). Yanomami: Shapori (Shaman), Hekura. Ye'kuana: Ademi (Shaman), Curandero. Warao: Wisiratu (Shaman), Hoarotu (Light Shaman). Quechua: Altomisayoq (High

Mystic), Paqo (Andean Priest), Curandero, Yachaq (Knower). Aymara: Yatiri (One Who Knows), Curandero, Amauta (Wise Teacher). Kallawaya: Kallawaya (Traditional Healer), Curandero. Aymara: Yatiri (Knower), Curandero, Ch'amakani (Medicine Person). Quechua: Paqo, Curandero, Altomisayoq. Quichua: Yachak (Knower), Curandero, Wishin. Shuar: Uwishin (Powerful Shaman). Muisca: Mohán (Shaman), Curandero. Kogí: Mamá (Priest-Shaman), Curandero. Mapuche: Machi (Shaman-Healer), Longko (Spiritual Leader). Atacameño: Curandero, Yatiri. Mapuche: Machi, Pillán Kushe (Sacred Grandmother). Tehuelche: Curandero, Medicine Person. Toba/Qom: Piogonak (Shaman), Curandero. Guaraní: Pajé, Karaí (Sacred Person), Ava Karaí (Sacred Man). Aché: Pajé, Curandero. Charrúa: Curandero, Medicine Person. Wayuu: Outsü (Shaman), Piachi (Medicine Person). Pemón: Taren (Shaman), Curandero. Arawak: Peaiman (Shaman), Medicine Person. Carib: Peaiman, Curandero. Trio: Piai (Shaman), Medicine Person. Wayana: Peleeito (Shaman). Wayampi: Pajé, Medicine Person. Emerillon: Pajé, Curandero.

THE LANDS OF THE QUETZAL (CENTRAL AMERICA)

Here's a partial list of the names people in medicine are called across Mexican and Central American cultures, including both English and indigenous terms where available.

Mexico - Nahua/Aztec: Curandero/a, Tlamatqui (Wise One), Nahualli (Nagual/Shape-shifter), Ticitl (Doctor). Otomí: Bädi (Medicine Person), Hmũ (Shaman). Purépecha/Tarascan: Petámuti (High Priest), Curítiecha (Healer). Zapotec: Pitao Cozobi (Priest), Bene zaa (Medicine Person). Mixtec: Iya (Medicine Person), Savi (Shaman), Tzotzil. Maya: Ilol (Seer), Poxlom (Curer), J'ik'al (Diviner). Tzeltal Maya: Hiloletik (Healers), Ak'chamel (Prayer Maker), Ch'ol Maya: Hierbatero (Herbalist), Aj k'in (Day Keeper), Tojolabal. Maya: Curandero, Rezador (Prayer Person). Yucatec Maya: H-men (He Who Knows), Chilam (Prophet), Ah Kin (Day Keeper). Itzá Maya: Daykeeper, Curandero. Huichol (Wixáritari): Marakame (Singing Shaman), Cantador (Singer).Tarahumara (Rarámuri): Owirúame (Medicine Person), Curandero. Yaqui: Pajko'ola (Deer Dancer), Maestro (Teacher/Healer). Mayo: Hitevi (Medicine Person). Mazatec: Chota chjine (One Who Knows), Sabio/a (Wise One). Chinantec: Curandero, Wiseman. Chatino: Curandero, Medicine Person. Guatemala K'iche' Maya: Aj q'ij (Daykeeper), Komadrona (Midwife-Healer). Kaqchikel Maya: Aj ilonel (Seer), Curandero. Mam Maya: Txumil (Daykeeper), Chimán (Priest-Shaman). Q'eqchi' Maya: Ilol (Seer), Aj k'in (Priest). Mopan Maya: H-men (Medicine Person), Bush Doctor. Garifuna: Buyei (Shaman), Duguchugu (Healer). Lenca: Curandero/a, Sukias (Healers). Pipil: Nawalli (Nagual), Curandero. Miskito: Sukia (Shaman), Prapit (Healer). Lenca: Curandero, Sukias. Garifuna: Buyei (Shaman). Miskito: Sukia, Prapit Nani (Medicine Person). Sumo/Mayangna: Sukia, Curandero. Rama: Medicine Person. Bribri: Awá (Shaman), Usékölpa (Medicine Person). Cabécar: Awá, Curandero. Boruca: Sukia, Curandero. Kuna: Nele (Seer), Inaduledi (Medicine Person), Kantule (Chanter). Emberá: Jaibaná (Shaman), Curandero. Ngöbere: Sukia, Curandero.

THE LANDS OF THE EAGLE (TURTLE ISLAND-NORTH AMERICA)

Here's a partial list of names people are called across North American tribes/nations, with both English and indigenous-language terms where available.

Lakota/Dakota: Wicaša Wakȟáŋ (Holy Man), Winyan Wakȟáŋ (Holy Woman), Pejuta Wicaša (Medicine Man).

Cheyenne: Mahpe (Medicine Man), Maahpe-hohpe (Medicine Bundle Keeper). Blackfoot: Natoas (Holy Person), Aokii-kitsikaki (Medicine Pipe Owner), Crow: Baaxpee (Medicine Person), Akbaatatdia (One Who Knows), Cree: Mask-ihkîwiyiniw (with regional variations) – literally "medicine man" or "one who uses medicine." Maskihkîwiskwêw – "medicine woman" Pêyâkwaskamikisit – "one who doctors" or healer Mitêwiyiniw/Mitêwiskwêw – refers to someone with spiritual power, sometimes translated as "shaman." Comanche: Puhacut (Power Person), Medicine Man, Navajo (Diné): Hataɫii (Singer/Ceremonial Practitioner), Diyin Diné'é (Holy People).Hopi: Powaka (Sorcerer), Qaletaqa (Guardian of the People). Apache: Diyin (Medicine Person), Gaan (Mountain Spirit Dancer). Pueblo: Cacique (Religious Leader), Medicine Man. Pima: Siikam (Shaman), Ma: kai (Medicine Person). Tlingit: Ikh.áat (Shaman), Íxt (Medicine Person). Haida: Sgaawaay K'uuna (Shaman) Tsimshian: Halait (Shaman). Salish: Sčətxʷ (Power), Sqaləlitut (Spirit Dancer). Makah: Tamanawas (Spirit Power Person). Yurok: Wok-hlew (Medicine Person). Tungva: Toypurino/a (Medicine Person). Chumash: Antap (Religious Society Member). Pomo: Moki (Dreamer), Yomta (Doctor). Yokuts: Tipni (Shaman). Ojibwe/Chippewa: Midewin (Medicine Person), Jiisakiwinini (Shaking Tent Practitioner). Potawatomi: Mètemo (Medicine Person), Menominee: Mitāwit (Medicine Person). Ho-Chunk (Winnebago): Wakan (Sacred Person). Iroquois: Hodenosaunee Faithkeeper, Medicine Person. Penobscot: Medoulin (Medicine Person). Mi'kmaq: Puoinaq (Shaman). Abenaki: Medawlinno (Medicine Person). Cherokee: Didanvwisgi (Medicine Person), Adawehi (Healer). Seminole: Medicine Man/Woman.

Choctaw: Alikchi (Doctor/Medicine Person). Creek: Hillis Haya (Medicine Maker) Inuit: Angakkuit (pl.), Angakok (sing.), Qimmiq-anyu (Dog Shaman) Yup'ik: Angalkuq. Shoshone: Poha'gant (Power Person), Boha'gande (Medicine Person). Paiute: Puhagim (Shamans), Doctor. Ute: Poowat (Medicine Person). Yakama: Spilyay (Power Person). Nez Perce: Tewats (Medicine Person). Colville: Skelalitut (Spirit Dancer). Inuit/Eskimo: Angakkuit or Angakok.

MEDICINE PEOPLE IN WORLD CULTURES

Here's a partial list of what medicine people are called across different cultures worldwide:

Siberia/Mongolia: Samán. South Africa: Sangoma, Inyanga, N'anga. West Africa: Babalawo (Yoruba), Marabout, Fetisheur. East Africa: Mganga, Waganga. Central Africa: Nganga. Korea: Mudang, Mansin. Japan: Miko, Itako. China: Wu, Fangshi. Tibet: Bon-po, Lha-pa, Pawo/Khandro. India: Jhankri (Nepal), Ojha, Tantrik. Southeast Asian — Bomoh (Malaysia), Dukun (Indonesia), Babaylan (Philippines). Northern Europe — Sami: Noaidi. Finnish: Tietäjä, Noita. Celtic. Druid, Ovate. Australia/Oceania — Aboriginal Australian: Clever Man/Woman, Kurdaitcha. Maori: Tohunga. Hawaii: Kahuna (Expert, Master, or Medicine Person). Middle East/Central Asia — Turkic: Kam, Baksı. Persian: Pir, Dervish. Central Asian — Bakhshi, Manasch.

BEAR MEDICINE

Bear medicine traditions are deeply woven throughout Indigenous healing practices across the Americas, representing one of the most widespread and revered spiritual healing systems among Native peoples. Most Native American tribes revere the bear, and at the core, the bear represents authority, good medicine, courage, and strength. Bear Clan members are renowned for their healing abilities and possess extensive knowledge of medicinal plants, including bitter root, bear root, flat cedar, sage, and many others. The bear's significance as a healer and protector is central to most cultures. The bear symbolizes awakening the strong force of the unconscious, with the strength of bear medicine being the power to restore harmony and balance–to heal.

Most traditional Earth-based religions view bears with deep respect and reverence, regarding them as powerful spiritual beings that deserve honor rather than fear or persecution.

• Death and Rebirth: Hibernation symbolizes spiritual death and resurrection.

• Wisdom Keepers: Bears as teachers of medicine and natural knowledge.

• Protective Spirits: Guardians of forests, mountains, and sacred places.

• Seasonal Cycles: Connected to agricultural and spiritual calendars.

• Healing Power: Associated with herbal medicine and therapeutic practices.

• Warrior Spirit: Symbol of courage, strength, and fierce protection.

• Shamanic Power: Bridge between human and spirit worlds.

From the Ojibwe and other Anishinaabe peoples of the Great Lakes region, where the Bear Clan are known as carriers of medicine, to the Plains tribes like the Lakota who honor bear medicine for protection and healing, to the Cherokee and other Southeastern nations who incorporate bear symbolism into their healing ceremonies, bear medicine healers serve as powerful intermediaries between the physical and spiritual worlds.

This tradition extends beyond North America, with various Central and South American Indigenous groups, including the Ukuku bear shamans in Peru, who maintain order and perform essential rituals. These groups from Central and South America also recognize bears and similar powerful plant and animal spirits, such as Ayahuasca and the jaguar, as sources of healing knowledge, creating a continental network of ceremonial practices that honor nature and the roles of her spirit allies as teachers, protectors, and guides in the healing arts.

Bear medicine traditions extend far beyond the Americas, forming a profound spiritual thread that weaves through cultures across Eurasia and the world. In Siberian shamanic traditions, where the bear is considered the shaman of their cultural, ceremonial, and spiritual practices, bears are regarded as spiritual mediators between humans and spirits. The bear ceremony is one of many practices in which humans can communicate directly with spirits without a third-party agent. Bear worship is found in many North Eurasian ethnic religions, such as those of the Sami, Nivkh, Ainu, Basques, Germanic peoples, Slavs, and Finns, with several deities from Celtic Gaul and Britain associated with the bear.

In the Celtic tradition, Artio/Andarta refers to the near goddesses of fertility and war. Bears represent sovereignty and royal power. In the legend of King Arthur, his name is associated with the bear king. It is linked to warrior initiation and transformation, as well as to the sacred lunar goddesses and seasonal cycles.

The Old Norse Viking warriors, known as berserkers, wore Bear Skins to frighten oncoming hordes and invoke the strength of the Bear in battle. Berserkers drew their power from the bear and were devoted to the bear cult, which was once widespread across the northern hemisphere.

Worshippers of the Goddess Artemis were found throughout the ancient Greek world. One of the most famous worshiping sites for Artemis was in Attica at Brauron. Artemis is said to have presided over all the biological transitions of females from before puberty to the first childbirth, along with their first moon-menstrual rites during which young girls danced for Artemis, in some places playing the role of animals – embracing and integrating their human-animal natures, and nature itself.

In Hinduism, the Jambavan (Riksharaj) tradition, as depicted in The Ramayana, features a bear king as a wise and powerful ally of Lord Rama. In the Hindu epic poem The Ramayana, the Asian black bear Jambavan is depicted as the king of bears and aids the title hero, Rama, in defeating the epic's antagonist, Ravana, and in reunifying with his Queen, Sita. In the Bhalu Avatar, some traditions include bears among the divine incarnations. Bears represent strength, wisdom, and devotion when aligned with dharma. Associated with the forest sage tradition and hermit wisdom

In Buddhism, bears symbolize the transformation of greed and negative emotions into wisdom and enlightenment. Represent beings capable of enlightenment despite their seeming aggressive nature.

In Tibetan Buddhism, bears are sometimes seen as protector spirits of mountain regions. Jataka tales include stories of the Buddha's past lives, which often involve bears.

In Taoism/Chinese Traditions, bears embody Yin energy - introspective, hibernating, and earth-connected, and are a symbol of contemplation and inner wisdom. Bear walking is a traditional qigong exercise associated with longevity and health practices.

In African regions with bears (historically found in the Atlas Mountains), they are seen as mountain spirits and are associated with ancestral wisdom, protection, endurance, and survival.

In the Ainu Religion in Japan, the Kamuy bear spirits are the most sacred of all animal spirits. Bears are seen as gifts from the gods, messengers between worlds, and are central to spiritual practice and seasonal ceremonies.

In Shintoism in Japan, the Kuma (bear spirits) are considered powerful kami (divine spirits). Mountain bears are seen as guardians of sacred forests. Bear ceremonies honor the spirit before and after hunting, and bears represent the wild, untamed spiritual power of nature.

BEARS IN POPULAR CULTURE

And how the bear's association with strength, independence, and fierce protection makes it a popular choice for representing territories, teams, and organizations that want to project power and determination. Some of these include sports teams like the Chicago Bears, Boston Bruins, Memphis Grizzlies, and the Baylor Bears, as well as territories such as California, Alaska, Nunavut, Igloolik, Churchill, Manitoba, and regions like Russia, Greenland, Finland, Romania, and the cities of Bern and Berlin.

Tribal bear symbols are featured in bear clan images, logos, flags, and seals throughout the Pacific Northwest, as well as among the Ojibwe, Chippewa, and Cree nations and communities, among others. Many Indigenous communities have traditional protocols governing the use of bear imagery so that official flags may be more subtle or feature stylized representations rather than realistic bear depictions. The symbols often carry profound cultural and spiritual significance that extends beyond mere identification.

BEAR POPULATIONS TODAY

American Black Bear (Ursus americanus): The most common bear in North America, found from Alaska and Canada down to northern Mexico.

Asiatic Black Bear (Ursus thibetanus): Also known as the "moon bear" for the white crescent-shaped patch on its chest. It lives in forests across Asia.

Brown Bear (Ursus arctos): The most widespread bear species, with a wide distribution across the northern hemisphere. Subspecies include the grizzly bear and the Kodiak bear.

Giant Panda (Ailuropoda melanoleuca): Native to south-central China, this endangered species is known for its distinctive black-and-white coat and bamboo diet.

Polar Bear (Ursus maritimus): The largest bear species, uniquely adapted to survive in the Arctic. It is a marine mammal that preys primarily on seals.

Sloth Bear (Melursus ursinus): Found in the Indian subcontinent, this nocturnal bear has a shaggy coat and a long snout for sucking up insects from their nests.

Spectacled Bear (Tremarctos ornatus): Also known as the Andean bear, it is the only bear species native to South America and is found in the Andes Mountains.

Sun Bear (Helarctos malayanus): The smallest bear species, living in the tropical forests of Southeast Asia. It is known for its long tongue and love of honey.

Mongolian Bear (Ursus arctos gobiensis). Also known as

the Mazaalai or Gobi Bear. An extremely rare brown bear subspecies found only in the Gobi Desert of Mongolia and China. Critically endangered (fewer than 40 individuals remain.

The extinct species of bears are: Giant Short-Faced Bear (Arctodus simus), Atlas Bear (Ursus arctos crowtheri), Cave Bear (Ursus spelaeus), Mexican Grizzly Bear (Ursus arctos nelsoni), California Grizzly Bear (Ursus californicus), Florida Short-Faced Bear (Tremarctos floridanus), and various extinct members of the genera Arctotherium, Plionarctos, and Agriotherium.

ANIMAL AND NATURE ALLIES

Zoroastrianism / Persia

In Zoroastrianism, dogs are revered as highly beneficial, righteous, and spiritual creatures, companions to humans and helpers of the supreme being, Ahura Mazda. They are considered vital to cosmic order and are believed to possess supernatural virtues, such as the ability to ward off evil spirits. Zoroastrian law and rituals, including the Sagdid ritual at funerals, mandate the care and protection of dogs, with mistreatment being a serious offense.

Ancient Egypt

Ancient Egyptians incorporated animals into their cosmology through religious symbolism, divine representation, and beliefs about life and the afterlife. By observing the animal kingdom, they attributed specific traits to their gods, depicting them as theriomorphic (part-human, part-animal) or fully zoological beings.

Judaism

Judaism has profound positive connections to nature, deeply embedded in its theology, law, and mystical traditions.

The Hebrew Bible establishes humans as stewards (not owners) of creation, holding that the Earth belongs to God and that humans are responsible for its care. In Kabbalistic thought, everything is interconnected through divine energy that flows from God and manifests in various forms throughout creation. Understanding this flow can lead to enlightenment and fulfillment.

Islam

The Prophet Muhammad's relationship with nature was profound and comprehensive, establishing him as one of the earliest environmental advocates in Western history. The three most essential principles of the Prophet Muhammad's philosophy of nature are unity (tawhid), stewardship (khalifa), and trust (amana).

Christianity

Jesus demonstrated a profound positive connection to nature throughout his teachings and ministry. His deep appreciation for the Earth was evident in his teachings, as many of his parables drew on agricultural life and natural phenomena that his audience would readily understand. The images Jesus uses in his parables are, for the most part, drawn from the natural world, including stories about seeds, vineyards, trees, mustard plants, and fields that illustrate spiritual truths about the Creator's queen/kingdom – ever present within, above, below, and beside.

The statement "The kingdom of the Father is spread out upon the earth, and men do not see it" originates from the Gospel of Thomas, an apocryphal gospel found in the Nag Hammadi library. The phrase suggests the Kingdom of Heaven is a spiritual reality present in the world, nature, and within oneself, but not perceived by people due to their worldly limitations, lack of inner spiritual awareness, or their expectation of a grand, external, outside, or someday event.

Francis of Assisi was a 12th-century Italian mystic, poet, and Catholic friar who founded the Franciscan order. His relationship with animals was characterized by profound reverence, compassion, and a belief in the spiritual kinship between all of God's creatures. Considered the patron saint of animals, St. Francis had as his life theme the love of nature, developed in all its forms, believing that all animals deserved respect and affection because they are also God's creatures.

In contemporary spiritual traditions, Mary Magdalene has become strongly associated with nature-based mysticism and the concept of the divine feminine. Modern spiritual practitioners envision her "in a lush garden, the air fragrant with roses and jasmine," radiating "a palpable energy of love, wisdom, and power"

The Abrahamic religions (Judaism, Christianity, and Islam) have several stories and interpretations that have, unfortunately, contributed to negative perceptions of bears throughout history. One such example is the story of the She-Bears of Elisha (2 Kings 2:23-24). This Old Testament story recounts the Prophet Elisha being mocked by children who called him "Baldy." In response, Elisha cursed them, and two female bears came out of the woods and mauled 42 of the children. This story has been used to portray bears as instruments of divine wrath and violence, reinforcing fears of bears as dangerous predators that attack the innocent.

Bears were also seen as symbols of godless nations. In the Book of Daniel and Revelation, bears are used metaphorically to represent destructive, godless empires and forces opposed to divine will. Daniel 7:5 describes a bear-like beast representing the Medo-Persian Empire. Revelation 13:2 describes the beast from the sea as having feet like a bear, representing worldly power that opposes God.

One can find representations, allies, and symbols of animals and nature in every country, religion, and timeline on Mother Earth.

74

Acknowledgments

Thank you to the Maskwa editors, consultants, contributors, and readers who helped shepherd this book toward completion.

Mario Mabe

Melissa Henderson

Tony Herbert

Sanjay Sharma

Kenneth Helmer, Esq

Deborah Cohen

Matthew Sharpe

David Cameron

Hannah Ceselki

Carlos Lanundery

Paige and Kate at Fiver

Annie Martin

TJ Marquis

William Davis

Brittany Schellin

Chris Ortiz

Ashleigh Haynes
Jennifer Lamb
Susie Hunt
Adolf El Assal
Jr Sketcher
Shawn Smallman
Jill Evlyn
Ahdam Wakil
Isaac Depeyer
Stephen James
Sol Mason
San Blakkert
Nirvana Anulekha
Paul Sand
T. Cook
Christina Le
Megan Rippey
Adam Dorsey
Stephen James
Cassandra James
Sonalii Castillo
Allesondra Helwig
Daniel Donham
Kayla Hendy
Alex Correla
Michelle Claremont
Michelle Mower
Elizabeth Avellan
Helga Douglas
Susan Mcconnell
Darryl Marshak

Alexandra Radlovic
Elton Bolden
Jake Cross
Andy Lee
Jennifer Betit Yen
Melissa Bickerton
Sky Redlove
Laura Hart
David Rottenberg
Book Cover Design: Deborah Cohen, Johnny Cole, and Mario Mabe

75

About The Author

I'm a Kuychi medicine carrier. Kuychi means 'Rainbow' in Quechua, one of the languages of Indigenous people from South America. Kuychi refers to the Rainbow-Winged Serpent, or the archetype of integrated wholeness, found within elder cultures and regions throughout the world, including the Americas, the Arctic, Africa, ancient Europe, Scandinavia, Ireland, Wales, Australia, the world's islands, and Asia.

It is worth mentioning that America derives from "Amaruca" (also spelled "amaroca"), which in Quechua and related Andean languages refers to a mythical serpent deity. In Inca mythology, Amaru is a giant double-headed serpent that dwells underground, at the bottom of lakes and rivers, and Amaruca is literally translated 'Land of the Plumed Serpents' or 'Lands of the Rainbow Winged-Serpent.'

I work with the Rainbow Winged-Serpent, or Kuychi, medicine to stay rooted, aligned, and connected to my human and divine natures and to my ever-emerging rainbow child-light unique essence within my own life.

As such, Rainbow Winged Serpent or Kuychi medicine is a

masterful healing ally to have on one's journey through life, encompassing all aspects – healing, creativity, relationships, parenting, community, career, business, politics, and nature. It has been foundational to my work as a filmmaker, writer, photographer, healing arts practitioner, & mentor.

At its core, rainbow wisdom medicine invites me to access and integrate all the colors and vibrations of the rainbow, including the deepest, darkest shadows and the highest, illuminated light, within, without, and with everything. Its medicine is practical and transcendent, rooted, and rising, and a simply good friend to have on one's path. It's also the optimal ally for protection within and around as we navigate and integrate the descending and ascending choppy waters of our unconscious underworlds, human-nature realms, and the 'upper' spiritual dimensions of reality.

The Rainbow Winged-Serpent is likely one of the oldest energies and images to emerge in world mythology. It remains an elixir of healing in many indigenous cultures today, and images of it can be found in the rock art of Australia, dating back to 40,000 BCE. Based on many older myths, traditions, and legends, it seems likely that the Rainbow-Winged Serpent first appeared in human consciousness in Africa, at least 100,000 years ago.

The Rainbow Winged-Serpent is often portrayed in world cosmologies as a deity that connects, weaves, and transmutes the realms of the underworld, nature, and sky into a unified whole. The Rainbow-Winged Serpent is regarded as the primordial, alchemical, cyclical life force. It's raw and honest, arising from within/without devouring people and all of nature, vomiting, and rebirthing them back up – symbolizing the cycles of birth, life, death, and rebirth. As such, rainbow medicine has historically been utilized to support individuals and cultures in integrating the various realms of experience across the cycles of transformation within oneself and on Mother Earth.

This Rainbow Winged-Serpent is associated with ceremonies related to fertility, abundance, and peace within the human, community, and ecological realms. It is depicted as masculine and feminine, yin and yang, and many meandering rivers are said to have been carved out by its body as it slithered across the Earth. Piles of rocks are also said to be the deity's droppings, and as such, have been designated as sacred places. They are also seen at the entry portals to the holy, both within and without, including dreams, spirit journeys, springs, mountains, and the threshold of anything. They also often arrive as a significant ally for healers or anyone who has undergone and continues after a series of initiations. They provide them with a rainbow ladder or staff, through which to ascend and descend, and integrate into the various realms and cycles of their lives.

In more modern times, the roots of rainbow medicine are deeply connected to Quetzalcoatl, the Rainbow Winged-Serpent (kundalini) master teacher from Mesoamerica. Cross-culturally, it is also linked to the alchemical caduceus (the spiraling serpents around a staff, blossoming with wings) or medical symbol. The cross-cultural names of the rainbow-winged serpent include:

· Oshumare Aido Hwedo, and Da in Africa.

· The golden Christed rainbow dragon of Yeshua/Magdalene.

· The deity/spirit of the Amazon River, known as Yacumama, and the deity/spirit of the forest, called Shachamama, are associated with the Rainbow Serpent. The balanced and spiraling interplay between these masculine and feminine life-giving twin deities fuels and sustains life in the Amazon, which in turn extends its breath or lungs of life to all of Mother Earth.

• Katari and Amuru — the illuminated rainbow serpent of the Andes.

• The rainbow Pleiadian frequency emanates from and is rooted in Ausangate, Peru.

• The spiraling plant vine Ayahuasca.

• The Hindu concept of the divine love between Krishna and Radha.

• The Ngalyod. Borlung, or Wa.gyl- the rainbow serpent of the Aboriginal Australians.

• The Pleiadian Rainbow Light Codes.

• The 144000 rainbow frequency of ascensions.

• Anguinum — the Celtic Druid's serpent-woven egg.

• The Chinese Hong yin and Yang emerging from the two-headed rainbow-winged dragon.

• Degei, the Rainbow Winged-Serpent in Fiji.

• The rainbow covenant of the kabbalah.

• The rising rainbow phoenix in alchemy.

• The North American Indigenous Rainbow Warrior Prophecies.

• White Buffalo Calf Woman, the Rainbow light of the Lakota.

• Kundalini activation and embodiment in various yogic lineages, as well as numerous unnamed traditions throughout the long history of Mother Earth.

I began my apprenticeship/initiation with Rainbow Medicine in my early teens, exploring plant medicines, working with bear medicine, and engaging in other healing activities. Not surprisingly, it was and is used in many elder cultures as an initiating energy for youth as they enter adulthood.

This medicine has supported, revisited, reinitiated, and guided (although sometimes unconsciously) my four-and-a-half-decade journey in medicine as a yogi, mystic, seer, healer, artist, writer, filmmaker, craftsman, entrepreneur, community health developer, and Earth guardian.

Over that time, I blossomed the roots of rainbow medicine through my practices of Ashtanga and kundalini yoga, meditation, study, travel, hands-on healing, Reiki, intuitive tools, and community holistic health services. It has also been working with me, wisdom teaching and initiating my path with circle medicine, essential oils, plant medicines, animal and nature allies, dance, creativity, ancestral connections, Ausangate of the Andes, Kilauea Volcano of Hawaii, Sacred sites in Ireland, Yacumama and Shachamama - the twin rainbow serpent of the amazon, Quetzalcoatl of the Americas, Ascended Masters, Yeshua/Magdalene, Hermes, Rumi, Mystics, Alchemists, Egyptian pyramids and mystery schools, and elder shamanic lineages and Indigenous wisdom teachings anchored and woven through nature and mother earth herself. An introductory guided meditation to activate rainbow medicine can be found here.

As for my background, I'm an initiate and an artist of Icelandic, Irish, Canadian, and American descent with over four decades of experience integrating healing modalities from Eastern, Western, and Indigenous traditions. A special shoutout to some of my beloved teachers:

Twayla Nitch - Seneca Nation

Vern Harper - Cree Nation
Pauline Shirt - Cree Nation
Lional Whitebird - Cree Nation
Wanda Whitebird - Mi'kmaq Nation
Jawee - Arapaho Nation
Jessica Ehret - Quechua Nation
Maestra Adela - Quechua Nation
Alberto Tazto - Yachag Nation
Godfrey Chips - Lakota Nation
Sky Redlove - Huron Nation
Gaspar Rengifo - Shipibo
Mu Uta Ku Mara - Maori Nation
Carrie Green - Cherokee Nation

WWW.DIVERGENCIES.COM
YOUTUBE
INSTAGRAM
TIKTOK
LINKEDIN

Thank you
Johnny